By Kathleen J. Wickman

Copyright © 2013 by Kathleen J. Wickman

All Rights Reserved

DEDICATION

To my family and friends who have encouraged me along the way.

MaryAnn Andrews and Maureen Grell, two of my best friends who happen to also be my sisters. Your words of wisdom and guidance will never be forgotten. Thank you for believing in me!

Eric Wickman, my brother and dear friend. Your business and marketing knowledge has given me insight I would've never had. Thank you for looking after the well-being of my dreams!

My parents: Dave and Jan Wickman. Thank you for always being there for me.

Taylor, Marcus, Jordyn, Jackson and Emma: my nieces and nephews who have given me permission to use their first names for the characters in my book. The characters themselves are not intended to reflect who you are and are completely fictitious in nature.

My friends, you are too many to list but I hope you know who you are when I say thank you for encouraging me along the way, even in the smallest measurement, it has meant everything!

This book is for you.

ACKNOWLEDGEMENT

Thank you to the following people who have helped me during the process of writing this novel.

Brittiany Koren, Editor – You have gone above and beyond to help me make this novel the best it can be. Your guidance, expertise and patience with my endless questions are truly appreciated! Thank you for all your hard work!

Carole Yakel, Watersmeet Chamber of Commerce – You were my very first resource three years ago when Phantom's Crossing was starting to come together. I will never forget your kindness and helpfulness. The information you sent me was very beneficial to my writing. Thank you!

Kim Wickman, Illustrator – My talented cousin who designed a truly awesome book cover for me. Seeing my cover for the first time made it seem very official and exciting. Thank you for all you have done!

Amy Vivio Photography – Thank you so much for taking such great pictures! It was very difficult to decide which one to use for my book. I normally despise having my pictures taken but you made it fun!

Barb Raffin, Author – Thank you for taking me under your wing and helping me get started with the editing process. Without you, I wouldn't have known about Brittiany at Written Dreams and my book wouldn't be what it is today. I will always be appreciative of your advice and guidance.

Chart of Accounts

Chapter One – The End	1
Chapter Two – Nothing But a Memory	7
Chapter Three – A New Dawn	15
Chapter Four – Dolly's Restaurant	33
Chapter Five – Paulding Light	47
Chapter Six – Sam	67
Chapter Seven – Disappearance	91
Chapter Eight – The Party	107
Chapter Nine – Holy Ground	127
Chapter Ten – Secrets	145
Chapter Eleven – Cursed	155
Chapter Twelve – The Scorching Truth	181
Chapter Thirteen – Bloodline	211
Chapter Fourteen – Visions	233
Chapter Fifteen – A Leap of Faith	271
Chapter Sixteen – A Sinister Mind	285
Chapter Seventeen – The Hand of Fate	307
Chapter Eighteen – Phantom's Crossing	341
Chapter Nineteen – The Ultimate Sacrifice	361
Chapter Twenty – Do or Die	369
Chapter Twenty-One – Broken	381

Chapter Twenty-Two – The Beginning	391
About the Author	405

CHAPTER ONE — THE END

Taylor, in all the years I have known her could out wit and outsmart anyone with her sharp tongue and her over-educated brain. Her steely gray eyes and raven black hair added to that predatorial beauty. And yet in one swift change of gears, she could soften her game face and morph into a persona of a child when it suited her. When she's around those who know and love her for the kind-hearted person she really is.

As far as looks go, some say we could pass as twin sisters even though we weren't related. We were only friends who looked similar except my hair was dark brown and my eyes were dark blue. Just back from a nursing conference in Texas, she sat cross-legged on the edge of my bed as I stuffed more clothes into an already packed suitcase. The bedroom Taylor and I are in now sits bare, save my bed, as well as the rest of the house. I was suddenly grateful I had not moved in with Dylan. Packing up my life would've been that much harder. At least in my own house, his absence wasn't everywhere I looked.

"Why do you really have to leave, Jade?"

"I thought we already went over this. There's nothing left for me here, Tay."

Without looking at her, I turned from the suitcase and walked back into the closet to grab more clothes.

"Gee, thanks. I'm glad I mean so much to you." Taylor dropped her gaze into her lap where her hands were crossed and started pouting as she stared at her chipped nail polish.

"Oh hell, you know what I mean." I said over my shoulder while grabbing an armload of blouses from the closet.

"No, I don't. There's more to this than simply losing a job. It just doesn't make sense. Don't tell me this is about *him*."

A sigh louder than I anticipated escaped my mouth conveying the mounting frustration within. I really should've prepared myself better for this kind of reaction from my loved ones when I told them of my decision to move. The 'him' Taylor referred to was Dylan; the man as of two weeks ago I had planned on spending the rest of my life with. When I didn't answer, Taylor went on.

"I told you to sleep with him, but you didn't listen to me. By the way, how the hell do you date someone for as long as you did and not sleep with him? There's your problem right there."

"No, Taylor. Believe it or not, that *wasn't* the problem. Dylan and I came from the same background, in a fast paced world where there is more complication and divorce than ever. We valued the importance of time and of waiting until the right moment. When we both knew we wanted to spend the rest of our lives together. Only then would sex have any meaning. Besides, it wasn't a big deal to us. Sure, at times it was difficult to abstain, but we weren't looking just to make love, we wanted to make love last."

"Well, a lot of good it did you. You're now single and packing your life away into a suitcase to move to Timbuktu for what? To escape the past? You know it will only follow you wherever you go. There's more activity in my sock than there is in that ghost town."

At that, I stopped packing and turned to my childhood friend.

"Look Taylor, I don't expect you to understand my decisions as of late. I simply ask that you support them. I'm not doing this to upset anyone, especially you. This is something I feel I need to do for now. I need a change. The time is right and I'm taking this opportunity. My Aunt Emma needs help with her restaurant. She's allowing me to rent one of her beautiful lakeside cabins for half of what she charges everyone else. I'm not going to pass this up."

"Jade, I get that. I really do, but a job as a waitress? You work for a newspaper. You're capable of so much more than this."

"*Worked* for a newspaper, remember? Besides, I was a photographer for them. I can freelance myself out now and continue taking pictures. Maybe I'll open up a shop in Paulding and sell my work. And what is wrong with being a waitress? It's hard work!"

She apparently was more concerned about where I was moving to then what I'd be doing there as she ignored my last remark and went on.

"Right. The ghost town. That should go over well."

"Oh, give me a break Taylor. Paulding is not that small. Sure, it's small compared to Billings but in reality it's a quaint little town with shops along Main Street. It has a movie theatre, recreational facilities, coffee shops, you name it. Just like we have here, but on a smaller scale, that's all."

"Okay. So back to Dylan, why did the two of you break up? You never told me."

"Yes, I did. Irreconcilable differences."

"You sound like a lawyer. What's the real reason?"

I had yet to tell Taylor the absolute truth. And how it all began after the accident one year ago. No one knew except for Dylan and myself. And apparently Dylan didn't take it too well since now I'm single and alone. I'll be damned if I go through that pain and rejection again. No, this secret is one I'll take to my grave.

"That is the real reason. The differences we had were monumental enough to end the relationship. I won't settle and neither should he. Can we drop it now?"

Taylor looked at me pensively, she started to say something more, but then decided against it.

"Okay, so I'm selfish." Taylor's face suddenly changed from seriousness to utter sadness and deflation.

"As far as you moving away on me, I don't want to lose you. You're my dearest friend, Jade."

"You're not going to *lose* me Taylor. You know I will keep in touch. I'll come home and visit and you can head my way anytime. I'm not even sure if this will be permanent so don't worry. No matter where the road takes me, we'll always be friends."

My suitcase and bags were now packed. The boxes of impertinent items and furniture had already been sent to the storage unit until I returned for them later. As of now, the cabin I would be moving to included furniture and amenities. My Aunt Emma took extra steps to make sure I had everything and would be comfortable despite my wishes.

The last thing I wanted was to be a nuisance or have special treatment. I could've cared less if she put me up in a tent in the back yard. I was just grateful to have someplace to go, anywhere but here. I placed the last of the luggage by the door and plopped down beside Taylor on the bed. I wrapped my arm around her shoulder as her head lowered into her lap. She appeared to me not as a twenty-four year old woman anymore, but as a young child helpless and lost. My heart broke.

A moment passed as we hugged each other and shed a few tears. The house is silent except for a few sniffles here and there. A car horn beeped somewhere in the distance.

Looking at my watch I realized it was only three o'clock and I had finally finished everything that needed to be done before the big move. I stood up suddenly and faced my old friend.

"I think we should go see *Fancy Pants* tonight. It's the last night they're showing it at the cinema and I've heard it's a real hoot!"

Taylor looked up at me from the bed with red-rimmed eyes and a hint of a smile.

"That has got to be one of the dumbest titles for a movie I've ever heard."

"No, that would be *Flem* which was released in 1996. Sounds appealing; doesn't it?"

"Yuck, we're not going to dinner first are we, because I think I just lost my appetite."

***

The two women chuckle and walk arm and arm down the stairs to catch the early show, oblivious to the hollow eyes peeking out from the closet and now fixated upon their backs as they descend to the landing below. Two car doors slam and an engine starts. The car drives away unaware of the ghost watching them from the second story bedroom window.

CHAPTER TWO — NOTHING BUT A MEMORY

The house is eerily empty and quiet like a hollowed out grave as I enter. Out of habit I almost drop the keys on the end table by the front door, but suddenly remember that I had loaded it onto the truck earlier that day. A flick of the switch and the front entry way lights up. Not a stitch of furniture remains as I climb the stairs and enter my bedroom.

I purposely packed a night bag for this last evening at home. The movie was just what Taylor and I needed. We laughed so hard at times that I was glad I relieved myself before the movie started. I smile thinking about our evening as I switch on the light to the bathroom.

I brush my teeth and wash my face as per the usual nightly ritual and as I stand up to grab a towel from the rail, I instinctually perceive a slight draft and the fine hairs on my neck begin to rise. I sense before I see a presence and like a passerby to an accident scene, not wanting to look but unable to stop, I drop the towel from my face and meet hollow eyes looking back at me in the mirror.

I jolted in shock as a scream tore from my lips followed by a few curses. I spun around quickly as the ghost jumped back, eyes widening further reflecting the surprise in mine.

"Stephanie, please don't scare me like that!"

Stephanie's wispy outline becomes denser as the translucent face fills with 'life' to appear more like my own. Her floating movements become those of solid footsteps as she turns and walks out of the bathroom and into the adjoining bedroom. There she stops, facing the wall with her back towards me.

"I'm sorry, Jade. I don't mean to scare you, but I'm not sure how not to."

"I know. It's okay, Steph. I just wasn't expecting you. I haven't seen you in quite a while. I thought you had crossed over."

It had been one year and four months since the accident that had claimed Stephanie's life and nearly mine as well. Another chill enters my bones, this time from the memory. It causes me to shudder as I remember pieces of that real life nightmare. Ever since that fateful day, I had been periodically and unexplainably visited by Stephanie's ghost. I know she's trapped here, I just don't know why. And neither does she.

"Why are you still here, Steph? Is there anything I can do to help?"

Her body is now completely solid, having lost all the ghost like features. At this point, she is as alive to me as the neighbor down the street. The only problem…she was just an illusion. Whenever I have tried to touch her, my hand passes through.

"I've come to give you one last message and to say good-bye."

"Good-bye? As in I won't see you anymore? I don't understand, Steph."

Confusion clouds my face as I walk over to the edge of the bed to sit down. Stephanie is standing in the corner of the room, just beyond the reach of the glow cast by the bathroom light. Her body is a silhouette now as it hides in shadow. Her voice is solid and strong when she speaks. She turns around to look at me.

"It's finally time for me to cross over. I'm going to the other side, Jade. And I've already seen what awaits me."

Even in shadow I could see her face light up with a smile and a far-away look in her eyes as if she was looking at something truly beautiful.

"Oh, Jade. If only the entire world could see where people go once they die, no one would ever mourn for their dead again. Their hearts would fill with happiness instead. It's so beautiful! Oh, how I wish you could see."

"Do you have to go Steph? Can't you stay just a little while longer?"

Tears started streaming down my face as I pleaded with her.

"I know how you must feel Jade. I never meant to torment you like this by my staying but I understand now why I couldn't cross over into the light right away. It's like a puzzle that all comes together in the very end but you don't understand the pieces until you leave this world and are able to see the bigger picture. You see Jade, when the accident happened, my soul was ripped from my body so quickly; I was dazed and confused all this time. Lost along a path I couldn't follow.

Not sure of which way to turn or where to go, I felt I still had unfinished business here, things to take care of. We were all so young after all, Jade. Naturally it wasn't my time to leave this world but life doesn't always march by the beat of the world's time clock. There is a much bigger clock, a celestial one that deciphers the time and place."

Stephanie had only appeared to me a handful of times since the accident and most of those incidents were just in passing. I'd see her at the dinner table at Dylan's house while we were having supper. Having not fully adjusted to my new gift at the time, I nearly choked on a piece of chicken the first time I saw her. And just as quickly, she'd vanish.

I suppose she wanted to check in on her brother. Make sure he was okay, that we were all okay. Dylan took the news of his sister's passing the hardest. It was so unexpected for all of us. He clung to me tightly in the months that followed.

I knew how grateful he was to still have me considering I had died also that night. But I had been fortunate enough to come back. Even though the encounters were short lived, I started to feel as if she were still alive. My brain couldn't make the adjustment to the fact that she was truly gone because my eyes and ears were deceiving it whenever she'd show herself. She looked so human to me. Not like the visions people shared on those haunted house stories, or like characters depicted in movies as translucent colorless forms.

It was difficult not to want to reach out and touch her, hug her, and just be near her. She was the kindest person I had ever met, with a gentle heart and loving ways. I fell for her before I fell for Dylan. She had been the sister I'd always wanted, but never had.

Her sudden news now about leaving took me off guard. I couldn't understand why now? Why did she have to go now? Even though deep inside, I knew it was the right thing to do. She couldn't stay earthbound forever. Her body had left; it was time for her soul to go too. Despite myself, I still wasn't ready to let her go.

"Was it terrifying for you, Steph? To feel lost? Were you in pain?"

"No, no, not at all. The best way I can describe it is like being in a dream. A surreal dream where everything is vivid yet trance-like. There is no pain here. And only happiness where I'm going now."

"You're talking about Heaven, aren't you? Why now, what has changed since the accident? I still don't understand."

"It's all dependent upon one's belief system and what they would call it. But yes, heaven indeed. It does exist! Just as happiness and love exist on earth, that is what heaven is made of. I've finally made peace with things of my past. Righted some Wrongs, persuaded some people to make healthy decisions, and now all I have left is to give you a message."

The last two comments confused me so I addressed the first one.

"What do you mean by persuading people to make healthy decisions, Steph? Can others see you too? Am I not alone?"

"No, I'm afraid there aren't many like you Jade. By persuading I mean…." She pauses a moment. "Have you ever found yourself doing something you felt you had to do but having no solid reason as to why you should? Like taking a right at a street you normally turn left on? Only to find out later there was an accident you would've been involved in had you not left the house late or taken that right turn?"

Not waiting for me to answer, she continued.

"While most call it dumb luck, I call it guardian angel work. Humans are surrounded by them each and every day. Doing little things here and there to help people get to where they're going without accident or delay. It's hard to explain but we all have a path to follow and sometimes a guardian touch is in order to help us along the way."

I tried to keep my voice steady to no avail.

"What is the message you have for me?" An audible crack in my voice had Stephanie walking out of the shadowy corner of the room to kneel down before me at the foot of the bed. My hands were clasped tightly in my lap, while my head hung low. I lifted my gaze to hers as she reached out with her hands and held them over mine in an attempt to comfort me. Instead of crying harder as I wanted to do, peace filled me instead and my dark blue eyes connected more squarely with her light blue ones.

She really did look like an angel to me. Her soft, billowy blonde hair hung long and silky down her shoulders. Her face was peach cream colored and flawless. Her lithe form like that of a dancer's as she knelt before me.

She wore a startling white satin type nightgown that hung perfect and long all the way down to her toes. It was a material of which the like I had never seen before. She looked even more beautiful than normal tonight. For some reason I thought of my mother, of summer days, of children's laughter and of all things good in this world.

"You have a gift for a reason, Jade. Try not to despise it regardless of how much pain it has brought you already. Accept it, for it will come in handy very soon. Trust yourself, always and stay strong and true to your beliefs."

"Others will challenge you; let them. Forgive my brother for he truly does not know what he has done. He was not meant for you and someday when the pain dies, you will realize that. His path is different from your own."

"And lastly, and most importantly, take heed of your gift. For with its powers, there is a price to be paid."

With that Stephanie's face grew somber as her last words sunk in and her eyes conveyed a seriousness that shook me to the core.

"What do you mean? What price?"

Without hesitation, she answered.

"His life."

My brow furrowed at her words.

"Whose life? Dylan's?"

Instead of answering, she stood up and walked towards the patio doors at the far end of the room. Somehow I knew this was our final good-bye. This would be the last time I would see her until I, too, left this world. The closest thing to a sister I ever had and she was leaving me. My heart ached in sorrow as a piece of me went with her. In final desperation, I called out.

"Steph! Wait! Don't leave."

Turning around to look at me once more, she smiled and whispered, '*I love you*'. Then she turned back and walked through the patio doors, past the deck and faded into a memory.

CHAPTER THREE — A NEW DAWN

It was early May and traffic was minimal at six a.m. on a Saturday morning. The air was crisp and dry. The sky was deep blue and endless.

I dreaded this last stop before leaving town not because of any negative feelings towards my parents. On the contrary, we have always been close. I just knew by the time they finished fretting over me, I would feel as if I were about to take a one-way dangerous and deadly journey to the far side of the galaxy rather than a short trip a few states away. Adeline and Michael McKenzy stood in the driveway in front of their two-story ranch as I pulled up.

"Do you have your cell phone with you, Jayden? Make sure you take some food with you in case you get hungry on the way. It's a long drive after all. Oh, and be sure to take your pepper spray in case you run into trouble!"

Adeline McKenzy was the Joan Clever of the 21st century. A Christian woman to the core and an incessant do-gooder, she always had a smile for everyone and volunteered for local charities whenever she could. But she tended to worry a bit much over her only child. She was also the only person to call me by my legal name.

"Mom, quit worrying. I have everything I need. I'm twenty-four years old and you're making me feel like I'm twelve. I promise to call you when I reach Aunt Emma and Uncle Marcus' house."

"She'll be fine, dear."

Michael McKenzy patted his wife's shoulder soothingly and walked over to check Jade's tires once more.

"Tire pressure is good. Fluids have been checked. You're good to go, kid."

My father hugged me one last time and walked back into the house. As tough as he seemed on the outside, he was a softy at heart and never liked good-byes. Mother and daughter exchanged a few more words, hugged and then said good-bye.

As I maneuvered the candy apple red Jeep Liberty out of the driveway, I couldn't help but look back at the house I had grown up in and the parents who had raised me so well. I felt it was a blessing to have such a close knit family, and the reality of not seeing them again for a while suddenly hit me like two fists to the chest. I actually felt like I was twelve again because of how insecure I felt at that moment.

"Oh, for Pete's sake, get a grip on yourself. You're a grown woman!" I chided myself out loud.

I angrily brushed tears away from my eyes while trying to focus on the road and maintain some semblance of control. Music was definitely in order so as to drown out my thoughts. An up-beat pop song was playing on the radio. I tapped my hands on the wheel after rolling the windows down to let the fresh Montana air in.

I have to admit, from Taylor's perspective; it was kind of crazy to leave such a beautiful place. The mountains were looming in the distance as I reached the edge of town, their glistening white caps like an artist's painting in all of its perfection. My family was here, besides Aunt Emma and Uncle

Marcus in Paulding. So were my friends and it really didn't make any sense as to why I had to leave. But something inside me kept insisting that I do, if only for a while.

I had no choice but to follow my instinct and migrate east. Besides, I was really looking forward to seeing Aunt Emma and Uncle Marcus again. I had been in high school the last time I visited them. It seems like decades ago.

But to move to a town in Michigan that hardly anyone has heard of seemed odd, especially compared to the bustling activity and massive size of Billings, Montana. The only explanation I could offer to myself was the need for peace, for solidarity between myself and nature at its most serene. Sure, nature exists in Montana, it's what the state is known for. Majestic landscapes and vast expanse of wilderness to be compared to none other, yet it's that massiveness that I've been feeling lost in. Swallowed whole, so to speak.

There was something really humble and modest about the endless quiet of Paulding, Michigan. Yet within that seclusion, a bustling little town exists, where life's pulse flows and everyone knows everyone. That in itself, breeds security and companionship. The permission was granted by my own accord and there was nothing my loved ones could do about that. I may always be a child in my parent's eyes, but I have lived more life these past few months than most people do in their entire lifetime. Some days I felt very, very old.

I hadn't realized that one song had ended on the radio and another began as I drove along highway 94. So much for allowing the music to drown out my thoughts. They were louder than my speakers were able to go. Ten hours later, a few stops for fuel, and I had arrived in Fargo, North Dakota.

The evening was young but I was exhausted and didn't want to chance falling asleep at the wheel. I checked into a hotel and a few hours later I was on the road again, somewhat refreshed but more determined than ever to get to my destination. I had another eight hours of driving and the last stretch was the worst because it was the most monotonous.

There was absolutely nothing to look at but trees. Mile after mile nothing but trees and then when I thought I was going to go insane from isolationism, a town appeared. The beginning of Paulding at last! Rural homes and farms dotted the sparse fields, a small hardware store with a crooked sign reading 'Sal's Hardware' hung above the front door where two gray haired gentlemen stood talking to each other. They looked at me as I drove by then resumed conversation.

A mechanic shop was on the next block, its two car garage doors were open revealing a Cadillac on one hoist and a beat up looking Ford truck sitting on the ground in the second stall patiently waiting to be worked on next. A few modest looking homes dotted the way, then an ice cream shop appeared around the next corner where kids were playing tag in the nearby lawn while trying to eat their ice cream, mostly missing their mouths and smearing their faces instead with the cold treat. As I approached the stop sign and came to a halt I couldn't tear my gaze away from their innocent faces, so happy and carefree. I remember being that kid many years ago and coming to this town, eating at that very same ice cream shop. Back then I didn't know how burdensome life could become.

How I envied those children and how I sometimes longed for those days again. I pulled away from the stop sign and turned right onto Melbourne Lane. I could just make out my Aunt Emma's house in the distance. The dark brown fence with ivy clinging to it lined the street. A mailbox built like a replica of their log cabin stood at the base of their driveway.

It was so intricately carved by the neighbor carpenter twenty years ago that people still commented on how iconic it was after all these years. Just then a siren wailed behind me. I jerked my head up and looked into the rear view mirror to see a police car on my tail with lights flashing.

"Great. Now what did I do?"

I didn't recall speeding or breaking any laws, maybe he's on his way to an emergency and it has nothing to do with me. I slowed the car down and pulled over and to my dismay so did the cop behind me. With a mix of anxiety and irritation of being stopped so close to my aunt and uncle's house, I reached over and got my driver's license and all necessary paperwork out for him to check, hoping it would speed up the process faster so that I could go to my new home. When I turned back to the window, he was already standing there waiting for me to roll it down. One look at his face told me he wasn't the friendly sort of fellow.

"License and registration, please."

Cripes, he sounds like Robocop. I nonetheless gave him a smile as I handed over the essentials. He did not return the smile but instead looked over my papers. I couldn't read his eyes as they lay hidden behind dark sunglasses.

"Did I do something wrong, officer?"

For a moment I didn't think he was going to answer me as he studied my license.

"Yes. You stopped at that stop sign back there."

"Excuse me? I stopped at a stop sign? Umm, isn't that what you're supposed to do?"

Finally he looked at me, and I suddenly felt like a bug under a microscope as he examined my face intently.

"Normally, yes. But this stop sign has a stipulation printed underneath which apparently you did not take heed to. Only traffic making a left turn or heading straight across the intersection has to stop. Traffic turning right as you were doing, has a thru way and is not required to stop."

Man, this guy needs a hobby. I've never heard anything more ridiculous in my life and told him so.

"You've got to be kidding me. Is this a joke? That is the dumbest thing I ever heard."

"No joke. It's the law. And by the way, your license is expired. I'm going to have to write you a ticket."

He was talking to me like I had killed someone and I was getting even more irritated. I was actually beginning to feel like a convicted criminal. I did nothing wrong and I couldn't wait to tell Uncle Marcus about this. My quick temper was rising fast.

"Listen. I just moved…am moving to my aunt and uncle's resort right down the street. You might know my uncle considering he's the chief of police in this county and your boss. I can see their mailbox from here. My new license is in transit to their house as we speak. I made sure to forward it knowing I would be gone by the time it arrived at my old house in Montana. Is a ticket really necessary? I've been driving for the past two days and just want to get to my new home."

"I know who you are Ms. McKenzy. And as far as my boss is concerned, he expects me to do my job and you've committed two violations. I'm going to have to write you a ticket."

At that he walked brusquely back to his squad car and left me sitting there with my mouth gaping open in incredulous disbelief.

Unbelievable! I've been in this town a mere twenty minutes, broke one tiny law which shouldn't even be a law and now I, the niece of the town's Chief of Police no less, am getting a ticket from Captain America! I was so frazzled, exhausted from the journey and sulking in my anger that I didn't realize he had come back to the window. When he spoke, I gave a slight start.

"I dropped the license violation and only wrote you up for the traffic violation."

Did he really think he was doing me a favor? Man, this guy is more in love with himself than I thought.

"Gee, thanks." Sarcasm dripped off my tongue.

A glint on his right shoulder caught my eye. Just above his breast pocket was a silver nameplate that read the name 'J. Butler'. I snatched the ticket from his outstretched hand, threw the jeep into drive and had to control the urge to take off fast enough to spew gravel in his face. I stole a glance in the rear view mirror. Officer Butler was still standing in the same spot watching my car drive away. A few seconds later I was thankfully turning into Emma and Marcus' driveway. My aunt must've been waiting for me by the bay window because she came running outside just as I was getting out of the car.

"Jade! On schedule as I had hoped. It's so good to see you again my dear!"

My aunt wrapped her arms around me in a warm embrace. Em was in her early fifty's, fifty-two last month if memory serves me well. Lately I have trouble remembering what I did the day before. Life has become a sporadic series of foggy days since the accident.

I drift through them as if I were in a waking coma. Seeing everything, going through the motions, completing the tasks of the day and speaking to people and hearing my detached voice as if it were coming from someone else's body. When I look at the sky sometimes, I see the sun but can't feel its warmth. Then the next day, I will have it all together and be on top of my game.

It's as if my batteries re-charge after a good night's sleep. My mental strength returns enough to get through that day coherently. The emptiness inside of me was going to take a long time to fill, that much was certain. Love still remains for Dylan, regardless of what I went through, and my heart ached for Stephanie. I missed them both very much.

"It's great to see you too, Aunt Em."

My mother and her sister Emma were like night and day in every way possible. Adeline has the dark brown hair and blue eyes that she passed along to me. She and her brother Charlie coveted the height from the gene pool that was also passed along to me. My 5'7" stature hovered over Aunt Emma's 5'4" as we stood facing each other.

The top of her head barely reached my chin. Emma's honey blonde hair was just beginning to thin ever so slightly; her light colored skin was such a sharp contrast to her sibling's darker complexion as well as my own. Em's baby blue eyes looked into mine as we walked towards the house. The only thing we all had in common was our slender physique.

Uncle Charlie had made the remark one time when he came to visit how Emma was the Milk Man's child. Everyone had a good laugh, including Emma. Aside from looks, the two sister's personalities were quite opposite as well. My mother, the incessant worry wart, always airing on the side of caution and more serious than her sister.

Aunt Emma would comment how my mother was born grown up. The worrying could have come from me being her only child. Emma having no children; was more light hearted of the two women. She was always joking and carefree and fun. A kid at heart, she took nothing seriously.

The only time I've ever seen her down and depressed was when she found out she couldn't have children. Her and Marcus were really upset about that. To try and fill that void, they compensated with three dogs, two horses, and a hamster named Chunk. Chunk likes food…a lot…and it shows. When they got him from the store, I was here visiting for the summer and had the honor of naming him.

What better namesake than that of the beloved character from The Goonies. Chunk actually took a break from running on his hamster wheel one time to stuff his face and watch that classic movie with me.

"How was your trip dear? Any problems along the way?"

"Everything was fine until I was pulled over just down the street. He gave me a ticket as my welcoming present."

"Oh no. What happened? Were you speeding or something?"

"No. I stopped at a stop sign."

Irritation was resurfacing as I rehashed the incident.

"That damn stop sign has always confused people from out of town. I'm guessing Jackson Butler was the one to give you that ticket. He's quite the stickler when it comes to those things. I'm sure Marcus will straighten things out for you."

We had mounted the few steps up onto the porch and made our way inside the house. Emma loved gardening. Flowers aligned the walkway leading to the huge wrap around deck. Two antique looking rocking chairs sat side by side to the left of the front door.

The deck ended to the right of the door where the two-car attached garage was. The rest of the deck wrapped around to the back of the house where a spacious backyard met the lakefront. Before I could kick off my shoes and plop down onto the overly plush couch, three fur balls came flying at me, assaulting me with wet kisses.

Bella, the yellow lab; Bruno, the chocolate lab; and Scooter, the Jack Russell Terrier. Scooter, the leader of the pack jumped up onto my lap while Emma went to the kitchen to pour me a glass of lemonade.

Being here again felt like I had never left, and talking to my aunt again seemed as natural and easy as friends who have known each other for years. I felt perfectly comfortable in her presence. She never makes anyone stand on ceremony in order to impress. 'My home is your home' she'd always say. I didn't realize how much I had truly missed talking to her until I arrived moments ago.

"Is uncle here? I'd like to do just that. I was being treated unfairly and it was an honest mistake. He could've cut me *some* slack."

I knew I was sounding like a petulant child but I didn't care. The last two days of traveling were catching up to me, and not to mention the weeks of packing prior to that. I was in desperate need of a nap.

"No, he's not here. He's out fishing on the lake and won't be back until dinner."

She walked into the spacious living room with two glasses of ice, cold lemonade and handed one to me. Sitting down next to me on the sofa, she tucked her leg under her and faced me.

"Don't let Jackson get to you, Jade. He's hard as nails on the outside but he's really a decent guy once you get to know him. Marcus will talk to him tomorrow at work. It'll be fine."

We caught up on what I've been up to since the last time I was here. Emma was glad to see I was completely healed from the accident and doing well. I was careful not to talk too much about Dylan, and I steered clear of the topic of my gift/curse. Whatever you want to call it. Thankfully, Em didn't prod me too much on the break-up.

She was a perceptible woman who could read people like a book and knew when to talk, what to say and when to say nothing at all. That's one of the reasons she did so well with the restaurant. She was exceptionally blessed with social skills and knew how to understand people.

There wasn't anyone who didn't like or respect Emma Hawthorne. After a few more minutes of idle chat, Emma took my empty glass and returned to the kitchen.

I took that moment to glance around at all the familiar sights, sounds, and feel of the house. I had always loved this home.

It had all the warmth and charm that most log homes have. It seemed wrong to call it humble, when in reality; the place was magnificently large. It was no secret my aunt and uncle were doing well just by the sheer beauty of this place and by the land they owned.

When Emma returned, she gave me a tour of the house. Some things had changed since the last time I had been here. The living room where we now sat had a large stone fireplace. The stones reached all the way up to the open concept ceiling. A staircase graced the right of the room leading up to the second level bedrooms. At the top of the stairs a balcony loft looked down over the living room. Another set of stairs was positioned just below the first leading down into the den area where a pool table, dart board and second living room including a wet bar resided. Half underground from the front of the house but opened in the back with a set of patio doors leading out to the back yard and lake.

Back on the main level, a small hallway led past the fireplace and into a kitchen big enough to cook for a small army. White cabinets aligned one wall, their glass fronts exposing the dishes inside. An island counter took up part of the slate gray marble floor with stools on one side. This was the one room that contrasted with the other rooms. It's white and yellow décor everywhere, giving the sensation of cleanliness and summertime. More flowers in a vase graced the small table next to the long counter space.

The kitchen table stood in a little nook with another set of patio doors just behind it, opening out onto the deck and into the backyard. Adjoining the kitchen was the dining area, separated by another small hallway. The dining room consisted of a long mahogany table rich in color that took up most of the room with tall backed white satin chairs on both sides. Floor to ceiling lace window coverings on the east wall overlooked the lake. The entire house was designed with deep, rich colors of mauve and hunter green and flowers of every kind filled the house, inside and out.

We walked outside and into the backyard. The dogs ran ahead of us, racing each other to the water's edge. Gardens graced the property and walking paths of stone weaved through it aligned with antique trinkets, watering cans, ceramic frogs and ornate decorations speckled throughout. I always felt like I was walking into a magical place when I toured the gardens. The backyard was spacious with a fire pit off to one side. A long narrow dock harbored a pontoon boat along with Marcus' fishing boat which was now somewhere out on the lake with Marcus in it.

A loud whinny pierced the air. I smiled at Gracie and Silky frolicking in the adjacent field. What I loved most about this place was the privacy it held. The nearest neighbor was at the end of the street and the only other noticeable evidence of humanity was the cabins scattered around the lake that my aunt and uncle also owned and rented out to vacationers year round. Many years ago my great-grandmother was in a position to buy this land when others couldn't afford it and much of the area was underdeveloped.

The lake was part of that purchase and has been in the family ever since.

This place emitted peace and serenity when the world seemed to be full of noise and chaos. It drove city folk wild with boredom after a time but I never got sick of it, even giving the city I myself had come from. Nature was in my blood.

I hugged the dogs and kissed them good-bye as Emma brought them back into the house then showed me to my new home. It was a short drive down a dirt road. Mine was the first cabin on the lake and from the water front, I could see the main house just to the right, through the trees. We turned off the dirt road and onto the narrow driveway that stretched on for thirty feet or so.

Trees created a canopy overheard as the road curved left then right as the cabin came into view. A quaint little home perfect for one person or a small family met my gaze. Two windows on either side of the front door each had window box planters where delicate pale flowers with strange leaves peeped out. Pink and purple tiny dots on the inside of each petal were colorfully displayed.

A small deck aligned the front side of the house. Em was talking about the vacationers that would soon be here.

"We have renters that vacation here every summer. You'll start to notice traffic increasing in a few days as they begin occupying the surrounding cabins. Each cabin was deliberately set back from the main road in order to provide privacy."

Summer was around the corner. The town would soon vibrate with extra life and the lake would fill with boaters and swimmers. To maintain that serenity my aunt and uncle only allowed people to use motorless boats on the water. Canoes, paddle boats, row boats and the likes are the only things permitted.

The lake was big but not big enough so that if every vacationer brought a motorboat, there would be complete chaos and possible injury. It wasn't worth the risk.

As we walked up the front steps to the deck, the pale white flowers caught my eye again.

"What are those, Aunt Em? I'm not a flower expert but I don't think I've ever seen this kind before."

"They're my experiment. I hope it's okay that I practice on you. None of the other cabins have them because this isn't their natural environment. They're called Ghost Flowers and they thrive best in desert washes and rocky slopes. I figured if they poop out on me, you wouldn't mind. It may look really bad for the other renters though if they drive up and see brown dead flowers hanging out of their window baskets."

"They're beautiful. I can almost see right through them."

Instead of dirt, I noticed rock and light soil aligning the bottom of the planter.

"I hope they survive."

"Me too."

Em handed me the key to the front door and then went back to grab something out of the car. I couldn't help but notice the irony of the Ghost Flowers gracing my windows; life at times could have a weird sense of humor. Or maybe it was just my imagination running away on me. I smiled to myself as excitement to see my new home enveloped me. I pushed the door open and jolted in shock to see a man greeting me in the doorway. His face was covered in blood and he had a stoic look in his eye. He raised his hand to reveal a knife. A scream tore from my throat, shattering the peaceful sky as he took a step towards me.

Kathleen Wickman

CHAPTER FOUR — DOLLY'S RESTAURANT

I tripped backward in a hasty attempt to get out of there, turned and fell flat on my face onto the deck. I whipped my head around to see him walking towards me with that same stoic look. He bent down with both hands stretched towards me. At that point, survival instincts kicked in as I kicked with all my might, catching him square in the stomach. I watched as he hugged his mid-section and doubled over.

"Jade!"

Emma had flown from the car upon hearing my scream. She approached the deck with a welcome vase of flowers in hand to see me drop the intruder to his knees. She put the vase down on the steps as I scrambled to my feet and into her arms desperately trying to pull her towards the car and away from the cabin. Never taking my eyes off him for one second.

"Oh my gosh Gus, are you okay? What are you doing here? I thought you were in town buying supplies?"

Emma resisted my pull and broke my grip to run and check on the man who was now slowly climbing to his feet.

"It's okay Jade, he's our overseer of the cabins. What happened to your head Gus? Did you cut yourself clipping the hedges?"

Gus was on his feet now. The knife I had first caught glimpse of before running like a mad woman was in actuality small clipping shears. He nodded his head slowly.

"I had an accident and came inside looking for bandages. I didn't mean to scare anybody."

"It's alright Gus. Come inside and we'll get you cleaned up. Gus, this is Jade, my niece. She's going to be living here for a while. Jade, make yourself at home while I take care of Gus."

I'm sure my eyes were still as wide as saucers as this information sunk in to my frazzled brain. I took a few cautious steps towards Gus as he continued to stare at me with a bland expression. There was no doubt from the way he moved, looked and spoke, there was something not quite right with him. Some kind of mental incapacity or affliction.

Part of my fear came from Gus' immense size. He was built like a bull, standing well above my head. His arms were muscular under his thin white shirt. His blue overalls were stained with dirt and grime as well as his hands and face. He was definitely not someone I'd want to meet in a dark alley. He still hadn't said a word to me after Emma introduced us. I felt bad for kicking him and said so.

"I'm sorry for hurting you. Are you okay?"

He nodded his head again but didn't say a word. He seemed to shrink from me slightly as I approached the front door. He turned and walked inside with me following behind. A small kitchen equipped with electric stove, refrigerator, and microwave greeted us upon walking in.

On the counter was a basket full of fresh fruit. Emma was already at the sink with a washcloth in hand. Gus had taken a seat at the kitchen table. I took the opportunity to survey the cabin. I walked through the kitchen and into the open concept living area with only the wrap around counter top acting as divider between the two rooms.

A fireplace graced one wall. A couch, loveseat and recliner created a 'C' facing the fireplace. And directly above the fireplace was a flat screen television hanging on the wall. Two sets of French doors took up space on each side of the adjoining wall facing the lake. The first set of doors was in the living room area and the next set was a few feet away. Behind the couch was a small dining room table and chairs.

A long deck lay beyond the doors with a few steps leading down to the yard and small beach area. There was also a fire pit off to the right. A small dock reached out into the water behind that. On the other side of the dining room table was a staircase leading up to the second floor. Walking up the stairs and down a narrow hallway, I ran my hand along the polished rail as I looked down onto the living room and dining room below.

Another crescent window overlooking the water was above the French doors, and as I walked down the hallway, I saw clear across the lake into the setting sun. The first bedroom I approached was small but quaint. I walked to the second bedroom at the end of the hall and was surprised by the sheer size of such a room in such a small cabin. A queen size bed took up the middle of the room and a small alcove containing a window seat displayed nothing but green, lush forest outside.

Skylights splattered the ceiling and a beautiful wooden dresser sat at the far corner with another flat screen television on the wall right beside it. I plopped my bags down and walked into the adjoining bath where a Jacuzzi tub and large shower awaited the next visitor. Everything was pristine and spotless. I was beginning to really like it here. This place was not hard to love.

"Gus is all taken care of and has headed back into town. He feels really bad about scaring you."

I jumped at the sound of Emma's voice. I hadn't realized she had walked into the room behind me. I turned around to face her.

"You must be so tired after that long trip. Don't worry about coming over for dinner; I'll bring some food to you. Get some rest dear. You look exhausted. Here are your keys for the cabin. Is there anything you need?"

"No, thank you. I'm fine here."

"Well, you have my number in your cell phone if you need anything. Don't hesitate to call, we're just down the road."

"Do you need a ride back to the house Aunt Em?"

"Oh no, I'm close enough to walk home. Get some rest. I'll see you later."

And with that she left. I dug out my cell phone just to be sure I had signal in this isolated place and to my relief, full bars displayed. I walked through the rest of the cabin just to get familiarized and then hauled the rest of my luggage from the car. I opened the fridge and my heart melted. My aunt was too kind.

She had fully stocked the fridge. I had told her not to do that. As hungry as I was, sleep was stronger. I climbed the stairs and plopped down on the quilted comforter. Within minutes I had fallen asleep.

***

Sunshine woke me up as it streamed through the windows. I stretched my achy muscles and rolled out of bed. To my relief, the bathroom was fully stocked too. Fresh clean towels were in the closet and soap on the sink. I grabbed my packed toiletries and got ready for work. My first day at my new job and I was excited yet nervous.

It felt like eons ago when I last worked at Dolly's Restaurant. After I cleaned up, I headed downstairs for breakfast. Last night's supper was in the fridge. My aunt must've stopped back sometime in the evening to drop it off for me. I hadn't even heard her come in. I grabbed a banana and headed out the door.

The air was crisp as summer nipped at its edges. Occasional warm drafts assaulted my face promising more heat to come. It was a relatively short drive to Dolly's and for the first time I got to see more of the town as I passed by. People were out walking the streets going in and out of storefront businesses. For a small town, the place was buzzing with activity.

The lawns were nicely manicured, the stores were immaculate looking and the windows glinted from the morning sun. A small water fountain sat in the middle of town- square. Nearby a park and basketball court already had kids practicing their lay-ups. Toddlers played on swings and ran every which way while their mothers watched nearby. A phone call was in order for Taylor. My childhood friend needed to see this place and how vibrant it really was. One visit here would change her tune.

Paulding was far from desolate. But after a few short minutes, I had passed through town and was just seconds away from Dolly's when I rounded the corner and saw flashing lights. An ambulance blocked my path as a police officer stopped traffic. An emergency crew assisted a car that had gone off the road and into the ditch. The front end was all smashed up and it was unclear whether the people inside were all right.

I had come to a stop three cars behind the scene. There was no way around. Great! My first day on the job and I was going to be late. I called Emma at the restaurant. I knew she'd be there by now. She always began her day bright and early.

After explaining the situation, she said she already knew. She had heard about the accident from Marcus and told me to sit tight. Whenever I could get there would be fine. I hung up and sat tapping my fingers on the steering wheel. I didn't know the area well enough yet to take a different route.

I looked over at the mangled car again and saw that they had finally extricated someone and were hauling him up to the ambulance on a stretcher. The steady rhythmic flashing from the emergency vehicles caught my gaze and brought me back to a crisp, clear February day on a barren road. Stephanie was behind the wheel of her car with myself in the passenger seat. I remember laughter and feeling happy.

My life had been perfect then. I had literally blinked once and in that instant, I had felt the car jolt to the left as if something had smashed into it with excessive force, sending us into a tailspin. I heard screams then felt myself being lifted out of my seat as the seat belt desperately and painfully held me to Earth. Cracking of metal or trees or some kind of material exploded in my ears...

Crack. Crack. Crack!!!

A knuckled finger banged harshly on my window. I snapped to attention and realized the cars in front of me had been waved on through the accident scene. I was holding up the line of cars behind me as a uniformed officer was staring at me strangely.

"Move along, Ma'am."

I put the jeep into gear and drove away with shaking hands gripped tightly on the wheel.

***

"You remember my niece Jade, don't you Sheba?"

"Of course! Jade, so good to see you again! Welcome back!"

Emma was introducing me to the recent hires and reacquainting me with the originals, such as Sheba who has been working for my aunt a little over a decade now. Sheba was in her early forties and had become good friends with Emma. Sheba trained in the new wait staff and had a smart business sense about her, often assisting my aunt in operating Dolly's. She could be shrewd and brisk, occasionally forgoing the mental filter most people have and saying exactly what comes to mind.

Usually when that happens, the person she's speaking to has it coming. Some of the girls have taken offense to her bluntness but most respect her because of her knowledge and professional mannerisms. Those who join Dolly's Restaurant learn quickly how intimidating she could be. There were three new faces I had not seen the last time I had been here.

Heather and Nikki were waitresses and best friends. Both of them were unfailingly kind and helpful to me as I tried to remember the ropes. The third new girl I took to right away. Jordyn was a few years younger than me and had a smile that could light up any room.

She welcomed me like a long lost friend and something about her came across very genuine and real. I liked her immediately and was looking forward to working with her.

"There's my girl!"

Uncle Marcus was sitting at a small table with a cup of coffee and the morning newspaper. He rose when he saw me coming and walked over to me and gave me a big hug.

"How's my favorite niece? Did you sleep well last night?"

"Hi Uncle! I'm doing much better now that I'm here. I slept really well, thanks."

"Em told me about Gus giving you a scare. I apologize for that. He may appear a bit odd but he's really harmless."

Uneasiness still rumbled low in my spine when I thought back to that incident.

"It's okay. Umm, he doesn't have a key to get into the cabins, does he?"

With a slight chuckle, Marcus grabbed both my shoulders at a distance and looked me in the eye.

"No, he does not. We were finishing up with getting your cabin ready and I had left the door open by accident. I went fishing and Em went back to the main house to meet you. Gus had been doing lawn maintenance around the cabins and ran to the closest one, that being yours, after he cut himself. We wouldn't have Gus around if we thought he was a threat."

With that he put his arm around my shoulder and looked at Em.

"Now go easy on Jade, don't scare her off with that leather whip you keep in the office."

He leaned conspiratorially into my ear.

"She's become quite the slave driver since you were here last."

"Oh Marcus, you're so full of it! Don't you have somewhere else to be? Jade, don't listen to him."

"Trust me, I'm not. Whatever kinky business you two have going on, I don't want to know." A coy smile tugged at the corner of my mouth.

With a hearty laugh, Marcus gave me one last squeeze and kissed Em before leaving. He called out over his shoulder as he was walking out the door.

"See you at dinner, Jade!"

"Bye."

I shook my head and smirked, thinking how my uncle hadn't changed one bit. Still a big ol' Teddy bear type of guy who has the ability to make anyone feel right at home. He struck me more as a big brother type, always kidding around and making jokes. I swear there were still remnants of a fifteen year-old kid soul stuck inside his fifty-five year old body.

The bond between him and my aunt was unmistakable. Aside from the bantering and sporadic arguments those two have shared, their love ran deep. They began as best friends and still behave as one. It was difficult not to be enamored with that kind of chemistry.

Lunchtime rolled around and I was slowly beginning to feel as if I had the hang of waiting on tables again. I had been working all morning and the steady breakfast crowd turned into a steady lunch crowd. By two in the afternoon, things slowed down a bit. Em called out from behind the cash counter to take a break and I gladly accepted the offer.

I refilled my water glass and sat down at the nearby bar and stared dreamily out the window. Jordyn plopped down right beside me and we chatted for a while.

"So, Jade, how's your first day going?"

"Not bad. I haven't dropped food or spilled drinks on anyone yet so I can't complain."

"I haven't been here that long but I love it. There's never a dull moment. Are you single?"

Her question was unexpected and out of place. I raised one eyebrow at her while trying to think of a way to answer. I kept it simple.

"Yes."

"Oh. I thought maybe you had a boyfriend back home or something."

"No." Was all I said. After a brief silence, Jordyn's face brightened a bit more.

"Well, you know some of your uncle's officers aren't too hard on the eyes, especially that Jackson Butler. I've had a crush on him since I first saw him. But he doesn't give anyone the time of day. Maybe you two might hit it off. Have you met him yet?"

"Um, yeah, we've met." I said bitterly, suddenly remembering I had yet to talk to my uncle about that damn ticket that miser gave me.

"He gave me a ticket my first day in town." And on a side note I couldn't help but ask. "Is he always that crotchety?"

"Only on Monday, Wednesday and every other Tuesday."

Jordyn choked on the sip of coke she had just taken as I spun around fast enough to nearly knock her and I off the bar stools. He stood like a tower over my head, just inches from my bar stool, looking directly down at me. I hadn't heard him walk up and could feel my face burning as I stared right back into his dark brown eyes. They seemed to reach right through me. I instantly felt uneasy.

I hadn't noticed the color of them before because of the dark sunglasses he had been wearing the day he pulled me over. Now I thought how perfectly they matched his brooding, rigid face. Before I could think of anything to say he proceeded.

"You can tear up the ticket I gave you. And thank your uncle for the reason. I don't give special treatment just because a person is related to the

Chief. If you break the law again and I catch you, you will be held accountable."

"Well, if it isn't Mr. Butler." Emma had come over as soon as she was free from her duties.

"Do you want a menu? Are you having lunch today?"

He finally looked away from me after Em's last comment and for the first time since I met him, his face softened into a faint smile.

"No thank you, Mrs. Hawthorne. I've got to be hitting the road again."

"I see you've met my niece, Jade?"

"Yes, I was just coming to tell her to discard her ticket."

"Oh, how sweet of you. Once she gets used to the roads and the area, I'm sure it won't happen again."

"I will count on that." His steely gaze locked onto mine once again and I couldn't resist the contempt I felt rising in my chest. *What was his problem*? He started to walk away when Em called out.

"Jackson, would you care to join us for dinner tonight?"

I whipped my head around to stare at Em incredulously. She either didn't feel the heat radiating from my eyes like lasers into her skull or deserved an Oscar for pretending not to notice. I faced Jackson again and without regret shot him a warning glare. *Don't even think about it, buddy.*

"That's really kind of you Mrs. Hawthorne but I'm afraid I have to pass. I have plans tonight."

Before she could stop him again, his long legs carried him swiftly out the door.

"Well that was a tad uncomfortable." Jordyn shook her head and laughed. "But I still think he's hot."

"Then he's all yours, I want nothing to do with that man. Aunty, what were you thinking? I told you how rude he was to me and then you go and invite him to dinner? I didn't deserve to be treated so coldly. He's condescending, coarse and conceited."

"Jade, my dear, you're judging a book by its cover. There's more to Jackson than what meets the eye. The past few years have been rough on him and he has no one to go home to lately. I asked him to dinner because he's a good man and a friend to us."

"Well forgive me, that may be the case but I still don't like him."

Emma reached over and tweaked my chin.

"Two more hours and call it a day Jade. Dinner will be ready by five at our house. I've got to get back to work."

A few minutes later Jordyn and myself were clearing tables and washing them down when I rehashed the subject again.

"Seriously. What is his problem?"

"Who?"

"Jackson. Does he have a beef with women or something? Or just people in general?"

"I'm not sure. I don't know him all that well but from what I've heard he was engaged once quite a few years ago. She was killed by an intruder late one night in their home."

"Really? Did they catch the guy?"

"Not that I know of. Apparently it was some random attack. A few breaking and entering complaints had been filed throughout the town but no one else was injured besides Annabelle. Jackson came home late that night to find the house broken into and her lying fatally shot in their home. The strange thing was…nothing had been taken. The house was a disaster of broken stuff but nothing was missing."

I stood there trying to absorb this new information.

"That's horrible."

"Yeah. That's when Jackson decided to join boot camp for cops. He wanted to become an officer. Some people think it was to cover his tracks, spruce up his bad reputation so to speak."

"What do you mean?"

"Well, although I don't buy it one bit, some say Jackson's alibi that night was confirmed but it smelled like someone possibly covered for him. They think he killed Annabelle."

CHAPTER FIVE — PAULDING LIGHT

A few weeks had passed since arriving in Paulding. Things were starting to settle down and a routine began to form. Heather, Nikki and Jordyn were becoming good friends of mine. We were all starting to get to know each other and calling one another on occasion.

There was no doubt how much quieter and secluded Paulding was compared to the bustling city of Billings, and more than once I ached for home. I missed Taylor, I missed my parents; I missed the familiarity of the life I've always known. Em had graciously given me the weekend off and I thankfully welcomed the time to myself. Weekends at Dolly's were always the busiest.

People traveling through town stopped in to grab something to eat, some of them visiting the area and the recreational activities Paulding has to offer. Hunters migrated from the south and west during waterfowl and deer season. The surrounding plentiful forest outside of town offered an abundance of wildlife year round. Emma's cabins attracted much of the visitors due to the private lake that harbors a variety of fish for the avid fisherman such as Bluegill, Brook Trout and Yellow Perch. Some of the known species to inhabit its waters.

Still in my flannel pajama bottoms and fuzzy slippers, I sat in one of the high backed rocking chairs on the deck with a blanket wrapped around my shoulders and a hot cup of coffee in my hands. The temperatures were climbing as spring awakened and the trees began to show more signs of fresh green life. I loved the early morning setting outside my window.

Every morning brought a soft billowing fog that caressed the forest floor and danced across the motionless glassy lake. Looking across the water made me forget where I was. The fog obliterated the surrounding characteristics and seemed to obscure time itself. And yet, with its subtle strength, it failed to dampen out the loneliness that sometimes engulfed my heart.

As serene as this place was and as busy as Em was keeping me, these waves of feeling hit me like anxiety attacks, strong at first then subsiding into emptiness. I felt them now and started to think of home and of Dylan. I wondered what might have been if he had never found out the truth. Would we still be together? Would we be happy?

I will never forget the look on his face when he came over after work one day and saw—what appeared to him—as me talking to the wall. Stephanie had appeared to me. I had been home from the hospital for a few months recovering and it was as if a light switch had been turned from ON to OFF in that split second. Dylan had been so genuinely comforting and supportive of my recovery process, helping me with anything and everything. It all changed when he stepped into the room.

"Jade…what are you doing? Who are you talking to?"

His gaze scanned the empty room then turned back to my startled expression.

"Did I just hear you say Stephanie's name?"

I couldn't think of an adequate response fast enough, one that would reverse the damage I could see I was causing. He looked at me as if I were mentally sick. A flicker of fear crossed his eyes for just a moment, then was replaced with a hesitant curiosity again. *The Truth Shall Set You Free.* I had heard that expression a few times in my life and when I tested that theory out, I found it to be quite accurate.

"Um, well, Dylan...I'm not sure how to explain this but something happened to me when I died on the hospital table. I saw Stephanie's spirit. She's still here, Dylan. I can see and talk to her. In fact, she's standing right next to me."

Stephanie stared at him helplessly, knowing he couldn't see her. He gave a convincing presentation of continuing to support me after that day, but he never looked at me quite the same again. His genuine concern over my welfare had vanished. It was like he had become perfunctory in his obligations to me, going through the motions of taking care of me robotically, yet devoid of any true feeling. And like I had feared, he did not believe me when I made my revelation. He countered it with 'head trauma' and 'emotional distress'.

We went through the motions of a normal couple afterwards but something just wasn't the same between us. I hadn't realized how desperately I had hoped he would trust and believe in me, I thought that was what love was all about. I also realized how much of a burden this was starting to be on him, on us. Arguments had broken out shortly after, mostly about me going into therapy.

I kept telling him I wasn't crazy or sick or in need of help. I tried so hard to convince him. Stephanie would sometimes appear behind him with a hopeless look on her face. Neither her nor I knew how to convince him otherwise.

Messages I gave him from her went unheeded. Things she told me about his childhood I thought for sure would be the answer to breaking past the brick wall he had built, but he always had an argument for everything.

"You two were good friends, she probably told you all about my life before she died and now you're trying to pretend that she's telling you these things from the grave? It's horseshit Jade! You need help and I'm afraid I don't know how to help you anymore. I'll go to counseling with you if it'll make a difference but otherwise, you need to stop. Just stop, I don't want to hear anymore."

I cried a lot that night; I could sense the end was near for Dylan and I. I had turned into a freak show to him and he had let me down when I needed him the most. We were a disappointment to each other. The next day he asked me again about therapy and I told him the same answer as always: '*No*'.

He said he was done, that he was sorry but he couldn't live like this. He didn't know how to give me the help I needed when I would refuse to admit I had a problem. I yelled back that he *was* the problem. His mind in all its inaptitude and simple ways couldn't comprehend that maybe, just maybe I was telling the truth. Why would I lie in the first place? What point would there be in doing so? Just then every ounce of energy, passion, love, frustration and even rage drained from my body and I was left standing there facing him, empty and resigned.

"Just go Dylan. We've already said our good-byes."

The Truth had indeed set us both free.

I slowly came back from my reverie to find I had started rocking myself back and forth on the rocking chair. The fog had lifted from the lake and the sun was breaking through the soon to be clear sky. I stood up and was about to call Taylor just to hear her voice when my cell phone rang from the kitchen counter.

"Hey Jade. It's Nikki! I have the day off and heard you did too. Heather is working the morning shift but is done at eleven. We wanted to see if you wanted to join us today in town for lunch?"

I had to admit, those two girls were something else. Impeccable timing to say the least for how much I needed someone at that moment and here they were to save the day. The two of them were so carefree and fun loving people. They were welcoming light and I was the moth, inescapably drawn to their charm. Nikki's husband was a deputy. Johnny Waters was known to be a straight-laced guy, serious more often than not but secretly had a laid back side when not on duty.

It was hard to believe that when I met him for the first time last week when he came into Dolly's for lunch. Despite his 'No Nonsense' disposition, it was easy to see he was a fair and cordial human being. Unfailingly polite and courteous and even-tempered. How he was drawn to Nikki or vice versa was still a mystery.

Simply put, opposites do attract. I've been told by the girls at work that Johnny's been teased by the fellow officers how much he took on when he married Nikki. Not known to be the best driver, she had run off the road a few times and had even taken out a street sign. A few innocent by-standing vehicles had received the brunt of her feeble driving skills as she backed into them on more than one occasion.

One of the more classic times was when she was leaving an automobile insurance agency and backed into a company vehicle, shattering the driver's side taillight and denting in the bumper.

"You've got your hands full with that one Johnny!"

His coworkers would tease and laugh. Johnny simply took it in stride. He'd smile and shake his head as if in agreement. Nikki also liked to have a good time, all within reason of course. Her love for Johnny, and his for her, would never be compromised. Their trust and fidelity for one another was strong and true.

Her and Heather loved to go dancing and have been known to visit the local dance club in town. Sometimes a band would be playing and other times a DJ would spin out hits all night long. Johnny deemed it a 'respectable' enough establishment where fights were few and patrons weren't of the law-breaking sort and so didn't put up much of a fuss when she felt like kicking her heels up. He probably wouldn't be able to stop her even if he did tell her 'No'.

Nikki could be strong willed when she wanted to be. But theirs wasn't the kind of relationship of control or containment, it was of mutual respect and an intangible understanding only those two shared. Besides, their nights out weren't an every weekend venture. The girls respected their husbands immensely. Whenever they spoke of them, it was always in good humor and admiration. For how little time has passed since arriving in Paulding, I feel I've become acquainted with the entire town through stories people shared of one another. Most of them I hear at the restaurant.

"I can pick you up Jade if you'd like, say around 11:30?"

"Thanks Nikki, but I've got some things to do after lunch and will need my car. I can just meet you guys at the restaurant."

I didn't feel like taking any chances just yet, riding with her sounded like a death wish and I had things to do yet before I died. We picked a cute little café in town with umbrella tables scattered on the sidewalk. The town was bustling with people and it was just past noon. We spent an hour prior to lunch scourging antique shops and window-shopping, then took a walk over to the park and crossed a stone bridge overlooking a small creek.

A narrow path had taken us a quarter mile through the park, twisting through trees and park benches then past a pond where ducks were swimming. By the time our walk was finished, we were hungry and relieved to be sitting at one of the umbrella tables with iced tea in hand.

Kathleen Wickman

"So, have you seen our town's infamous phantom light, Jade?"

Strangely enough in the few times I visited my aunt and uncle, I had vaguely heard of Paulding Light but had yet to see it.

"Actually, I have not."

"Well then, I say it's time we introduce you to the eighth wonder of the world. Let's go tonight. Weather forecast shows clear skies, perfect conditions to view it."

"Ugh, we're going there again? I'm burnt out on that place. You two go; I'm going to paint my nails or something."

"Oh Heather, don't be a boob. You know you have nothing else to do tonight considering Eric and Johnny will be playing cards with the guys. They're having a guy's night, why shouldn't we have a girl's night? Would you really rather sit at home alone doing nothing?"

"Fine! I'll go."

I looked at both women then back down at my salad plate. I was not nearly as enthusiastic as Nikki was to go. But I kept my mouth shut for in reality, I would've preferred avoiding anything paranormal for the rest of my life if I could. Like Heather, I also did not relish the idea of sitting at home by myself tonight either. That's all I seemed to be doing lately when I wasn't working. Maybe a girl's night out is just what I needed.

"So, it's settled then. I'll pick you up at dusk. No need for directions, your aunt told me which cabin you're staying in."

"Uh…." I started to say something but Nikki cut me off.

"No arguing, just have your spook pants on."

Heather rolled her eyes then gave Nikki a look before turning to me.

"There's no point in resisting, Jade. Just go with it. And don't worry, it's not that spooky so you won't need a change of pants as she's trying to imply."

She patted my shoulder consolingly then turned her attention to a car that had slowly rounded the corner.

"Hey, there's Jackson and your hubby."

Heather waved her arm in the air in an attempt to draw their attention our way. My fair mood changed gears swiftly as the patrol car turned down the street we were on and pulled up alongside our outdoor table.

"Hey stud muffins! What are you guys up to?" Nikki called out as the car came to a stop.

"Hi, ladies. We were just cruising by to check out Eric's work on the culvert." Johnny Waters smiled at us as he spoke.

Heather's husband Eric LeClaire worked for the city of Paulding and was kept busy throughout the week fixing water mains and patching up roads where they had to dig.

"He told me they were done with that job. Was there a problem?"

"No, no problem. They are done with it. It looks great. They did a good job as always. Speaking of your husband, is he still planning on meeting us tonight for our poker game? It's at Jackson's house in case he forgot."

"Yup. Wild horses couldn't stop him, which is good because he's driving me nuts this week. So keep him as long as you'd like. We've got our own plans tonight anyway."

"Really? What trouble may I ask, has my wife corrupted you into now?"

Johnny gave Nikki a wink, then looked back at Heather.

"Hey now, don't be giving Jade any wrong impressions of me. She thinks I'm a saint, don't you Jade?"

"Of course."

"Too late I see; she's fooled you. So what's on the agenda?"

"I'm taking her to see Paulding Light. She's never been there before."

I glanced up from my untouched plate of food and locked eyes with Jackson. He hadn't said a word since they pulled up. Other than smile at Nikki and Heather, he said nothing but I noticed he was now watching me closely. I began to feel uncomfortable. Why wouldn't he just go away?

Johnny looked my way "Jade, have you met Jackson yet?"

Apparently I wasn't going to get my wish just yet.

"Yes, we've met. I pulled her over on her way into town."

Jackson's response cut mine off.

Johnny elbowed Jackson in the ribs. "Oh, you're harsh Jackie."

"I voided it out afterwards to appease Marcus."

He really knew how to bring out the worst in me and before I could bite my tongue I blurted out.

"Well, I really didn't think I deserved it. I never heard of not stopping at a stop sign before. It was an honest mistake."

The girls looked at me, at each other, then down at their plates at my sarcastic comment. I instantly regretted giving him the power to piss me off. I was making a fool of myself in front of my new friends.

"I know. That's another reason I tore it up. I realize I went over-board. No hard feelings I hope."

It was the first time he had displayed any sense of decency towards me and it confused me deeply.

"Not at all."

I didn't know what else to say.

"Have fun tonight ladies." Jackson tipped his hat at us then nodded at Johnny to drive away.

"See you later, babe!" Nikki called out to Johnny.

He waved, smiled at us and drove away.

"What was that about, girlfriend? You two got something going on?"

Nikki leaned over to me with overt interest, awaiting an answer.

"Yes, do tell! He really got under your skin. Did some hanky panky happen while you were here and he never called back, or what?"

"Or 'what' more like." I replied.

They continued to stare at me, hoping for more tidbits.

"Cripes, I just moved here! It's not even possible to hook up that fast! He just rubbed me the wrong way initially but it's fine now. No big deal."

"He is pretty strict when it comes to his job. He has to be. But he's really a good guy once you get to know him." Heather said.

"You sound like my aunt."

"I just think he has a wall up since Annabelle's death. Who can blame him with all he's been through."

Jordyn's comment that day at Dolly's came back to me about the conspiracy and how some people thought Jackson was the killer. Curiosity got the best of me.

"I heard some people think Jackson had something to do with Annabelle's death. Is that true?"

Heather scraped her plate and answered with a mouth full of food.

"That rumor has been floating around for years. More than likely stemming from small town boredom and people having nothing better to do than talk. The truth is that there's nothing that can link him to the crime and more importantly, he'd never be able to become a cop if he was truly believed to be guilty of doing something to Annie. They go through rigorous training and background checks. Jackson joined the police force to bring justice and peace to the world and maybe even capture the true killer."

"Is that really why he joined? Johnny never told me that."

"No, but it's what I think."

The waiter came and gave us our bill.

"Okay Jade, see you tonight!"

We paid our bill and said our good-byes. I wasn't quite sure what to expect and still wasn't all to at ease with the thought of seeing some kind of weird phenomenon. Ironically dread filled me more than fear. Steph had told me ghosts couldn't hurt the living. Most of the time they didn't even notice us as they drifted in between worlds.

Strangely enough, I did not fear my gift; I simply dreaded it. I'd imagine most people would go insane if they were stuck with the abilities I had. I just adapted as best I could with something I could not explain nor change. Perhaps that was part of the gift in itself, strength to bear the hidden burden. And courage to go on.

Nikki picked me up just as the day drew to a close. I was told it would be about a fifteen-minute drive outside of town. We followed the main highway for a while until all signs of habitat disappeared completely leaving only forest surrounding both sides of the road.

"Remember Heather, when Paulding Light was featured on an episode of Unsolved Mysteries?"

"Yeah, that was neat. And the Ripley's Believe It or Not people were out here too doing experiments to try and figure it out."

I sat in the backseat listening to their chatter. As a teenager I remembered my aunt telling my mother about the light and how it would appear from the woods, then mysteriously vanish. At the time I figured it was just pranksters up to no good. When Dylan and I met in college, I had tried talking him into coming with me to see it. But like many of our plans, it fell through the cracks, forever lost.

"Ready to be amazed, Jade?"

Nikki's cheery voice cut through my thoughts as she abruptly steered the car off the highway and onto a gravel road.

"Hang on, we're almost there!" She straightened the wheel as gravel kicked up behind the tires.

"What exactly is this place again?" I asked without looking away from the window.

"It's a ghost light that's been said to haunt these woods since the turn of the century, over a hundred years ago. No one can explain what it is exactly, but rumor has it a train derailed here long ago causing the death of the Brake Man as he failed to switch the tracks in time. Supposedly, the mysterious light is that of the ghost train."

I nodded my head as if I understood even though it sounded far-fetched to me. Then again, who was I to judge that subject? I was grateful to have met Nikki and Heather so soon after moving to Paulding. I didn't realize how much I needed a friend after leaving everything I had ever known behind.

"I hope the light shows for you Jade."

Heather turned around from the passenger seat of the car and looked back at me.

"Sometimes it stays dormant for long stretches of time, or it may show but it's so faint that it's barely detectable."

I glanced away from the window towards Heather.

"So how do you know it's not some kids playing a prank on the town, or something?"

Nikki answered before Heather could.

"Scientists have been up here several times to investigate the light, as well as other specialists from various fields. All hoaxes were ruled out."

"But there will always be those who doubt anything paranormal, who believe that car headlights are the true cause or that some chemical from the ground is causing a mysterious fog. Or light refraction from glaciers are reflecting somehow into the valley."

I looked at both girls and said, "So, what do you think it is?"

Heather, the feistier one of the two said, "Hell if I know, but it's cool to look at."

The car was cruising at a quick rate up a steep hill at that moment.

"Nikki, slow down! You're gonna hit somebody!"

"Chill out Heather, I'm slowing down." Nikki tried to hide the smirk on her face while Heather sat there clutching the door handle for dear life.

The girl's personalities were like night and day, yet they made the greatest friends. Their bickering was so comical at times it was easy to see how close they really were. Heather was the less patient one, while Nikki could be stuck in a New York City traffic jam and make a game out of it by singing show tunes just to pass the time. Nothing ever seemed to bring that girl down. I envied her for that.

The sun had already taken cover behind the hills in the distance. Its beautiful orange hues quickly fading from the clear night sky. As we approached the top of the hill, I could see we weren't the first ones on the scene. There were already a few people gathered at the guardrail located at the east end of the valley. On the other side of the guardrail was a long clearing that swooped downward then leveled out across a glittering stream. It gradually climbed back up to the other side of the valley where a wall of trees marked its end. The railroad tracks had long since been removed.

Nikki parked the car near a vacant spot next to the guardrail, and we all climbed out. The forest was everywhere. It seemed to suffocate the tiny clearing the ghost light is normally seen in. We found a spot to stand by the rail as I glanced around. There were people of all ages standing nearby. Kids playing tag, not really concerned about spooks at the time. Retired folk staring intently down the hill hoping to catch a glimpse of something, anything. Some brought binoculars and almost everyone had cameras. There were empty beer cans all over the place. I thought to myself what a shame it was that someone couldn't at least provide a garbage can out here. After all, this place was as close to 'No Man's Land' as I'd ever seen.

It was getting colder. We had been standing for at least forty-five minutes now as the day faded into darkness. Not even the moon was out. A few stars dotted the sky. I wanted to head back home because my feet were getting cold. It was early May and the ground was barely thawed from the harsh winter. The evenings were still chilly and even the fleece jacket I was wearing seemed to be too light for the continuous drop in temperature. But I stood there, not wanting to be the party pooper. Heather and Nikki chatted about their husbands when all of a sudden a gasp broke out in the crowd. I couldn't see anyone's faces anymore. I could only make out Heather's shadowy profile only because she was standing right next to me.

Far down the hill a faint white glow had appeared. So soft it was barely recognizable. It slowly grew in brightness, then danced from one side to another. It looked so small, as if it were many miles away.

To my amazement, the light suddenly seemed to lock on to us and started to drift closer, becoming brighter as it did so. Within half a second it had grown so close and so bright, I thought it would swallow us whole. I couldn't wrap my mind around how fast it went from miles away to mere feet before us in such a short span of time. And what amazed me further was not just the softness with which it moved; so obscure and graceful as opposed to fast and brutal, which is how it should've been considering the distance it just covered, but moreover the quality of the light itself.

There was no doubt in my mind this was definitely *not* the product of a vehicle's headlight. It was just too transparent, elusive. Like at any minute it could disappear. And as if it could read my thoughts, it did just that.

The crowd had grown silent over the occurrence but when it vanished everyone started talking excitedly. Some teenagers nearby mocked the incident and made crude remarks. While others were looking at their digital cameras hoping they had caught the spectacle.

Heather leaned over and gave a soft jab to my side. "Pretty cool, hey?"

"Yeah, that was neat. Will it come back?"

"Not sure. I hope so."

"I wonder if the lantern will appear?" Nikki pondered out loud.

I looked at her, wondering what she was talking about. She proceeded to tell me about the Brake Man and the red lantern he carries. And how he haunts these woods as well. Every now and then you could see its red glow swinging back and forth along the path of where the train had once been. The white light of the train sometimes accompanies the red lantern as the two lights sway in an ethereal trance like beauty.

Then, as if on cue, another light appeared on the horizon. This one was different from the first light. It had the erubescent hue of the so-called lantern.

"There's the lantern Jade!" Nikki was bouncing up and down like a kid in a candy store, clapping her hands feverishly.

For a twenty-five year old woman, she certainly had the heart of a child. I couldn't help but laugh.

The 'lantern' did indeed swing as Nikki had predicted. It was swinging closer now to the left side of the guardrail where I was standing. My laugh died quickly as the red lantern swung into the woods then back out again, each time drawing closer to me. I wanted to move but my feet wouldn't budge.

Heather grabbed my arm. I could feel her fingers digging in. Off to the right of the red glow, the white light appeared. Strong as before and hovering just behind the red lantern. My breath caught in my throat.

Is that really what I think it is? Please, not again...

A shadowy outline of a man holding a lantern stood facing me. I couldn't see his face clearly but the hairs on my neck told me he was looking straight at me. For reasons I couldn't explain, an intense sadness gripped my heart and almost brought me to my knees. My whole body ached with it. I wanted nothing more than to crawl into a hole, wrap myself into a ball and simply cry.

Then both lights and man vanished instantly before my eyes and so did the sadness that just seconds before ravaged my soul. I knew their answer before I even asked but I had to know. Just maybe this time, it would be different.

"Did you guys happen to see that man holding the lantern?"

Heather and Nikki looked at each other with confused expressions then back at me. Neither said a word at first, then Nikki busted out laughing.

"Yeah, yeah, nice try Jade. You almost had me."

"I'm serious. So, you didn't see anyone?"

"Just the spook lights. Come on. Let's get out of here."

As we walked back to the car, the girls walking ahead of me, I couldn't shake my mind of the silhouette lantern man. And that incredible sadness I felt. I thought my heart would truly break from it. I knew that feeling once before, not as brutal but just as debilitating.

That was why I had left Montana, to escape the pain and sadness. But apparently I wasn't able to escape my gift. Two things I knew for sure as we got into the car and drove away. For reasons beyond comprehension, my ability to see and talk to the dead was expanding into something bigger than merely communicating to Stephanie's spirit as I once had. It now seemed to extend to all ghosts. And one of them was trying to tell me that something horrific happened here long ago.

CHAPTER SIX — SAM

It had been over a week since I saw the shadowy figure of the presumed lantern man standing in front of the eerie white ghost light. He was the first ghost I had seen since Stephanie. As much as I wanted to forget about the incident, I simply could not, or that crushing sadness I had felt when he appeared. I swear since that moment, a phantasmal floodgate had opened and quite periodically, I'd see a salient form walking down the street. As solid and vivid as my hand in front of my face. The only difference between live flesh and the fact that it was a ghost was the graceful, fluid continuous type movement it was making.

The legs would be moving as if in a natural walk and yet the ghost seemed not to fully touch the ground as it moved. The first thing that came to mind when I saw a ghostly woman dressed in forties style clothing was not the eccentricity for how she looked but that of how she moved down the sidewalk on Main street. I envisioned the sliding walkway at Chicago O-Hare Airport as a comparison and how people seemed to be flying or floating across as they walk to catch their next flight. Chills always crept into my bones when I saw a ghost.

They'd disappear into thin air within a matter of seconds but the chills I got lasted for much longer. Most of them were unaware of my presence, or the presence of anyone else for that matter. For on one occasion, I had witnessed a ghost walking through someone else. Neither being aware of the other as they made their way to unknown destinations. The most disturbing time was when a man had been sitting at a corner table at Dolly's. I had just come in for my shift and saw him staring down at his hands, which were covered in grease and dirt.

He had stained overalls on and a worn out, ripped long sleeve shirt. His boots were old and torn and full of mud. I groaned inwardly thinking about the mess I was going to have to clean up when he left. When he suddenly looked up and stared directly at me with the clearest eyes I had ever seen. I froze on the spot and tried to look away to no avail. A strange and ominous feeling washed over me. I immediately felt ill. The kind of sickness I had felt when I realized Stephanie died in the car crash.

"You should leave this town now while you still can."

His voice was raspy as he spoke. My eyebrows furrowed in confusion. I was about to ask him what he meant by that but before I could, he faded into nothingness. I blinked a few times in surprise. The entire experience was unnerving to say the least.

In an effort to escape the unworldly chaos my life had become, I had suggested a road trip to Green Bay to see a Josh Groban concert. I was a fool in thinking my gift was restricted to a centralized locale. The realization of my blunder took effect within a half-hour of the performance. It turned out Josh's large fan base wasn't limited to those with a pulse. I anxiously gripped my chair while I watched in horror from the fifth row as a group of overly excited young women raced onto the stage from the wall behind them. A young brunette in the lead tripped on some unearthly object and fell right through him, dropping into the floor on the other side. The other girls disappeared shortly before reaching him. His amazing voice never missed a note as I sat in shocked silence. It was then I exhaled deeply remembering I was the only one who could see what had just happened. I glanced over at Nikki, Heather and Jordyn. All three were smiling at Josh and singing along to his music, unaware of anything out of the ordinary. Here I was, with three good friends in a crowd of hundreds of people and I had never felt more alone. In time, I would learn to accept what I could not change.

***

Our road trip weekend had really been wonderful, despite the celebrity haunting. I was back to work at Dolly's. Emma had hired college students for the summer, which was why I was fortunate enough to have those few days off. I was making up for lost time in the hours she had me scheduled during the week though.

Each night after my shift I would plop down in my soft bed and instantly fall asleep just to wake up a few hours later and do it all again. I was beginning to wonder if Uncle Marcus was right after all; my aunt may indeed be the slave driver he had talked about. But I didn't mind. I loved the work and I appreciated the exhaustion at the end of each day for that meant haunting thoughts couldn't trouble my mind.

I even found time to continue taking pictures as I had once done at my old job back in Montana.

Kathleen Wickman

The scenery was becoming more beautiful as flowers blossomed, trees bloomed and spring turned into summer. It was late June and the weather was starting to feel like summer. I was told the Upper Peninsula of Michigan had its own seasons…winter and 4th of July.

Summers came late and were fleeting, winters lasted for what seemed like an eternity, and if you blinked your eyes, the seasons could change overnight. I was mentally preparing myself for that bridge to cross. But for now, I welcomed the sun as it warmed my skin and kissed my face. There was a commotion inside the restaurant. A few screams reached the deck where I was serving table five.

I excused myself, told the patrons to stay where they were when I noticed customers standing up from their chairs, and ran inside to see what was going on. A deranged man was running wildly through the restaurant, with gun in hand, desperately trying to escape from his fate. Just then, Jackson rounded the corner in full pursuit with gun drawn. They were both heading directly at me and I froze on the spot. The empty tray I had been holding dropped with a clang to the floor.

No one else had moved, the entire restaurant had frozen in place, watching in shocked disbelief. The fugitive saw me and threw his arm around my neck as he ran to the door. His speed toppled me backwards and spun him around as my back collided into his chest. A cold piece of metal pressed into my skull. Every drop of blood drained from my face as Jackson screeched to a halt a few feet away, gun poised on us both.

"Get back! I swear I'll shoot her!" His words came out gruff as his grip tightened on me.

Jackson never took his eyes off the mad man as he slowly dragged me step by step out onto the deck. People who were sitting near the door saw what was happening and scattered. The tables further away stayed awestruck in terror, watching helplessly. For every step the man took, Jackson took one too.

"You're caught sir! Back up is on its way and when it comes, you'll be surrounded. Let her go!" Jackson's tone was steady and strong as he commanded the man to drop the gun.

We were outside now nearing the back steps off the deck. The woods were just beyond, beckoning anyone to become lost within its shadows. I was clutching at his arm, the gun still jammed against my skull. Just to the right of us a table sat inches away, and sitting at that table was a lone man in his thirties. I wasn't sure why he caught my attention but he did. Sitting there, closest to us, all by himself.

He had been leaning forward over the table when we walked past him. When I glanced his way again his face implored mine. He mouthed the words *"Let go"* and leaned distinctively back in his chair. Nine out of ten times I more than likely would not have had a flipping clue as to what he was talking about, nor would I have been able to shut out the terror gripping my body in order to think straight. But the fact that we were on the edge of the top step and that my captor was facing an eight-foot drop to the grass below, something just clicked in my head.

Survival instinct kicked in. I knew exactly what that patron meant when he mouthed those words and leaned back into his chair.

At this point it appeared I was dead either way whether I went into the black forest with my captor or took a bullet to the brain, it didn't matter. My candle was about to burn out. I said a quiet prayer, inhaled deeply and pushed backwards with all my might. My assailant was completely caught off-guard as was Jackson.

The hand holding the gun went into the air as he desperately fought for balance. I braced myself for the fall as both our bodies tumbled down the wooden steps. The soft cushy grass caught us both. Before I even rolled to a stop, Jackson was on top of the assailant and had him in handcuffs. Back up was just rounding the side of the restaurant and Johnny ran to my aide.

"Jade! Are you alright!?"

I slowly sat up and tested my limbs.

"Yeah, I'm okay Johnny."

A delayed reaction of nerves set in and I started to tremble. I tried to stand up only to be met with a searing pain in my ankle. A yelp escaped my mouth and I crumbled back down as Johnny's arm wrapped around my shoulder.

"Whoa, easy Jade. Don't move; you may have broken something."

Jackson's back up was assisting him with the irate thief who still refused to be caught. When they walked by us with the man handcuffed, Jackson looked down at me and stopped.

"Johnny, your muscles are bigger than mine, help Duvall and Hawk haul his ass into the brink. I'll take care of Jade."

Johnny patted my shoulder.

"You've got guts kid, doing what you did. I'm glad you're okay."

At that he walked away to help his fellow officers.

I looked for the man who had inspired my escape and found him standing near the doorway speaking to Gus. Then he took one last look my way and disappeared inside the restaurant as more and more people poured out to gather by my side. A few of the waitresses had run outside to see if I was all right, Jordyn being one of them.

"Jade! Oh my gosh! I can't believe you did that! Are you okay?"

"I'm fine, Jordyn. Just hurt my ankle."

"Your aunt's going to flip when she hears about this!"

She was wound up like a ten- day clock, half excitement on her young face, half fear for what had just happened, what could have happened. I was thankful my aunt was running errands today. It would be bad enough once she found out. I didn't want her to see me hurt. She needed to know I was okay. The same went for Heather and Nikki who wouldn't be coming in until dinner shift.

"She'll be alright ladies, go back inside." Jackson waved off the ensuing crowd of onlookers.

To my surprise, he put one knee on the ground and leaned into me with one arm bracing behind my back and the other under my legs.

"Jackson, I'm fine! You don't have to carry me, I can walk." I tried not to sound rattled as I spoke.

"Yeah, I noticed. You crumpled like a pancake on your first attempt to stand. Just relax, you don't want to put pressure on it until a doctor examines it."

"Fine! Just don't call an ambulance please, I can drive myself."

"And how do you suggest you do that when it's your right foot that's hurt? I won't call an ambulance but I am driving you to the hospital. Now put your arm around my shoulder."

The close proximity of his body as he scooped me effortlessly into his arms alarmed me. Granted he was a solid man but his strength surprised me given his thin stature. I was also astutely aware of the smell of his skin, musky and strong. He smelled like the Montana Mountains during a spring rain, fresh and intoxicating.

I turned my face away. He carried me to his patrol car and gently sat me in the front seat. My ankle was throbbing painfully at this point and I was visibly cringing at every movement.

"Ice would do just fine, Jackson. I don't think the hospital visit is necessary."

He climbed into the driver's seat and shut the door.

"No sense taking any chances. Your foot is swelling pretty badly."

He waited outside the hospital room as the doctor examined my ankle. To my relief it was only badly sprained. Doctor's orders were to stay off of it for a few days. Jackson drove me back to my cabin and followed me inside as I hobbled on my new crutches.

"Your uncle had to go to the next county this morning. He's rushing back as we speak to check on you. Emma is on her way over as well. Marcus called her on his way home."

"Great. I'll be here."

I was making a weak attempt at humor to lighten the mood in the room. The look on Jackson's face was all seriousness. I hobbled over to the couch, plopped down and picked up the remote for the T.V. He stood in the living room for a moment while I flipped through the channels. My attempt at ignoring his presence was feeble. I dropped the remote and looked up at him.

"You know Jade," he started "that was an incredibly foolish thing you did today. You could've gotten yourself killed. What were you thinking?"

I lifted my injured leg onto the coffee table in hopes of relieving some of the pain. The drugs the doctor had given me unfortunately hadn't kicked in yet. I shrugged my shoulders and answered honestly.

"I didn't think I had much choice. Either way, I felt I was going to get hurt. Besides, how would you have stopped him with me in the way?"

Jackson walked over to where I was sitting and grabbed a soft pillow from the end of the couch.

"It was my job to stop him, not yours. You took a dangerous risk."

His hand gently lifted my injured leg while the other one placed the pillow under it. His closeness was doing strange things to my pulse again. I tried to ignore my nerves as I continued defending my actions.

"It may have been your job, but it was my life. What's done is done Jackson. You nabbed the guy, that's all that matters."

A loud sigh escaped his lips as he stood over me with his hands on his hips. He was about to say more but relented and shook his head. He turned to walk away then stopped.

"Can I get you anything before I go, or are you stubborn enough to get it yourself?"

"I'm stubborn enough."

I gave him a smug grin then turned back to the program on T.V. There was still a part of me that rebelled against him for reasons I didn't understand.

"Is there a reason for your attitude or does it just come naturally?"

"Ha! That's the pot calling the kettle black."

I don't know why I was being so flippant with him; he just had a way of bringing the worst out in me at times. I felt harassed over my decisions today and there was nothing I could do about it. He had made an attempt to be cordial though lately, especially today with how he took care of me, duty or not. I softened a bit.

"Look, Jackson. I'm sorry. I'm tired and in pain. Thank you for everything you did today but I think I'm going to lie down."

"Suit yourself."

With that he turned and walked outside, letting the screen door slam behind him.

***

Uncle Marcus and Aunt Emma checked in on me from time to time but overall gave me my space to recover. They offered to let me stay with them until I healed but I declined. My aunt and uncle were blissfully not as overprotective and suffocating as my parents could be, but they still worried.

I could see it in their eyes whenever they'd stop by my cabin. My aunt had been horrified to hear what had happened.

"I should have been there." She had told me shortly after the incident.

"Auntie. There was nothing you could have done. Besides, no one was seriously hurt. That's all that matters."

She looked at my injured ankle when I had said this, then wrapped her arms around me in a tight embrace.

A few days later I was climbing the walls with boredom. It was a beautiful Saturday morning and I knew Aunt Emma would be home so I decided to get some fresh air. I didn't need my crutches anymore; I was healing faster than expected. A large plastic brace encased my right foot and I hobbled along slowly down the dirt road. The other cabins were now occupied as tourists inundated the area.

Cars passed me occasionally as they left their cabins or returned from some remote excursion. Boats dotted the private lake and children were swimming not far from shore. Their laughter filled the air and made me smile. I loved summertime. Within a few short minutes I had reached the main house and was greeted at the door by Scooter, their Jack Russell Terrier.

"Hey boy."

I scratched his head and peeked through the screen door into the house.

"Aunt Emma?"

A voice replied somewhere in the garden, behind the back deck. I turned around and walked down the porch steps, following the stone path around the side of the house. Bella and Bruno were sunbathing near the lake and jumped up when they caught sight of me. All three dogs now accompanied me, jumping and dancing on the remaining walk to see Emma.

"Don't tell me you walked over here, Jade?"

Emma had been kneeling down in the dirt, weeding out her flowerbed when she sat back on her haunches and wiped the sweat from her forehead with the back of her hand.

"I sure did. My ankle's not that bad anymore. I'll be happy when this blasted brace comes off on Monday. Can I help you with anything?"

With a slight grunt she stood up and smiled.

"No, thank you dear. I think I'm going to take a break now. I've been at this thing all morning. Why don't you have a seat in one of the patio chairs and I'll get us some cold drinks."

I plopped down on the nearest chair and Scooter hopped up into my lap. The vacationers were making well use of the lake. Two people kayaked past the dock and waved when they saw me. I smiled and waved back.

In the distance a few boats were hovering over fishing spots as the anglers made ready their tackle in hopes of connecting with a large mouth bass or walleye. Em returned with iced tea and took the chair next to me. She had changed out of her garden clothes and into a light flower skirt and white tank top. It was hard to picture her as anything over forty not because of mere looks alone but by her personality and light-hearted ways. Her skin was still fair and without blemish, her eyes sparkled with mischief every now and then. She seemed more like a friend than relative as she sat down in the chair next to me. Sometimes I felt I could tell her anything.

"We're going to have a 4th of July party here on the property. We host one every year for friends, neighbors, restaurant employees, anyone really. Marcus goes out and buys the best fireworks he can and we light them off over the lake. Could you help me get the place ready?"

"Sure." My mother had told me once about their parties and how much fun they were. This would be the first time I'd get to see for myself.

"Could you pick up a few things for me on Tuesday? I have something to do at Dolly's and won't have time to get them myself. I'll give you the list and my credit card."

"Are you sure that's a good idea? Giving me your credit card? I may end up in Fiji."

We joked with one another and chatted more as the sun sank lower in the picture perfect sky. Tuesday evening I parked my car on Main Street within town square and walked, brace free to the party store with list in hand. I was looking at some red, white and blue party favors and added a select few to an already growing basket.

"Shopping for your aunt's party Jade?"

I turned around to see Sheba standing one aisle over.

"Hi, uh yeah, she asked me to help her out."

"That's nice of you. Her parties are lots of fun. The whole county turns out for it, or so it seems given the size of the crowd."

I smiled and turned back to look at streamers.

"Are you liking it here so far?"

"Yeah, I am. It's a beautiful area and everyone's been really nice."

"Yes, it is. I'm sure being the Chief's niece doesn't hurt in making new friends."

I gave her a sideways glance then resumed with my shopping. She followed me to the next aisle.

"Don't get me wrong dear, you seem like a really sweet girl and your aunt is one of my dearest friends. Marcus is a darling as well. It's just that it's no secret Emma and Marcus are one of the more affluential families in town, in the county even. Although they don't flaunt it. Sure, they have a big house but that's all you see of their comfortable life style. Dolly's has been the most popular business for a few generations now. Why, Marcus doesn't even need to work if he didn't want to. Neither does your aunt. They've done well for themselves. I'm sure they're glad to have you taking over the business for them."

Why was she telling me all this? What is she talking about?

"I'm not taking over the business. She needed to hire someone and I needed a job."

"Of course Jade, I didn't mean anything by that. You've been a big help to Emma. She's already told me how lucky she is to have you here."

Sheba glanced out the window and her face scrunched up into disdain. I followed her gaze and saw Jackson in civilian clothes across the street talking to a stunning blonde who looked like she just walked off the cover of a glamour magazine. My jaw dropped slightly then slammed shut as I continued to stare from inside the store.

What was she doing here when she could be walking the streets of New York City heading to her next photo shoot? She wore a short strapless summer dress that clung to her perfect figure. Long legs stretched down into high-heeled sandals. Her blonde hair hung long and straight over tanned shoulders.

She brushed it back with delicate hands as she laughed at something Jackson had said. He looked impeccable too. I had never seen him outside of his uniform and to my dismay had to admit how ruggedly handsome he was. He wore plain blue jeans and a gray t-shirt that gave a glimpse of the muscle hidden beneath. I could see the defined upper arms now as he reached up to scratch the back of his neck while smiling back at her.

"Watch out for that one, sweetie. He may be charming and handsome as hell on the outside but nothing but a womanizer within. You see the problem with him is he knows he's handsome. And yet he gives off airs that he's unattainable."

I had to admit, the high and mighty part of her comment I agreed with wholeheartedly. Some people just oozed it whether they knew it or not.

"Is that his girlfriend?" I had never heard him talk of having one nor had I heard anyone else referring to him dating anyone either.

"You never know with him. That's Sophia talking to him. She's been sweet on him for years."

Sheba scoffed at the two of them chatting then turned her back on the scene. The bombshell blonde was nodding her head at something he said, her radiant smile not as strong as before as she leaned in to hug him. He wrapped his arms around her too and patted her back; then they both walked separate ways. I finished my shopping and quickly paid for my things at the counter.

I said good-bye to Sheba then walked out the door. Jackson was getting into his truck parked just down the street. I had to wait for traffic to clear before crossing the street to get to my own car. I could see he had pulled away from the curb and was about to drive past me.

He saw me and waved without smiling. I politely smiled and waved back. As I jumped into my jeep and drove away I couldn't help but puzzle over how hard he was to figure out. He came across quiet, reserved and very distant then seeing him laugh and talk to that woman across the square was out of place for the man I had conjured up in my head.

He was relaxed and happy and it added an even deeper appeal to his characteristics. For someone who I had pegged as a mere jerk upon arriving here had now displayed a lighter side to that woman. A human side, as he laughed with her and relaxed his uptight demeanor. More importantly, it disturbed me more to realize I was a bit too curious about someone whom I virtually knew nothing about except for what others had said. Who gave me an unsettling feeling in my stomach.

Ironic, really, given his profession but intuition had yet to steer me wrong. I found myself wondering as I drove home in the dusk how much different he was than Dylan. I had met Dylan my junior year of college. He was so shy. But I knew he was interested in me so I finally asked him out.

He was cute and humble but never gave the impression of being weak or insecure. He just didn't follow the crowd by jumping into things head first and moving quickly only to limp away injured. As we had seen too many of our friends and even family do when it came to relationships. I guess you could say we were jaded at a young age not by our own experiences, but by the failure of others. So we broke modern conventions and marched by the beat of our own drum.

My reverie brought me back to Jackson and the differences between the two men once again. Yes, Jackson emitted danger and recklessness; Dylan was safe, secure and reliable. Up until the end of course.

Just then, my car began to hiss and steam streamed from under the hood. I glanced at the temp gauge and saw it was in the red. How long it was overheating, I did not know. I needed to stop daydreaming while driving, or else I would end up just as I had been before.

I shuddered at that thought and pulled the car over. Night had fallen by this time and it dawned on me how much time I had overspent in town. I'm sure Emma was starting to wonder what was taking me so long. The road I was on was completely deserted. I had decided to take the long way home and now regretted it. I estimated to be roughly ten miles from my aunt and uncle's house. Too far to walk in this darkness.

To make matters worse, there wasn't a house nearby, nor was the moon out. I was left in utter darkness alongside the road. Just ahead was Robbins Pond Road, the dirt road leading out to Paulding Light. I rifled through my purse to grab my cell phone so that I could call my aunt to come and get me. A loud sigh escaped my mouth as I looked at the screen.

Crap! No signal. Just then the interior of my car filled with light as a vehicle approached from behind. I heard a door slam then the crunching of footsteps on the gravel behind me, slow and deliberate. I glanced in my mirror only to see the shadowy outline of a burly looking man approaching my driver's side door. His face obscure as he walked in front of his vehicle's headlights.

Nerves danced in my belly as wild visions filled my mind. What if this person is a convicted felon, a psychopath, a rapist, or all of the above and here I am a lone female, trapped on a desolate road with no phone signal. He stopped just outside my window and peered down at me saying nothing at first. Panic seized me and I said the first thing that came to mind.

"I called for help already, they'll be here any minute!"

My voice sounded shrill to my own ears. I prayed he didn't hear the panic within.

He smiled faintly, his clear eyes sharp and penetrating.

"I'm sorry if I've frightened you ma'am. I only want to help. I'm a mechanic. I work next to Sal's hardware store in town. Maybe you've heard of it?"

I vaguely remembered the store on my way into town. It had been the first sign of civilization on my long journey. I remained silent nonetheless because I still did not know if this man was safe to trust, and yet it looked as if I had no choice. If he wanted to harm me, he could easily break through the thin glass separating us and drag me out. Still, there was something about his eyes as they implored mine. Something familiar…

"You don't have to open your door ma'am. Just pop the hood so I can take a look. Your help may take a while to get here."

Well, it beats just sitting here or having to walk into town. I don't know why, but looking into his eyes, I felt I could trust him. That was insane to think so I knew, but what other choice did I have, beat him to death with my phone? I was helpless. I pulled the lever that released the hood and sat there while he poked around. After a few minutes he walked over to my window again which was now rolled down just a crack and peered inside. Then all of a sudden it hit me.

"I know you! You were at Dolly's the day I was taken hostage. You told me to 'let go.' Why did you say that?"

He gave me a once over before answering.

"Yes. I was there. Why did you listen to me is more the question at hand?"

When I didn't answer he continued.

"I thought I was helping you. It seemed like your only chance and I could see that gunman wasn't paying attention to you or me, just that officer who was trying to disarm the situation. I didn't think you'd do it but I'm glad you didn't get hurt."

I didn't know what to say so I sat there staring at him dumbfounded. He brushed his hands off on a dirty rag before continuing.

"You're out of coolant. That's why your engine is overheating. I have some in my truck. I'll fill it up so you can get home."

"Thank you."

He tipped the brim of his hat at me, smiled again and walked back to his truck. He returned with the jug of coolant and began pouring it into my car. At this point, I was reasonably sure he wasn't out to hurt me. I opened my door and stepped out.

"So, did I damage anything? Should I take it to a shop tomorrow?"

I gazed under the hood. I hated to contribute to the stereotype of girls not knowing mechanics but my knowledge of vehicles was indeed limited. I recognized the engine of course and where to pour brake fluid, oil, washer and tranny fluid and how to check these levels. I had a feeble education on how to change a tire many years ago but had yet to change one on my own. And anyone that tells you that you're out of blinker fluid is just being an ass. Other than that, I was clueless.

"No, it looks fine. I don't think you were driving long enough to do any permanent damage."

He finished what he was doing, checked to make sure everything else was fine then wiped his hands on a rag as he closed the hood. I hadn't noticed before but looking closely at him now, I saw that he was a young man, maybe a few years older than myself. Yet upon first glance, he seemed ravaged a bit. Like he had been through hardship.

Therefore giving him an older look. His face was crisp from long hours in the sun and lines appeared around his eyes when he smiled at me. Despite the disheveled appearance he presented now, there was a definite beauty to his face. He had a strong set jaw and thick dark blonde hair that hung just past the top of his ears.

The wind had tousled it into a wild mess, which surprisingly was not unbecoming on him. It was the kind of hair someone would want to run their fingers through. His shoulders were broad and strong like he had done a lot of heavy lifting in his life. His chest was equally wide.

Overall he was solidly built man, tall and lean. His smile captured me the most. It radiated his face and had the power to make even the crabbiest, ill-tempered person on their worst day smile in return. Ironically, despite the smile, a sadness lay hidden within those clear eyes of his.

The smile seemed to be a cover up of something more. Something just out of reach. I found myself wondering what stories followed his steps. What had life done to him?

"I'd like to pay you for your trouble."

I jabbed my hand into my pants pocket to withdraw a twenty.

"No need to pay me, ma'am. It was no trouble at all. Please, keep your money, it'll do me no good."

He seemed to be looking through me again and a slight chill ran up my spine as the wind began to pick up. I stuck my hand out to shake his.

"I'm Jade."

"They call me Sam." He grasped my hand firmly and smiled that radiant smile.

"Are you new here Jade? Don't think I ever saw you in these parts before."

"Yes." I nodded.

" I just moved here from Montana."

"Got family or friends here I assume?"

"Yes. My aunt and uncle; Emma and Marcus Hawthorne."

"Ah, yes. I know them. Good people. Well, Jade, looks like a storm is blowing in. You better get home. Stop by the shop if you need any more work done on your car."

"Okay. Thanks again, Sam."

"Anytime."

He tipped his hat again and walked back to the truck. He waited until I jumped into my jeep and started it up. I put it into gear and drove away. He followed for a while until I reached town then his headlights disappeared.

By the time I reached the main house, the wind had picked up violently and huge raindrops began to splatter the windshield. I grabbed the bags from the seat and ran inside the house.

"Where on earth have you been? I tried calling your cell and you didn't answer. I almost sent Marcus out after you!"

"I'm sorry Auntie. My jeep broke down on the side of the road twenty miles outside of town and I had no cell service to call you."

"Oh dear. Nothing serious I hope?"

"No, nothing serious. I just felt bad knowing you were wondering where I was. A nice man stopped and helped me."

A blinding streak of lightning struck nearby followed swiftly by a deafening crack of thunder. Bella and Bruno tore out from under the kitchen table and hightailed it down the stairs into the basement. Only Scooter remained behind to valiantly jump up onto the back of the sofa and bark challengingly out the window at the encroaching storm. Just then the lights went out and the house went dark, spare a few candles that had been lit.

"Oh great! I'm glad I lit those candles beforehand. I had heard a storm was on its way. Come on Jade, lets head downstairs for a bit just in case this thing turns into a tornado. Scooter, get off the couch! Come here!"

Scooter obediently gave up his attack position on the sofa and followed us downstairs. My encounter with Sam temporarily forgotten as the wind tore viciously throughout the night.

Kathleen Wickman

CHAPTER SEVEN — DISAPPEARANCE

"Steph!!!"

My voice was hollow and detached as I helplessly watched her turn the wheel in a desperate attempt to avoid the approaching pine trees. The car just seconds prior was on flat pavement and now we were careening off the road straight into a mass of trees, bending the guardrail completely back as metal hit metal. The crack of branches reverberated through my skull. The air bags inflated then popped as glass broke and branches clawed at our faces. The sky was spinning, and then there was nothing.

Sound ceased to exist, light vanished to be replaced by darkness and I was suddenly positioned over my body in the hospital room.

How did I get here? What's happening?

There was no fear, no pain at this point, only confusion. I looked down at my still body lying on the hospital bed, while medics frantically tried to revive me. My eyes were closed and my head was bandaged. Tubes were coming out of my body and more blood than I have ever seen covered the sheets. Why was I not scared? Just then the doctors looked at each other and the nurse read the clock.

"Time of death, 2:15p.m."

My body suddenly felt like it was being pulled away as I tried screaming to the doctors and nurses to go back and try again!

Please, don't give up on me!

In one blink I was sitting on a bench next to Stephanie at Lake Eda. The sun was beginning to set. We were the only ones on the beach. Lake Eda was our favorite spot to visit every summer. Located just outside of Billings, our families would grill out and swim in its crystal clear waters with the glorious snow-capped mountain backdrop.

"Why are we here Steph? What's going on?"

Stephanie looked away from the glassy lake and the setting sun and smiled at me. Her voice was peaceful and steady when she answered.

"You have to go back, Jade. It's not your time. But I will see you again. Don't be afraid. Things are about to change. You are to be given a great gift Jade. Use it well."

That familiar tugging sensation was surrounding me again. I was pulled off the bench while Stephanie sat calmly and watched me go.

"No! Wait! Steph, what's happening? Help me!"

But she continued to sit silently with only a hint of a smile. Darkness enfolded me again and this time I gasped real air and opened my eyes. I looked into the blinding overhead lights of the operating room.

"Doctor! She's back!"

A flurry of movement and my bed was completely surrounded by all kinds of emergency staff.

"You're one lucky girl. Now just try and relax, you're going to be just fine."

I jolted awake in a cold sweat and looked around.

Where the hell am I?

As the dream slowly vanished from my mind's eye, objects in the overcast room suddenly brought me back to reality. I wasn't in a hospital bed. I was in the spare bedroom on the lower level of the main house. The storm had kept me here all night.

Emma had insisted I stay with them until it passed and I was too tired to argue. Scooter was lying next to me with his head cocked to one side as if to say *'Are you alright?'* I rubbed his ears and propped myself up in bed. A small silver box wrapped in a white bow sat on the bedside table.

It hadn't been there the night before. A smile crept across my face. I didn't think they knew or even remembered. Although I didn't want anything, it was a nice surprise. Today was July 4th, the day America and I celebrated a birthday.

Scooter wagged his tail, gave me a wet kiss then jumped off the bed and out the door. I opened the lid of the gift box and inside was a uniquely ornate necklace, delicate in design. A 1/2 inch emerald stone with sparkling matrix hung from a thin silver chain. Suspended from the base of the stone hung an intricate glass like opaque feather which glinted in the sun light streaming in from the bedroom window. I gently lifted the pendant out of the box and held it in my hand. Pushing the covers aside I walked over to the dresser mirror and clasped the chain around my neck.

"I was just about to wake you."

I turned at Emma's voice in the doorway.

"Is this for me? If not, where can I get one?" I lovingly touched the rich green stone.

"Of course it's yours. Happy Birthday dear. I'm glad you like it. It's a family heirloom. Passed down from Dolly Sturgis, your great-grandmother. It was a gift from her husband who was from the local Ottawa tribe. His ancestors passed the necklace down to him. Granted that was many years ago and the necklace changed in design but the stone remained untouched. A sterling silver chain replaced the original leather one and a family member hand crafted the feather some years later to add to it."

"I didn't know that. I mean, I knew we were connected to the tribe by blood but I never made the connection to grandma Dolly until now."

"Well, back then your great-grandmother's parents weren't overly thrilled about the marriage. They had moved young Dolly from Ohio a few years after the Crash of '29. Lucky for them, most of their assets were not tied up in banks and they made off with much of their livelihood still intact. While most people were heading south to escape the cold of approaching winter—considering they had lost their homes, jobs, everything— Dolly's parents were moving up here to settle. Dolly's father had plans for the area once the depression passed. He was a brilliant man. A 'jack of all trades'; an architect and engineer with a scientific brain and common sense to boot. He managed to stay one step ahead of the game despite the desolation and depression around them. They hunkered down and waited out the ten-year storm. Dolly's father began working on a railroad system that had been constructed in town prior to the depression. They also ran a rooming house, or boarding house if you will, for the local railway workers and loggers to eat and rest. In later years Dolly herself salvaged a railway car and turned it into a boxcar diner, which today has been changed yet again into what is now known as Dolly's restaurant. Clayton was of the Ottawa clan and very young when he met your great-grandmother. Dolly's parents didn't feel Clayton was a worthy match for her. They saw him as a rebel, a troublemaker but Dolly was stubborn, a trait she passed down to all Sturgis women and nobody was going to tell her who to love."

Emma and I had walked up the stairs and into the kitchen. I sat down on one of the island stools, propped my elbows on the counter and fingered the stone again as it hung from my neck.

"So do you know where this stone came from? I've never seen anything like it before."

"Unfortunately, I can only provide the legend as it was once told to me. I was told a small nomadic tribe had converged with the local Ottawa tribe here in some sort of peace agreement many years ago. This nomadic tribe claimed to have magical powers to heal and protect. Those powers benefited the Ottawa clan and in return, the Ottawa's provided protection and land to the 'Phantom tribe' or so they had been deemed. No one knows where they had originated from, not even your great-grandfather. Some kind of conflict had taken place long before your great-grandfather was even born. Much of the original clan vanished or died taking their history with them into oblivion. As far as the stone, legend has it that a young phantom tribesman saw the peculiar stone from a base of a mountain during a rainstorm and brought it back to the chief leader, Keeja. He was a shaman and collector of stones to assist him in his healing rituals. But the chief felt the stone exuded peculiar energy waves and so saved it to present to his bride at a later time as a gift. The stone was deemed 'The Wounded Healer's Stone' and is said to be the most powerful healing stone in existence. It was also said the stone had great powers to protect the tribe and inflict harm on enemies that drew near. It only answered to one master, Keeja. Others had stolen it only to find it useless and defunct of any magical abilities. The stone somehow always found its way back to him. Keeja supposedly used it in the great conflict and many lives were lost on the enemy side. But like most wars, casualties are great on both sides, magic or not and the repercussions of war haunted both sides for years to follow. The stone was then passed on to Clayton after the last of the Phantom tribe perished, and now it is yours."

"So, what was the conflict about? Did it happen here?"

"It was over land as most battles had been about between white man and Native Americans during that time. And yes, it happened not far from here. Now, that is all I know so eat up. We've got a big day ahead of us. It's the 4th of July after all and we're going to the parade today."

After breakfast I hugged my aunt and thanked her again for my present. I patted the dogs good-bye and leaving my car at the main house decided to jog back home to my cabin to get changed for the parade. The sun was rising high into the sky and the day was starting out crisp and clear.

Last night's storm clung to the leaves as rain drops dripped onto my head and into the ground.

There was lightness in each step I took and a smile on my lips. I hopped up the front steps to the cabin and noticed the Ghost Flowers hadn't wilted yet considering they were out of their natural environment here. The delicate petals were raised to the sky above and seemed to be thriving. Gus, the caretaker must make sure all the flowers are taken care of as well as the surrounding lawn. And yet, no one ever sees him do as such.

I hadn't seen him personally since my first day here when he scared the pants off me. He's just as elusive as these beautiful flowers. I quickly changed and headed back to meet my aunt for the parade. Downtown was festive and colorful. The wonderful smells from nearby food vendors wafted through the street and people of every age aligned the sidewalks anxiously awaiting the Paulding parade. Red, white and blue balloons were tied to every kid's wrist as they skipped along the sidewalk with their parents holding tightly to their hand. Their laughter filled the air.

Emma and I made our way through the crowd, stopping every so often so she could introduce me to people. It seemed I made the acquaintance of the entire town by the time we reached our destination. I couldn't wait to plop down into my fold out chair and relax.

"Hey stranger!"

A familiar voice called out from behind me and I turned around to see Jordyn standing a few feet away. I waved and invited her to join us. Emma and I scooted over to make room for her to sit.

"I think Jackson's looking for you." Jordyn said.

"What for?" I asked, getting comfortable.

"I just saw him a few minutes ago a couple blocks from here and he had asked if I had seen you or Emma here. At the time I hadn't and told him so. I think he might want to join you guys."

"Isn't he in the parade with Marcus driving one of the patrol cars?"

"I asked him that and he said he's not big on driving in the parade. He'd rather be a spectator than a participant. He didn't really want to be here at all except he got bored sitting at home and felt the need to be here, if anything, just to pass the time until the party tonight."

"So, he's going to Em and Marcus' party at the main house?" I feigned dull interest, ignoring the flutter in my chest.

"Sure! Everyone will be there. I can't wait!"

"Jordyn, are you even old enough to drink?"

I chided her because she really did not look a day past eighteen.

"Of course I am! I'm twenty-two, ask your aunt if you don't believe me."

"I believe you. You just don't look it."

"Speak for yourself."

She playfully elbowed me and both of us continued scanning the crowd as more and more people filed into the street. A sharp whistle cracked through the air and caught my attention from across the street. My ears actually hurt from the decibel level it reached. Nikki was hailing me with arm flailing wildly in the air, and Heather scrunched down next to her deep in her seat what looked like an attempt to sink into the pavement from embarrassment.

Heather looked up from shading her face with her hand to give a smile and meager wave towards us then she turned and glared at Nikki, smacking her on the arm. Half the block had stopped talking momentarily. Apparently Nikki's whistle caught everyone's attention. Nikki remained oblivious to the stares and shouted my way.

"Hey girlfriend!"

"Hi!" I called back and laughed out loud at Heather's crimson face.

"Damn that girl's got a set of lungs on her."

Jordyn chuckled and nodded her head in agreement. Shouts filled the air as the parade approached us. Drumbeats sounded in the distance and sirens wailed sporadically. A playground and small parking lot were just behind us. Most of the kids jumped off the swings and slide when they heard the sirens.

One small child remained with hands to her ears not at all enthused about the excitement and increasing noise. She looked to be about five or six years old and unaccompanied by an adult. Just then a young woman walked over to her and tried enticing her to join the other kids at the curb but she refused to budge. She looked to have her hands full as a small boy ran to her for attention and tripped, falling flat on his face and skinning his bare legs.

His painful wail filled my ears and my heart went out to him as the young woman turned her back on the little girl temporarily to comfort the boy. She scooped him up into her arms and tried to grab the little girls' hand in order to lead her back to the parade, but the girl was obstinate and refused to budge. Instead she ran the opposite way towards the swings and pushed herself back and forth, still covering her ears. Another child approached the young woman and tugged at her pant leg while pointing at something within the group of people along the roadside.

I could almost hear her sigh loudly and with a last glance at the little girl swinging on the swing, she walked back to the parade and disappeared from my view.

"Jackson, you made it! So good to see you! Come, have a seat, I brought an extra chair for you."

Emma's voice speaking Jackson's name turned my head from the little girl and I found myself glaring into the sun at his towering form.

"Ladies."

He nodded at Jordyn and myself, then returned Emma's hug before sitting down next to her.

"Will you be at the party tonight Jackson?"

Emma really did see Jackson as a son that she never had. It was easy to see the apparent love and compassion she displayed towards him.

"Yes. Don't ask me how I got the night off. It's rare that I'm not scheduled for patrol on any holiday let alone the 4th. But Hawk and Duvall won't be able to attend. They have to work tonight. They said they might stop in later to make sure Marcus is staying in line and to give you a taser gun in case he decides to dance on tables again."

Wow. So Mr. Jackson Butler does have a sense of humor after all. I laughed out loud at the picture he mentally painted of Marcus dancing on tables. Jackson turned to look at me and smiled. There was something peculiar about that smile.

I couldn't quite place it. Trumpets and drums boomed through my skull distracting my thought process as the local marching band walked by us in perfect unison. I turned my head to look back at the playground. The little girl was nowhere in sight. She must have finally relented to her mother's prodding and re-joined the group near the parade.

Sirens wailed ever louder as the fire truck rolled past. The driver whom I had never seen before waved at Jackson and Emma. Directly behind him followed the patrol cars, county and state. Marcus was behind the wheel of the car nearest us and turned the siren on as he drove past. He smiled and waved at us sitting together near the curb.

A subtle cry hovered slightly above the siren blast. It was faint but audible and I instinctively turned to look at the playground. The young woman was running frantically around the park calling for the little girl. Two little boys hovered together nearby. I got up out of my chair and ran over to her to see if I could help.

"My baby girl! I can't find my baby girl! Oh my God, how could I let this happen!?"

She was hysterical and all alone save for the two boys huddling together. It was apparent there was no one else here to help her. Perhaps she was new in town and didn't know anyone and as far as the father, it wasn't clear if there was one. All I knew was that she was young and frightened for her lost child.

"Try to stay calm. I'm going to help you. We'll find her. Now, where did you see her last?"

"Right here! Just a few seconds ago. My son fell but he didn't want to leave the parade. It's the first time any of them have seen a parade and I just wanted them to enjoy it. He had superficial scrapes on his knee so I decided it'd be okay if we stayed but I couldn't get my little girl to leave the park. I was watching her the whole time the parade was happening but my boys distracted me for just a moment, and then when I looked back, she was gone! Could someone have taken her?"

Sobs wracked her worn out body and I ached for her.

"We'll find her. What's her name?"

"Rose."

Jackson was by our side at this point and Emma had taken over watching the two little boys. Jackson looked at me point blank, casual persona gone to be replaced by the usual hard face of an officer on duty.

"You go this way and I'll go over here. If we split up, we'll have a better chance of finding her."

I ran to the north end of the park, furthest away from the parade and started calling out to Rose. Gus, the cabin caretaker and Sam were in what looked like hurried conversation by the park bench.

Gus looked at me then walked the opposite direction as Sam began walking quickly towards me.

"Sam! Have you seen a little blonde girl about five or six years old, wearing a purple sun dress?"

His eyes were still as clear and captivating as they were on the night he helped fix my broken down jeep on the side of the road.

"Yes."

A cold wave of relief washed over me putting out the fire of mounting despair. He pointed in the direction of the parking lot where about a dozen vehicles were parked.

"She's in the dark blue van with tinted windows. I saw her climb in from across the park. At first I figured her mother would follow shortly and all would be fine, but then I saw that she had lost track of her and given the heat of the day, I knew the girl would not last long in that vehicle. If it's eighty degrees out here, it's got to be over a hundred in that van."

"We've got to get to her!"

Sam and I started running towards the van. Jackson was on the other end of the park and I called to him that we found her. He stopped in his tracks at my voice then ran as fast as he could to meet us. Sam and I arrived first at the van and sure enough, a faint cry emanated past the window. I couldn't see inside as I desperately yanked on the door handles. They were all locked. By now the young mother and Emma had arrived with the two boys in tow.

"Your keys! Where are your keys?"

"This isn't my car! I don't know how she got in here! Oh my God, my baby, please get her out!"

Jackson had arrived at this point. He looked around for something to use and his gaze locked onto a large rock sitting nearby. He dug it frantically out of the dirt and before hauling it through the window, looked in to make sure Rose was in the backseat. With enough force he punched the rock into the passenger side door, furthest away from Rose.

Glass shattered, Rose cried harder and Jackson stuck his arm in to unlock the door. The young mother yanked her daughter out and to everyone's relief, Rose appeared to be fine. Her cheeks were flushed from the heat but she was crying which was a good sign in itself. Jackson looked her over and called for the paramedics anyway just to check her out and make sure she was re-hydrated.

A small group had formed during this time and chaos reigned for a few minutes. When some of the commotion had passed Jackson turned to me with a question burning in his eyes.

"How did you know where to find her Jade?"

"I didn't at first but then I ran into a friend, Sam. He said he saw Rose go into that van. I'm thinking she just wanted to get away from all the noise of the parade. I had been watching her earlier and saw how that mother struggled trying to get her to join the others but she didn't budge. She just wanted to stay by the swings."

"I'd like to meet him, shake his hand for all he's done. He saved a life today."

"Sure. I just saw him over there. Come on, I'll introduce you."

The crowd was starting to disperse, the ambulance had left and Sam was nowhere to be found.

"He was just here a second ago. Maybe he wanted to stay out of the mad house this place turned into after we found her. Next time I see him, I'll be sure to give him your regards."

Jackson looked at me pensively. He started to say something then changed his mind. The parade had ended and the town was emptying out.

"Okay. I'm taking off. See you at the party."

I watched as he abruptly walked away and disappeared around the corner.

Kathleen Wickman

CHAPTER EIGHT — THE PARTY

The hot sun was starting to make its way westward, slowly sinking in the afternoon sky. People were starting to arrive at the main house and the backyard beach area was becoming inundated with kids. Emma and Marcus had half a football field of a yard and already a third of it was filled up as more and more people arrived, dishes in hand as the barbeque got under way. I had spent half the day finishing up with decorations and party preparations, setting tables outside and also trying my hand at cooking in the kitchen under Em's close supervision.

Most of the food was being grilled outside and that was being taken care of by Marcus and a few of his buddies. Extra grills were brought in and the guys were in their glory with beer in hand and a basting brush in the other. Many neighbors and friends brought their own dish to add to the buffet.

"Jade, go relax. You've done plenty to help me. Help yourself to a margarita, there's a full pitcher already made in the fridge."

"Thanks, but I'll grab a soda instead."

How I had avoided the college tidal wave of partying, I still don't know. I wasn't a prude by any means. I had a few beers over time but I had never acquired the taste of it. I only drank because of a few situations where I'd rather have pretended to party than let on that I didn't like alcohol at all. Some of my friends figured it out and would tease me that I didn't quite fit the bill of a naïve nerd type.

"You're way too hot to not want to party Jade! Come on dude, have a shot with us, you'll like this stuff!"

Whatever the hell that was supposed to mean. I'd politely shrug them off and make my exit. Dylan partied more than me but he never got carried away. He had a way of staying focused too on his schoolwork.

After all, his scholarship had depended on it. I walked out onto the back deck overlooking the yard and spotted Nikki and Heather talking to some people by the fire pit. The air was saturated with spices and delicious meat smells that made my mouth water. I descended the steps to the yard below and made my way over to the girls. Sheba stopped me halfway there.

"I heard about that little girl at the parade and how you found her Jade. Thank God you were there!"

"Yeah, it was scary. But I technically wasn't the one who found her. Sam saw her climb into the van from across the park."

"Sam? Who's Sam?"

"A local mechanic who helped me out last night when my jeep stalled on the side of the road."

She gave me a puzzled look, then her eyes lit up briefly.

"Do you mean Sam Newman? He has a small shop on the outside of town."

"I'm not sure, but he sounds like the same guy. I never did catch his last name."

Sheba's eyes dropped to my birthday present resting at the base of my neck.

"Beautiful necklace, Jade. Where did you get it?"

"Thanks. It was a gift from my aunt. It's a family heirloom."

She seemed to eye it up rather intently and for a moment, I thought she would reach out and touch it. But her hand fell back to her side. She blinked a few times and connected her gaze to mine once again.

"Well, it's very lovely." She said politely and smiled.

I thanked her again as a deep voice reached my ears from behind.

"There you are love. And who do we have here?"

Cayden Hendricks, Sheba's husband approached from behind and wrapped his free arm around his wife's waist while the other hand brought a cold beer to his lips. His eyes never left mine. What I saw in them gave me an unpleasant feeling in my stomach. He winked at me and an unsettling feeling coursed through my veins.

It was hard to place his age but if I had to guess, I'd say he was in his late thirties. Most seemingly he appeared a few years younger than Sheba. When he smiled, deep creases appeared around his dark brown eyes and on his forehead whenever his thin eyebrows would raise; as they did now at the once over look he was giving me. He wasn't an unpleasant looking man, but the way he was looking at me certainly was.

"Cayden, this is Emma and Marcus' niece Jade. She just moved here from Montana."

He freed up his hand to shake mine. It felt cold just as I'd imagined it would be, and not because of the beer he had just been holding.

"Nice to meet you." I mumbled softly.

He smiled a crooked smile that some may find dashing; I found it creepy.

"The pleasure's all mine."

Sheba seemed distracted and either didn't notice her husband's oily sexual overtones or didn't care, but I was crawling with distaste and tried to make my escape.

"Cayden, where's our son?"

Sheba was looking around the yard.

"He's over by the dock."

"Excuse us Jade, we need to tell our son it's time to eat."

I subtly shook my shoulders to rid the chills I still had and walked over across the yard to Heather, Nikki, Eric and Johnny. Glancing back I watched them walk over to a small boy around eight or nine. He was playing with other kids around his age and seemed dwarfed by either his small frame or their much larger ones. Sheba had leaned over to tell him something while Cayden's gaze drifted over to where I was standing next to Heather.

Our eyes locked briefly as he winked my way, followed by that crooked smile of his. I shivered and broke the glance, quickly turning my focus on the conversation at hand. The barbeque turned out fabulous. I had stuffed myself to the point I couldn't move. A good crowd had showed up and some of them brought fireworks that they were now starting to light off.

The sun had yet to set but the sky was turning a deep pink as night encroached. I don't know why but I found myself looking for Jackson throughout the afternoon. I was beginning to wonder if he was going to show up at all. Then I chided myself by giving a damn in the first place.

He wasn't someone I wanted to waste too much time on. He was too mysterious for any type of trust to form and his past was too insidious and precarious for my peace of mind. A local acoustic group provided reggae and light pop music that they now began to play. Some of the outdoor lights were turned on and the yard glowed with soft beauty.

A large American flag graced the top deck and waved impressively in the light breeze off the lake. Tiki torches were lit and a few people had even begun dancing. My aunt and uncle love the Caribbean and incorporate some of its attraction in most of their parties as they had done now. Maui was where they were wed and celebrated their honeymoon.

"Where's your drink, Jade?"

Nikki, Heather and their spouses had drinks in hand and were heading over to the band area.

"Um, I'm not much of a drinker."

"Well then you've never tried our famous Malibu concoction. Come hither, we'll make you one."

Heather had put her arm around my shoulder and was leading me to the tent.

"Thanks, I'm sure it's great. But I'll pass for now."

"Heather, leave the poor girl alone. You're going to corrupt her."

Eric was trying to pry his wife's arm off my shoulder but she threw her hip into him, knocking him back a step.

"Oh, please. Don't listen to the hypocrite. He's the corrupter, he got me to marry him after all, didn't he?"

She gave him a wink as her hips bopped to the beat of the music all the while guiding me towards the tent. Nikki joined us and threw her arm around my shoulders so that both girls now had me in an arm/shoulder lock with me in the middle.

"It's your birthday and we've got to celebrate! I promise I'll go easy on the booze and add more soda than liquor."

"Well I would hope so!"

I laughed at both girls and somehow broke their grip.

"Look, I really appreciate it but I'll stick to plain soda for now. Maybe later okay?"

Just then Jackson appeared from the side of the house looking better than he deserved to. My heart did a little skip much to my annoyance, but I didn't dare deny my sight the vision he presented. In casual clothes he looked really good. Blue jeans hugged his waist in a perfect fit, not too tight nor too loose.

He was wearing a crisp white shirt buttoned down at the front with a few of the top buttons open to reveal just a hint of chest hair. His hair was dark and thick with a mild attempt at tame given the lightly slicked look. Nikki waved her hand in front of my face.

"Hello? Earth to Jade? You're going to burn a hole through Jackie with the look you're giving him."

I blinked a few times, blushed slightly then felt my head turning back in his direction. I turned in time to see a stunning blonde walk out just behind him and wrap her arm through his as they began talking to another couple. It was the same blonde I saw at town square yesterday while shopping for decorations. Jackson seemed to have come alive when he was talking to her. Some kind of feeling inside me started to make a devastating plunge downward, taking my good mood with it. I looked at both girls and threw my arms around their waist.

"How 'bout that drink?!"

***

Night had fallen and the air became cool as the stars lit up the sky. We were sitting at a table near the music. I had consumed a few Malibu's at this time and had to admit, they were really good.

"I heard it was someone's birthday."

I sputtered on the last sip as Jackson approached with a tray full of red, white and blue jell-o shots. I could feel the buzz begin to set in and shook my head in decline.

"I've had my limit, thanks."

He sat down next to me and I found myself tensing a bit at his closeness. That enticing musky scent of his cologne invaded my senses and had my pulse quickening.

"They're not strong, trust me. Your aunt asked me to bring them out to you."

Eric and Johnny grabbed theirs and Nikki and Heather had theirs in hand waiting on me.

"Hey Sophia, grab a shot and have a seat."

Johnny waved the beautiful blonde over.

"Oh hell, give me that!"

I grabbed the shot out of Jackson's hand and he leaned forward to grab another one off the tray for Sophia and himself. The band stopped playing long enough to announce my birthday then began singing 'Happy Birthday' as all faces turned my way.

Dammit Emma!

I slunk into my chair and prayed for it to end quickly.

"Your face is turning red, Jade."

Jackson leaned into me and clinked his glass to mine. I looked at Sophia then raised my glass in quick thanks at everyone's stares and loud applause then downed the shot. Huge fireworks started shooting off over the lake and all eyes turned towards the display. Marcus and some of his buddies were in charge of lighting them off near the dock. All around the lake campfires glowed and cheers broke out from nearby camps at the conclusion of the firework display.

Afterward the band hyped up the tempo and people were starting to dance again. More guests joined the party from the neighboring cabins. Sophia grabbed Jackson's hand and pulled him onto the grassy dance floor. He bulked considerably, leaned into her ear then broke her grasp on him. She watched him for a second as he disappeared into the crowd then Nikki and Heather joined her.

The guys stayed behind at the table and I felt the same way they did; there's not enough liquor to get me out there. I excused myself and walked over to the garden path where it was quiet and secluded. At one point it edged the water. I exited the garden to follow the beach- front a ways. The moon was brilliant tonight, its glow cast shadows on everything around me. A branch cracked behind me and out walked Cayden from the shadows.

"What are you doing out here by yourself? Need some company?"

I stopped dead in my tracks and turned to face him. Unfortunately he was in my path back to the main house and there was no way to get around him discreetly. He walked right up to my face with bottle in hand and I could smell whiskey on his breath.

"No thank you, I was just heading back to the main house."

He grabbed my arm as I walked past him.

"I must say; you are one stunning woman. You're the talk of the town; do you know that? Sheba was saying how all the guys want you, even that Jackson fellow. And that the ladies should lock up their husbands. I think she's right."

Those shifty eyes looked over my body again and my skin turned ice cold.

"Please let me go Cayden, are you forgetting who my uncle is?"

"Yes, he's a good friend of mine and he's not here right now, is he?"

He surprised me by yanking my body into his; the smell of tart cologne stung my senses. He held me fast with one hand while taking a swig with the other. I pushed at him with all my might but his grip was intensely strong.

"Don't make me slug you Cayden! Let me go!"

I had never hit anyone before and was hesitant to do so now even though he deserved it immensely. The only reason being I knew my strength already compared to his was puny and punching him I feared would only make it worse. Nonetheless my fist hardened into a ball and I leaned back to throw. He dropped the bottle and caught my fist just as I began to swing and in a stunning move, he had me on the ground with his hard body on top of mine.

"Oops, sorry I tripped."

His words were a bit slurred and tinged with amusement as he continued holding me there against my will. A scream began to well inside of me but just then he stood up and grabbed my hand to pull me up as well.

"One little kiss and I'll let you go, I promise."

That crooked smile was back and I turned my head to avoid the whiskey on his breath. He still had me by the arm; his fingers were starting to dig in painfully. My fist swelled again as panic broiled inside of me. To my amazement the white glow from the moon increased in brightness and concentrated on a shadowy figure approaching from the woods just behind Cayden.

The closer the man got to us, the brighter the moon became casting shadow to conceal the man's identity. Something clicked inside of me and I gasped. This was the ghost I saw at Paulding Light. Except this time that sadness did not grip my chest as it had done before.

I felt an intense anger now instead and somehow I sensed it was coming from the ghost. Cayden saw my eyes grow wide and followed their stare behind him into the black forest beyond. He turned back to me with confusion on his face.

"What's wrong with you? What are you looking at?"

His grip dug deeper into my arm sending pain up my shoulder.

"I can read his thoughts Jade. And I could kill him for what he wants to do to you. When the time is right, run!"

The words were but a whisper in my head and the voice that carried them was rugged and angry. I looked at the ghost and could barely make out his features but the one thing I did notice was he was glaring directly at Cayden. Just then the bottle of whiskey Cayden had picked up off the ground whipped violently upward connecting directly into his face and the sound of glass shattering filled my ears. His grip loosened as he stumbled backwards in shock and pain.

I wasted no time taking advantage of my freedom. I ran as fast as I could back to the house sparing one look backwards only to see the ghost had vanished and Cayden on his knees with hands to his face. The party was still going strong when I got back to the house. Cayden never returned and Sheba was nowhere to be found.

I was more shook up over the ghost sighting than I was with Cayden's drunken behavior and given the fact that Sheba and my aunt were such good friends, I decided to keep my mouth closed on this incident. Next time he tried to pull something with me, I was going straight to Marcus. Besides, the bottle in the face was warning enough to leave me alone. How that happened is beyond fathomable, but so are most things in my life these days.

It was getting late and all I wanted to do was go home. The events of the day were finally catching up with me and exhaustion was wrapping around me like a warm blanket. I headed past the bright lights from the party and into the shadow cast by the house when footsteps ran up behind me. My heart skipped again traitorously at the sound of that voice. I turned around to see Jackson's imploring look.

"Leaving so soon?"

"Yes, I'm tired."

I couldn't help but notice Sophia was nowhere to be seen.

"Where's your date?"

"She left with some friends."

"Harsh."

"It's not like that. We didn't come here together. We just arrived at the same time. She's just a friend. Where's your date?"

His question threw me.

"I don't have one."

"Now that's hard to believe. No boyfriend? No one back home waiting for you?"

"No."

My face fell as Dylan's image appeared in my mind.

"See you around Jackson."

I started to walk past him when he called out to me.

"How about one dance before you leave?"

I hadn't noticed the music was slowing down for the night. People were starting to leave the party but a few couples remained and were slow dancing. My mind beat against him for reasons I had yet to understand but my heart betrayed reason as it upped its tempo.

"I'm not a very good dancer. Especially after having a few drinks."

"I'm not either so we can look bad together."

He took my hand and it was hard not to ignore that spark at his touch. I tried not to trip over anything in the shadows as we walked down the slight incline where the band was still playing. He turned to face me abruptly and I nearly crashed into his broad chest. His arms wrapped around me and mine encircled his neck as I looked up into his face. He was smiling down at me. After a few seconds he spoke.

"You liar. You dance just fine."

I shook my head in resignation and leaned into him as we swayed back and forth.

"So tell me, why do you hate me so much?"

I pulled back a little to look at him.

"I don't hate you Jackson. I barely know you."

"Well, I can tell you don't like me very much. Is it because of the ticket I gave you?"

"You know, I could ask you the very same question. Do you enjoy being arrogant?"

"Arrogant? Where did you get that idea? Look, I'm sorry if that's the way I come across but you really don't know me at all."

"You're right, I don't. But I know how people make me feel and you came across high and mighty on more than one occasion. You were even rude at times. I started to feel like a convict or something."

"Jade, I don't expect you to understand, but given my line of work, I have to maintain control. If I waltz into every scenario acting like a clown, no one would take me seriously."

"Really?"

I arched one eyebrow and tilted my head with amusement.

"You know what I mean."

"Well it's funny how control and arrogance coincide."

He shook his head and chuckled softly.

"Okay, judge me as you wish. Who am I to stop you?"

A few more silent seconds passed.

"What's wrong Jade? You're really tense and on edge."

"Nothing. I'm fine."

I could feel his eyes sear into the top of my skull as I averted my gaze. I tried not to think about the moonlit lantern man on the beach. The song ended and more people began to leave.

"I think I better go home."
"I'll walk you home if you'd like."
"No, I'll be fine…actually…"

The unsettling memory of Cayden flashed into my mind and I digressed.

"Sure, that would be nice. Thanks."

We said our good-byes to everyone and made our way along the dirt road. For a while neither spoke a word and only the sound of crunching gravel under our feet filled the night air. A wolf howled somewhere in the distance, it's lonely call hauntingly beautiful. After a few more minutes of silence I looked at his shadowy profile.

"Where's your car?"
"I walked here. I don't live far from here."
"Oh."

I stumbled on something and Jackson caught my arm and steadied me.

"This road is unstable."
"I think it's you my dear, who's unstable."
"I can walk just fine."
"I see that. Did you have fun tonight?"

I didn't answer right away and Jackson turned to look at me inquisitively.

"What's wrong?"
"I had a great time, except…"
"Except what?"
"Tell him!"

I swung around at the whispered words and almost lost my balance if Jackson hadn't had such a tight hold on me.

"What is it? Did something happen?"

"I went for a walk down by the beach tonight and Cayden confronted me. He was just being a drunken idiot, but it sort of scared me."

Jackson stopped walking and turned my arm so that I would face him.

"What did he do?"

"Nothing. He was just creeping me out with some of the things he said and it was more the way he looked at me. Like I was a piece of prime rib or something. How can Sheba be married to that?"

"Did he hurt you?"

"He grabbed my arm at one point as I tried walking away from him and when I went to punch him he lost his balance trying to stop me, knocking us both to the ground."

"He's walking a thin line. I'll have a talk with him tomorrow. How did you get free from him?"

I couldn't tell him the truth because I wasn't really sure what had happened myself. But I did know a ghost was involved.

"I kicked him and he let me go. Please don't tell my aunt about this, her and Sheba are good friends and I don't want there to be any hard feelings between the two. It was nothing really. I'm not looking to cause trouble."

"No but he is. I'm still going to talk to him privately. I won't say anything to Emma and I'm sure he won't mention our soon to be conversation to his wife."

We continued walking. I could see the porch light to my house in the distance.

"By the way, you did a great thing today helping that lady find her daughter. If it wasn't for your diligent observance of your surroundings, we may not have found her in time."

I couldn't help but laugh.

"What?"

"Man, do you ever sound like a cop. And it wasn't just me, it was Sam too."

"Who is this Sam guy anyway and how do you know him?"

"He helped me out the other night when my car stalled on the side of the road. I think his last name's Newman."

"Sammy. Yeah, he doesn't go out much. Good fellow though. Strange though, I didn't see him at the parade or in the parking lot once we found the girl."

"Yeah, I know. He was in the park when I saw him prior to finding the little girl. Then he must've left shortly after when the crowd gathered."

"He is kind of a recluse. Doesn't like crowds much. I'm surprised he even went to the parade."

We reached the porch steps and he saw me to my door. I thanked him again for walking me home then turned the key under the knob and stepped inside. Jackson followed close behind.

"What may I ask are you doing?"

"Checking out your place before I leave."

"Don't be ridiculous, I'm fine. I locked up before I left."

He ignored me and brushed past poking his head into each room. Then he mounted the steps two at a time and checked upstairs. A few seconds later he returned to the main floor.

"Looks good. Lock up when I leave." His voice was all seriousness.

"I may look like I'm made of glass but I'm no wuss. I can take care of myself."

"I'm not disputing your wuss level but I wouldn't feel right leaving you here if someone had broken in."

"I also know how to handle a gun, Jackson."

"Do you have one here?" He asked matter-of-factly.

"Well, no, but…"

"A lot of good that does you then."

"You piss me off sometimes you know that?"

"What now? What did I do?" Amusement played across his face at his obvious attempt to bait me.

"That! I don't know…your attitude. You're flippantly annoying."

"Thanks. I try just for you." A smirk tugged at the corner of his mouth.

He winked then turned to leave. I followed him to the door.

"Thanks again for walking me home."

"No problem. Happy Birthday, kid."

He pulled me in for a hug that was meant to be quick but lingered ever so distinctly. A strange magnetic field seemed to hold us together. His cheek brushed past mine as our heads pulled back from one another and for one moment, I thought he would kiss me. Instead he cleared his throat and put back the wall he carried around with him. His voice was distant when he spoke again.

"Take care."

And with that his long strides carried him off the porch and into the shadows of the night, as the lone wolf in the distance howled its lonely call one last time.

Kathleen Wickman

CHAPTER NINE — HOLY GROUND

"Men! And they say we're complicated!"

It was break time as the girls and I sat outside on the deck at Dolly's. It was a slow day and we had the deck to ourselves. Heather's feet were propped up against the rail and she was shaking her head at me.

"Why do you even bother with him, Jade? He's like Fort Knox. No one can get passed his blockade, although I was quite impressed to see you two dancing last night. He wouldn't dance with Sophia, maybe he's grown tired of her."

"Look, you asked for details about what happened between him and I and I told you. He asked me to dance, then walked me home. You make it sound like I'm chasing him all over town. And as for Sophia, he said they're just friends. I don't think there's anything going on between them. I just don't get that vibe."

"It's because you're smitten. Your radar is foo-barred by hormones and is giving you an inaccurate reading."

Nikki chimed in at this point.

"I don't think he's a player kind of guy either. It's because he's good looking and single and that's the real reason he gets such a bad rap. He happens to have a female friend who's hot and everyone automatically thinks they're sleeping together."

Jordyn was sitting with us too and added her two cents.

"What I don't get is the conflict inside of him. He treats Jade coldly in the beginning and not just by what he says but by his demeanor towards her like he decided long ago not to like her, then a flick of a switch and he changes his tune. Just as quickly he flips it off again. I think he's afraid of getting too close to anyone since he lost Annabelle."

For a young girl, Jordyn could be incredibly astute and attuned to human behavior whether it was the truth or not, her theory that is, was irrelevant. She surprised me sometimes with the maturity in which she speaks.

"Well, whatever the case I wash my hands of it. Besides, I think he sees me as a kid."

"Why do you say that?"

"Because he called me kid last night. And sometimes I feel as if he treats me like one."

"You're five years younger than him. That's hardly an age gap."

"It doesn't matter. We're like fire and water and something about him still sets me on edge."

"Annie's death?"

"I don't know, maybe."

Just then Sheba stepped out onto the deck, unsmiling and apparently not in the best of moods.

"Jackson's here to see you Jade. He's out front."

I could almost feel the questions buzzing at my back as I left the table. My friends had yet to learn of what Cayden had done and I had no doubt that was what Jackson wanted to see me about. I walked inside and out towards the waiting area where he was standing tall and regal in his crisp uniform. I inhaled a deep breath, squared my shoulders and walked up to him.

"Hey." I gave him a subtle smile.

"Can you come outside with me for a minute? I need to talk to you in private." His expression was unreadable.

"Sure. I still have a few minutes left of break."

He led me through the front door and out into the parking lot next to his squad car. The lot was nearly empty on such a quiet clear afternoon.

"I just spoke to Cayden. I warned him actually to watch himself and that I knew what had happened on the beach between you two. The first thing that struck me when I saw him was his face. It was scratched all to hell. I asked him about it and he blamed you for it. He said you smashed him in the face with a bottle. Is that true?"

"No, of course not. He had me by my arm and wouldn't let go. I had to kick him to get free."

"Even if you did Jade, I wouldn't say he didn't deserve it. I know his type and it gets worse when you add booze and stir. I'm just trying to figure out what really happened."

"I don't care what he says. He harassed me that night and if he does it again, I will smash him in the face with whatever I can find."

"I believe you Jade. I'm not here to interrogate you. I just wanted to tell you he's been warned. You can press charges if you'd like but given all you said to me the other night, I'm guessing you won't."

"Not this time. Next time is a different story."

"Let's hope there won't be a next time."

"Does Sheba know?" I lowered my voice even more in case we were being listened to.

"Not that I know of. I just left their place and whether he tells her or not is beyond my control. You did the right thing by telling someone, Jade. Leave the rest to me."

I thought about the look Sheba had given me just a few minutes ago like she knew something was up. Or maybe now she's realizing what a dirt bag she married. My sympathies rested in their son. One could only hope he doesn't follow his father's slimy footsteps. A few cars began filing into the parking lot for the early dinner specials and Jackson's radio buzzed on indicating some kind of house call.

"I've got to run."

He started to get into his car, hesitated then reached for his pen and scribbled on a piece of paper.

"Here. Call me if you need anything."

I thanked him and headed back into the restaurant, trying hard not to figure him out, wondering if I ever would.

***

Somehow Marcus and Emma stayed oblivious to the incident on the beach. It was better that way because I didn't need them worrying about me like a second set of parents. I knew how to take care of myself. I was twenty-five now. My shift ended early and I felt like experiencing nature this place has an abundance to offer.

I went home, changed and grabbed a small backpack to fill with snacks and water. Then I walked over to the hallway mirror and fingered the necklace I had received on my birthday. I had decided to wear it today at work and wanted to check to make sure it was still clinging to my neck. I headed for the door then stopped abruptly. I didn't think it was necessary but backtracked into the kitchen closet where the mace was stored and stuffed it into my bag.

Might as well take it just for the hell of it. I drove my jeep out to the county park on the outside of town where I knew some walking trails were and began my short trek up the hillside. Rivers and streams snaked near the trails. The wilderness was alive with the sound of birds chirping somewhere from the cover of dark, lush green leaves. I made my way past rocky cliffs and man-made bridges. I had brought my camera with me and was snapping shots here and there of anything that caught my professional eye of interest. The way the sun gleamed off the brook made the water appear almost golden as I captured one moment with the push of a button. Another was captured when I spotted an eagle soaring high and proud in the open sky. Its body was statuesque-like as it glided smoothly on the soft wind, flying in circles with its large wings.

The sun glistened down through the trees casting slivers of light onto my upturned face. I smiled and continued walking with my face pointing skyward as the smell of pine trees and wildflowers invaded my nostrils. A raspberry bush caught my attention, its bright red berries lush and inviting. I stopped to pick a few.

A burst of sweetness exploded in my mouth as I bit into each one, savoring their pure, un-altered taste. I had been walking for a while and was getting tired. I sat down on a nearby rock and rested for a few minutes. No one else was around. It was easy to imagine myself being the only one left on the planet and as peaceful as this was, the thought was mildly unsettling.

At this point, I thought it best to make my way back home. A rustling sound caught my attention and I turned to look into the dark underbrush just off the trail. A brown blur of a body scurried out from a bush and made its way hastily up a tree. Chipmunks, for such small creatures, could make quite a raucous.

Smile still on my face I headed back to the jeep. Another rustling sound occurred not far from where the first one was. I ignored it thinking another chipmunk was in pursuit of the first. Until I heard the deep guttural snort and a huff of air exhale like a short burst fan. I froze on the spot and slowly turned around.

My blood didn't just run cold; it froze into icicles at the sight before me. A mammoth black bear had sauntered out onto the path and was eyeing up the raspberry bushes I had just picked from. It lifted its huge head in the air then turned in my direction. I stopped breathing and stared back wide-eyed. My brain began to rapid fire like a super computer and ideas flashed before my eyes, each one being ruled out quickly.

Should I run? No, too far, I'd never make it.

Play dead? No, your movement might provoke it.

Scream? Definitely not...not yet anyway.

My mace! If only I had time to grab the mace out of my backpack.

But I knew it was too late. I had read somewhere the difference between the black bear and grizzly and what to do in either situation upon meeting one. But for the life of me, in this moment of fear, I could not recall which action I was supposed to take. And so I stayed frozen, praying to God he wouldn't notice me or wouldn't care. I was wrong. He stood up on his haunches and snorted the air.

I could feel a slight breeze blow my hair from behind, sending my scent his way and I closed my eyes and started saying my good-byes. Another snap from the heart of the woods across from where the bear was standing had my eyes riveted wide open but not out of fear. Out of amazement and awe and wonder. I temporarily forgot the fact that I was about to die and stared incredulously at the most beautiful creature I had ever seen.

Fur as white as the first fallen snow and a rack that would make any hunter fall to their knees in appreciation was the most glorious buck to ever exist. Nothing in Montana compared to this and I was sure nothing ever would. The buck stepped out of its leafy cover and lifted its head higher than I thought possible. First staring at me, then at the bear that had now stopped its advance towards me and focused its attention on the deer. The buck let out a loud snort and pawed the ground with a long muscled leg, kicking up dirt as it did so.

I didn't want to watch this, I didn't want to see this beautiful snow-white animal be killed by this massive bear but I couldn't tear my eyes away. I couldn't believe any of this was happening. My camera hung from my neck, the weight of it begging to be picked up and used to capture this rare moment but my arms and hands were frozen to my sides. All I could do was stare.

The buck stood its ground. The bear snorted once more, looked at me one last time, then turned and headed back into the forest from which it came. My shoulders sagged in relief and my knees began to shake. I was lightheaded and weak and I needed to sit down. I hobbled over to a rock and plopped down still watching the deer as I did so.

It had not moved but continued to stare my way. It's delicate pink nose tested the wind then ever so softly, it took one step towards me. Then another. My heart began to race again. I didn't think deer were aggressive and it would be a shame now to read the headline.

'Girl gets trampled to death by deer.'

But my heart was not beating madly out of fear. I felt no alarm for my safety anymore, only anxiety for this impressive creature. I stayed my muscles and kept completely still. Another step. And another. He was now five yards away and still approaching. This couldn't be happening.

Maybe this deer was someone's pet and had gotten loose. That's the only explanation as to why it harbored no fear towards me. But then again, it would be unlikely that someone could keep such an animal confined. No, there was a freedom about this animal, an elusive carefree spirit that at any moment could and would disappear back into the woods never to be seen again. He was an older deer, not timid, small and jumpy as the younger ones are.

I swear I could see a wise soul in those golden eyes as they continued to look into mine. I wanted to reach out my hand but kept it firm by my side as it lowered its head. I leaned my own head far back to avoid being jabbed by the antlers as its pink nose sniffed the necklace hanging around my neck. And for just one split second, we made contact as it nudged the stone ever so softly then withdrew a few inches and stood tall looking down at me. I instinctively reached out my hand slowly so as not to startle it away.

He continued to stand in place. Just before I could touch the soft fur, he turned and in two giant leaps, vanished behind the trees leaving barely a rustle in his wake. As I made my way back to the jeep I wondered if I had possibly witnessed my first animal ghost. Could it have been real? I sensed he was.

I had felt the warm breath on my neck as he touched the stone necklace. I saw the light in his eyes as he looked into mine. And yet the beauty this creature emitted was like a vision, a dream of some kind. I had heard of and seen albino animals of different species existing but none struck me as incredible as this one had.

I still couldn't get over its size alone. I wondered now if that black bear had indeed met its match in battle. Stranger things have happened. I was heading back to the jeep contemplating all this when someone approached me from the south near the ridge. The trails branched off every so few feet and if it weren't for signs as to where to go, I'd have been lost a ways back. The stranger was walking towards me on a separate path and as he came into better view recognition spread across my face.

"Sam! Hi, it's so good to see you!"

"Jade, how are you?"

"Better now that you're here. I had a close encounter with a bear a few miles back."

"That's unsettling. Although now that it's berry season, they come out to store up for the impending winter. I'm sure we'll see a few of them during the search."

"Search? What search?"

"Mrs. Jenkins reported her husband missing. He went fishing yesterday and never came home. A search party has formed and are scattered throughout this vicinity where he was last seen."

"Is there anything I can do to help?"

"Sure. If you could spare some time, we could search together. I'm heading downriver where the waters meet, there's a place no one has checked yet."

As we made our way off the trail and into a clearing near the water's edge, voices were getting louder as people called out to the missing man, hoping to get some kind of response. Along the bank there were people here and there. I could see Johnny making his way up a nearby hill and Jackson was just behind him. Both men spotted us and waved and I waved back.

"I'm over here! Please, you have to find me!"

In unison, Sam and I spun around to face a white haired man wearing a red and black short-sleeved shirt, jeans and fishing waiters. He was holding a fishing pole in his right hand. It was Mr. Jenkins and my heart sank for I was looking at the person not as flesh and bone, but in spirit. He would haze in and out of solidity and every so often. I could see the forest backdrop through his shirt. His voice sounded distant as well, like spoken from a tunnel or across a room. I looked at Sam startled to see him staring at Mr. Jenkins too.

"Please. Help me."

Mr. Jenkins pleaded as he first addressed me then Sam.

"I know you can hear me."

"You can see him too, can't you?"

I implored Sam as I desperately tried to read his clear gray eyes. He looked sad as he answered me.

"Yes."

"Unbelievable! I'm not alone after all! Okay, we're going to talk about this later but for now, Mr. Jenkins, show us the way."

The three of us picked our way through the thick brush as we headed the opposite direction when something made me turn around and look up at the nearby hill. It was Jackson. He was standing there, staring down at us. His brow furrowed, even at this distance I could see the questions in his eyes. I didn't understand at first what had him looking so perplexed. It was then the breath caught in my throat at the sudden realization. I was just speaking to Mr. Jenkins, a man only I and now Sam could see. There was no doubt in my mind as I turned back to follow Sam and Mr. Jenkins through the trees, Jackson had just saw me talking to the dead.

***

Poor Mr. Jenkins had suffered a heart attack while fishing off the banks of the Ontonagon River and had died on the shoreline. After we had found Mr. Jenkins, I shouted to a small group of people nearby then stood back at a distance watching the paramedics remove his body just as the rain began to fall. His spirit was still with us and was watching the scene unfold. When it was over, he looked at me and smiled.

"Thank you for helping me. I'm ready to go home now."

He looked out across the river at something only he could see then began walking across the water and with a startling flash, he was gone. I blinked my eyes a few times then wiped stray tears off my cheek. I turned to face Sam who had been standing next to me the entire time.

"I think we need to talk."

A few minutes later I was back at my cabin listening to the pounding rain outside my window. I quickly changed into dry clothes and descended the stairs to see Sam sitting at the kitchen table, cup of hot coffee in his hands.

"Is there anything else I can get for you? Something to eat? I'm sorry I don't have any thing for you to change into. I can get you a blanket if you'd like."

"No, thank you. I'm fine."

I filled up my own cup and sat down across from him. Rainwater was still dripping off the tips of his hair. I started to get up to grab a towel for him when he spoke.

"You must think I'm crazy."

"Not any more than you think I am. So, how long have you been able to see them?"

"Ghosts? Since my accident."

"What happened?"

He stirred his coffee around, having yet to take a sip.

"I got hurt on the job. They said I died yet here I am. Ever since then, strange things would start happening to me. Voices in my head and glimpses of people moving but when I look, no one was there. I thought I was going insane for a while.

I couldn't make sense of anything. Then I would see apparitions vividly and they would talk to me, ask me to help them sometimes. At first I'd completely avoid them but after I realized it wasn't going to stop, I decided to make the best of it. People see me talking to myself a lot. I try to be discreet but sometimes it can't be helped."

"Do you have family? Do they know about this?"

"No. My wife died a while ago."

"I'm sorry to hear that. Did you two have any children?"

He paused a moment longer before answering.

"My son died too, when he was just a baby."

"Sam, I'm really sorry."

"I've made peace with everything now. It's okay."

The rain was beginning to let up and a ray of light found its way through a broken cloud.

"So what about you? What's your story?" Sam looked at me imploringly.

"Pretty much the same as yours except my accident didn't happen on the job. I was in a car accident. Doctors told me I went into Hypovolemic shock caused by loss of blood, which resulted in temporary heart failure from over exertion. They tried to revive me and just when they gave up, a pulse registered on the monitor.

Despite the seriousness of the crash, I suffered minor contusions, an ankle and clavicle fracture and bruising to my lungs and a few broken ribs. They believe my air bag and seat belt saved my life. I must've had guardian angels watching over because it could've been so much worse despite my safety restraints. I should be wheelchair bound or paralyzed or dead right now."

"Then there must be a reason why you're still here. Sounds like you were very fortunate Jade. I'm glad to have met you."

"Same here."

"Do you have a family of your own Jade?"

"Just my aunt and uncle here. My parents are back home in Montana."

"No husband or children?"

"No. I had someone back home that I thought I wanted to spend the rest of my life with but it turns out my new gift of seeing ghosts was a deal breaker. His sister was a dear friend of mine. She died in that same car crash I was in. It was winter and we hit an ice patch and careened off the road. She did her best to keep the car on the road but it was too late."

"I'm sorry for your loss."

"Yeah, me too."

The clock on the wall was the only sound for a while as it ticked away each second. I brushed my hair back behind my ear and took a sip of my coffee.

"I'm curious, Jade. How are you not deathly terrified of driving again after what you've been through?"

"I was scared. I never wanted to touch a vehicle again, let alone get in one. But the fact of the matter was unless I wanted to revert back to horse and buggy and allot myself months to get from point A to point B, I had no other choice but to face my fear. After a few months, when I was fully healed, I did just that."

He nodded his head in understanding. I gave him a sideways glance with a burning question of my own in mind.

"It's weird how every time we meet, someone happens to be missing. Don't you find that a funny coincidence?"

"Well the first two times we met, you were either held hostage or broken down on the side of the road. But yes, I know what you mean. It is odd."

He fell silent again but focused his sight on my necklace. I had noticed him glancing at it every now and again. I didn't think much of it at the time for I had received many compliments from customers at the restaurant and from my friends who found it charming. But Sam was studying it now with intense fascination as we continued sitting across from one another.

"That necklace. I've seen it before but I can't remember where. It's very pretty. Where did you get it?"

I rubbed the stone between my thumb and forefinger.

"It was a birthday present from my aunt and uncle."

"Family heirloom I take it?"

"Why, yes. It is actually." I gave him a peculiar look. I was about to ask him how he knew that but the sound of a car door slamming interrupted us.

I stood up to look out the front screen door to see Jackson walking up to the house. Sam stood up too and seemed to be sizing up Jackson with the same interest he had in my necklace a moment prior. His eyes squinted then grew wide when he saw that Jackson was in uniform, his name badge glinting in the sunlight.

"I have to go Jade."

"But…wait!"

He was away from the table and moving quickly towards the back patio when Jackson knocked on the door. Sam left the house shutting the door behind him with a bang as Jackson walked in. Jackson was staring at the patio door in apparent surprise then looked at me.

"Am I interrupting something?"

"Um, no. Come in. What's up?"

"I've come by to say you certainly have a knack for finding people. Mrs. Jenkins was saddened yet relieved to have found some closure concerning her husband. He was suffering from a heart condition for years she said. It was only a matter of time."

"I'm glad I could be of help." I offered him the same chair Sam had been sitting in as I took the one opposite at the kitchen table.

"It can be dangerous territory around here if you're not careful. People get lost and sick all the time out in these woods if they don't know what they're doing. Some people may tell you it's haunted out here but don't let them scare you, especially when you consider in Paulding Light. There are many different theories on that subject, who knows if any are true. The natives will tell you its holy ground. You'll come to learn a lot about this place the longer you stay."

I wasn't sure why he was telling me all this. It almost seemed like he was giving me a lecture possibly because I was out hiking by myself earlier? I couldn't be sure. Although when he saw me, I was with Sam.

I hadn't been alone. Either way, I'm glad I'm hearing this now and not before my hike. The albino buck entered my mind as he mentioned holy ground.

"The real reason I'm here is because a few of us at the station are going to see a comedy act at the local casino tomorrow night. I thought maybe you'd like to join us. I have an extra ticket if you do."

"Um, sure. Yeah, why not."

"Are you sure because if you already have plans."

He said this while scanning the room then back at the door Sam had just left.

"No. It sounds like fun actually. Thanks."

"I'll pick you up at seven then?"

"Sounds good."

He stood up, his tall frame walking towards the front door as I followed him. I watched him walk down the steps to his vehicle. He turned around to face me, smiled then got into his car and drove away.

CHAPTER TEN — SECRETS

Jackson was at my door at seven sharp. He had on casual attire yet still managed to look debonair and down-right handsome. He had on a crisp pair of dark blue jeans that fit him ever so right and a form fitting black and white plaid button down shirt with short sleeves that were rolled at the elbows.

"Hi. Are you ready to go?"

"Yeah, I just need to grab my purse."

I walked back into the kitchen and grabbed my purse off the table. I wasn't much of a fashion queen but I always liked to look good nonetheless. What woman didn't? Especially being around someone who makes your pulse rate quicken as Jackson seemed to be doing to mine.

His entire frame filled my door way as he stood there waiting for me. I caught one last glimpse of myself in the wall mirror and smoothed out my black v-neck blouse. It was short sleeved, light and airy, perfect on this warm evening. I had just bought a new pair of khaki Capri pants last week that I was wearing now with black spaghetti strapped sandals.

Somehow I felt over dressed as I joined Jackson at the door. I touched the stone lightly my aunt had given me just to be sure it was still hanging loosely around my neck. I wore it often these days.

"You look nice."

He smiled briefly then held open the door for me.

"Thanks."

Why was I resorting to grade school girl mentality as if this was my first crush? I suddenly felt awkward and shy and my mind went blank with things to say.

Oh for heaven's sake girl, get a grip on yourself!

I chided myself mentally as he opened the passenger side door for me. His truck was a bit on the huge side. It was a newer cherry red Ford F-150 and I had to hike my leg up to step onto the side rail. I went to reach for the handle bar located near the top of the door when my foot slipped off the rail and my hand completely missed the bar. Jackson caught me before I tripped backwards and made a bigger fool of myself.

That was graceful. Nice one Jade.

I needed to get a grip on myself. It wasn't helping that he was holding me closely from behind as he assisted me into the truck. This time I climbed up with little help. I was still chiding myself thinking of all the times I've climbed into trucks with no problems whatsoever. Damn nerves.

We headed out of town on the short drive to the casino where the comedy act was scheduled to be held in one of the showrooms.

"You're quiet Jade. Everything okay?"

He looked me over from the driver's seat, then focused back on the road.

"Yes. I'm fine." I tried to think of something else to say.

"So, who else is going to the show?"

"We're meeting Hawk, Duvall and their wives in the lobby. Johnny and Nikki will be there, too."

I hadn't talked to Nikki in a while. Our shifts have been so diverse and hectic lately that we've been like two ships passing in the night. It was a relief to have someone be there whom I knew. The others were relative strangers to me. I had to credit much of my nerves to the fact that it was Jackson's world I was about to enter into briefly, people he was comfortable around and knew and here I was the outsider. I stole a glance at Jackson to see he was looking at me with a smile on his face. I smiled back feeling re-assured.

A few minutes later we pulled into the parking lot and walked into the large front lobby area. A small group was sitting at a table waiting for us. Nikki saw me first and sprinted over.

"Look at you girlfriend! You look great! I was so excited to hear you were coming!"

"Wow! You too, I can't believe you cut all your hair off. I like it."

Nikki made me feel a bit better about feeling over-dressed considering the short black skirt she had on and red silk blouse. Her once shoulder length blonde hair was now short and styled into a pixie look. She looked even more hip and cool with a side dish of sexy. She introduced me to the group. I felt relaxed within minutes.

They were all very welcoming and warm. The show was better than I expected. I laughed so hard at times my stomach was beginning to hurt. By the end of the show, we were all chatting and joking as if we were long lost friends.

Some of us had to work in the morning including Jackson and myself and so we declined the invite from the others to play pool over at Spud's Tavern. After saying our good-byes Jackson and I made our way to the truck. He was teasing me about being called up on stage for one of the comedian's act much to my humiliation.

"Well, if you guys wouldn't have all been pointing at me like a big red arrow, he wouldn't have picked me to go up. That was asinine of you throwing me under the bus like that!"

I jabbed him in the side as I said it and he surprised me by catching my arm and linking his hand into mine. His chuckle and my pounding heart the only sound in the brightly lit parking lot. Because of the crowds appearing for the show, we had to park near the far side next to the tree line and it was quite a walk. The lights weren't so bright on this side of the lot and a slight wind had picked up from the north sending chills down my spine.

Jackson pushed a button on his key ring to unlock the door as we approached. I glanced over my shoulder only to see nothing but vehicles and the casino in the distance. There wasn't a soul around.

"Do you need me to boost you into the cab or can you handle it this time?"

He was still in a joking mood as he stood there holding the passenger door open for me.

"I think I can handle it." I scoffed at him.

He held me by my elbow nonetheless as I started to climb inside. A crackly voice from behind startled us both.

"A lesson unlearned is a mistake repeated."

A little old woman with gray hair and a hunched back stared at us from the tailgate of the truck. I scanned the lot trying to figure out where in the blazes she had come from. She looked old and haggard and wore a faded wool dress that hung from her bony shoulders. Her mahogany face was deeply lined and her eyes were black.

A satin shawl with ornate colorful eagles stitched on its delicate cloth hung from her shoulders. Beadwork hung loosely from her neck. She must have come here from the local tribal establishment nearby. She walked with a cane, which she now pointed directly at Jackson.

We were still standing outside the truck as she advanced on us rather quickly despite her frail appearance. I instinctively took one step backwards bumping into Jackson's chest as he leaned against the open passenger door. His arm dropped from the door and around my waist protectively as he continued staring back at the old woman. She turned her gaze from Jackson and focused on me.

"You too will be cursed if you stay by his side. Evil runs through his veins and the hand of fate will claim your life as its own, just as it had with the others. Leave now, before it's too late."

She took one more step then stopped, her eyes dropping from my face. My neck began feeling warm where my emerald necklace hung. A soft green glow distracted me from her withering gaze and I looked down to see the stone had begun to glow ever so faintly yet brilliantly in its own right. I clasped my hand around it and held it up to my face.

Jackson had noticed too and his eyes grew wide as the stone pulsated with color then faded into nothing. The entire occurrence lasted but a second. The old woman let out a slight gasp then glared at me with squinted eyes. The black recesses of her pupils widened then she staggered back, turned abruptly and walked into the tree line alongside the parking lot, disappearing into the forest beyond.

Jackson's entire mood from that point onward shifted gears drastically. He sat stoic and cold behind the wheel of his truck as we drove back towards town. His face a mask of solidity, revealing not a single emotion. Every so often I could faintly make out the twitching of his jaw muscles as he spoke not a word. The incident left us both quiet at first but questions were burning in my mind as to what just happened.

"Did you know who that lady was Jackson? Have you seen her before?"

"No. I have never seen her before. Just some nut bag old woman, we have a lot of those around here."

He was bitter about something. I could feel tension radiating off him and I could see his knuckles as they turned white on the steering wheel. He never took his eyes off the road to look at me once the entire ride home.

"What's with your necklace?"

His only query for the night was the mysterious glow my necklace had given off.

"I'm not really sure. It's never done that before."

"Well, I'm glad it scared her off because I was about to back over her in order to get the hell out of there."

"Jackson, what's happening? What was that all about?"

"I don't know Jade."

He snapped the last part out at me like a hissing snake. He knew something but didn't want to tell. If he really didn't know what was going on, he wouldn't be so on edge as he is now. He would have just brushed the incident off like it was just another weirdo to deal with.

Despite his apparent irritation, which I knew had nothing to do with me; I nonetheless felt a sting from his tone and was mildly hurt by it. Then again, did it have something to do with me and I was simply being naïve? What did the old woman mean by being cursed? And 'evil running through his veins'? I wondered if this had something to do with the death of Annabelle, Jackson's fiancée.

Was she referring to the rumor that he had something to do with her death? All I knew for sure was I had more questions than answers, and the harsh realization came back to me that I truly did not know this man sitting next to me at all. That faint alarm in the pit of my stomach began buzzing ever so softly, persistent and demanding to take notice and heed caution until I could figure out what was going on, if anything at all. I stole one more glance Jackson's way in the dark interior of the cab and tried to envision him committing such a horrific act such as murder.

I simply couldn't fathom it. There would be no possible way for him to have achieved and maintained his current status as an officer of the law if there were any doubts in anyone's mind as to who killed Annabelle. Or was I wrong? Marcus must know more about what had happened that night; I'll talk to him first thing tomorrow. The truck pulled into the driveway and jolted to a stop. He kept the engine running and for the first time since leaving the casino, he looked my way. I didn't like what I saw in his dark brown eyes.

"I'm sorry about tonight Jade. You should go inside now."

His rugged face was shadowed and hard, and his eyes emitted a silent warning.

"Jackson, you're acting strange. What's wrong? Tell me, I want to help."

He looked straight ahead and the muscles in his jaw twitched again. Without looking back towards me he answered in a monotone voice.

"If you want to help, then you should listen to what that woman said tonight. Stay away from me, and I'll promise to do the same."

"What? What are you talking about? I thought you said you didn't know who she was?"

"I *don't* know who she is, but she obviously knows me. And what she was trying to say is bad things happen to people who get close to me. Call it a curse, call it bad luck, whatever, it doesn't matter. What matters is she's right, I have worse luck than most and it's not worth hurting anyone else in the process.

It was hard not to be drawn to you Jade and because of you, I forgot about everything that could possibly go wrong. Tonight, that old woman brought it all back and I'm not taking any more chances."

"Jackson, you can't be serious? Bad things happen to everyone but if you're going to think negative thoughts like that then yes, you end up placing bad luck upon yourself. You're no different than anyone else who's suffered loss. I can't believe you'd listen to that woman; she's just a nut bag like you said. I never knew you were so superstitious."

"There's more to it than just bad things happening Jade. Look I'm not going to go into it anymore. You should really go inside, it's getting late."

My voice softened and I implored his face. Warmth flooded my heart and I stepped out onto a limb of faith when I spoke.

"Okay, I'll go. But if this is about Annabelle then I hope you realize it wasn't your fault. You shouldn't carry guilt around thinking you're cursed because of it. It was a freak accident and it could've happened to anyone."

This time his head slowly turned in my direction and the warmth iced over into alarm as the warning bell inside my gut began to ring even louder.

"You don't know anything Jade. Annabelle's death was not a freak accident; it was planned. Cold and calculating with the killer running free. Some say I had something to do with it. What if I told you they were right? What if I told you I killed her?"

My voice cracked nervously.

"Did you?"

The longest thirty seconds I've ever experienced ticked by before he answered.

"Yes. And if you don't believe me, just ask your Uncle Marcus. Because of our lies, Annabelle is dead."

CHAPTER ELEVEN — CURSED

Knock, knock, knock…

My aunt was in deep concentration when I gently rapped on the door to her office. She looked just as stressed and haggard as I felt when she looked up from the computer at me. Her face lifted ever so slightly in recognition.

"Hi my dear, what can I do for you?"

Her eyes averted mine as she furrowed her brows in confusion and stared back at the monitor.

"Is this a bad time? I can come back later."

"No, no. Nonsense. Sit down. I could use a break." Emma leaned back in her chair.

"You look distressed. Is everything alright?"

"Yes. No. I'm not sure. I was wondering if I could talk to you about something."

"Sure. What's on your mind?"

"It's about Jackson."

I told her about meeting the old woman in the parking lot and what she had said. About Jackson's drastic change in mood right after and the words he spoke to me when he dropped me off at the cabin. She seemed to ponder this a second, then reiterated what I had just said.

"You're saying some woman threatened you last night and now you're talking about Jackson being cursed? And that both him and Marcus have something to do with a murder?"

"I know how it sounds. I'm not sure how to put it delicately to be honest. But Jackson became someone else when that woman threatened him….us. He went from an open, funny, genuinely nice guy to cold and distant and unfriendly in a single instant. He said he's cursed and that Annabelle is dead because of his and Uncle Marcus' lies. I need to know what he's talking about."

"Was he drunk?"

"Auntie, come on. No, he wasn't. Neither of us were."

"Well, I just don't get it Jade. It doesn't make sense to me either. I have no clue what he means by lies. But I do think I know what's going on concerning the curse he feels is following him. But he should be the one to tell you this, not me."

"That's the problem. He won't talk to me about it. He told me to stay away from him if I know what's best for me. He won't explain much else."

I was sitting across the desk from Emma sleep deprived and anxious as I awaited any kind of feedback that would unlock this mystery. I had awoken from fitful sleep before the sun even arose across the lake. Dressed myself for work haphazardly and made my way directly to the main house to speak to Marcus. Aunt Emma had told me I just missed him by five minutes. The disappointment and anxiety had been mounting as the day wore on. I was getting nowhere and I wouldn't be able to speak to Uncle Marcus until lunch break, three hours from now.

"If you're concerned about Jackson being dangerous, don't be. Marcus and I had been friends of his parents for a long time and Jackson is like a son to us. He's a good man and he wouldn't be where he is now if he was guilty of any crime. What happened to Annabelle shook the town. Jackson and Annie were a very close, loving couple.

He would have died for her Jade. He loved her that much. It devastated him tremendously when he learned of her death. The police conducted a full investigation but turned up with not a single clue.

Their house had been ran-sacked but nothing was reported stolen or missing. Some break ins had been reported around the time of Annie's death and a few weeks after her funeral, more break ins were reported in the next town. They caught the kids who were breaking in but cleared them of any murder. Turns out they were stealing loose change off of kitchen countertops and electronic devices.

They left jewelry and weapons untouched. Very petty, novice type work yet dangerous nonetheless had someone decided to take the law in their own hands, which some tend to do in small towns like ours."

"Where are Jackson's parents? Do they still live in town?"

"They're gone. Jackson's mother died when he was only five years old and his father died of cancer just shy of Jackson's nineteenth birthday."

"How did his mother die?"

Emma seemed to hesitate before she answered. I could see I was treading on un-easy territory, a subject that made her visibly tremble.

"A local convenience store had been robbed in broad daylight. Jackson's mother was in the wrong place at the wrong time. She pulled into the parking lot unaware of what was going on inside the store. The robbery was so fresh; the police hadn't even had a chance to arrive yet. She walked up to the store as the robber was coming out.

He decided to take her hostage when he saw the squad cars pulling up. She fought him and he shot her. He was killed shortly after by police but after that tragedy had occurred, it destroyed Jackson's father completely. Mr. Butler didn't know how to go on without her and suffered depression for many years after.

We helped out as much as we could in raising Jackson. He was still too young to understand what was going on but it affected him deeply regardless. He was so sad and confused when his mother never came back home."

I listened in horror as my aunt spoke. I couldn't believe so much sadness could happen to one person in one lifetime.

"What about Annabelle? Did she die recently?"

The questions were like a train wreck; they kept spilling forth from me out of morbid interest.

"Five years ago. Her and Jackson were both twenty-five years old when she died. She was a very sweet young woman, vibrant and full of inhibition. She had the most beautiful red hair, funny how certain things stand out in one's memory. Jackson once told me how it was her hair shining in the sun that first caught his attention. He said it looked as if it were on fire. Radiant and shimmering, just like her."

I still wasn't convinced of the so-called curse upon him but I was starting to understand now why he pushed people away and placed that wall of his up. If he didn't become close with anyone, then he wouldn't feel the pain of loss anymore. If no one could get in, no one could hurt him. But it still didn't explain why that old woman painted Jackson as an evil person or why he thinks he killed his girlfriend.

Maybe there was more to the puzzle than meets the eye. I was still leery. I had to be. My aunt's fondness of him could impair her judgment in which he could do no wrong. I had to find out what lies he and Marcus told, maybe then I'd make some peace with all of this.

"It's strange how I never knew any of this before, given the few trips I've made this way to stay with you. I never even knew Jackson until now."

"You wouldn't have, honey. He was off to college when you were here. He and Annie were attending the same university and were living in Marquette at the time. You weren't here when his father or Annie died. And it's a subject we don't talk about much in our family. The memories are just too painful."

It was apparent to me seeing Emma's strained face how hard this was for her to talk about, even after all these years.

"I'm sorry Auntie for making you rehash all of this. I just don't know why Jackson would say something like that to me. Or why he keeps pushing me away."

"Give him time, sweetie. He's been through more than what most of us go through in an entire lifetime. But he's a strong man, he always has been. Marcus and I were there if he ever needed us but he was always so self-sufficient. He's not one to open up quickly to others and because of that, he's easily misjudged. He'll come around in time, just don't expect too much from him."

"I'm not. And thanks again. I'm going to head over to the station on my break and talk to Uncle Marcus."

"He'll appreciate your visit. He's swimming in paper work today and hasn't left the office much. Sheba will in the office here when you get back. She helps me out with some of the book keeping and ledgers so if you need me, call my cell."

"Thanks. I will."

I got up to leave the office when one more thing popped into my mind.

"Aunt Em?"

"Yes?"

"My necklace gave off a soft green glow the other night. Is that normal?"

She blinked a few times then squinted her eyes at the stone resting upon my chest.

"That's odd. Can't say as I've ever noticed that before. Are you sure it glowed?"

"Yes, of course. Well it did for only a moment."

"Hmm....I have heard of some minerals giving off a light during sunset rendering the appearance of a glow. Others have absorbed radioactive energy thus emitting afterglow. But unlike common portrayals of a 'green' glow on cartoons and such, it actually emits a bluish color."

"Great."

"Oh Jade, your necklace is not radioactive I can promise you that."

Emma smiled at the look on my face.

"You know, I read somewhere that rare earth ions can activate phosphorescent pigments of alkaline earth aluminates thus causing an imminent glow. Maybe some crystals found their way into your stone? Remember how I told you of the legend of our tribe and how a young tribesman found the stone shining in the rain? Maybe that's the reason why."

"I have no idea what you just said but I feel as if I've entered a parallel universe just now."

Emma laughed.

"It's amazing what odd things my brain can recall sometimes. I wouldn't worry too much about it, Jade. I'm sure it was just a fluke incident."

As I walked out of the office, I stopped at the door and looked back over my shoulder. Emma seemed more preoccupied and burdened than normal and I couldn't help but ask.

"Are you alright Auntie?"

She didn't seem to hear me at first, then glanced up in surprise.

"What? Me? Yes, I'm fine."

I remained quiet while looking at her pensively. She picked up my drift and stopped the charade.

"I'm just trying to figure out some finances here, a few things aren't adding up. Math never was my strong suit, as ironic as that sounds being a Business Major and all."

I could see she was trying to make light of it but the creases in her forehead contradicted her attempt at flippancy.

"Can I help at all?"

"Thank you sweetie, but there's nothing you can do at the moment."

My mind was still swimming with questions as I drove across town to the police station later that day. I dreaded having to possibly run into Jackson while there but that couldn't be avoided. This was something I needed to speak to Marcus about in person and it couldn't wait. I pulled into the station and looked around but no one was outside.

I walked into the front lobby and was directed to Marcus' office. The entire time on the lookout for Jackson, but he was nowhere to be seen.

"Jade! How are you my dear? Have a seat. Em said you needed to speak with me."

"Hi uncle. Yes, I do. I only need a few minutes of your time."

"No problem. What can I do for you?"

"I'm not quite sure how to explain this without it sounding odd but…I need some answers."

I told him everything I had told Emma.

"…and that's the reason I'm here. To ask you what in the blazes he's talking about."

Marcus was shaking his head up and down slowly like an attentive, understanding person would. His big hands were clasped in front of his belly as he leaned back in his chair. After a few moments of silence he finally answered.

"I don't want you worrying yourself over nothing my dear. Jackson could be talking about any number of things. But I'm here to tell you first hand, neither he nor I were responsible in any way, shape or form for what happened to Annabelle."

"Uncle…I didn't mean…."

"No, no, it's okay Jade. I'm not upset with you for coming to me about this. I understand the confusion he must have placed upon you. Jackson's not entirely healed from Annie's death. He carries around a lot of guilt for what happened. He felt he should've been there to protect her."

"His father and I were very good friends and I looked at Jackson as one of my own. Emma and I couldn't have any children and so we gradually took to Jackson and his family. They were good people and Jackson is proof of that. He's a good kid. So don't take everything he says so seriously."

I tried accepting what Marcus was telling me but something still felt off. I'll never forget the look on Jackson's face when he warned me to stay away. But for now, I had no choice but to accept it. My uncle is a wonderful man, always has been and does not contain a malicious, deceitful bone in his body. If he had, my aunt would've kicked him to the curb a long time ago. I exhaled deeply and shook my head in resignation.

"Thanks for your time, uncle. I appreciate it."

"Anytime, Jade. Will we see you tonight for dinner? Em's making her famous Chicken Piccata dish and Tiramisu for dessert."

"Sounds great. See you then."

I should have been satisfied with what Marcus told me but I wasn't. I still couldn't shake this unsettling feeling I had.

***

A week had passed with no sight or sound from Jackson. I managed to push my questions and concerns to the back of my mind as I plugged away at the restaurant. I didn't know what I would do if I saw him strolling in. A part of me would uncontrollably delight at his presence, but another part did not want to have anything to do with him.

I understood a threat when given one and even though I didn't buy into it completely, I ascertained his need to want nothing to do with me. A delicate flash of pain coursed through me at this notion and my mood dropped considerably. Jordyn approached me at Dolly's on Friday morning with a huge grin on her face and mischief in her eyes. Emma had asked me if I could utilize my Arts degree and create a flyer for a banquet that was coming up. I was sitting in her office in front of the computer when Jordyn knocked on the open door.

"You have a delivery!"

"Of what?" I asked, half interested in her answer.

I continued to stare uninterested and expressionless at the monitor, punching keys every now and then.

"Flowers silly. They're out front, on display so everyone can see. Come take a look!"

I gave her a sideways look, one eyebrow raised.

"I'll be right there."

I finished what I was doing first, stretched my arms over my head and arched my back, trying to loosen stiff muscles. I had been sitting at the computer all morning and could use a break. Jordyn, Heather and Nikki were impatiently waiting next to a stunning array of flowers sitting perfectly arranged in a glass vase.

"Hurry up, slow poke. Open the note, I want to see who it's from."

Nikki looked at Heather and winked.

"I bet I know who they're from."

I gave a knowing look at Nikki, walked up to the counter and snatched the note from the plastic clip.

"I bet you're wrong." I said smiling sarcastically.

The flowers were a summer fun bouquet full of Chrysanthemums, Daisies, Freesias, Geraniums, Orchids, Carnations, Belladonna Lily, and Sun flowers to name a few. And they smelled wonderful.

I ripped open the envelope and my face went blank with shock.

Nikki grabbed it from my hand and held it up.

"Ha ha! I was right! They're from Jackson."

Inside the note was a short message.

Jade, I'm sorry for my behavior. I needed time to think. I'd like to explain everything if you'll let me. ~Jackson

"Uh-oh, lover's quarrel?"

I gave Heather a searing look and headed back to the office leaving the flowers behind. Before I reached the door a voice had me turning.

"Nice flowers."

My traitorous heart slammed clumsily into my chest then dropped to my stomach where it lay fluttering pathetically. I still had control over my face, which I kept cool and aloof at his approach.

"Jackson, nice to see you. Would you like a booth or table?"

"I'm not here to eat Jade. I came because you asked me to."

I gave him a deer in the headlight look.

"You wanted to speak to me about something?"

He looked over at the flowers again with curiosity.

"What the devil are you talking about? I didn't ask you anything."

"I have your text right here Jade."

He handed me his phone and I stared incredulously at a message that someone sent from my cell phone.

Jackson, I need to talk to U. Plz come by the restaurant today if U can. ~Jade.

"Huh! I'll be damned…"

I looked up at him. His look always made me uneasy as it was doing now. Direct and intruding like he was analyzing every inch of me.

"I don't know what to tell you Jackson, but I didn't send this. Someone must have gotten a hold of my phone and sent this to you."

I knew that wasn't possible because I always carried my phone with me at all times. Unless, someone dug into my purse while I was waiting on tables and sent it to him. But who would do such a thing? And why?

"And why would someone do that?"

"I honestly don't know, but I'm telling you that I didn't write that."

He stared at me. A few silent seconds passed before he continued.

"I'm not into playing games Jade, keep that in mind."

"I swear to you I don't know who did that. I don't play games, either. I'll lock my phone in my car from now on."

He must have heard the genuine, desperate quality to my voice and seen how upset I was becoming because his tone softened, as well as his ruggedly handsome face.

"Okay. I believe you."

He looked like he was about to leave then hesitated.

"So, who sent you the flowers?"

I wasn't sure if I detected a tone of jealousy in his voice as he glanced around the restaurant then back at me.

"Are you serious? Wow, talk about games."

I handed him the card and his eyes squinted in intensity at the words.

"This isn't my hand writing and I never sent you flowers."

"Oh." was all I managed to say. I sat down heavily on the nearest bar stool as he handed the note back to me.

"Well, it appears as if we have a scoundrel on our hands. Someone who likes to play pranks on people. Keep your eyes open and let me know if anything else strange happens would you, please?"

"Yeah. Okay."

I had my head down with the note twirling around and around in my hands. If only he did want to talk to me. If only he would open up to me and tell me what's really going on. Why he feels the need to keep me at bay. But it was no use. I'd have better luck getting blood from a rock than crack open his solid constitution.

It was hopeless. In another time, we may have had a chance at developing a relationship of some kind, but some things just aren't meant to be. He started to walk away then stopped and reached out his hand to caress one of the flowers.

"I saw this exact arrangement the other day and thought of you. It's kind of bizarre actually how they ended up in your hands after all. Now I wish they really had been from me. You deserve every kind of happiness Jade."

I couldn't help but notice Nikki, Heather and Jordyn leaning over the counter behind Jackson, eyes wide, taking in his every word. In another time and place I would've found this comical but as it were my face began to flush as his long strides suddenly brought him dangerously close to me. I stood up from the bar stool to face him as he leveled me with that look of his.

"It's really not about you, Jade. You did nothing wrong."

His voice lowered to a whisper as he continued.

"But I realize now that I'm not the only one who has suffered tragedy and loss. I know about your accident back home in Montana and the friend you lost."

"I know about the relationship you were in and how that ended shortly after the accident. Don't be upset. I asked your uncle because I care about you and I didn't think you would tell me yourself. You seemed to have had a vendetta against me when we first met."

"I could say the same of you." I whispered back.

"Fair enough. But I do think you deserve an explanation after all, as crazy as it's going to sound. You can take it or leave it."

He asked when I'd be done with work, then we agreed upon a time in which he'd stop over.

***

A few hours later I was pacing back and forth in my living room when I heard tires on gravel approaching the cabin. Jackson had changed out of his uniform before coming over. He looked fresh and clean-shaven as I held the door open for him.

I offered him a soda before leading him out onto the back deck facing the lake. A small fishing boat floated nearby by as its lone inhabitant cast out his line a few times then sat back waiting patiently for a bite. A man and woman in kayaks paddled near shore. They turned around and headed out across the lake in the direction of a cabin where a group of people were sitting next to a bonfire and laughing. Their jovial voices floated across the lake mumbled by distance, yet edged with obvious happiness.

Everything here felt peaceful and normal. I sensed that was all about to change with what Jackson was about to say to me.

"I'm not sure how much you know about this area but there's a deep history here. Many still do not know that a battle once took place here and quite

Kathleen Wickman

a few lives were lost. Like most towns, some stories lie hidden, waiting to be told."

I took a sip from my glass, waiting patiently for him to go on.

"In 1887 my third great-grandfather, Andrew Sampson Butler, worked for the Chicago and North Western Railroad Company.

A railroad was being constructed at the time through the town. It was a time where the logging industry was booming and railroads were being built and maintained throughout upper Michigan. Andrew was young back then and a hard worker. He was a part of a migrant group of men that traveled with the railway systems, taking their families with them in some cases.

A dissension began to form between the loggers who were clearing the land and the local Ottawa tribe who inhabited the area nearby. My father once told me that despite all appearances, the Ottawans weren't the ones who started the conflict; that another nomadic tribe from the north did. They had joined the Ottawa people in some sort of peace agreement many years prior and lived together in harmony before the loggers came in and disrupted their serenity. It was this smaller nomadic group that convinced the Ottawa nation to revolt for the land they were about to lose.

They claimed a sure victory for although they were small in numbers standing alone; they boasted to have magic in their blood and the strength of the Ottawa people to back them up. News began to spread throughout the camp that a revolt was on the brink and to be prepared for any kind of ambush. So

Phantom's Crossing

the white men went out every day with pistols holstered and axes swinging as they continued cutting down the forest making way for the railroad system. Months went by without any kind of disruption and the men began letting their guards down believing it was all some kind of empty threat.

None were too worried to begin with considering they had an industrial revolution on their side that was essentially a wild fire spreading out of control. The nearby towns were developing more and more every day and nothing could stop it from happening, or so they thought."

A screech of laughter from a small child split the quiet afternoon air. It broke the spell Jackson's story had on me as I turned my head briefly in the direction the sound had come from. Jackson paused as well to look out across the lake to see kids playing hide and seek. In unison, we turned back to one another, our gazes locking onto each other's.

"The presumed ambush was now just a joke to the men who spent day and night expecting something that never happened. Andrew had continued to stay in the area. His family resided a few towns over.

He was now assigned as a train crewmember who performed railcar and track management for Paulding and Watersmeet where the roundhouse was located. The details have become blurry over time as to what exactly happened next. But from what I gather, the ambush did happen when they least expected it, and the leader of the nomadic tribe was killed by Andrew's hand. It was at this time a curse was placed upon my great-great-great-grandfather and all who are direct descendants of his lineage. After that, my ancestor's loved ones have all died an untimely death.

I didn't believe it myself, not even when my mother died. It was only after Annabelle that I believed this could all be more than simple fate. My father's stories of the battle and of his ancestors haunted me. I knew turning my back on the facts was just no longer possible."

I hadn't moved a muscle when he began telling me his story, and now that he finished, all I could do was blink at him dumb-founded.

"I know you think I'm crazy. I can't say as I blame you. It sounds crazy saying it out loud."

My voice came back to me as my brain finished digesting all this information.

"You'd be surprised at my crazy threshold."

We sat in silence a while longer before I continued.

"Why did only the females die? Shouldn't the curse have taken the lives of the men who descended from Andrew seeing as how he was the one to take the Chief's life?"

"I don't know. Unless it was meant to be this way in order to inflict more pain. What greater suffering is there than watching those you love die before you?"

"I wonder if this isn't just all self-inflicted bad karma caused by a false belief in magic that doesn't exist. There are women in my family who have died before their husbands too but that doesn't mean my family is cursed."

"Yes. But were all the females exactly twenty-five years old when they died? My mother, Annabelle, my grandmother, and so on. Don't you think that's a little odd?"

"I think the whole thing is odd."

"Tell me about it. And the weirdest part about the whole thing is that each and every one of them died by gunshot, the same way the chief tribesman perished. Coincidence? Doubtful."

"No way."

"Yes way. From the third greats down to the greats down to my father, lastly with me. We've all lost the women in our lives to gunshots. It's as if the Butler line is destined to be stamped out come hell or high water. Yet, somehow, we've managed to carry on into the next generation. It's still a far-fetched mystery to me."

"This is ridiculous."

"It is what it is Jade. Take it or leave, like I said."

He seemed insulted somehow and I lightened my tone.

"I don't mean to be flippant about this but it all seems very overwhelming at the moment. You actually believe you have a curse lingering over your head?"

"Believe me when I say, I'm the last guy to buy into fairy dust, witch and warlock type stories but *something* strange and unusual has happened down the bloodline of the Butler family and it hasn't stopped. I don't think it ever will. That is why I've been so closed off to the world and to you as much as it kills me to. You are the hardest to keep out and it's because I care for you that you have to stay away from me. You're twenty-five now which is even more reason that we can't be together, ever."

"So...if that's the case and they all died at twenty-five...then just choose someone older. It sounds as if it's an age oriented curse so if you date someone older, problem solved."

It disturbed me to say that out loud. To suggest another woman for him when I wanted him to choose me. Stay with me. Love me. I blinked a few times to regain focus as his words reached my ears.

"That would be beautiful if only it were true. The curse strikes when the iron's hot mostly when a loved one turns twenty-five because most people marry young as they did in my family but it does not stop there. It is feeling oriented too, not just age. Two years ago a buddy of mine kept persisting I go out with this girl who worked at the station as a dispatcher.

She was twenty-eight, smart, funny, and easy to like. Annabelle had been gone for three years and the wounds were still fresh. I wasn't interested in getting serious with anyone any time soon and wanted to keep things casual for a while. We had some similar interests, one of them being hiking.

After a few weeks of dating, I began to have feelings for her. One day, we took a hike by Bond Falls. The air was motionless, not a breeze stirred as a branch above us suddenly snapped free and fell towards our heads. I yelled for her to watch out, she jumped ahead and I fell backwards. She lost her footing on some loose gravel and tumbled down the hill hitting rocks along the way before stopping in the shallow creek below."

"Jackson, that's awful. Was she okay?"

"No. Not at first. She was in critical condition and in the hospital for a few weeks before she started to recover. After that, we drifted apart and she ended up moving to Florida to accept a new job. We no longer keep in touch."

"Don't you think it was just an accident, nothing more, nothing less?"

"Possibly. But why risk it? It's not worth anyone getting hurt anymore. When no one is in my life, no one gets hurt. Simple as that. I'm not afraid of being alone for the rest of my life. I can handle it."

"Why twenty-five?"

"What?"

"I'm just thinking, why that age? Why did the spouses of the Butler men have to die at twenty-five?"

"Not sure. That's one question I have no answer to."

We sat in silence for a moment as a loon called out over the lake, beckoning its mate to return.

"Well...there's got to be something you can do. Someone who might know how to reverse this? Maybe you could talk to a family member of the tribal leader and explain what happened and ask for forgiveness."

"He was from a very small tribe within the Ottawa community, many were killed that day in battle and I highly doubt any of his kin are still alive or even in this area anymore. The tribe was said to have either been killed or retreated to another location after the massacre. Only the Ottawa natives remain in the area to this day."

"I still think it's worth a shot. What do you have to lose? I'll go with you to the reservation for moral support."

He gave me a look at that and the first signs of a smile played at the edges of his mouth.

I know that smile...

The thought teetered delicately in my mind then subsided. Jackson sat up straighter in his chair as a thought came to him.

"I'll talk to Sam. He knows this area like no one else. He also knows the people on the reservation. I bet he even knows that little old woman who warned us in the casino parking lot. She knew about the curse. She might be able to help me."

"Sam knows the area?"

"Yeah, he's a regular historian as well as a mechanic."

Sam didn't strike me as a historian but I shrugged my shoulders and stood up simultaneously as Jackson did.

"I'll go with you."

"No, Jade. Stay here. I'm not sure what to expect and this is something I need to do on my own."

"I'm not afraid of getting hurt Jackson. I'm not afraid of you or your curse. Let me go with you, please."

He had walked back into the house with me right on his heels. He put his empty glass in the sink then turned to face me.

"You've done enough. Besides, I can see you don't believe me anyway so why on earth would you want to come along?"

"I never said I didn't believe you! I care about you and I want to help. Why do you have to be so bullheaded?"

He was trying to keep me at bay with his cutting words. I sensed it but angry tears started welling in my eyes nonetheless as I painfully granted his wish.

"Fine. Leave and don't bother coming back. If space is what you want, then space is what you'll get."

I was being childish and petulant and yet I didn't care. It killed me every time he pulled me close then shut me out again. I turned my back on him but not before one tear escaped to run down my cheek. I stormed away heading back to the patio when a hand on my arm stopped me and the other hand turned my body back to face his close proximity. In just two strides he had caught up to me and was looking down into my tear soaked face.

"I can't do this anymore. I don't know how to be your friend."

The words tumbled out of my mouth and I didn't care that I sounded like a babbling fool.

"Let me go. Just leave!"

I turned my face valiantly trying to hide my tears to no avail. I took a step back towards the wall attempting to release myself but his tight grip followed me. His face was twisted with raw emotion and his eyes held a deep longing that not even his bravado could hide. I saw the vulnerability reflected back like two mirrors facing each other, the loneliness a prowling hungry wolf that's been on its own for far too long. The air sizzled and grew warm as my pulse quickened with every breath.

His chest was rising and falling and I couldn't tell if it was my heart I was hearing or his, as the pounding grew more intense. He leaned into me; I closed my eyes and our lips melded together in a sensual dance. He pushed his body against mine pinning me to the wall as his arms dropped from my shoulders to wrap around my waist. I reached up and locked one hand behind his neck while the other tangled into his hair. His body was hard and massive against my subtle frame and it felt like minutes before either of us resurfaced for air.

I gasped as his lips continued down my jaw line leaving a blazing trail of heat down my neck. No one had ever made me feel like this before, nor one kiss bring me back to life as this one did. I had not one hesitation or fear of taking this as far as it could go which was why I had to stop before we delved ourselves into a delicious all-consuming fire. I tried forming the words but my throat was dry and scorched, the only sound was my breath coming in gasps.

"We shouldn't do this. I'm sorry."

His voice was like velvet, soft, deep and sensual. My eyes opened and locked onto his.

"I know. I can't do this either." I had yet to let go of him.

With much effort, he took a step away, breaking the connection our bodies had as they molded together. His head was down and his breaths were heavy and heated. He walked over to the couch, sat down and ran his hands through his dark unruly hair with elbows propped onto his knees. I stood there not knowing what to say. And so I said nothing and waited, hoping for an absolution that may never come.

"Alright. Come with me then. To be honest, ever since that day you came into town, I haven't been able to get you out of my head. You became a part of my life whether I liked it or not, or whether you knew it or not. As far as I see it, the damage is already done. Whatever happens next, just know there's nothing I won't do to protect you. You have my word."

I saw determination in those eyes and a fierce resignation to fate. He stood up, walked over to me, and held me tightly in a time stopping embrace. I burrowed my face into his chest, closed my eyes and let the world outside slip by.

Kathleen Wickman

CHAPTER TWELVE — THE SCORTCHING TRUTH

"Hello Jackson! Haven't seen you in a while, son. What brings you to my neck of the woods?"

When Jackson's truck pulled into the gravel parking lot I expected to see a familiar face but instead a gray haired man limped out of the garage with a walking cane. This wasn't the Sam I knew. Not only was his hair gray but thinning as well. He walked with a limp thus rendering him the use of a cane. And when he shook Jackson's hand, his was jagged and bony. Sam's face was deeply lined but he had a strong set jaw and shining blue eyes that defied his age. Those eyes were locked on me now as he smiled a crooked smile and gave me a once over glance.

"You're Sam?" The bewildered question flew out of me before I could stop it.

He turned his quizzical eyes towards me again.

"Last I checked."

"Uh, Sam, this is Jade. She just moved here from Montana."

His eyes glowed in recognition.

"So you must be Emma and Marcus' niece. Nice to meet you."

I took his weathered hand in my own and was surprised at the strength with which he held mine. He was a strong man despite his appearance. He seemed to be about mid-seventies and still plugging away on cars.

"I was under the impression you two knew each other but now I can see I am mistaken."

Jackson looked first to my blank expression, then to Sam's jovial one.

"Not officially, until now that is. But I had heard that you were moving to town from Fenton."

He nodded his head back towards the shop where another man was half under the hood of a rusty pickup.

"He knows your uncle real well. You know how small towns are. News travels fast."

He winked at me and I hesitantly smiled back, traces of confusion still flittering across my face.

"How do you like our town so far, Jade?"

"It's great. I'm a bit confused; the Sam I know said he works here. Is there anyone else by that name who works with you then?"

I peered my head over Sam's shoulder trying to get a better look into the shop.

"Nope. Just myself, Fenton and Joe."

The one named Joe was walking out of the shop and to a nearby car. He was in his late forties with light brown thin hair. I knew instantly, he wasn't who I was looking for. Fenton had pulled himself out from under the hood at this point and was looking our way. He spotted Jackson and gave him a wave.

Even from this distance I knew he wasn't Sam I knew either. I started to assume that possibly, Sam had given me a false name for some reason and that he was here in the shop somewhere. But why he would do such a thing? It was beyond my capacity of logical reasoning. Unless, of course, there was another auto shop in town, which could very well be the case although I did not know of any offhand. But I hoped so for Sam's sake. Like the real Sam said, it's a small town. And lies had a peculiar way of coming about face in a rather short period of time in small towns.

"Mr. Newman, do you know anyone who fits this description?"

I described a young man, late twenties or possibly early thirties who is about 6'1", broad shouldered and solid frame with dark blonde hair and gray eyes.

"No, can't say as I do."

"Well, is there another shop in town?"

"Nope. There's one in the next town over though. Why do you ask?"

Both Jackson and Sam were staring at me and I suddenly felt like I was losing my mind.

"It's nothing. I must've misunderstood something, never mind."

"Still dinking with cars, hey Sam?"

Jackson nodded back towards the garage.

"Beats staying home with the wife."

Both guys chuckled at the long-standing joke then Jackson changed subjects.

"Sam, we're here because we have to ask you something. I'm looking for someone and am hoping you could tell us where to find her."

Jackson described the old woman in the casino parking lot and spared any extraneous detail regarding what she said to us.

"Unfortunately, I did not catch her name at the time and was hoping you'd know."

He thought about it for a minute, scratching his head as he did so.

"You must be talking about Matilda Choate. She was the oldest on the reservation and always wore the necklace you describe."

"Was the oldest?"

"She passed away yesterday afternoon. I was fixing a broken water heater for a neighbor of hers when the news spread throughout the community. I spoke with her a few times over the years and found her to be kind and witty."

Jackson's shoulders visibly dropped as the breath exhaled out of him. I could see the last shred of hope leave his body on the winds of despair. He shook his head in understanding and sympathy at Sam's reminiscent tone.

"I'm sorry to hear that. She sounded like a great lady."

"She was."

"Did she have any relatives?"

"None living as far as I know. I didn't really know her all that well. If she had family, they've either passed on or live elsewhere."

We had hit an immediate dead end. The men chatted a bit more about miscellaneous things, including me in their discussions here and there, then the conversation fizzled out. Sam looked up at the sky then nodded at Jackson.

"I better get back to work. Nice to see you again Jackie boy."

"Nice to see you, too. Thanks for your help. Take care."

"Anytime. Take care of him now, keep him in line!"

Sam winked at me, then nodded his head at Jackson. When we climbed back into the truck I gently laid my hand on his shoulder.

"I'm sorry."

He put the truck into gear and pulled onto the road.

"Don't be. It was a long shot anyway and a feeble attempt at finding some closure. There were no guarantees that she could've helped us anyway, even if she had not passed on. One thing I do know is that this stops with you. Whatever fluke, coincidence, accident, or curse, it stops with you. If I have to put you into a bubble and lock you in a dungeon, I will."

"Please don't. I'm afraid of bubbles."

My weak attempt to lighten the mood seemed to work for a time. His anger of moments ago fizzled out to be replaced with a subtle smile. My hand dropped from his shoulder and was caught in his as we drove back home.

***

The next day everything changed. An ominous cloud seemed to hang over the day, literally and figuratively. I woke up early from a restless sleep to an overcast sky. The air itself seemed to be taking on a slight variation as summer rolled to a close and fall began creeping in. The air was still warm but tinged with a slight crisp as I walked into the restaurant.

As soon as my shift began, rain started to fall outside and the sky grew dark. The mood inside Dolly's reflected the darkness outside. Nikki's shift had just begun too; she caught me as I headed out of the break room.

"Be warned; your aunt's in a foul mood today. Try and stay out of her way if you can."

She gave me a knowing look, then walked out ahead of me into the seating area. The door to Emma's office opened and a white faced Jordyn walked out, shoulders stiff, head held high as she brushed past me without greeting and began waiting on tables. No one seemed to be in the greatest of moods today. Of course the customers that came in throughout the morning were none the wiser as Jordyn, the other girls and I put on a happy face in greeting and waited on them graciously.

But in the shadows of the day, when no one needed impressing upon, there was a definite aura of gloom. I did my best to shrug the feeling off, blaming the weather for drowning everyone's spirits.

The bell on the front door gave a quiet buzz indicating another patron had just walked in. He walked past the 'Please Wait To Be Seated' sign and plopped down at a small private table near the window. It was Gus, the resort maintenance man. Every time I saw him I couldn't help but wonder if he had forgiven me for kicking him the day of my arrival when he startled me half to death.

I shoved down the resurfacing guilt I always felt upon seeing him and walked over to his table. Gus came in a few times each week for coffee and two pieces of rye bread toast. His looks were a bit on the frightful side given his massive build and hollow eyes but overall, he was a gentle soul like my aunt had said. He looked up at me when I greeted him.

"Hi Gus, how are you?"

"The Peking Geese are doing well. Yeah, they're going to be fine today."

He was nodding at something outside when he answered me. Most times, Gus was coherent and attentive, but then there were rare days when he would get lost inside his own mind. This apparently was one of those days.

"That's good, Gus. Glad to hear it. Can I get you the usual?"

"Yup. The usual."

As I walked into the kitchen, a light bulb went off in my head and I hurriedly returned with Gus' coffee and toast.

"Here you go Gus. Hey Gus, I have to ask you something. Do you know where I can find Sam?"

He didn't answer right away and so I persisted.

"Do you know who I'm talking about? You were talking to him at the Fourth of July parade, remember?"

Another moment passed as he buttered his toast and sipped his coffee. Just when I felt it best to give up, he looked at me and his eyes seemed to shine a bit clearer when he spoke.

"Just call him and he'll be there."

"Great. Do you have his number? What's his last name, by the way? Do you know?"

He resumed eating his toast and remained silent. Before I could press him a little more, Heather walked up brusquely and interrupted.

"Jadester, the lunch crowd is arriving and we have a group of twenty people coming in shortly for a meeting in the banquet room. Could you grab table five for me, please?"

"Sure thing. Be right there."

I turned back to Gus who was now engrossed in the rain outside and smiled at him even though he couldn't see. There was a peculiar maternal feeling I had for him as strange as that sounded given the fact he was a good twenty years my senior. But now that I was beginning to know him better, what some may perceive as him being 'different' was actually refreshing in the fact that symbolically he represented a simpler time, a simpler man. He harbored no resentment or animosity nor judgment towards any soul. Jealousy, conspiracy or materialistic wealth was not in his vocabulary. I found myself admiring Gus' spirit and his way of life. What I wouldn't give now to have that kind of freedom in my own world.

"Take care, Gus."

I was answered with only the crunching of toast and the rain outside. As I approached table five, an older man in his fifties sat across from a young boy. They were in deep conversation about the Paulding Light. My ears perked up and a smile crossed my face.

"Hi there. Sorry for the wait, I'm Jade, your server. Can I bring you anything to drink?"

The older gentleman was a shrewd looking man who looked up and over his bifocals at the sound of my voice.

"My grandson and I would like a Pepsi please and we'll both take number seven on the menu, hold the pickles."

"Sure thing. Coming right up. By the way, I couldn't help hearing your conversation about Paulding Light. I was there myself not too long ago and found it fascinating. Do you live around here?"

He glanced at his grandson and some kind of hidden signal was passed between them before he answered me.

"Yes, we live nearby. I own a recreational facility a few miles away and know the area pretty well."

My eyebrows raised in interest as I asked him another question.

"Do you happen to know what Paulding Light is?"

He paused for a moment as if debating on whether or not to answer. After a few seconds, he sighed noticeably then answered.

"Well, I'd have to say the Light is pretty obvious."

Crickets started chirping somewhere either outside or in my mind, I couldn't differentiate at the moment.

"May I ask what you mean by that?"

"Well, looking at the map of the area a person may think they're facing south when they're actually facing west…."

He was rambling on about directionals and going off subject completely. I struggled to follow along and couldn't help but wonder if he was a politician on the side. I excused myself when he had finished and walked away.

Thanks for nothing pal.

I had to bite my tongue not to say those words out loud as I headed for the counter. Today was not my day for questions answered that was for sure. People were flooding in and the place had become a madhouse as I scrambled to keep up. A few people from the group of twenty were already arriving as I met Nikki behind the counter.

"Do you think anyone would notice if I lock the doors now to stop people from coming in? Or at least put up a sign outside that says **No More Crazies!**"

"Yeah Nikki, I don't think that would fly very well with my aunt."

"It was worth a shot."

"So you're getting some dandy customers too?"

"Hell yes! One woman bit my head off because there wasn't enough ice in her soda. And then a ten-year old boy slapped my butt as I passed by his table while his mother glared at me like *I* slapped *his* butt. There must be a full moon or something for all these Fruit Loops to come out of the woodwork like this. I'm tempted to flush myself down the toilet to escape this insane asylum."

"Nice visual. Just keep talking about toilets and flushing out loud and that should clear the place." I chuckled at the disgusted look on her face.

"At least more help is arriving. You and I have been assigned to the banquet by the way. Yay for us!"

The last comment was loaded with sarcasm. I laughed and grabbed a tray full of food and headed back to my tables. The banquet area was large and private, situated off from the main dining and bar area. Nikki and I walked down a small hallway that led to double glass doors that opened up into the banquet area itself.

The room was well equipped with flat screen television and Internet hookup for presentations or Webinars. A pull down projector screen was available as well as a small chalkboard. Long tables graced the room leaving space for people to navigate around and down the center aisle if need be. A private set of restrooms were just outside the door and a patio ran parallel to the room with two sets of French doors leading outside to a wide veranda.

At the back of the room where Nikki and I now stood was a mini bar fully stocked and ready for use. There was a secret door out of plain sight near us leading directly into the kitchen. I considered this the greatest invention of all seeing as how because of its creation, a long detoured route through the main lobby and dining area could take time and cause congestion during busy hours such as this one. It also eliminated any chance of dropping a fully stocked tray of food due to collision, which had happened in the past prior to the installment of the secret door.

People were filing in now and taking their seats. The greatest part to this huge assignment was that everyone pre-ordered before arriving. All Nikki and I had to do was take drink orders and deliver their meals and remain in the back in case called upon. Forty-five minutes later everyone was full and happy as the presentation began.

Nikki had said Mr. Lennon; the president of the local bank treats everyone to a yearly lunch and progress report of the company. Each department manager was standing up to give a status update and to talk about upcoming goals and reformations. I listened partially in between runs to and from the kitchen but during one dull moment where I stood task-less I began to daydream until a voice caught my attention.

"You there, young lady? Would you mind coming up here to help with my demonstration please?"

"Ha Ha."

Nikki's sarcastic laughter reached me, so light only my ears could hear it. I gave her a searing look and turned back to stare into twenty sets of eyes plastered on me. I gulped noisily as my face started to drain of color.

"Uh, I don't know."

I stammered uncomfortably while Nikki's soft chuckle turned into a snort. Her lips were pressed together in an attempt to remain straight faced. I had confessed to her once before how much I hated being in the spotlight.

"Oh, come on. Be a sport. You don't have to do much I promise." The man was beckoning me forward.

I slowly made my way down the center aisle towards the finely groomed suit and tie man who had called me over, as all eyes followed my every step. It was then I realized to my horror I had forgotten to leave the coffee pot behind as I held it in a death grip.

"And what's your name young lady?"

"Um, Jade."

"Nice to meet you Jade. I'm Dan. Now if you'd just stand here a moment while I call Jason to the front of the room. Jason, could you join us please?"

A debonair slicked back black haired man in what looked to be his late thirties straightened his tie and walked stiffly up to Dan. He was gorgeous to say the least as he smiled perfectly straight white teeth first at me, then at Dan.

"Now Jade, you be the customer for us and Jason is going to try and sell you a product. We're going to do a little role-playing here. I want you to start by saying to Jason that you don't have time to open an IRA and we'll go from there. Just keep giving him reasons why you don't think purchasing a product is best for you."

Oh my dear Lord, may the ground open up and swallow me whole. Any distraction will do. Just get me out of here.

The Good Lord must've heard me because no sooner did I make my silent plea when the air in the room suddenly changed. It went from stagnant to cool and wispy, like a soft caressing touch. Goosebumps danced up my arms and I looked around to see if any windows had been opened. All were shut tightly and no one seemed to take notice but me. Halfway through Jason's well-rehearsed spiel a beautiful woman appeared behind him. Her hair was black like his and her eyes were a bright green. They were focused intently on Jason.

"Cheater!"

She spat the words at his head as he continued on, oblivious to her ghostly presence. Then her searing eyes locked onto mine.

"Tell him! Tell him I'm here and I know the truth! Tell him Isabelle says he's a dirty rotten cheater! I know about Joleen. Tell him I found out the day I died that he had been seeing her for months. Tell him!"

"No. Stop!"

My words were a hissed whisper and Jason hesitated before going on. Dan interrupted him and asked if I was all right.

"Yes, I'm fine."

I averted my eyes from both men and from Isabelle as silence filled the room. Isabelle's anger was penetrating as she moved next to me.

"I'll make you tell him!"

I felt the pressure of her touch much to my incredulity as she shoved my arm holding the coffee pot. My hand flew up and hot coffee splashed out onto Jason, covering the front of his shirt and burning his skin underneath. A sharp yelp escaped his lips as he jumped back in surprise. Dan leaped back also, leaving me standing solo with an empty pot in my hand.

"What the hell!? Why'd you do that?"

Jason was staring at me wide eyed with his arms outstretched as hot coffee dripped off his shirt onto the floor. A woman from the third table back had run up with a towel and handed it to him as she too stared at me with a bewildered look on her face. In fact, as I glanced around, the entire room had the same expression on their faces. I could hear hushed whispers amongst each other no doubt debating on whether I had lost my mind. My face drained of more color if that were even possible. I was sure I looked as white as a sheet standing there dumbstruck.

"Why did you do that?"

Dan had stepped up and grabbed my arm, demanding an answer.

"I…I have a message for you."

My eyes were locked on Jason's as I said the words. His hand that held the towel stopped dabbing in mid-air.

"Message? Are you nuts? What are you talking about?"

In a gust of nerves, I unburdened Isabelle's message and instantly felt ten pounds lighter.

"Isabelle told me to tell you that she knows about the affair you are having with Joleen. She found out about it the day she died. She's angry with you."

The woman who had handed him the towel quickly returned to her seat and I presumed she was Joleen as both her and Jason exchanged a hasty glance then looked back at me. He looked me up and down trying to ascertain what I had just said.

"My wife passed away a few months ago, who are you to disgrace her memory by saying such ludicrous things?"

"*He* disgraced my memory! Tell him about the email I saw him type the day I died to her saying how much he missed her and wished she could be there to comfort him. And how he kept thinking about their 'business' trip together in Colorado and the wonderful night they spent together. Oh, he makes me sick! And to think I spent nine whole years with that rotten, son-of-a…"

"Okay, okay, I get the point! I'll tell him. But then you have to let this go; it does not matter anymore. You're destined for a better place."

I turned back to Jason.

"Isabelle saw you type that email to Joleen the day she died. She watched you tell Joleen how much you needed her company at your time of loss and how you were thinking about the night you two spent together on your so called business trip to Colorado."

Jason's face went placid as I shared all Isabelle had told me. He seemed to stutter in his recovery to this news, then regained control.

"Who were you just talking to? How do you know my wife?"

"She's here with us as we speak Jason. I can see and talk to her spirit just as I can see and talk to you. She was adamant that I give you this message."

"So she spilled the coffee on me?"

He let out a high-pitched guffaw of astonishment.

"Yes. I think she needed you to know how much you hurt her. It sounds like you owe her an apology. She may need that to cross over."

It was strange really, how light hearted and carefree I was feeling while unleashing all of this. It suddenly did not matter anymore that people looked at me oddly. I didn't care what they thought. My secret was out and it was an incredibly liberating moment. Sure a straightjacket may be in my future but I would cross that bridge when I got to it.

As of now, I just didn't care anymore what anyone thought. It felt refreshing to be able to help people. To try and bring them closure no matter how uncomfortable the moment was, or how intense the problems were. Jason's pride was of immense proportions as his look of shock and surprise turned to self-defensive anger.

"I don't know who you are or what you're talking about, but this conversation is over. I could have you arrested for harassment lady."

"Jason!"

Joleen stood up from her chair with a pleading look on her face.

"Just tell her you're sorry."

Her eyes pleaded with his as she confirmed the accusation.

She looked back at me.

"We didn't mean to hurt anyone, I swear. It just happened and we fell in love on accident. Tell Isabelle we're sorry."

"Like I'm going to take anything either one of them says for face value? They're liars, both of them. They're only sorry they were caught. I'm not going anywhere until they pay for what they've done."

Isabelle was still standing next to me as she spoke. I tried pleading with her to find forgiveness but she had too many unresolved issues to hear a word I said. Her life was taken much too quickly and without warning and for the time being, she seemed to be stuck here with a near decade of rage and betrayal fueling her energy. In one flash she stood an inch from Jason's face and swung at him, her arm sliding through his head without connecting. Nonetheless, he must've felt something because he raised his hand and brushed it softly past his cheek.

Then Isabelle faded out again to re-appear next to Joleen standing at her table. Isabelle swiped at the plate in front of her, somehow connecting with the silverware and sending it flying onto the floor. Joleen let out a yelp and jumped back in surprise, as did those sitting around her. My head jerked to the back of the room where Nikki had stood witnessing the entire event.

Her hand was up to her chest and I could see the whites of her eyes from across the room as she took everything in. Isabelle appeared right next to Nikki and in a last ditch display of tantrums, knocked the napkins and glasses from the bar counter onto the floor just next to Nikki's feet creating a loud clatter as debris scattered everywhere. The bank meeting didn't need any more encouragement than that to wrap up and ship out. The group had left the building within a few minutes.

Jason and Joleen were the last to leave, never taking their eyes off of me as they walked passed where I had joined Nikki at the back of the room. When Nikki and I were alone, she turned to me and simply stared as I bent down to pick up the broken glass.

"Holy shit! I can't believe what I just saw! Are you for real?"

I paused momentarily to look up at her.

"You're not afraid of me? You don't think I'm weird?"

"No, I'm not afraid of you, and yes, I always thought you were weird. That's why I like you. But damn girl! That was awesome! I felt like I was in a movie or something. Can you do that again? Wait, how the hell do you do that and what is it that you do exactly?"

Nikki was going a mile a minute with the questions and I started to laugh.

"I didn't *do* anything, Isabelle did. I really don't know how to explain it. I was in a car accident a while back and the doctors had to revive me. A few weeks into my recovery I was able to see and talk to spirits. This new found ability scared me immensely at first, but now it suddenly feels natural. Like it's a part of me, and I'm not scared anymore."

I could see a thousand more questions burning in Nikki's eyes but before she could open her mouth to ask them, Emma burst through the door.

"What happened in here? I just had a red faced Mr. Lennon telling me you spilled coffee on one of his employees, that you were talking crazy nonsense about ghosts and that you were pulling pranks on them by making things fall off tables and breaking glass. Would you mind telling me please when my reputable restaurant became a circus act for you, Jade?"

Emma had been under unusual stress lately with problems she had yet to disclose with anyone so I tried keeping that in mind as her strict tone cut into my chest. She had never spoken that way to me, *ever* and I instinctively reeled back from the sting of her words.

"I…Uh, I'm sorry Aunt Em. I had no control over what happened in here. I can explain everything if you'll let me."

"You're damn right you're going to explain everything. Mr. Lennon has been a long- standing customer of ours and so have many of his bank employees. But now we'll be lucky if any of them show their face in here again or any of their friends, once word gets out what happened in here."

A hint of fear entered my heart, turning my blood into ice. This could be the beginning of the end for me in so many ways. I fought to maintain control as I answered her in a professional manner.

"With all due respect Auntie, I think you're overreacting about all of this. I'm sure they'll be back again."

Apparently that was the wrong thing to say, for her features hardened and the red in her neck began to rise up into her face. Yet her voice remained level and controlled as she responded.

"Clean up this mess, then please see me in my office, Jade. We need to talk."

She spun on her heel then marched out the door, closing it swiftly behind her leaving Nikki and myself alone in the room.

"Crap. I'm done for. It was nice knowing you, Nikki."

"Oh, don't start with the melodrama now. She's not going to fire you. Just tell her what happened. You're her niece; she'll believe you over Mr. Suit and Tie."

I gave her a sideways look of partial amusement.

"I don't gamble but I'm betting the pill I'm about to deliver to her is going to be hard to swallow. Mr. Suit and Tie will win this round and I'll be out on my butt."

"You don't know that. Besides, I don't think she's really upset with you. She's upset about some missing money from the business account. Some financial records have gone missing as well from her computer. Sounds like someone has been dipping their fingers into the melting pot if you ask me."

I dumped the remaining broken glass into the garbage and stopped to stare at her, trying to digest what she had just said.

"How do you know this?"

"Someone overheard a phone conversation one night Emma was having and spread the word to us that troubles were brewing and someone was pocketing money."

"That's awful! Who do they think it is?"

"No one knows for sure. But don't tell Em I told you any of this."

"Of course not, if you don't tell anyone about my gift. I want to keep this on a need to know basis."

"Scouts honor." Nikki held up her hand in salute.

"Well, wish me luck. I have no idea how I'm going to say all of this so that she believes me."

"Just be yourself and know that I'm on your side. You need anything, just holler."

"Thanks. That means a lot."

Just outside of Emma's office door I took a deep breath in and let it out in a whoosh. Here goes nothing.

"Come in Jade. Have a seat and close the door behind you, please."

My hand hadn't even rapped on the door yet. It levitated just inches away from the smooth wooden surface. She must've heard me approaching. I walked in, closed the door and slowly sat down in one of the two plush chairs. Emma had yet to look up from some papers in front of her.

Her thin reading glasses perched nimbly on the crook of her nose. It was hard to believe at this moment we were of the same blood. When she looked at me, none of the warmness caressed her smile or lit up her eyes as it usually did when she saw me. Panic gripped me in knowing some people's opinions really did matter, hers being one of them.

I craved her approval and not because of my job. I needed to make her understand somehow. I respected and looked up to my aunt always, ever since I was a little girl. I needed her acceptance more than I had realized.

"I apologize for snapping back there Jade. I know you would never deliberately sabotage business, but I do need to know what is going on. I need to know the truth. Mr. Lennon said you claimed to be able to talk to ghosts?"

I paused for a brief moment as something shiny glinted softly from the dark interior of the safe located to the right corner of the room. Its door open just enough to see papers, a rather large stash of money rubber banded together and that tiny glinting object which now began to glow ever so softly. The delicate curve of my throat where my necklace hung began to feel warm. I instinctively lifted my hand to cover my stone's answering glow. Emma's eyes widened at the sight of the aura my necklace was omitting but she remained silent with subtle fascination written all over her face.

"Aunt Em, your safe is glowing."

She tore her eyes away from my necklace to look over her shoulder at the safe. Rising slowly she walked over to it and reached in to pull out the object in question. It was a necklace just like mine except the chain was made of thick gold unlike my delicate silver one. And the stone was exactly like mine except slightly bigger.

"You have one too?"

I exclaimed in surprise, still feeling my neck pulsate where the stone rested in answer to Emma's radiating stone in her upturned hand.

"So you knew they glowed all along then? Why did you act indifferent when I had asked?"

"Yes, I have one too. They are one and the same stone it's just that a smaller piece had broken off at one time and was crafted into a second necklace. And no, I didn't know they glowed until recently, when I had given you yours. They had never done that before and I had kept them together for years."

She scratched her temple then put the jewel back in the safe, leaving the door slightly open.

"Huh, that's pretty neat."

She shook her head slightly before continuing more directly.

"But we need to focus here Jade. I didn't call you in to talk about jewelry."

"I know."

I lowered my head like a puppy about to be spanked for peeing on the carpet.

"What in the devil is this accusation I'm hearing about regarding ghosts? Mr. Lennon said you were talking to someone who wasn't there in the banquet room. Is this true?"

I inhaled sharply, squared my shoulders, lifted my head to make direct eye contact and dove in head first on a wing and a prayer.

"Yes, sort of."

In explicit detail I outlined everything that had happened to me from the day of the accident and the appearance of Stephanie's spirit and how it terrified me at first to see her. I told Emma the real reason of Dylan's and my break up and how my new gift was too much for him to tolerate. This wasn't something I asked for but it was something that I couldn't ignore. There are many things in life that harbor no rational explanation and yet they exist.

Paulding Light for example. No one really knows what it is. Haunted houses we hear about with doors slamming and lights blinking and visions of ghostly people visitors swore they saw. It was essentially up to each person's individual belief system to accept it for what they were, unworldly mysteries, or deny paranormal and devoutly link arms with science until the end. This was no different.

"They say we only use ten percent of our brain. Maybe the accident awakened a deeper part of my brain's capacity allowing me to see *all* things living and dead. Like a dog's heightened sense of smell that no human obtains. Well, this is a heightened sense of sight if you will."

"So what you're saying is that the commotion that took place in the banquet hall was the result of a ghost?"

"Not just any ghost. A ticked off ghost who found out her husband of nine years had been cheating on her with a co-worker. Her spirit body read a private email he was typing to his lover and she became infuriated. Somehow her anger gave her energy to knock the coffee pot out of my hand. She also knocked things over as she left the room. I don't know how she did that."

Emma stared at me with nothing less than expected disbelief. A flush of irritation washed through me.

"Oh come on, Aunt Em! Do you really think I'd be making all of this up? Why would I deliberately throw hot coffee on someone? How in the world could I have rigged a stunt allowing utensils and glasses to be knocked off their resting spots just inches from people? And why would I go through the trouble even if I could? What is there to gain? You know I'm not a jokester. I'm a businesswoman like yourself. Ask Nikki if you don't believe me. She saw the whole thing and knows I had nothing to do with this."

"Fine, fine. I believe you Jade."

"Really?"

"Well, I don't think you did anything on purpose and I don't think you're crazy but I do need time to digest all of what you are saying. I don't necessarily buy into this ghost thing and to be honest I'm not sure how to take all of this right now. I've got a lot on my plate at the moment. The real reason I called you in here actually is not just to talk about the ghost incident but to ask you a question."

"What is it?"

"I'm missing some money from online accounting files. Either something wasn't recorded properly or someone's been tampering with the till. You didn't happen to change anything on my computer by accident did you, when you were working on that flyer yesterday?"

"No, of course not. I know better than to mess with your stuff." My spine stiffened at her query.

"Don't get defensive Jade. I have to ask everyone who works here. Do you know anything about this? Have you seen anything suspicious with any of the cashiers and/or wait staff?"

"No. I haven't."

"I know you have friends here Jade, so I promise to be discreet with any information that is shared here. But I have to find out the truth to this mess. This could cost me my business, a business that's been in our family for generations. Do you want to see that happen?"

"Of course not. I'm not hiding anything if that's what your implying and if you think my friends here trump you, my family, then you don't know me as well as I'd hoped. Now if I'm not fired, I'd like to finish my shift and go home."

I stood up to leave with more than a hurt look on my face. Emma's voice softened.

"Jade, I'm not going to fire you, the thought never crossed my mind. You only have half an hour left of your shift, just bag it and go home dear; I'll still compensate you for the time. You've had a long day."

A traitorous tear escaped my valiant attempt at blinking them away and I turned my face towards the door before answering.

"That's not necessary. I'd like to finish what I start if it's all the same to you. A half hour won't kill me."

Unleashing my unconventional secret took more out of me than I had realized. Emma heard the crack in my voice and stood up to approach me. She grabbed my shoulders and gently turned me to face her as tears from a long stressful day spilled down my glossy cheeks.

"I didn't mean to upset you sweetie. You're not one to cry often, just like your mother. Two strong and sturdy rocks, the both of you so to see you like this tells me I must've went too far. I'm sorry. You're looking more and more like your mother every day."

She said the last part while wiping tears from my face.

"I'm fine, really. I just got some sand in my eye that's all."

"You prideful pathetic liar, you. You can't fool me child. Go on, get out of here, I don't want my customers seeing you looking like a wet dishcloth. Why don't you accompany me to the movies tonight? Marcus is working late and I need a break from all this bullshit that's going on around here. My treat."

"I don't know if I feel up to it…"

"I'll take that as a yes then. Oh come on, we'll go to the early show, please? I don't want to go alone."

"Okay then. If you insist."

"Good. Do me a favor, will you? Tell Jordyn she can have her vacation next week. I was a bit harsh on her this morning over some closing procedures that weren't done properly last night. Maybe if I give her time off, she'll forgive me for biting her head off. Got to try and balance out 'good guy' with 'bad guy' sometimes, as hard as that can be."

"Sure thing. If there's anything I can do to help at all, I'm here for you."

"Thanks, Jade. You're a doll."

Emma wrapped me in a quick fierce hug then walked me to the door. I took a few steps out and nearly bumped into Sheba who had been standing by the door and who was now staring over my head at something in Emma's office. I turned in time to see Emma walk back over to the safe and shut the door, locking the necklace within.

"Ah, Sheba. Just in time. Come in!"

The women convened in Emma's office once again shutting the door behind them as I collected my things from the break room. With my jacket and purse in hand I walked down the hall and nearly plowed into Jackson.

"Hey there. You look like you're a million miles away. Everything alright?" he asked.

"Oh, hi. Yeah, I'm just tired. It's been a long day. You're early."

He was here to pick me up from work and take me home. I had told him it wasn't necessary but secretly was feeling like a schoolgirl again on a first date when he insisted.

"I got off work early. You've been crying."

"Is it that obvious?"

"To me it is. What's wrong?"

We walked side by side towards the door. I couldn't help but notice more than a few stares as we made our way to the exit. Two elderly ladies were watching us leave, and one began shaking her head in disapproval. Jackson followed my gaze and chuckled softly.

"Once a suspect always a suspect. Gotta love small towns." He scoffed.

"Some people still think you killed Annabelle?"

"Well, there's no one else to pin their suspicions on. Just ignore it, I do. Now tell me what happened today?"

I shrugged off conflicting thoughts and downplayed the day leaving out the ghost part completely. He opened the door for me as I stepped out into the cool afternoon air. The rain had stopped but the sky remained overcast. I hugged my thin jacket to my body and climbed into his truck. He jumped in, started the engine then on an afterthought, turned to me and caught me off guard with his next words.

"You shouldn't let one little haunting ruin your day Jade. Besides, there's no such thing as ghosts."

CHAPTER THIRTEEN — BLOODLINE

"What?"

The truck rolled along the county road on the way back to my house. Jackson's face was filled with amusement as he countered my serious one.

"Like I said, small town. News travels fast. I went to the bank earlier and overheard some of the tellers talking excitedly about a haunting in the banquet room today. Did you catch the person who did it?"

"Did what? I don't follow."

"It's obvious someone was messing around. Things don't just fall by themselves."

"Did the tellers say anything else?"

I wondered if he had overheard them talking about me, or if they even knew who I was and more importantly, what I claimed to have seen.

"No. They stopped chatting when I walked up. Were you in there when it happened?"

I knew it was wrong to fib. But being completely honest at this moment just didn't feel right and the questions I was sure would follow were ones I wasn't ready to face.

"No. I just missed it. I had to clean up the mess though."

It was ironic really—his belief that curses exist—but ghosts do not? In my mind, they went hand in hand. Yet not all minds are alike as Jackson was proving to me now. My heart sank knowing I would never be able to share this private part of my life with him. The look on his face told me he thought the whole incident comical.

"So, you don't buy into strange occurrences or the afterlife at all?"

"I can't say I don't believe in anything that's not solid. I feel curses exist, so to say I don't buy into the unexplained is just plain hypocritical but I can say that once we die, we die. *The end*. Ghosts are just illusions in people's minds of what they *want* to see and not what's actually there. The things that go bump in the night and supposed haunted houses are just various energy fields from the ground clashing amongst themselves."

"What about Paulding Light?"

"What about it?"

"No one can explain that. All have conflicting reasoning behind their hypothesis. What's yours?"

"The same thing that causes those little white globes to appear on photos. They look spooky but they're just light refractions and dust particles. Besides, the Light has been solved. Some Michigan Tech students have concluded that Paulding Light is the result of car headlights."

"Day in, day out, 24 hours? Rain, snow, sleet, hail conditions year round?" I was cautiously trying to find a crack in his solid, matter-of-fact constitution.

"Traffic is year round and ceases to exist just because of bad weather Jade."

I could see my attempt at wavering his beliefs was to no avail. But I continued anyway, feeling slightly flustered yet determined to convince him otherwise.

"Okay, but I read that the earliest eyewitnesses of the Light was at the turn of the century. There were no roads here at that time. How do you explain that?"

"That's not true. There weren't any highways at that time but there were roads, dirt roads."

I shook my head in frustration and stared out the window. Jackson's laughter filled the truck.

"Now what? Is this a touchy subject for you my dear?"

His tone was light and chiding, playful even. And somehow it irritated me even more.

"Well, it's just difficult for me to understand why you believe in curses yet not ghosts. I mean, both are unseen, untouchable entities that can affect people in different ways."

"To me, they're completely different. Curses are simply a form of bad luck brought on by certain choices. Karma if you will. Yet unlike bad luck, which is random, I feel curses are surrounded by strange and unusual patterns that link each misfortune to the last. As for ghosts; they are simply what you see in the movies, white blobs floating around scaring people."

"Thank you for that technical analysis, but I beg to differ."

"Look, some say the Kennedy's are cursed. Two brothers, one President and the other running for President both are shot and killed. Not to mention the weird facts surrounding JFK and Lincoln's career in the White House and their assassinations. Both were shot on a Friday. Both were shot in the head. Lincoln was elected to

Congress in 1846, JFK in 1946. Lincoln elected as President in 1860, JFK in 1960. Lincoln's secretary was named Kennedy, Kennedy's secretary was named Lincoln…"

"Yes, I've heard that before."

I interrupted him, knowing our conversation was getting off track and going nowhere. And yet I implored one more opinion to find common ground with him.

"Whether all of that information is even accurate or not is beside the point. We're not really talking about a high profile family here. Their lives were in the spotlight so it's natural to assume their tragedies were displayed for all to see. As unfortunate as those circumstances were, they did nothing to provoke a curse or bad luck or whatever you want to call it any more than a human wishes to be earthbound after they die."

"Earthbound? Where did you come up with that?"

Jackson gave a quick sideways glance, one brow raised slightly higher than the other before resuming full attention to the road.

"I guess it doesn't matter. Why are you so against curses?"

"Why are you so against ghosts?" I retorted emphatically in answer to his question.

"Okay. This is getting ridiculous. I really don't want to argue about such a trivial subject. I'm sorry I brought it up. I didn't mean to make your bad day worse. Let's talk about something else."

I broke the ensuing silence, resignation in my voice.

"You're right. This is foolish. I didn't mean to take it so personal. I'm more stressed out than normal, I guess. And if it makes any difference, I do believe in curses. I have since the day you told me about your family and I'm sorry for what happened to them."

"It's no big deal really, but thank you."

Without taking his eyes from the road, he reached over and grabbed my hand, giving it a gentle squeeze. I hadn't really expected him to say the same to me regarding ghosts but secretly had hoped he would. Just for the sake of wanting his faith in me. Something I desperately longed for and never had.

Sam crossed my mind as I continued to stare out the window at the passing trees. He understood me. He *believed*. I started to wonder if Jackson ever would. The thought of losing him so soon after giving in to that magnetic pull between us was painfully breathtaking. I couldn't bear to ponder the thought for long. At least there was Sam, a man I knew nothing about yet shared one common colossal secret. One shared isolating ability that separated us from the rest of the world.

I found myself longing to see him again. To find out why he lied to me. What or who was he hiding from? I needed to see that smile of his that assured me everything was going to be okay. The truck pulled into the driveway and Jackson walked me to the door. I had already told him my plans to catch the early show with Emma, much to his disappointment.

Now that we had given in to our attraction, it was almost impossible to stay away from one another. But somehow we managed to maintain balance and control. He leaned in to kiss me goodbye and within seconds the kiss ignited into flame. I found myself pinned against the doorframe with his hard body holding me there, strong arms securing me to his broad chest. Warmth flooded through my body from my center outwards like reaching fingers as I subconsciously leaned further into his chest to become impossibly closer to him. After what seemed like eternity we broke the connection.

"Sorry."

His words were labored with much strain in between breaths.

"I'm not." I said softly.

He smiled a seductive smile then took another step back as his hands remained holding my arms.

"You're quite intoxicating. Everything about you draws me in."

He brushed dark strands of hair away from my face as he continued.

"I honestly can't recall ever being this captivated by someone. With you, I feel more myself and more at home, almost as if I've known you forever and yet at the same time I feel like a new person, like I've come to life for the first time since being born. It's hard to explain."

I shook my head slightly and raised my eyes back towards his.

"You don't have to. I think I understand."

He kissed my forehead then turned and headed back to his truck and drove away.

***

My aunt, as discombobulated as she was, knew when to take a break to clear her mind and decided a comedy was in order. We hit the early show walking out two hours later with lighter spirits and a slight spring to our step.

"I'll see you tomorrow Jade!"

Emma had just dropped me off from the movies and I waved good-bye as she made her way back to the restaurant. She seemed to be spending most of her time there lately. I had gone over to the main house a few nights the past week to cook dinner for Marcus and couldn't help but notice the concern on his face whenever he spoke of her.

We both knew she was working too hard fixing the errors that seemed to resurface every day at Dolly's. Uncle Marcus didn't discuss it much with me over dinner nor did I ever ask. I hinted one time to see what his thoughts were but quickly realized it was an open and shut door. He'd answer briefly and noncommittally then change the subject altogether.

I sensed they knew more than what they were letting on but decided they wanted to keep it between themselves. And that was their prerogative. I just hated to see how much time it was consuming from my aunt these days. She was the first at the restaurant every day and the last to leave at night. None of my attempts to help in any way were heeded. So I was left standing on the sidelines hoping the matter would clear itself up in due time.

The days were growing noticeably shorter as the sun had already taken cover for the evening leaving dusk to settle in. It was a full moon tonight and its brilliance was already awe-inspiring. I climbed the stairs to the second level without having to turn on a single light due to the moon's white glow as it poured in strongly through the half crescent windows above the French doors from across the lake.

It guided my way down the hallway and into my room where I flicked the switch and changed into comfortable flannel pants and long sleeved shirt. I descended the steps into the kitchen and opened the fridge. My aunt had given me a bottle of Pinot Grigio she had ordered from France that was now sitting open on the top shelf. At the time I didn't have the heart to decline the gift but after we shared a glass, my taste buds were surprisingly pleased with its crisp, slightly sweet taste. I poured myself a glass to take out onto the deck.

Grabbing a blanket off the sofa, I made my way outside to the back deck and seated myself in the nearest rocking chair within plain view of the moon overhead. The lake was as still as the night sky and the remaining clouds from earlier in the day were clearing out. An owl hooted nearby and the leaves rustled slightly from a breeze only the trees could feel. I took a sip of wine and pulled the blanket tighter around my body, my legs pulled tightly against my chest.

I rested my head back against the rocking chair, closed my eyes and gently rocked while listening to the night sounds. Behind closed eyelids the light from the moon grew brighter as if someone had turned on a flashlight and was shining it a few feet from my face. I opened my eyes and set my glass down on the table, hastily flinging the blanket aside. I walked up to the railing and rubbed my eyes before refocusing them on the growing moon above.

In an instant the moon exploded in brightness and I shielded my eyes with my arm, turning my head away from its glare. The blinding light subsided and I whipped my head back to stare across the lake as to what looked like a headlight across the glassy waters. It was moving from the forest beyond across the lake heading in my direction. Tilting my head upwards again I spotted the moon in the exact same spot, the same brilliance as before.

It radiated its glow as if nothing had ever happened. And yet the smaller white orb continued to make its way across the lake, the closer it got the brighter the light. It dawned on me that I had seen this vision before. It looked to be a replica of Paulding Light and how I had witnessed it upon arriving here.

But what was it doing here? This time unlike last, I harbored no fear, no alarm of any kind as it approached nearer the beachfront just yards from where I was standing. Now instead of growing brighter, it morphed from white to red and shrank in size. I squinted my eyes to get a better look and thought I deciphered a hint of green within its aura. It was now on dry land and still advancing towards me.

My knuckles were hurting and my mind snapped out of its reverie to tell my body to let go of the railing. I was squeezing the ledge harder than needed out of sheer adrenaline yet remained surprisingly calm with regards to my safety. From the smaller reddish green aura a shadowy outline of a man stood just behind it. His body tall and lean, his arm raised where the light now followed.

I tilted my head to one side trying to get a better look when he exited the shadows of the tree line and into the light from the moon above. It was then his face became clear and the lantern he had been holding vanished within his grasp. His arm dropped back down to his side and so did my mouth in vivid astonishment.

"Sam?"

He walked up to the railing just beside the stairs and looked up at me.

"Hi, Jade."

A few babbled incomprehensible words escaped my lips before I recovered enough to make sense.

"This isn't possible. You were real. I felt your warmth."

"I know this isn't easy. Jade, sit down before you fall."

"I shook your hand...I..."

I suddenly felt very light headed and weak as I took a hesitant step away from the railing. Sam had ascended the stairs in two short leaps and was by my side. I drew back from his touch in a protective manner. He dropped his outstretched hand and stepped back as I found my chair and plopped down.

"This isn't possible."

I kept repeating over and over. Sam took the chair next to me and bided his time. After a few seconds he spoke softly yet firmly and captured my attention with his rugged voice.

"Yes, I am real, but not in the way you think. I only misled you because I knew you weren't prepared to hear the truth just yet."

I felt the earth come back to me or I to the earth, and the storm clouds in my head began to pass as I caught my bearings and looked at him. The way he was looking at me had a peculiar effect on my heart as it skipped in time. That intense stare and crystal clear eyes. I had never before seen eyes like his, so soft in color yet hard around the edges like an eagle or a hawk. They cut right through me. His hair was still ruffled and thick, curled slightly at the edges and his handsome face was creased with lines branching from the corners of his eyes from long days in the sun. It was still hard to guess his age.

"So you're a ghost then?"

"In a manner of speaking. I left this world in 1887 and have been stuck here ever since."

"How is it I could feel you then?"

"It's a long story and much of it I don't fully understand myself, but I'll tell you as much as I know."

I sat there in awe and wonder, waiting for him to proceed.

"When I knew I had died all those years ago, I couldn't remember anything about my life or how I even died. I didn't know who I was at first. I felt nothing, knew nothing and was as lost in a strange old new world. I say 'old' because it was what I had come from but 'new' because I could no longer touch, feel or be a part of it as I once had been."

"That sounds awfully sad."

"More disconnected of a feeling than sad. After all, my life had ended abruptly. I was only twenty years old when I died. Most people who live a long life are ready to leave this world and aren't surprised when death takes them by the hand. I knew I had died young and that I wasn't ready...that's all I knew. The rest was a blur for a while."

"Then what happened?"

"Like a puzzle, pieces began falling into place one by one. The great thing about dying is you can go anywhere, anytime in a blink of an eye. Just think where you want to be and you're there. I began to remember bits and pieces of home. The next thing I knew I had been sent there, to my old house.

It was empty and cold and items from my life were scattered here and there: none of them holding any significance or remembrance. They might as well have belonged to a complete stranger save one item: a photograph of me standing next to my wife and unborn child. Grace was seven months pregnant with our firstborn. It was then I remembered.

I remembered having a family but they had died shortly before me. I remember feeling my first twinge of an ancient emotion; sadness."

I started to reach out to touch him in comfort then thought better of it and held my hands still. He stared up at the moon before continuing.

"After that a tidal wave of feelings and memories raced through my mind, most of them in a jumbled mess. I had worked for the Milwaukee Lake

Shore and Western Railroad system for a few years first doing odd jobs and cutting trees then progressed into the railroad system itself eventually becoming a brakeman for the engineer. Trouble had begun to brew with the installation with one particular railway system that was being integrated just west of what is now the Ottawa National Forest. Rumors began circulating that where the railroad was being built was considered holy ground by the natives. They were unhappy with the construction and desecration to their lands and a revolt floated upon the winds."

The story had a familiar ring to it but I remained silent as Sam went on.

"There was an alleged tribe called Arkaleaux, so small and discreet that most tribes had never heard of them before. Nor does anyone know where they had originated from. All that is known is that they befriended the local Ottawa tribe here and integrated with them for a time being.

The locals claim this small nomadic tribe was different than most. That they were a magical tribe of great healing. The land that they had settled upon was of no accident and that the great spirits of beyond morphed into white deer and guided them to this spot where the land was rich with power. A few of the townspeople claimed to have been healed by the chief himself. They called him Keeja.

The only person to give back life to those who were losing it was Keeja. A young woman nearly lost her only son when she sought out the chief and begged for him to save her boy's life. She had told some of the people in town of the miracle he performed with only a single stone that he waved over the boy's body. The wounds vanished before the mother's eyes and the boy fully recovered.

Her story made its way to the boarding houses where we would stay when far from home. Most of us shrugged it off as an old wives tale but some took the story very seriously. This was the same tribe that began the revolt which inevitably caused the derailment of Raven and the reason I'm still here."

"Raven?"

"That's the name I had given to the train I worked on before its demise. I had a tendency to secretly name the trains I worked on. Raven was pitch-black, full of power yet smooth as a bird. Majestic in its own right."

He smiled reverently then bowed his head once more seemingly focused on his gruff calloused hands.

"I was aboard her when we were attacked. All of us were prepared because we knew we had to be but none of us expected it. Raven had just left port when the attack came just before twilight. The men ran out of the nearby roundhouse and makeshift camps to defend the shipment of raw materials Raven was carrying. I had orders to stay inside the cramped cabin where the brakes were located in the caboose with my lantern handy in order to give signals to the engineer when needed.

I heard the gunfire before I saw anything at all. Then out of the forest like shadows in the night came the Arkaleaux people, along with the local Ottawa tribesmen as their ally. I readied my gun while keeping watch ahead knowing that the best thing to do was haul out of there as fast as possible, giving Raven open rein to fly like the wind. Arrows and spears hit near my head as I tried desperately to shield my face behind the steel wall that encompassed the caboose window.

A few times I fired shots back to help out my fellow man. People were everywhere and shouts filled the air. A full-blown battle had broken out around me as the train roared on. I saw friends of mine fall during hand-to-hand combat as knives were plunged into their bellies. Someone at one point set off an explosion nearby causing deaths on both sides in an attempt to thwart the attack.

Yet the tribe plunged on surrounding the train. It was then the ground began to shake and I knew something bad was about to happen. There was Keeja, standing on the tracks just ahead, with some kind of weapon in his hand. I signaled the engineer that we had to stop and hauled back on the brake switch. Squealing metal against metal filled my ears as I jumped out of the moving train. But it was too late, the tracks ahead cracked in two and the ground heaved upwards, sending Raven off kilter and onto her side where I was standing. That's all I remember. She must've crushed me on her way down."

The frogs were purring their late night song and the crickets sang in rhythmic unison as the night grew deeper, darker. I reached for the blanket again and wrapped it around my shoulders to stay warm. Sam's story riveted me to endless silence as I waited for more. Finally, I persuaded him to continue.

"Why are you still here, Sam?"

With haunted eyes he looked up at me and spoke plainly.

"Because of the curse."

The wind picked up slightly and howled through the deck where we were sitting. Sam turned his face back towards the moon.

"Jackson said his family was cursed by an event very similar to the one you just told me. But his ancestor worked for the Chicago and North Western Railroad. You said you worked for the Milwaukee Railroad. Is there a connection?"

"Yes. Chicago bought Milwaukee in 1891. He's referring to the same railroad system I speak of."

"So this curse is real then? It's not just affecting one family but the entire crew who worked on the system?"

"The curse is very much real unfortunately. As for it affecting others: that I do not know. A good friend of mine who died in the same battle told me in the afterlife that I was the reason the curse had been placed because I was the one who controlled the train. Therefore it was up to me to break it. None of what he said made any particular sense to me. There wasn't a single person solely responsible for what happened that day; we all had a part in Raven's destination and only one person was responsible for her destruction and that was Keeja. But my friend faded away before I could question him further. I imagined he must've moved on to wherever he was supposed to be."

"So how do you break this curse?"

He smiled his brilliant smile before answering.

"If I knew the answer to that question, I wouldn't be here. I'd be with my family in heaven."

Another mystery burned in my mind that I just didn't understand.

"Sam, how is it Gus can see you? You were talking to him that day at the parade when we were looking for that little girl."

"Yes, yes, I remember. Are you really surprised Gus can see ghosts? He's always been different. He was born that way. Most children have imaginary friends that they eventually grow out of. Well, Gus' friends were never imaginary, at least not to him. To everyone else they were make-believe but to him, they were as real as you and I. He just never grew out of it. He's always had the ability to see and talk to ghosts."

"But how is it that you were so real? I mean, if I touched you now, would I feel anything?"

"That's the tricky part. The answer is in the heart. It has to do with love, as does everything in this world. You can touch me if you'd like. I'm still here."

Our chairs were a few feet apart. His hand lingered outwards ever so slightly as mine cautiously reached for it. I felt a slight tingle in the air around us, like my fingers were about to get a static shock but instead I connected with flesh and bone and warmth. Only our fingertips touched at first, then I slowly caressed the back of his hand as he continued holding his steady.

I could feel the pulse of his veins and rough edges of bone through his skin and never flinched as he turned his hand palm up and clasped mine in a firm embrace. It was bizarre to think just moments ago, he was but a white orb floating across the crystal clear lake.

"I just don't understand." I said with incredulity.

"I guess being able to see ghosts pales in comparison to this. Your world has been flipped upside down Jade, ever since your accident. Yes, I know about you. I've been watching you for a while now. It was me actually who led you here although you didn't know it. You are important in a way I have yet to understand.

I prayed for an end to this wretched curse and you answered that prayer. I've learned every decision we make is influenced by something, someone. A simple thought to avoid walking by a dark alley at night is the work of those who have died and gone before us. Some call us guardian angels. For within that alley, danger was lurking in the form of a rapist or murderer. Those decisions we make are a part of our everyday life.

Some walk into danger or tragedy so that they may help others still stuck here on earth. It's an endless circle, but it's starting to make sense now for me. And it will for you in due time. Sometimes our work calls for more than a pale wispy form to float around in, sometimes it calls for passion, life renewed. I needed to make you see me, the *real* me. And that longing was granted by the powers above."

"You've come back then?"

"Only for a little while to see my work here is done. You needed me Jade, twice now and yet you have failed to realize it. I don't blame you. Humans can't see anything but what's in front of them. No one can see the future, just the past and present."

"What do you mean?"

"That night on the road when you broke down. A semi-truck was ten miles behind you traveling at a high rate of speed. It was destined for a blowout, which would've caused a freak accident, where the driver would've lost control and headed directly for where you were parked. Luckily, I was able to get to you first and get you on your way before he came through. And lucky for him, he was able to stop his rig safely on the side of the road where you had once been."

I drifted back to that night and shivered slightly. My eyes grew wide as I recalled the second time.

"That was you at the party, wasn't it? You were the one who saved me from Cayden!"

"Yes."

"He was going to hurt me, wasn't he?"

"He can be a dangerous man when he's drinking."

"Why didn't you show yourself then?"

"I wanted to, believe me. But I thought it more effective to scare the man by making him beat himself up rather than me having to do it in the flesh. Plus it was fun to see him shake in his boots. You're the only one who's meant to see me this way Jade. Don't ask why, it just is."

Sam's eye twinkled and a devilish smile crossed his lips at the thought of catching Cayden off guard the way he did.

"Besides, I wasn't ready to tell you that I'm a ghost."

"So who are you really? And why are you so interested in me?"

He let go of my hand and was now brushing back his thick hair from his face.

"You called for me today as Gus told you to do. I heard your cry and answered. You needn't feel alone. I understand you the way Jackson will someday. I knew it was time to show you who I am. As of recently, the last of the puzzle piece has fallen into place. The reason I'm still here is because of two people who can break this curse. One of them is you Jade."

"Me? Why me?"

He pointed to the necklace I wore around my neck.

"Because of that."

"This? It was a gift from my aunt for my birthday."

"I know. I recognized it the day you took me in to your home after we found Mr. Jenkins by the river. It's the same stone Keeja had in his hand when he broke the tracks in two."

As if on cue the stone around my neck began to glow again. Ever so softly it emitted light to the sound of its previous master's name.

"You're of his blood, Jade. Magic runs through your veins. More than likely it's the reason you can see and talk to spirits. The accident you had was just a portal entering you into that world so as to make the connection between this life and the next."

My hand glowed green as it protectively held the jewel while it continued to pulsate. Sam's eyes stayed riveted to it until it finally stopped. He saw the question in my eyes and answered before I could ask.

"My real name's Andrew Sampson Butler. People used to call me Sam. The other I speak of is my kin. Jackson and you are the keys to unlocking a century old curse. What hate has inflicted, love will undo."

Kathleen Wickman

CHAPTER FOURTEEN — VISIONS

That smile of his. I had known it somehow. Jackson had Sam's smile. They were of the same blood. How I never saw it before was beyond me. Granted they didn't look exactly alike but after Sam's revelation, I was beginning to see similarities between the two, the most obvious was that beautiful smile.

Jackson's hair was darker but they had similar builds. Tall, lean and solid with muscular shoulders and a wide chest. Each were beautiful in their own right which was probably why I was so drawn to Sam, not because of his secrets but because of his tie to Jackson. They seemed to share the same personality at times, even when I looked back on it. How eerie I had never noticed it before.

"But you said your wife and child died. How can that be?"

"Simple. I was mistaken. When we sat at your kitchen table that day and I recognized your unique necklace, something else came to light. Jackson came to your house shortly after. I saw his badge on his uniform. It said Butler.

Something inside of me clicked and I just knew. I knew he was from me. I could feel a pull from across the room, which was why I had to get away. I was afraid that maybe, just maybe, he'd see me. I didn't want him to know who I was."

"Would he have recognized you even if he could see? Not many people know their great-great-great-grandfather unless shown a picture."

"I couldn't be sure but I didn't want to take a chance either."

"Well that explains your abrupt departure. I thought you were wanted by the law at first."

He chuckled and even his laugh sounded like Jackson's.

"No. I was just scared I guess. I had always assumed my child died when Grace did. I was wrong."

"I still have so many questions."

"I still have an eternity of time to answer them." He smiled wistfully.

"You're the Paulding Light then? That was you I saw at the guardrail overlooking the clearing?"

"Partly. Yes, that was me you saw holding the lantern. Raven was behind me. She's trapped here, too. Her light is what attracts thousands every year nationwide. Never thought a train could be stuck in between worlds but she's there, doomed to run the same short route over and over, hell bent on delivering her supplies."

"I still don't see how Jackson and myself have any control over reversing this curse. No one from that time is alive nor are any of their kin around here to make things right. We've tried already with Matilda but we were too late."

"It's never too late to make things right. You and I live in different worlds, seemingly far apart yet you're only one breath away from where I am: one instant, one moment. I've been confined here in order to set things straight but I couldn't do it without your help. I've waited a long time for you."

"What do you want from me? What is it I'm supposed to do?"

"You're already doing it. Your feelings for Jackson and his for you can end this. It's as simple as that. I don't fancy myself as the match making type but I did my best to give you two the push you needed. There's still doubt in your heart regarding his past and he is still afraid to let you in completely for fear of losing you. Once that barricade is down and nothing but unconditional trust and love exist, the curse will end."

"What I'm feeling for Jackson is because of what you did? Did you put a spell on us or something?"

Sam chuckled.

"No, of course not. I'm a ghost not a warlock. I merely attempted to break the barriers between his cold distance and your jaded heart."

My mind raced back then stopping abruptly at something in the archives.

"The flowers. Those were from you? You sent the message to Jackson's phone pretending to be me, didn't you? How the hell did you do that?"

"Please don't be upset. This is just as difficult to admit as it is to hear it. I did what I thought was best for my family. Jackson, in a way, is a son to me. And a parent would do almost anything for the protection of their child."

"But how?"

"Gus. He's a good man. He knew my plight, knew it for quite some time now. I asked for his help and he obliged. His job and friendship with Mr. and Mrs. Hawthorne allowed him easy access to not only the cabins but the restaurant as well. He borrowed your phone to send that message. And he bought the flowers when he and I saw Jackson looking at them that day on the street."

I mulled all of this over, feeling as if my head was going to explode. So much had come to light in the past few weeks that I was running out of space in my brain to take any more in. My life had become a paranormal soap opera.

"What, am I supposed to force myself to speed up this romance or something, walk down the aisle with him before taking a bullet in the chest?"

Sam could see how upset I was becoming. How trapped I was beginning to feel and how scared that I played such a big role in something that I didn't fully understand.

"This is exactly why I didn't want to tell you who I was in the beginning. I had to lie about who I really was because I knew you'd never believe something like this coming from a ghost. It would be like empty air falling on deaf ears and I didn't want to scare you off. When you thought we had the same connection and gift, it was then I felt you would trust me enough to hear me out."

"By lying to me, you figured I'd trust you?"

Sam scratched his head and sighed.

"I reckon that does sound deceiving when you put it that way."

I shoved the blanket off me and walked down the porch steps and to the water's edge. The moon was making its slow journey across the night sky and I watched its reflection upon the water. The sound of Sam's footsteps reached me from behind a few seconds later.

"I'm sorry." He said softly.

I turned to face him and shrugged my shoulders.

"I guess I can see why you did what you did. But you have to understand how much pressure this puts on me. I mean, what if Jackson and I don't work out? What if what we're feeling isn't real?"

"But it is real. Please, have faith. That's all I ask."

I wanted to believe him. I really did. But something else gnawed at the back of my mind.

"Did he kill Annabelle?"

He closed his eyes tightly trying to remember.

"Unfortunately just because I'm dead doesn't mean I'm all knowing. I see what I'm meant to see and where my heart guides me. I wish I had an answer for you but I don't. What I do know is he came from good people and I would wager he is innocent."

"Sometimes good people do bad things." I whispered almost to myself.

Sam remained silent as I turned to face the lake again.

"There's one more thing Jade."

"Oh Sam, I don't think I can handle 'one more thing' right now."

"You're in danger."

I turned to face him.

"What do you mean?"

"Something's coming, I can feel it in the winds. The mark of death is heavy above you."

"Because of the curse?"

"Yes, and because of fate itself. The curse knows no boundaries. What your people failed to realize at the time was that spells cast in anger can and will eventually rebound to hurt those we love. You must take extra care to protect yourself. I may not always be here to help you."

I slowly made my way past him and back to the porch steps and heavily sat myself down on the second one. The night was growing colder.

"I don't know what you expect me to do with all of this Sam."

He stood over me with nothing less than compassion in his eyes.

"I know it's a lot to take in. I'm sorry to have to be the one to tell you this. I'm sorry for what I've done to your people."

His voice was fading and I raised my head from my hands to see he was no longer standing in front of me. He had faded back into the light that was now glowing softly by the tree line.

"I'm sorry for everything."

His voice was so far away and thick with sadness and regret. I rose from the steps and called out.

"Sam!"

But he was already gone. The light was now a small speck deep in the woods, eventually diminishing into the blackness beyond.

***

I awoke to the sound of Canadian geese flying overhead. The sun was bright and intrusive forcing my scratchy sleep filled eyes to open. The skylight was directly above my bed where the geese were flying past in their usual 'V' formation. I flung one arm over my head while watching them leave the area for the winter.

I burrowed my face into my pillows then rolled my body out of bed and stumbled into the shower. Sam's visit from the night before was unsettling and I found myself scrubbing my body painfully hard trying to forget the things he said. I refuse to let fear and worry dictate my life. The future was out of my control and I was determined to have a good time today. It was Friday, the start of Labor Day weekend and a welcome relief to have four days to do as I pleased. We had all been working at a constant pace the past few weeks as summer came to a close. As unconventional as it sounds, Emma liked to close up the business for Sunday and Monday every Labor Day weekend to take a much-needed hiatus before the rush of the travelers hit the area for skiing, ice fishing and snowmobile season.

Em didn't schedule me at all in case I wanted to join them on their camping excursion. Her and Marcus had left this morning to go camping with friends in the next county. Had I protested of course to the lack of hours she would've happily obliged and I would now be slaving over tables and wishing I were anywhere but here. So I thankfully accepted the mini-vacation I was given, declined their invite and made my own plans.

Kathleen Wickman

They wouldn't be back until Sunday afternoon and I secretly wanted to be near Jackson. The girls and I were going to head downtown today, do some shopping, go horseback riding at Heather's aunt's farmhouse then visit the fair that was in town. Heather talked me into joining them to see the local bands that night in the grandstand so I was off to pick out some new chic clothes to wear for the occasion.

Besides, Jackson was on duty walking the fairgrounds this year with Hawk and Johnny. Despite all the drama of the past few days, there was a spring in my step and a flutter in my heart when I thought about seeing Jackson again. It was hard not to think about him, and despite what Sam had said and how much it unnerved me, the pull I felt when I was with Jackson was hard to resist. I knew I was falling into the cliché of women loving men in uniform, but damn! He really looked good, and not only when he was dressed in his work clothes but all the time.

He carried an ease of style and I noticed a few times different women turning to look at him as he passed by. Yet underneath the surface was what ultimately attracted me to him the most. Jackson seemed humble. He hid it behind a staunch shield that many mistook for arrogance but deep within he didn't think he was any more special than anyone else and would scoff at me when I told him how nice he looked.

On more than one instance, he'd even made the remark of wondering why I liked him given there were so many other guys whom I could've chosen, never believing he had anything to offer me. This subtle insecurity did not make him possessive or co-dependant in any way. There was very much a strong independent constitution about him portraying a capable man who had survived much loss in his life and still had the courage to go on. Much like myself, we had that in common.

Our lives were defined on what we believed not who we believed in. People fade. Faith, strength, and love live on. I hurriedly changed into blue jeans and a scarlet camisole, made a quick breakfast of frozen waffles and orange juice, grabbed my jean jacket and headed out the door into the warm hazy air.

I bent down to tie my shoes then stood up and slowly turned around. The Ghost flowers that had been thriving all summer next to the entrance were now wilting right before my eyes. They changed from bright and perky to brown then black as they cracked and crumbled into ashes amongst the bed of dirt and rock they had grown from. I took a hesitant step towards the basket and peered inside to see nothing but black soot where the flowers had been.

Not even the stalks remained. A gust of wind swept through and carried the ashes away as I jumped back out of its path. I stood there for a moment in bewilderment, feeling the wind suddenly die just as quickly as it had started. I hugged my jacket tighter to my chest and made my way to the jeep.

***

A piercing scream filled my ears and all I could do was hang on for dear life. I shut my eyes tightly and prayed. My body began falling and my stomach climbed into my throat as my teeth gritted tightly together. The scream filled my ears again and I busted out laughing as tears streamed down my face.

Nikki was strapped in next to me on a ride that plunged us straight towards the earth and came to a sickening stop ten stories down. She was screaming in uncontrollable terror until the ride came to an end.

"Oh shit! Get me the hell out of here!" Nikki was yelling at anyone who would listen.

Heather was laughing just as hard as I was while Nikki sat between us cursing the whole time.

"Relax! It's over!" Heather was trying to console her to no avail.

The minute Nikki was unhooked from her seat, she jumped out and ran to the nearest railing for support as we followed behind her chuckling to ourselves.

"I could spit on you for talking me into that death trap!"

Heather took a few cautious steps back.

"Hey, no one forced you to go. You said you could handle it."

"Yeah, because you called me a wuss and I had to prove you wrong!"

Heather winked at me.

"Oldest trick in the book. Nikki is still a child at heart. You want her to do something, just call her a chicken."

Nikki wobbled unsteadily over to the railing while holding her stomach. Heather slapped her on the back victoriously.

"Come on, let's grab a slimy hotdog and hit the Scrambler."

Nikki's face turned visibly green at the sound of food and more rides. She slapped her hand to her mouth and took off for the nearest restroom as Heather and I exchanged looks of amusement.

"Well, she's done for the night. We'll be lucky if she goes on any more rides with us. So, which one do you want to try next?"

We decided to walk in the direction of the restrooms to check on Nikki when a group of officers walked up to us. My breath hitched at the sight of Jackson looking all regal and debonair in his crisp, clean uniform. His face lightened into a smile when he saw me.

"What did you do to my wife? I just saw her running into the bathroom."

Johnny greeted us with a smile and Hawk tipped his hat as we stopped to chat on the midway.

"She turned into a cream puff on the first ride we went on. Now we're one man down." Heather still looked amused as she answered Johnny.

"What ride did you take her on?"

"That one."

Heather nodded towards the Giant Drop.

"Nice. Should've saved that one for last. She can handle all the others. If she's still sick when I get off work at midnight, I'm calling you to take care of her!"

"Sure thing. I can be there in six hours."

Page 243

Heather's tone was full of amusement and sarcasm.

"You should've seen the look on her face though. Priceless."

He shook his head and snickered.

"Stay out of trouble."

"Always do."

Jackson had walked over by me during their exchange and touched my hand ever so lightly and briefly.

"Hey."

"Hi."

"Having fun?"

"Yeah. I haven't gone on rides since I was a teenager. Wish you could join us."

"No, you don't. I'd be in the bathroom with Nikki if I had. My stomach's not as strong as yours."

He looked over at Hawk and Johnny as they began walking the strip again.

"I gotta run. But I'll be around if you need me. Stay safe. Have fun."

He brushed my hand again and jogged to catch up with the guys.

Nikki had recovered in due time. We took a break to sit down and buy some water for her until she felt well again. In a short time, she was back to herself and actually joined us on a few more rides. She chose carefully this time though and only accompanied us on the gentler ones.

We walked around the fair as the day began drawing to a close. The girls didn't want to walk into the animal barn and I wanted to see the horses. I always had a love for horses and would ride sporadically near the mountains in Montana but never owned one myself. My photography work had taken me on many journeys in which I'd never be able to properly care for an animal. Hence I never owned any.

I told the girls to meet up with me later at the grandstand and I went off on my own. After spending a half-hour with the horses and watching some of the arena showmanship I decided it was time to head back across the fairgrounds to meet up with the girls. I took a short cut through the Exhibition building and glanced at some of the products on display. One particular table caught my eye. Or more so, one particular vendor caught my eye.

It was Sophia, the pretty blonde whom I had mistaken as Jackson's date to the 4th of July party. She was surrounded by gorgeous works of ceramic figurines. All of which were hand made. Above Sophia, hanging on the wall was a large picture of her shop and a group of people cutting ribbon on opening day. The picture looked to be a few years old. People viewing her merchandise surrounded her table. Sophia was deep in conversation with a nice looking man who seemed to be devouring every word she said.

Sophia laughed at something he said showing her perfect straight, white teeth. She delicately brushed her blonde hair behind her shoulder and a small twinge of envy stabbed my chest. Jackson wonders why I chose him and the same question burned in me now as to why he never chose her. Even her laughter was beautiful as it hung on the air like French silk. I slowly made my way over to the table as some of the crowd dispersed. The man seemed hesitant to leave as she began packing up her display for the evening.

"Hi there."

I tore my gaze from an angel figurine holding a weeping child in her arms to meet Sophia's stare.

"Hi." I said rather shyly.

"You're Emma's niece, right? Jade is it?"

"Yes."

She had a warm smile as she continued to look at me. I stumbled for something to say.

"You're work is beautiful. Did you do all this yourself?"

"Yes, well, most of it." She beamed with pride.

"My mother and I own a store outside of town. We carry all kinds of home décor and have a ceramic shop out back where we teach classes during the week and on weekends."

I nodded my head and gazed at a figurine of a dark haired man dancing with a red haired woman. Her flowing red locks and delicate blue dress captured in a frozen twirl as he held her tightly in his arms. Her ceramic face smiled up at his. I reached out and touched the statue man on his shoulder. A jolt ripped through my body starting at the point of contact and radiated from my head to my toes.

Everything around me dissolved into shadows and I felt I was moving even though my feet remained planted to the ground. I blinked a few times and found myself in a strange place. The figurine I had touched was no longer in my hand but in the hand of a woman I had never seen before. The room we were standing in was blurred yet distinctive enough to make me ascertain that I was standing in someone's living room.

The lady stood in front of a sofa and coffee table while staring at something in horror. I tried to turn my head to follow her gaze, but something kept me locked onto the figurine in her hands and that crystal clear look of terror on her face. I could see beads of sweat forming at her temples. She raised the figurine in her hand and yelled something incomprehensible.

I felt as if the entire moment took place under water and her words were garbled, lost amongst an invisible thick wall between us. I crossed the room looking straight at her as if I were the subject of her fear then a bright flash filled my sight. I blinked rapidly and found myself on the ground next to her lifeless body. Blood was pouring out of her chest and the figurine lay clutched tightly in her hand forever locked in an immortal blissful dance.

I gasped in air as the present surroundings rushed back to me in a tidal wave of awareness. My ears were ringing and sound was muffled momentarily. But as I inhaled my next breath, the noise of the fair came in clearer, louder.

"Jade! Are you alright?"

I must've grasped the figurine of dancing man and woman in my hand while zoned out. Like a poisonous snake in my hand, I reflexively released it and jumped back as it hit the cement floor, shattering. The sound resonated throughout the hollow building. Sophia rushed next to me and grabbed my arm to steady my balance.

"What's wrong? Are you having a heart attack? Should I call an ambulance?"

The thought of emergency personnel surrounding the area, attracting all kinds of attention made me snap out of it.

"No! Please, I'm fine. Really. I just felt light headed for a moment."

I placed the flat of my hand against my cold and clammy forehead.

"Would you like to sit down? Peter, grab that chair!"

The man Sophia had been talking to was standing in the same spot with a look of surprise and helplessness on his face. At Sophia's voice, he rushed to grab the chair behind the display table.

"No, thank you. I'm so sorry about the mess. I'll pay you for it."

My words sounded far away and weak like they were coming from someone else.

"Forget about it. I really think you should sit down though."

Sophia coaxed me over to the chair, out of the path of pedestrian traffic. I placed my hands on the back of the chair she offered and leaned over to catch my breath. People had gathered and were watching the whole scene much to my embarrassment. Panic at the ensuing crowd brought me to my senses.

I didn't want Jackson seeing me like this. I stepped away from the chair I had been leaning on and looked at Sophia's worried face.

"I'm sorry. I have to go." I blurted out.

With that I ran out of the building, Sophia and the small crowd staring after me in surprise. I didn't care at the moment. I needed air and the wide, open space the outdoors had to offer. Somehow, that figurine was connected to Sophia. And so was that lady in my vision.

Aunt Emma's words rang in my ears. That day I sat in her office asking her about Jackson. She had told me Annabelle had beautiful red hair that burned like fire in the sunlight. I remember feeling a pang of jealousy. Emma made her sound so perfect. And I felt far from that status. Jackson seemed to have had it all when he had Annabelle. I had no doubt now the red haired lady in my vision had to be her. Her hair matched that of the woman in the statue; long flowing red hair. Which made me wonder if the dark haired man was Jackson. The faces didn't resemble them but the color and cut of the hair did. I jogged along the midway towards the parking lot when I heard someone shout my name.

"Jade! My God in heaven child! What's the matter? You look like you've seen a ghost."

Sheba had seen me running out of the Exhibition building and hurriedly tried catching up with my frantic gait. I stopped at the sound of her voice and leaned over to catch my breath. I just wanted to get away.

"Sit down, dear, before you fall over."

Her stern motherly tone had me sitting down obediently on the nearest bench. I locked my hands behind my neck and stared down at the dirt.

"You dropped this back there in your frantic dash from God knows what."

I raised my head to see her holding my purse in her hands.

"Oh. Thank you. I didn't realize I had dropped it."

"Is everything alright? What happened?"

"I'm fine. I just had a near fainting spell that's all. I haven't really eaten much today and we went on a few rides. I'm sure that's all it is."

My strength was returning to me and my head was now clear as I gathered the last of my bearings.

"You look frightened."

She was assessing me with keen eyes.

"I dropped a ceramic sculpture in the exhibition building when I thought I would faint. The crashing sound startled me I guess."

I could see my feeble excuses were not being bought but I refused to say any more.

"I better get going." I said while standing up.

I started to leave then froze to the spot. I looked back the way I had come. Sophia was standing outside the building talking to Jackson. Concern written all over his face. He scanned the thick crowd with his steely gaze then gave his attention back to her. Sheba followed my stare and her eyes hardened.

"I'm going to get Jackson. You really shouldn't be driving in this condition."

"Sheba, that's not necessary. I feel fine now."

I started to walk the opposite way, when her voice stopped me.

"I thought maybe you were upset because Sophia was at Jackson's house last night."

I stopped and turned around.

"No. Why would I be upset about that? They're friends."

An unsettling feeling was beginning to grow inside my gut but I couldn't tell if it was because of Sheba or of him.

"Yes, I know. They're just friends. Actually, Sophia was Annabelle's friend before Jackson entered the picture. Now those two are as close as Annie and Sophia used to be."

"What are you trying to say, Sheba?"

She seemed genuinely perturbed by her blunder.

"Nothing. I'm sorry. My mouth gets carried away sometimes. I just think of you like a daughter and I don't want to see you get hurt. Jackson is a nice guy but there's something about him I don't quite trust. Just be careful, dear."

Maybe she should take a look at her own husband if she wants to talk about trust issues. I kept my thoughts silent and stared at her pointedly.

"Thanks. But I'm a big girl and I can take care of myself."

She walked up to me and gently placed her hand on my shoulder.

"I know you can."

A young boy ran up to Sheba accompanied by three of his friends.

"Mom! Can I have some money for food?"

"I didn't hear a please in there, Isaac."

"Please!"

He bounced up and down, anxious to be on his way. Sheba lovingly smoothed his hair much to his embarrassment.

"Well, I have to feed my kid. It looks like Jackson is on his way over here anyway. Take care, Jade."

Sophia had pointed in the direction I had gone. Jackson locked eyes with me as he broke into a run. I still had time to slink away given the dense crowd with hundreds more pouring in. I just didn't have the heart to deal with him at the moment and craved the solace of home. I felt bad ditching the girls, knowing they were probably wondering where I was. I'd explain everything to them later.

I turned and jogged quickly through the crowd, cutting off people as I went, hell bent on reaching the gate. A few feet from the exit, pounding footsteps from behind grew louder as Jackson grabbed me by the arm and spun me around with surprising force. A few onlookers undoubtedly presumed they were witnessing some kind of law breaking gone bad. My face began to flush.

"Hey, didn't you hear me calling for you? Why the *hell* did you run?"

Anger flashed in his eyes and his grip dug deep.

"I didn't hear you."

"You scared the crap out of me, Jade. Nikki's trying to reach you on your cell and you're not answering. You were supposed to meet them by the grandstand a half hour ago."

"Would you please let go of my arm?"

"First tell me what the hell is going on? Nikki got a hold of Johnny on his phone in the hopes we had seen you somewhere. I just started to look for you when Sophia found me and told me you had an episode of some kind and nearly fainted? What happened to you? You had me worried!"

"Oh for Pete's sake, calm down! I'm not twelve years old. I don't feel well, that's all. I didn't hear my phone ring. I'll call Nikki now and tell her I'm going home."

He let go of my arm but stood a few inches in front of my face.

"I'll drive you home then. Come on."

He grabbed my hand and led me back through the crowd towards the police trailer where all the squad cars were parked.

"I'm quite capable of getting myself home."

"I know you came here with the girls. Your car isn't even here."

I tried peeling my hand from his to no avail.

"I have two feet and I live in a small town. I can walk home. I don't need to be patronized like a child."

"Humor me."

He shot a warning look over his shoulder and I knew it was pointless to argue but I was stubborn.

"I wish you would stop treating me like a baby. I'm not made of glass you know!"

Anger was broiling and spilled forth in my words. This was twice now I was humiliated in front of a crowd. Once was beyond my control and now this! Yes, solace was looking pretty good right now.

Jackson remained silent as he continued leading me to his vehicle. He opened the passenger door and guided me in.

"Stay there."

His order was sharp and direct and I scowled back into his face as he shut the door on me. I watched him walk up the steps of the trailer, disappear for a moment then walk back out. It was only when we were on the road heading away from the fair that he spoke.

"Look. I didn't mean to snap at you but when no one seemed to know where you went, I panicked."

I didn't bother looking at him but continued staring out the window into the darkness beyond.

"Sheba's husband took off. No one can find him. He's wanted for molesting a fourteen year-old girl. Sheba told us she had a fight with him and kicked him out of the house last week. He's on the loose and possibly dangerous. I thought maybe he decided to finish what he had started with you at the party."

"I was perfectly safe. He would be stupid to try something here."

"Disappearances in large crowds aren't as uncommon as you may think. It's dark, there are plenty of hiding spots to prey on innocent passer-bys and you had broken off from the girls. It could've been a perfect setting for him to attack you."

My anger dissolved slightly and I looked over at his shadowy profile. The dashboard emitted a soft glow showing the strain on his face.

"I had no idea. I'm sorry. I'll be more careful."

His next words he spoke delicately.

"I don't want you to be alone tonight. I want you to stay with me."

"Jackson..." Nerves entered my voice when I answered.

"I'll sleep on the couch. Just please, stay with me."

"You can't protect me all the time. It's impossible." My words were but a whisper.

"No, but I can protect you while I'm here. And I'm here now so please don't make me spend a sleepless night worrying about you. We can stay at your house if it'd make you feel better."

I pondered the idea cautiously.

"You know Bruno could guard me just as easily if I take him home with me. Then you wouldn't need to stay."

I was referring to my aunt and uncle's chocolate lab.

"Ha! He runs and hides when someone knocks on the door. Scooter is a third his size yet could take down anyone who crosses his path. I'd feel much better if you took Scooter over Bruno. But I'd still like to be with you all the same."

Something in his voice had me relenting.

"Fine. If it'll make you feel better. I'll stay at your house."

His eyes locked onto mine in the dark interior of the car and my skin began to tingle. The remaining drive was quiet as he dropped me off at my cabin to collect some things. A few moments later I was back in the car. A mile and a half down the road later, he turned into a hidden driveway just off the main highway.

The dirt driveway was long and narrow and seemed more like a tunnel than a road as the dense branches from the trees created a dark canopy above. Within seconds the driveway widened and the overhang broke revealing a small ranch style home nestled among Pine and Fir trees. A yellow four-wheeler was parked next to the garage along with a rustic army green jeep. The headlights from the patrol car flashed into the woods as it followed the road up to the house.

Glowing eyes reflected back from the darkness as the lights illuminated a bait pile full of apples and corn. Alarmed deer raised their grazing heads to stare back in surprise then scurried into the forest in leaps and bounds. The car stopped in front of the garage as I got out, slinging my bag over my shoulder and looking around at the vast expanse of dark shadows and slivers of moonlight. A sensor light popped on near the front porch as Jackson led the way to the entrance taking my bag as he did so.

The night was thick and silent with only the occasional hoot of a nearby owl. Inside, I was surprised at the open concept and abundance of space the home consisted of given its humble exterior. Skylights graced the peaked ceiling allowing slivers of moonlight to rest upon plush furniture and a glass coffee table at the center of the room. A spacious kitchen hugged the far corner wall.

A long island counter was the only object separating the two rooms from each other. Just off the right of the main entrance from which I now stood was an open door leading down to the lower level. Jackson led me through the living area and I immediately stopped at the patio doors facing the back yard.

"Wow." Was all I managed to say.

He walked up behind me as I stepped next to the glass and peered out beyond. The view from this spot was incredible. I could only imagine what it must look like in daylight. Jackson's house rested on the edge of a cliff or hill. A few feet of cut lawn gave way to a panoramic expanse of open wilderness.

Massive black hills towered in the distance. Farms and trees dotted the expanse in between Jackson's house and the hills beyond. Tiny lights from dozens of houses gave the impression of a city viewed from the passenger window of a passing plane. I felt as if

"What an awesome view."

His breath caressed my ear as he answered.

"This is what sold me on the place. Not a neighbor in sight. I value my privacy."

His closeness was suddenly unsettling and I took a step to the side in order to look at him more squarely.

"It's beautiful."

He smiled in return. His dark eyes soft and warm. He brushed my arm tenderly.

"Come on, I'll give you the grand tour."

I nimbly followed him from room to room. There would be no need for anyone to sleep on the couch even if an army was staying here. Jackson had no shortage of spare space. Three spacious bedrooms were on the main level. One room had been converted to an office area and two others were located downstairs. One of which was used as an exercise room. The room was equipped with weights, treadmill, exercise bike, flat screen T.V and stereo.

The Master bedroom at the end of the main hall was magnificently large. A king size bed graced the center of the room and a Jacuzzi tub was nestled in the corner of the room on a tiled area facing double patio doors and a small deck overlooking that stunning scenic backyard.

I hugged my arms across my chest as he led me out of the room and back down the hall talking all the while about when he bought the house and what repairs and additions he made to it. It turned out Jackson was quite the carpenter when he wanted to be. He also was a very meticulous man when it came to his lifestyle. I noted not a single mess of any kind spare some dirty dishes in the sink.

Other than that, no clothes had been thrown haphazardly over the floor nor were there any dirt or grime to be seen as one by one, the interior lights were flipped on. The house was rather meticulous. After the tour I sat down on the couch and stared at the large flat screen T.V on the wall above the stone fireplace Jackson had turned on.

"Do you want something to drink?"

"No, thanks."

I continued staring at the images as they scurried across the screen not really paying attention to what I was watching. After a few minutes,

Jackson sat down next to me on the sofa with two steaming mugs in his hands.

"Here's some coffee in case you change your mind. You look cold. Is everything all right?"

I smiled, giving him a grateful glance as I reached for the mug. I shook my head 'yes' before taking a sip.

"Cayden can't hurt you here. Besides, we're on a trail to finding him. It won't be long now until he trips over his own two feet and we nab him."

"It's not that. He doesn't scare me."

"Are you still ill from your fainting spell?"

"I didn't really faint. I think it was the result of too many rides and an empty stomach. But I'm fine now. Really."

He set his cup down and rubbed his calloused hand soothingly along my neck.

"Wow, Jade. You're tense. I can help with that you know."

He moved his body closer to me as both hands now covered my shoulders and neck in a rather effective massage. Still I struggled to shake the inconclusive emotions twirling inside of me. Something just didn't feel right. I wish I knew what it was.

The logical explanation was that here I was, sitting in Jackson's home, delving into his private world, feeling things I wasn't sure I wanted to feel anymore given how powerful they had become and how vulnerable it all made me. This was indeed unchartered territory for me.

I had never felt this way about Dylan or anyone for that matter. That would be enough to set anyone's nerves on end. I hastily set my coffee down spilling some of it on the glass table in doing so and stood up abruptly. His hands dropped from my shoulders.

"What's wrong?"

His voice was full of concern and confusion. I spun around to face him.

"It's actually Sheba. Or something she said rather."

I could feel my face begin to burn again and so I turned away from him and walked back over to the glass doors facing the hills. Jackson made no move to follow nor spoke any comment as he sat patiently waiting for me to go on.

"It's stupid, really. But she said Sophia was over here last night. Now, I know you two are friends but if there is anything more going on or even if you have feelings for her, I really need to know before this goes too far. You don't strike me as that type of guy but I've been wrong before."

Dylan was someone I swore would never let me down or turn against me. We had been a solid pair knowing each other's deepest thoughts and wildest dreams. In the end, it turned out that I had given myself to him blindly. And to do that again would be more devastating than the first.

Jackson stood up and walked over to me. He put his hands on my shoulders, turning me around to face him, and looked straight into my eyes.

"Sheba is married to someone she doesn't even trust. She has become bitter about all relationships and sees others as she sees herself: A victim of broken promises. I feel sorry for her in a way. Even though she made her own choices in life, but I beg you not to let her words tarnish what we have."

He grabbed my hand and gently coaxed me back over to the sofa, sitting down to face me while holding both my hands in his.

"Sophia was Annabelle's best friend since childhood. When I entered the picture, she welcomed me like family. Annabelle looked up to her and admired her greatly and so do I. She is one of the kindest people you'll ever meet. She would never dream of forsaking Annie's trust or hurting anyone. Not even a fly. It was only after Annie's death did our grief bring us closer together."

"So there is something between you two then."

I nodded my head in acceptance and eased my hands out of his. But his grip tightened and held.

"No. Only the thought of a relationship existed at one point in time. It was six months or so after Annie's death when both her and I toyed with the idea of dating. It never went anywhere outside of coffee and lunch on occasion. But something was missing. The connection just wasn't there. It felt wrong almost to pursue a romantic relationship with my fiancés best friend. And I believe Sophia knew it too. We decided not to sacrifice our friendship further and agreed to end the casual dates. Annie and Sophia were like sisters and that is what she has become to me over the years. A sister."

"So it's common then for your sister to make late night calls?"

He snickered and showed his perfect smile once more.

"I love your fiery wit, you know that?"

I arched one eyebrow, attempting to hide my smile while turning back to stare at the empty fireplace. My heart told me he was being honest so far. I had no choice but to trust it for I was no longer in control.

"I had kept some of Annie's things but over time gave away some of the things that did not hold any priceless value. Our pictures taken and gifts we gave to one another I'll keep forever, but some of her stuff needed to be sorted through and given away. One item held too much sentimental value in which I just didn't have the strength to keep. Every time I looked at it, it invoked pain. It had become a burden in a matter of speaking.

I asked Sophia if she would take it off my hands even though she was the one that had given it to us. It was an ornate figurine that Sophia had made to present to us as an engagement gift. It pained me to ask Sophia if she would take it from me, knowing she had put many long hours and loving touches into its creation. And also knowing how much Annie had loved the gift when it was given to us. But it had to go and Sophia understood completely.

Besides, I thought she might have wanted it back rather than some stranger having it. She was supposed to stop by the station to pick it up but I had left the house that morning in a rush and forgot to take it with me. I told her I'd bring it by later but she said she was passing through town and would get it on her way home. She didn't arrive until nine last night to collect the figurine along with some other items she offered to take off my hands. We talked for a brief while then she left."

I listened quietly as he regaled his story and spoke nothing even after he had finished.

"That is the truth and nothing but the truth."

He smiled faintly trying to ease the tension.

"Why did the figurine bother you so much?" I said after a moment.

Like the sun going down behind the hills, his smile faded and hardness filled his eyes as he looked passed me into another time.

"Because it was what Annie was clutching in her hand the night I came home and found her body, still in one piece having never been thrown at the assailant. A dancing man and woman in our likeness. She had grabbed it off the mantle in a desperate attempt to protect herself."

My vision flooded back to me, and I realized the figurine I had held at the fair was the same one Jackson was referring to now. I shuddered visibly. Jackson seemed to take notice as his face softened. He stood up and grabbed a blanket out of a nearby basket that was resting next to the sofa.

"Here."

He wrapped the blanket around me and rubbed my arms to increase my circulation.

"I'm sorry for upsetting you. I simply ask that you trust me. I'd rather hurt myself than lie to you, Jade. You're that special to me. Please."

All I could do was nod my head as exhaustion began to set in. The events of the day and Sam's words the night before were catching up to me. I began to feel as if I could sleep for a week and not care about anything.

"Would you like something to eat?"

I could see he was suddenly uncertain as to what to do and was attempting to put me at ease any way he knew how. The mood had become heavy because of my inquisitions and now he looked as if he had said too much and that I might flee like a scared rabbit. Food was the last thing on my mind at this point and I nodded in decline. The look on his face appeared genuine and unsure. I couldn't help but reach out and smooth his ruffled hair.

"I'm sorry for making you rehash painful memories. I just needed some semblance of peace of mind, I guess."

"I know what it's like to be let down. I know what he must have done to you, how much you trusted him to be there for you. Jade, he couldn't have loved your spirit as much as I do. I won't let you down."

It was the closest Jackson had come to saying the words "I Love You". I felt them as much as I heard them being said. Perhaps I was a fool for giving in to the unseen force pulling us together. Perhaps we were under some kind of spell Sam failed to mention.

Or perhaps for the first time in my life, I was about to get it right. For at this moment, as much as the questions and mysteries still remained unanswered, I was being transcended into a place where only his face was the only one I saw; his voice the only thing that mattered. His touch the only guidance I needed.

It was all too easy to follow him anywhere. My head began to reel as he leaned in closer and placed his lips upon mine. His hand tangled into my hair as he drew me closer, made the kiss deeper. The blanket fell off my shoulders as my arms found his neck and locked tightly behind him.

My own fingers slid through his dark hair then made their way down his back as he leaned his body into mine, forcing me to lie down on the sofa. My legs drew up under his body as he positioned himself over me. His broad chest rested heavily on mine as my legs straddled his waist. I felt his hands run down my body, their heat burning through my shirt and thighs as he grabbed my hips while moving over me.

The weight of him became heavier as his body bore down on mine. I could feel his badge cutting into my chest. His hot breath scorched my ear as our kiss broke off and ragged breath invaded my starved lungs. I arched my body against his instinctively as his teeth and lips grazed my neck, seducing the outer rim of my ear.

A groan escaped him while his hands fumbled with my shirt finding their way underneath to the fullness of my breasts. The realization of how far we'd come in such a short amount of time had my senses spinning out of control as I attempted to regain some composure. My heart was pounding madly and my conscience was muddled and distant as it screamed at me from some hidden recess in my mind to stop. The fact that this time I was not afraid to give myself completely to Jackson as I had been with Dylan should have alarmed me. But the fact that it did not was an alarm in and of itself. I had every reason to take caution and tread lightly and yet, here I was unabashedly throwing myself at him. My hands pushed against his chest while my mouth continued its heated dance with his.

"Ow. Jackson, your gun. It's digging into me."

I tried moving away from him as he continued pinning me to the sofa.

"My gun's on the counter."

"Oh." Was all I could manage in between breaths.

"You fool! Don't you know a warning when you hear one? Don't do this!"

The voice came out of nowhere, loud and shrill causing my eyes to open wide. I physically jolted from the sound of it. Jackson jerked back at my startled gasp and followed my gaze over to the fireplace.

"What!? What's wrong?"

Jackson looked startled at my sudden movement as I pushed out from under him and sat up straight on the sofa. I rubbed my eyes in astonishment hoping my sight was failing me but no, she was still there. Isabelle. The woman from the banquet room at Dolly's who demanded I tell her cheating husband what a dirt bag he was. I hadn't seen her since that day and now here she was, standing a few feet away in Jackson's living room with nothing short of panic in her eyes.

I just couldn't believe she was still here. And why did she insist on tormenting me now? Why this moment? Anger began boiling inside of me at her impeccable timing. I shook my head and looked at Jackson's perturbed face.

"I'm sorry. I thought I saw a mouse run across your floor. It startled me."

"Where?"

He started looking around the room. He stood up and began pacing the floor the whole time searching for a mouse that wasn't there.

"I think I saw him head for the stairs."

"Dammit. The joys of living out in the country, I guess. I'll go check. Will you be okay up here?"

"Yes."

He left the room and the second he was gone so was Isabelle.

"Hey! Wait a minute. Where are you? Why are you here? *Dammit!* Isabelle, *come back!*" I hissed vehemently.

I marched outside onto the deck. The cold night air slapped my face and cooled my lungs as I stood there looking over the valley below. Isabelle reappeared beside me. I quickly shut the door after making sure Jackson had not come back yet.

"What are you doing here?"

"We girls have to stick together you know. I know something about Jackson that you don't. I couldn't let you make a mistake like the one you were about to make. Men just can't be trusted, Jade."

"Look, Isabelle. I don't know you and you don't know me. I'm sorry for what your husband did to you but you can't go sticking your nose in other people's affairs! I know what I'm doing. Besides, not like it's your concern, but I wasn't about to let it go that far."

"Sure. From where I was standing smoke was beginning to rise from how steamy you two were getting."

"And that's another thing! Just because you're a ghost doesn't mean you have the right to show up at any time, especially very personal moments such as that one."

She smiled her devious smile and winked before answering.

"I don't want to see that…" —She waved her hand in the direction of the living room— "…going on with anyone. I'm not a pervert. That is why I stopped it when I did. You're in danger, girl."

"Oh, not you too! I can decide for myself when I'm in danger. I don't need you or Sam or anyone interfering with my life."

"Fine. I simply felt it was my duty to protect you from a grave mistake."

"Your *duty* is to cross over."

"Oh no. Not yet. I haven't had my revenge yet on Jason for cheating on me."

"Isabelle, don't…"

And with another wink, she was gone before I could begin to argue or ask what she knew about Jackson. It was cold and the sound of the door opening had me turning to face him.

"No mouse. But I set a trap just in case. What are you doing out here? It's cold."

"I needed some air."

I walked back inside and sat down.

"Jackson…"

He sat next to me and placed his arm around my back.

"We shouldn't do this. I mean…I think we're moving too fast and I'm not ready for this yet."

He lowered his head briefly then brushed a strand of hair away from my face.

"Okay. I don't want to force you into anything, or make you uncomfortable in any way. I can wait as long as it takes, Jade."

I shook my head as conflicting emotions haunted me.

"You can have my room. I'll see you in the morning."

He kissed my forehead then stood up to lead me into his room.

"Jackson?"

"Yes?"

"Will you stay with me for a while until I fall asleep?"

He stood there for a moment with a hint of a smile in his eyes.

"I'm going to change out of this uniform then I will stay with you as long as you like."

He disappeared down the hall as I wrapped myself up into a ball on the sofa while the T.V droned on softly. Regardless of what tomorrow may hold, tonight I was going to shut the world away and all its warnings, fears, and uncertainties and give myself to the longing of a perfect kind of love. Jackson came back in the room wearing jogging pants and a Green Bay Packers sweatshirt as he climbed in behind me, pulling the blanket over us and wrapping his arm around me tightly. He kissed the top of my head and within moments his chest was rising and falling heavily. The soft sound of his snore filled the room.

I carefully turned my body to look at his sleeping face and mine softened in response. He looked peaceful, the lines on his forehead smoothed out. A faint smile played on his slightly open mouth. He looked like a young boy and purred like a harmless kitten as unbridled love swept through me. Like a floodgate opening, this revelation washed through me, and it suddenly did not matter if it was right or wrong.

If love meant dying, then there was no other way I wanted to go. Despite Sam's warnings of danger ahead and Sheba's distrust in Jackson. Regardless of Annabelle's unsolved murder and the gossip of a small town. Even Isabelle's most recent unsettling visit…these people were no longer a part of the living. Sam and Isabelle in the true sense of the word and Sheba's poor choices that had led her to an empty life full of regrets and bitterness. Therefore, a part of her no longer lived because of her constant fear of falling, of failing. But I was alive. And I was no longer afraid.

A sort of energy coursed through my body, one like I had never experienced before. It was revitalizing and empowering. And it all came from walking up to that unseen ledge that divides faith and fact, and taking a leap. It was the very essence of life itself, of love. And I had decided to dive in headfirst. For it wasn't the ending that mattered the most, it was the living.

CHAPTER FIFTEEN — A LEAP OF FAITH

The morning sun streamed through the window and woke me. At first I had no clue where I was as I squinted my eyes trying to accustom them to the unfamiliar room. I sat up cautiously and looked around while my brain slowly processed that I was in Jackson's home. It dawned on me that Jackson was no longer beside me on the sofa. I rubbed my neck and stretched out my back. The house was incredibly quiet as I rose to my feet.

"Jackson?"

Silence met my call. The breathtaking view from just outside the patio doors grabbed my attention as it had the night before. I walked over to the windows and peered out over the landscape. Even more in awe than before, now that the light of day washed over the terrain. I felt as if I were standing inside a castle looking out over the village as the hills in the background transcended me to another place, foreign and far away. I wanted to stand in place and look out into that fairytale like setting forever. But the curiosity as to Jackson's whereabouts pulled me away from the windows and had me venturing into nearby rooms.

The tour from the night before couldn't display the brightness for which each room appeared now. Cream colored paint covered the walls giving the entire house a bright and airy look and feel. The kitchen was pristine with shiny stainless steel appliances. I noticed fresh coffee brewing and helped myself to a cup. Jackson couldn't be far. There was no note indicating he had left.

I decided to check to see if his car was still here. Maybe he had been called into work and had to leave in a hurry. Although I couldn't imagine him not waking me to tell me as much or at least leave a note. I had a vague memory of movement just before the sun rose above the hills as I felt him leave the sofa but then must've fallen back to sleep. Before I could walk across the room to look out the front window a cold breeze whisked past my body sending familiar shivers down my back. I stopped dead in my tracks and turned around slowly.

"Isabelle."

Her face was as pale as ever with those brilliant green eyes cutting into my soul. She still wore that look of betrayal, anger and something else.

"What are you doing here Isabelle?"

My voice was heavy, relenting.

"We girls gotta stick together. He's hiding a secret, Jade. One you should know about."

And with that, her lithe form faded down the hall like a graceful cloud. My heart did not want to follow but my feet obliged. I followed her down the hall into Jackson's bedroom. There I found her standing next to his bed looking down at a small mahogany table. She looked down at the table and I followed her gaze as the top drawer slid out slowly before my eyes.

It suddenly felt as if all time slowed as one foot dropped in front of the other. When I reached the open drawer I saw a .38 Smith and Wesson handgun resting inside. My hand was no longer connected to my body as I reached down and touched the hard cool metal. I picked it up and was immediately transported down the hallway. The sun and moon set and rose over and over rewinding time backwards to a scene I found all too familiar. It was the same vision I had of standing in a living room watching a red haired woman holding a ceramic figurine.

Except this time, the hazy outer-lying details of my surroundings suddenly melted away into crystal clearness. I had been transported a short distance down the hall into Jackson's living room. It was dark outside but I could see every detail of the room including that same look of vivid horror on Annabelle's face as she stood facing me, still clutching the dancing man and woman figurine in her upraised hand.

"Why!? I trusted you!"

Tears of fear and betrayal streamed down her face. Once again I had become the very object of her terror and confusion. A shot rang out and I jolted in place. I tried to scream out as Annabelle's white face went rigid, the light in her eyes slowly faded. She dropped in slow motion to the floor, and a bright flash filled my vision as I was once again taken to her side. It was then I tore my eyes away from her still body and looked up into the face of Jackson, holding the .38 caliber pistol. He had a look in his eyes I had never seen before.

"Jade! What are you doing? Can you hear me? Hello!"

Jackson's voice came from somewhere far away then hit me like a ton of bricks as I whipped my head in the direction of his voice. He was standing in the doorway with a million questions in his eyes watching me hold his gun in my hand. With all the calm I could muster, I placed the gun back in the drawer and closed it firmly.

"I...I was looking for you."

He was assessing me with that unsettling look of his.

"I was outside working on the jeep. Why were you going through my things?"

"I...Um, I have to go."

And with that I walked quickly towards him praying he'd move and let me pass. To my dread, he did not move. His hand went up against the doorframe blocking my escape as he continued to look down at me. Cold sweat began to break out on the back of my neck.

"Jade, what aren't you telling me? I can tell you're hiding something from me."

His face had become cold and rigid and the first incline of fear tickled down my spine. Isabelle had reappeared next to me, gave me a wink and vanished. A second later a loud clatter came from the kitchen as if something had fallen. That noise was just the distraction I needed, for Jackson had taken a step backward into the hallway to see to the noise.

"Run!"

Isabelle didn't need to tell me twice. I bolted past him as he stood staring after me in surprise. He didn't stand there long. His footsteps echoed behind mine as I tore through the front hallway. Another loud noise had me whipping my head back to look over my shoulder. Isabelle had knocked a pile of books off a nearby shelf, which came in direct contact with Jackson.

"What the *hell*?"

His startled surprise bought me a few more seconds as I tore out the door and through the woods. I ran as fast as I'd ever run in my entire life heading in the general direction of the cabins. My lungs were screaming in pain and yet I continued to run. Every now and then I'd steal a glance back, only to find Jackson had not followed me. A few times I tripped over branches and rocks and slammed into the ground, narrowly missing a boulder with my head at one point.

Before even taking a moment to catch my breath, I'd be on my way again. Shock and disbelief coursed through me at the realization that Jackson had indeed murdered Annabelle. But why? I just didn't understand. Hot tears streamed down my face as the forest gave way to the familiar dirt road that led to the cabins.

I didn't stop running until I reached the door. I threw myself inside and locked the dead bolt behind me. There I sank to the floor and gasped in air as sobs wracked my body. This couldn't be happening. I couldn't have fallen in love with a killer. Marcus. I have to tell Marcus.

"*Sam*. Why didn't you tell me?"

The words were but a jumbled mess as they poured forth from my tear-stained lips. A desperate panic clawed away at my insides like a rabid monster. I scrambled across the floor unable to physically pull myself up just yet. My purse hung on the kitchen chair as I fumbled for my cell phone.

Before dialing I tried desperately to maintain some sense of control so that I could be understood but it was no use. What I was about to say would be hard to explain without revealing how I knew. My fingers clumsily punched numbers on the phone.

"Oh no!"

A quick look at my screen told me my battery was dead. I was cut off from the outside world and from help. Why did they have to go camping now when I needed them the most?

"*Sam*! Are you here? Sam, I need you, please!"

Silence filled the house.

"I'm scared."

Bang, bang, bang!

A scream tore from my lungs at the sudden sound of someone knocking on the kitchen door.

"Jade! Open up! Talk to me, Jade. What's going on?"

It was Jackson and he sounded angry. Phone still in hand I crawled further away from the kitchen and towards the stairs. When I reached them, I hauled myself up two steps at a time, running into my bedroom, shutting the door and locking it behind me. From there I ran into the closet and closed the door, hands shaking and breath coming in rigid gasps.

This can't be happening...

How stupid could I have been? The writing was on the wall the entire time but he hid behind a false shield to serve and protect. His charm and mystery had drawn me in like a moth to a flame. And now I was about to feel the pain of that fire. I sat huddled in the back of the dark closet, daring not to breathe just so I could listen for any noise in the house. All was quiet.

"I'm sorry Jade."

The voice was so quiet I didn't even feel her presence until she was next to me in the dark closet. I jumped at the sound of the whisper and whipped my head to the side to see Isabelle's profile next to me.

"Why are you doing this to me? Why won't you just cross over and leave me alone?"

"I thought I was helping you. You helped me speak to Jason when no one else could. But now I realize I've made a terrible mistake. I've put you in danger by showing you what I saw when I found his gun. I felt I had to warn you."

"Why were you there in the first place? What business is this of yours?"

For the first time since meeting her, Isabelle's hard, revenge-determined façade crumbled.

"You're right, it's none of my business. I had no intention of bothering you again after you helped me speak to…them."

She seemed to be struggling even now to say Jason's name.

"I was hell bent on getting my revenge by destroying the very thing they took from me; a chance at happiness. I had been following them all week, haunting them more like. They never had much peace while I was around. I was truly awful to them."

Isabelle had become pensive and paused a moment, reflecting on the past before going on.

"Somehow, my anger and passion gave me focus. It allowed me to touch things of this world. In the middle of the night, I'd knock a glass vase down from a shelf and watch with glee as fear gripped them. I watched as they pretended everything was fine while they continued with their normal routines. I noticed as the zest for life drained from her each and every day. She didn't want to do anything anymore.

The fair had arrived and Jason had encouraged her to go. Just for something to do, and if anything to get their minds off the trouble I had created for them. I followed them there this morning. Within the hour I watched as Joleen's face twisted in pain and she dropped to the ground.

Jason was next to her in a heartbeat holding her in his arms. They looked at each other as a crowd drew near. Something passed between them, some hidden secret that I could only vaguely sense. Then the pain wracked her body again and she closed her eyes against it, waiting for it to pass. It was then I saw it.

A tiny white ball rose up from her flat belly and hovered briefly over her body. It was the most beautiful tiny white light I had ever seen in my life. As I strained to look closer, the light took shape into that of a newborn baby. It was looking down at its mother with open eyes as if to say good-bye."

Isabelle's face crumpled in pain and for a moment, I didn't think she would go on.

"To my horror and shock, I realized at that moment, she was carrying life. And I was responsible for taking that from her. There's nothing worse than what I did. That child may not have had the chance to grow, develop or even resemble a human form but the brilliant breathtaking light told me there had been life.

It's beyond explanation how much life exists around us. Things too small to see or even care about. I see it now that I'm dead. Soft glowing auras around you, the trees, the grass, the sky, even around seeds in the earth…or inside a person. To explain it now is beyond words. Only those who are on this side understand completely."

She shook her head to regain focus.

"The important point being that revenge never hurts those we seek to hurt, it always backfires and destroys the one who inflicts it. And in my case, it destroyed an innocent soul in the process. What Jason did to me was wrong. Those sins they'll have to answer for someday. But the life they had created, unknown to me was not a mistake. No life ever is.

I watched in amazement as the baby was gathered in an angel's arms. We hear of angels but until actually being able to see one…well, it's beyond words. She was glorious, and lovingly scooped the child into her arms. She smiled at me from above as the infant clung to her neck. I sensed an overwhelming feeling of happiness and love where they were going."

"After Joleen was taken to the hospital and the crowd dispersed, I floated around feeling empty and lost. That's when I saw it again. It had been following you on occasion, hiding always near the forest edge, waiting and watching you. He was standing on the outskirts of the fair beckoning me silently to follow him. When I did, he led me here to be with you now."

"Followed? By whom?"

"Not who. What. It was a snow white deer."

I would've have laughed at how ludicrous it sounded if not for the look on her face. I thought about what she was saying for a minute then recalled the white deer I saw in the woods all those weeks ago. I wondered if there was a connection of some kind. But this deer sounded more like a spirit and the one I saw was real. Then again, what did I know of reality. I thought of Sam again.

"Why would it lead you to me? How do you fit in to all this?"

"Redemption is my guess. Quid pro quo. You scratched my back, I scratch yours?"

I looked at her with nothing short of madness as one eyebrow arched at her.

"What?"

"I don't know for sure. But I feel I was sent here to protect you and by doing so, right my wrongs so that I can cross over. I think that deer was your guardian angel of sorts. He showed me the curse that hovers over Jackson and how it affects all he touches. You Jade. I'm here to do my part."

"Someone already beat you to that assignment. Except he has a curse on him, too."

"Yes, I know. Sam's never far from you."

My eyes grew wide in the interior of the closet.

"You know Sam? Where is he?"

She chuckled softly.

"Yes, I know of him. You forget Jade that you may be able to see us, but we can see each other, too. I know of his burden also. Somehow, I just knew. I didn't know any of this when I was alive. But somehow all becomes clear after the last breath is taken. Sam will be here soon. He's heard your call."

Isabelle said the last part somberly then took one last look at me.

"Jackson seems to have a lot of secrets Jade. Just take heed. I've done all I could here and now have to leave you. I'm being called home, finally. Sam will watch over you from here."

"Wait! Don't leave just yet! I'm scared. I don't know what to do."

But she was gone. The gentle brush of wind on my face and arms told me so.

"Jade? Where are you? We need to talk!"

It was Jackson's brisk voice carrying up the stairs. My blood turned cold and I crossed my arms over my chest huddling as far into the corner as I could.

"Oh Sam, where are you? I need you!"

I whispered the words then fell silent as footsteps stopped outside my bedroom door. I heard the handle shake then a fist pummeled the wood paneling.

"Jade, *come on*! I know you're in there and that you're scared of me. I just don't know why. Open up so we can talk about this. You know I won't hurt you, *please*!"

"Go away Jackson! I don't want to talk to you."

"Why not? What did I do?"

I said not a word but carefully stepped out of my closet and walked over to the other side of the room far away from the door.

"Jade, I will break down this door if I have to. Now open up!"

"I'm calling the cops Jackson if you don't leave."

"I am the cops, honey."

No answer.

"Oh for Christ's sake, I'm coming in!"

In one loud kick, the wood splintered and Jackson was through the door in full uniform, gun hanging in his belt and eyes locked on me. His face was pinched and white and full of anger. He began walking around the bed to where I was standing. I lunged to the side dropping my phone in doing so as I desperately tried jumping over the bed and away from him. He caught me in mid-flight and wrapped his arms around me to restrain me. My back pressed firmly into his chest as I fought to break free.

"Let me go, dammit! I could have you arrested for breaking and entering!"

"Not if I report that I heard screams coming from inside the house which pardons me from any illegal intrusion."

He turned me around so that I was facing him. His hands held my arms down firmly at my sides. I glared up at him in contempt.

"Oh, you wicked conniving murderer!"

He blinked in surprise and his face contorted in shock.

"What?"

"You heard me, now let me go! I saw what you did to Annabelle. She loved you and you killed her!"

I started struggling again and managed to kick him in the leg. He yelped in pain then pushed me back against the bed. When my legs hit the sides, I automatically fell backwards onto the mattress with Jackson's body falling on top of mine. He pinned me down with his body and hands so that not one inch of me could move. His face inches from mine, and his eyes were as cold as ice.

"You're just like the rest of them, gossiping mindless know-nothing hypocrites. I thought you were different, Jade. I was *wrong*. Now I want you to listen to me and listen good. I did not, nor have I ever had anything to do with my fiancés murder. I did not kill Annie. I loved her. And now it seems she was *still* the best thing that ever happened to me. Get your facts straight."

His words cut into me like a venomous snakebite and deep down there was still a longing to believe him. Whether it was for the sake of not having to be wrong again in love, or because he was being truthful was a blurry distinction and one I could not place.

"Now, before I walk out of this room and leave you alone forever, I want you to tell me what set you off? Who told you I killed Annie?" His voice wavered ever so slightly. Irritation and something else conveyed heavily in his eyes. Sadness? Disappointment?

We were at an end so what difference did it make now in revealing the most sacred secret I had ever carried? His weight on me was making it hard to breathe as I stared into the eyes of a killer. He in turn, I'm sure, saw me as a shallow, untrustworthy small town follower who believed anything and everything she heard.

"You may think you know me so well but I don't need records, or evidence, or small town gossip to convince me of the truth. I saw it for myself when Annie showed me from the grave."

Hot tears were streaming down my face now and my voice began to crack.

"I have a gift. I can see and talk to the dead. I've had it since my accident in Montana. A ghost named Isabelle led me to your room this morning. I saw a vision of you standing over Annie's body holding the gun I found. I know you killed her. The dead don't lie."

CHAPTER SIXTEEN — A SINISTER MIND

My face was saturated in tears and I could no longer make out his face from my blurred tear soaked vision. I blinked a few times then felt his weight lighten as he moved off of me to stand up. He took a few steps back and continued to stare at me in silence. I sat up on the bed and wiped my eyes, not daring to look at him anymore.

I wasn't even sure if I cared to see what thoughts may be portraying on his face. My head was down and it felt like hours had passed. I was staring into my lap and still crying softly when I saw a tissue being handed to me. I looked at it in his hand then up into his face. He was standing over me, waiting for me to take it. His expression was unreadable. I grabbed the tissue, careful not to make contact with his hand then blew my nose.

"I don't know what to say Jade. But your vision is wrong. I didn't kill Annabelle. I'm sorry you believe that."

His voice was no longer stern but soft and full of regret. He started to walk to the door, stopped and turned around to face my back. I had yet to move off the bed and was now staring out the window.

"You are partially right though. I was standing over Annie's body that night with the gun in my hand because I was the one who found her like that. I had come home and saw the door cracked open. I had looked into the window from outside prior and saw a lamp overturned. Alarm gripped me knowing someone had broken in.

Earlier that night Annie and I had gotten into a big argument. I left to blow off steam. It was looking more and more as if we shouldn't get married. We had been drifting apart. That night brought all our differences to a peak. It upset both of us to see our relationship was becoming a failure; that it was never meant to be.

I was in the academy at this point and not yet an officer. The gun you found was in the same drawer you saw it in the night I left. Someone found it and used it to murder Annie. I entered the house expecting to find the intruder but instead found Annie lying on the floor already dead. What you didn't *see* is that in my panic I compromised the crime scene by holding her body in my arms then picking up the gun, which was lying on the floor next to her and inevitably portraying myself as the killer.

It was a stupid thing to do, picking up the gun like that. I was distraught and not thinking clearly. I couldn't understand how or why this had happened. I left my prints all over it of course. Marcus was the first one on the scene and was afraid I would be pinned for the crime he knew I did not do. He didn't want to see me get kicked out of the academy or spend my life behind bars.

He couldn't be my alibi. No one could because I was alone that night driving around in circles, not really going anywhere. So he jeopardized his career by wiping my prints off the gun and covering for me. Marcus and my father were good friends before he died. He watched over me when my father's health failed. My father couldn't live without my mom and felt guilty over her death.

Marcus had become the rock and role model I needed and so he took it upon himself to watch over me as he did that night. I didn't want him to do it but was in such a state of shock that I couldn't find any words to stop him. I stood there like a dazed idiot watching him clean up the mess I had made and inevitably destroying not only my prints, but also those of the true killer. Nothing else could be found, no hairs or fabric. Whoever did it was careful and calculating. Deep inside I still feel like the killer you accuse me of being."

I had remained motionless during his retelling but at that statement, something in his voice made me turn around on the bed to look at him. My eyes were now dry and red rimmed from crying.

"I tried to warn you off in the beginning because what I felt for you was like nothing I had ever felt before. As much as I tried to stay away from you, I couldn't. I was somehow being pulled back to you like a magnet. That's why I told you I killed her and that Marcus lied to protect me. Your uncle is innocent in all of this. He did what he thought was best for me like any father would do for a son."

There was a profound sadness in his voice now as he beseeched my understanding. We were asking the impossible of each other, faith in one another against all odds. I looked down at the floor by his feet and said not a word, feeling the battle raging inside me.

"I can't walk out of here Jade until I know that you believe me."

He took a few steps forward.

"I need you to believe me."

I had been staring at the floor as he finished speaking. Yet, out of the corner of my eye, I noticed he had taken a few steps closer to me and was now standing on the other side of the bed looking over at me.

"I believe you have a gift, Jade. I believe you. You've helped us find lost people when no one else knew where to look. I thought you were talking to yourself that day in the woods when we found Mr. Jenkins body. I contributed it to your eccentricity and possibly post-traumatic stress disorder from your accident. But now I know otherwise."

I said nothing but looked up into his beautiful face that I just could not stop loving. He smiled wanly and rubbed his head.

"The books falling on me say it all. I believe you, Jade."

Sam had appeared behind Jackson. His eyes were shining with pride yet hidden underneath was a palpable sadness as they focused on me.

"Sam. What's wrong?"

Jackson followed my gaze as it appeared I was talking to emptiness beside him. Sam had stepped up next to Jackson and answered me.

"It's Emma. Jade, she's been hurt."

I stopped breathing as he spoke. At that moment, the world stopped turning.

"Where? Where is she Sam?"

"Sam?"

Jackson looked from me to the air beside him in confusion.

"He's your great-great-great-grandfather, the one the curse was first placed upon."

"What?"

"It's a long story. I have to go. My aunt, she's hurt. Sam said she's been shot and is at Dolly's right now, dying."

I was scrambling for the door with Jackson on my heels when his radio went off. It was garbled and static filled but a few words had my blood running cold.

"10-4" (static) "...gunshot..." (pause) "...victim...Dolly's Restaurant on 1504 Kremlin"...(static)

"No! Em, hold on. Oh God, please..."

Jackson caught my arm when in my panic I missed a step and almost fell face first down the stairs.

"Easy, Jade! The ambulance is on its way, we'll get to her."

"I'm coming with you!"

"Jade..."

"She's my aunt. Either I'm coming with you or I'll drive myself. But I'm going!"

He made no attempt to stop me as we climbed into his patrol car and tore off down the road, sirens blaring.

Jackson and I were one of two respondents on the scene. Marcus' car flew up gravel as he tore in right behind us.

"What in the...Jade, you shouldn't be here! Jackson what the hell were you thinking bringing her here?"

Marcus had his gun drawn and had pushed me behind him while growling at Jackson.

Jackson ignored Marcus and had his gun drawn too.

"Jade, get back in the car and stay there."

Jackson's order was non-negotiable as I strained not to run into the restaurant full bore.

"Listen to him, Jade. Get in the car."

Marcus and Jackson secured me in the backseat then turned their focus on the restaurant as the other officers arrived on scene. Within minutes, the building was surrounded. All of the patrons and staff had run outside when the assailant had walked in and shot Emma in her office. A small group of employees were huddled together on the far side of the parking lot.

A few of them were already talking to police. Jordyn was with her co-workers and pointed into the woods. The officer talking to her radioed his partners as I sat there watching helplessly while Marcus and Jackson entered the building. A few minutes later a shout rang out that the building was secure. The assailant had apparently run off into the woods. Emma was being wheeled out on a gurney to be taken to the waiting ambulance. I tore open the car door and ran towards her.

"Auntie!"

"Jade. Are you hurt?" Emma managed to mumble the words through her oxygen mask.

She looked pale and weak and was wrapped in a sheet. Blood was smeared on her face and stained the sheet covering her. She was more worried about me than herself.

"No. Who did this to you? Will she be alright?"

I asked the paramedic closest to me the last question as I followed them to the ambulance.

"We don't know yet ma'am. If you'll just step aside so we can stabilize her."

"It's okay, dear."

Her voice was hollow. She seemed to be fading into shock but she managed to squeeze my hand before being lifted into the ambulance.

"I don't know who he was. He was dressed all in black, wearing black gloves and a black ski mask. It all happened so fast."

She turned to Marcus who had joined us after securing the building.

"The gunman ran off but we'll find him." He said.

His eyes were full of concern and worry over the health of his wife.

"I'll see you soon love. You're going to be alright."

Marcus' larger than life demeanor suddenly became small and frail as his voice fought control not to crack with strain. He had climbed into the ambulance and squeezed the hand I had let go of before conversing briefly with the paramedics. Emma had caught the bullet in her left shoulder. She was not out of the woods yet and her injury could potentially be life threatening if not stabilized soon.

Jackson walked up behind me when Marcus climbed down from the ambulance as the paramedics shut the doors and drove off.

"Jackson, will you drive Jade to the hospital and watch over her until this monster is caught? I'll be there in a few minutes. I don't know what we're dealing with here but I want my family protected as much as possible."

"Of course."

Marcus squeezed my hand, gave me a weak smile then walked over to the witnesses while the rest of his team continued investigating the crime scene. Jackson's hand brushed lightly behind my back guiding me towards his car. I was numb inside.

"Who could have done this?"

I asked more to myself than to Jackson as we drove to the hospital.

"Someone who needed money apparently. Cash was stolen from the till and the safe in Emma's office was broken into. An undisclosed amount of cash and an emerald necklace were taken from it. But I didn't tell you any of this. This is classified seeing as how a full investigation is pending. I'm not really at liberty to be telling you any of this but I guess I don't care at the moment.

She's your family and you have a right to know. Emma just happened to be in the wrong place at the wrong time. She was sitting in her office while the robbery took place. She heard the commotion outside her office and when she went to check on it, that's when the assailant walked in and shot her. Whoever it was broke into the safe then turned and ran out the back, hopped on a four-wheeler and drove off onto a nearby trail. We're trying to track him now."

Jackson's voice was heavy and almost wistful when he continued.

"Something is definitely fishy though. Emma was the only victim and shot for no apparent reason except that she was in the wrong place at the wrong time? He had what he wanted. There was no need to harm her. It makes me wonder."

"What? Makes you wonder what?"

I implored his face but his focus was on the road in front of him. At the ensuing silence in the wake of my question, he blinked as if suddenly remembering I was in the car with him and threw me a sideways glance.

"Nothing. It's nothing. We'll find this guy. Don't worry."

"Emma had told me she was having accounting issues at the restaurant. Money was missing and her ledgers were off. She was getting really stressed about it as the weeks went on."

"I know. That's why her and Marcus came home from camping today instead of tomorrow as originally planned. She told Marcus she had a hunch and needed to check something out at the office. She said she thinks she knows what happened. I guess we'll find out soon enough. It may help in solving this crime."

They worked on Emma for what felt like eternity. I wasn't permitted to see her when I first arrived at the hospital. Jackson left to head back to Dolly's once Marcus arrived. My uncle appeared utterly drained as he plopped down beside me in the chair. We were the only two in the waiting area of the ICU department. Neither one of us spoke at first as the clock on the wall ticked away the minutes.

"That was a very dangerous thing you did Jade, coming onto the scene like that when we didn't know what we were dealing with yet."

"I know. I'm sorry. Did you catch the shooter yet?"

"No, not yet. There are quite a few of our guys out there on foot, road patrol and on ATV's looking for him though. We'll find him soon."

At that point a nurse came in and permitted just one of us to see her. Marcus jumped up and followed her out of the room while I stayed put, hugging my knees to my chest in an attempt to get warm. My blood seemed to have stopped flowing the past few hours.

"Jade! Oh my gosh, I just heard what happened! How is she?"

Sheba rushed into the waiting room and sat down next to me. There were dark circles under her eyes like she hadn't slept in days and her forehead was crinkled with worry lines. I told her all I knew about Emma's current status as tears welled up in her eyes.

"That's horrible! Who could have done this and why?"

"They don't know yet."

"I was out of town when I got the call this morning from one of the waitresses that Em had been shot. I drove like mad to get here. I hope they catch the bastard who did this."

Sheba was very distraught as she sat there wringing the strap of her purse in her hands. The fear and anger in her voice mixed as one when she spoke. Sam had appeared and stood in front of us staring intently at Sheba. There was an ominous light to his eyes that had my head turning to one side in question. Sheba continued talking as Sam turned to look at me.

"She did it. She's the reason your aunt has been so stressed. She's been stealing from the business, Jade."

"How…?" I gasped.

"I found out she has been diverting funds into her account for the past few years and successfully covering her tracks until now. Emma had a hunch and I followed it, too. I watched Sheba when Emma couldn't and found the missing paper trail. That's when I knew how long this had been going on for and how she kept it hidden from her."

My face drained of all color as the room began to spin. I couldn't hear any more of what Sam was saying.

"Jade, what's the matter? Are you ill?" Sheba's question had me slowly turning to glare at her.

"You. It was you."

Sheba stared at me like I had lost my mind.

"What?"

"You stole from my aunt. Did you shoot her, too?"

The words tumbled out of my mouth. I was helpless to stop them, nor did I want to.

"Excuse *me*? How *dare* you throw such a senseless accusation towards me! Do you even realize how long your aunt and I have been friends? She's like a sister to me. *How dare you!*"

I stood up hastily, not daring to take my eyes off her.

"She was out of town, Jade. She wasn't the one who hurt your aunt."

Sam tried putting his hand on my shoulder but all I felt was unstoppable anger rising within me.

"Just stay away from me. My uncle's going to hear about this."

Sheba's mouth nearly hit the ground at my rigid tone of voice. My eyes were unwavering and neither were hers as she continued to sit there in shocked silence.

"Jade, you can go in now."

Marcus had appeared in the doorway weathered and worn. Sheba rose slowly and went to him, wrapping her arms around him in a comforting hug. Marcus returned the embrace and rested his head on top of hers ever so briefly before straightening up and drying his eyes. I fought the urge to scream at the top of my lungs. *Liar! Thief!* But this wasn't the time or place and the look on Marcus' face told me he couldn't stand much more drama at this point. He had nearly lost his wife today.

"Jackson is on his way to bring you back home Jade. Don't worry; she's going to be okay."

Stiff-armed and livid with rage, I walked past them and down the hall, uttering not a word. My visit was brief because Emma was still very weak.

She didn't speak except to say she was fine. Her worry for me shone in her glassy eyes.

Once again, I kept my mouth shut until the opportune time to unleash Sam's revelation. I didn't want to be responsible for sending my aunt over the edge with a coronary at the news that was burning a hole inside of me.

"You're turning into my mother Aunt Em, relax! I'll be okay. I'll take Scooter home with me."

At that she grinned and closed her eyes. I refused to take the ride back home from Jackson when he arrived. I debated on telling him about Sheba but would have to be alone with him again to do so. And that was something I could not bring myself to do just yet.

Not until I figured him out. Something unsettling still rolled deep in my gut and I just couldn't fathom trusting him completely again. Besides, this was something I needed Marcus to hear first and foremost. After politely declining his attempt to bring me home, I watched as his shoulders became heavy, his footsteps echoing out of the waiting room and down the hall.

"Jade, there's no need for you to stay here all night. I'll be with her and you need to get some rest." Marcus walked up next to me, his hand on my shoulder.

Exhaustion enfolded me at Marcus' words and I felt ten years older. Finally I conceded and phoned Nikki to ask if she'd pick me up and take me home. She attempted to persuade me to stay at her house but I declined. I just wanted to be alone with my thoughts. Although I did ask her to swing by my aunt and uncle's house so I could get the dogs.

I fed Chunk, the hamster and made sure he was taken care of then packed up the dog's food and toys and led them into Nicker's car. I stifled a weak smile at her less than pleased look, especially when Bella, in her eternal happiness at all things, licked Nikki quite affectionately in the ear.

"Sorry." I said.

"Oh no, it's alright. Just not used to having a zoo in my backseat."

Bruno's big butt pushed against Nikki driver's seat as she spoke as the tiny car plunked along the dirt road to my cabin. Once pets and I were settled in and Nikki drove away, I changed into more comfortable clothes and plugged in a movie for the night. All the locks on the doors and windows had been checked and I felt reasonably secure as the beginning credits of the movie started to play.

Jackson frequently entered my thoughts and within twenty minutes I had lost the thread of the storyline as I analyzed everything that had happened to me since arriving in Paulding. Could he really be dangerous? If so, why didn't he attack me when he had the chance? He had me alone a few different times and never threatened me in any way.

Was it because of Marcus? Or simply because he had no reason to hurt me…yet? Could he be behind what happened to Emma today? That seemed absurd. Or was it? If not, who? Does it have something to do with the curse?

I wish Annie was still here. I wish I could talk to her now. Find out the truth once and for all.

More so, I wish Sam knew. I wished Sam could've stopped Sheba from all the damage she had done. But ghosts, like he had said, are not all powerful or all knowing. Besides, Sheba will pay the hefty price real soon, just as soon as Marcus comes home tomorrow.

I'm going to tell him. Sam's knowledge of this dreadful truth regarding Sheba was confounding. Maybe he feels protective of not just me, but all my kin. Maybe this is part of his reconciliation. Too many questions once again, my head began to hurt.

Scooter's high-pitched bark nearly had me jumping out of my skin. I hadn't realized how deep in thought I was or how dark it had become outside. Bella joined in by letting out a deep bark. Bruno let out one big 'Woof!' then went and hid behind the chair.

"You big baby."

I chided him as I stood to look outside. My nerves were a bit on edge given the last twenty-four hours. I fought the instinct to grab something heavy to use as a weapon. The air whooshed out of me when I saw it was just a car passing by heading down the dirt road to one of the other cabins. I watched it go by, then tried to settle the dogs down.

A few minutes later the same car presumably, came back up the dirt road heading for the main highway. I knew the dirt road ended at the last cabin with a huge turn-around for cars looking to head back to pavement. I watched closer this time to see the vague outline of red and blue lights on top of the roof. It was a patrol car.

It was impossible to see who was behind the wheel. I'd imagine it was Jackson but in reality, it could be anyone. Marcus had asked that I be watched over until the shooter was caught. Perhaps he placed one of his rookies on the job.

The sound of tires on gravel was a regular one throughout the night much to my chagrin. For each time it went by, whether it was a patrol car or one of the renters, the dogs would bark feverishly which woke me several times. I slept in later than normal that morning. But Scooter would not have too much of it.

His tiny frame pounced on the bed and licked my face until I surrendered. Getting up, I proceeded to feed him and the others. A short while later I loaded the car with their things ready to take them back to the main house before heading back to the hospital when the sound of a four-wheeler approached. The dogs were running around the yard playing and chasing chipmunks when the dark helmet rider approached. He waved his hand in salute as he drove past, then as if on second thought, turned around and drove down my driveway.

Visitors always seemed to get lost out here whether on bike, boat, ATV, or on foot. So it didn't alarm me at first when he stopped. I simply concluded he was looking for directions as he turned his head in various degrees as if trying to locate something or someplace. He looked utterly lost as his machine came to a stop and he lifted his helmet off his head. A gasp escaped my lips as recognition filled me.

"What do you want?"

I said the words flatly trying to hide my fear.

"Now is that anyway to greet an old friend? I just stopped to say hello." Cayden smiled his slick smile in return and shook his head.

"You're wanted by the police for molesting that girl."

"I'm innocent. They'll come to see that in time. I just happen to like talking to pretty girls such as yourself."

I ignored him as I reached for my cell phone hoping against hope that I had some signal.

"Who ya calling?"

"A friend."

The dogs ran past me to check out the new visitor. Scooter stopped a few yards short and sniffed the air while Bella; the loveable one, ran up to Cayden with tail wagging. Cayden reached down and patted her on the head. Bruno hung back a few inches and wagged his tail too, waiting his turn to be petted.

"I wouldn't do that if I were you."

His voice had me stopping in mid-text. I had been trying to send a quick message to Jackson but my hands were shaking too badly. When Cayden spoke, I stopped to look up. In a flash Cayden grabbed Bella by the collar and with the other free hand reached into his black leather jacket to pull out a gun. He stuck the gun to Bella's head and with a voice as sinister as hell itself demanded I drop the phone.

"Put it down, Jade. There'll be no visits from your boyfriend cop today or from any cop for that matter."

I dropped the phone as if it had burned my hand. My face contorted into a thousand different emotions as I watched Bella stop wagging her tail in an effort to pull free from Cayden's death grip on her collar. She squirmed a few times then gave up and plopped her rear end down on the dirt in peaceful resignation. She watched a butterfly swoop by with no inclination that she was in any kind of danger. My heart dropped at the sight before me.

"Please don't!"

Scooter began to growl softly, his wiry body poised and waiting. With a lion's heart of courage he waited for an unseen command from his internal instincts to attack. Cayden let out a loud guffaw and let Bella go. She tromped off after the butterfly in the nearby woods.

"What do you think I am, some kind of sadist? Why would I hurt innocent animals when you're the only one I'm interested in?"

He took a step away from the ATV towards me. Bruno lost interest in being petted and trotted a few feet away to smell the grass. But he kept picking up his head sporadically to look my way as if he sensed something too. Bella had come back and joined Bruno by his side. When Scooter saw that Cayden was advancing towards me, he let out a sinister growl and stepped between us.

"Whoa! Leave it to the pip squeak to defend thy honor!"

Cayden sounded deranged as he ignored Scooter's warning. He raised the gun at Scooter as if to shoot him but before he could aim, Scooter was off like lightning and attacking Cayden any way he could.

"*Ow!* Son of a bitch!"

I looked around frantically at the diversion and knew I could make it to the jeep if I could just get around Cayden. I started to run screaming at the dogs in a desperate attempt to save them.

"Go! Get out of here! Run!"

Bruno and Bella continued to stand there staring at me with absolutely no clue as to what I was saying. Instead they twitched nervously, watching Scooter fight Cayden off. I no sooner made it to my car when Cayden got free of Scooter's toothy grip. He flung back his leg and kicked Scooter as hard as he could, connecting with the dog's ribs. Scooter looked like a rag doll as he went flying across the yard. His little body came to a rest and stayed motionless.

"No!"

The scream tore from me as I struggled to open the car door. Too late. Cayden was already coming after me and I knew my best chance to escape was to run. Bella and Bruno were barking behind me and then a gunshot rang out. My blood turned to ice as I looked back.

The bigger dogs were trying to run after Cayden until he shot at them, missing Bruno by a hair. He didn't need any more warning to turn around and run into the woods. Bella followed close behind as Cayden fired another round at them hitting a nearby tree where Bella had just been.

Cayden picked up the pursuit towards me. I screamed for help as his footsteps grew louder and louder behind me. I felt something heavy hit my shoulders, knocking me down hard as I tore my skin and clothing on the sharp rocks of the dirt road. I tasted blood on my lips as he aggressively turned me over so that my back was on the road. He then straddled me with all his weight crushing down.

I clawed at him and kicked as he yanked me up by the shirt. He pulled me towards the four-wheeler as something jabbed into my back. A hand clamped over my mouth to prevent me from screaming while his pistol urged me onward.

"Do as I say or I will shoot you right where you stand."

He shoved me over to the four-wheeler where I was then directed to drive. I sat on the machine and refused to move even as the hard cold metal stabbed further into my back. Cayden had already climbed up behind me and pushed himself up against my back. He reached over and flicked the switch to start up the engine.

"Drive, damn it!"

I spared a glance over my shoulder to where Scooter had been laying. To my immense relief, he was back on his feet attempting to hobble our way. Out of the corner of my eye I saw Cayden's hand extend as the gun focused in Scooter's direction.

"No! Please! Okay, okay I'll drive anywhere you want. Just please leave him alone!"

I quickly turned the machine around and away from Scooter's feeble attempt to catch up. I cranked the throttle as Cayden's grip tightened around my waist in an effort to hang on.

"Head for that trail."

His voice was raspy and harsh and I nodded affirmatively at his command. My body jolted at the sudden unexpected shot that rang out. I glanced furtively behind while attempting to maintain control of the machine in time to see Cayden had fired a shot backwards at Scooter.

"No!"

A sob tore from my heart. The quick glimpse I had was of a little white and brown body lying still near the cabin.

Kathleen Wickman

CHAPTER SEVENTEEN — THE HAND OF FATE

"Easy now!"

Cayden must have pocketed his gun in order to reach around me and steady my arms.

"Why did you do that?"

"That little shit's tenacious. I was just trying to ward him off. I can't help it if he got in the way of the bullet."

We had been riding deeper and deeper into the woods on a trail I had never seen before. The trees created a canopy overhead blocking out the intense sunshine from above.

"Jade. Hold on, I'm going to get you out of here!"

Sam filled my blurry tear-soaked vision as he stood next to a nearby tree a few yards ahead of us. A wave of relief and resounding strength flooded through me in monumental waves. I maneuvered the machine past him as our eyes locked. I desperately wanted him to return to physical form to help me take down this lunatic riding with me but instead he vanished. A half hour later we came across a camp in the middle of a small clearing.

"Stop here."

I pulled over where he directed and cut the engine. The gun was again positioned at my back as he led me towards the front door and into the camp. Cayden yanked me through a small living room and past a door leading down to the cellar. A small cot sat in the corner and next to it was a long, thin pipe coming up from the cement floor to the ceiling above. He tossed me onto the cot then hand cuffed one of my wrists to the pipe.

"You give me any guff and I'll finish off your aunt. And I'll take down your uncle too."

"I knew it! You're just demented enough to do something like that. Why?"

He snickered before answering.

"Because she had it coming. Now keep your mouth shut if you know what's best for you."

Sam had re-appeared in the room but stood off to one side as Cayden spoke. His eyes filled with anger as Cayden waltzed by, strode up the stairs and slammed the door. I rubbed my neck and temple with my free hand then sat up further on the cot with my back against the cold, brick wall. Silence floated down from upstairs making me wonder if Cayden was still in the camp. The sound of birds chirping outside was the only noise I heard in the dank, cold vicinity of the basement.

"You should've punched him in the head like you did by the lake. Or knock over a fridge or bookshelf onto him."

"I can't kill him, Jade and had I connected with him in any aggressive type of way, it would've only aggravated him more. Nothing's going to scare him off. He's terribly unstable. Even temporarily interfering with him would've enacted the full intention of his plans. I couldn't jeopardize your family like that. But I have already gone for help."

"Who?"

"Gus."

"You went to Gus? I just hope he is in a normal state of mind today to help."

"I told him to get Jackson. Marcus is still with Emma at the hospital, which is ideal. He should stay with her for now; it's the only way she'll be safe. There's no telling how far Cayden will go to get what he wants. He's done it before."

"I don't trust Jackson, Sam. I saw him kill Annabelle."

"What choice do you have at this moment?"

I sighed loudly.

"Fine. As long as someone gets me out of here, that's all I want."

"I have to go, but I'll be back soon with help. Gus needs me to lead him and Jackson to this place. We're deep in the woods, nestled among thick underbrush and rocky crevices. He picked a well hidden fortress and it'll be difficult to get emergency personnel back here."

"Don't leave me! What if Cayden comes back?"

"I won't be gone long, I promise! I won't let him hurt you again, Jade. I'll do whatever it takes. Trust me."

"I do trust you. I always have. Just hurry please!"

And with that, Sam vanished leaving me alone to my thoughts and fears.

What if he doesn't come back in time?

What if Cayden decides to kill my family and me just because he's crazy enough to?

What if I'm stuck here forever?

No! I mustn't think this way. Panic was beginning to rise in my chest at the innumerable questions and 'What Ifs' burning in my brain. My breath was coming in short gasps. I forced myself to close my eyes, clear all worries and fears from my thoughts and breathe in deep breaths. I exhaled verbally hearing the soft whoosh of air escape my lungs until my heart rate began to slow and the panic began to subside.

I had to keep a level head if I was to get out of here. Okay, now think! There has to be a way to escape or attempt to while waiting for help. I noticed a small window just to the left of my head where the sun was shining through. It was large enough to squeeze my body through and didn't appear to be locked.

Now, if I could only figure out how to get out of these stupid handcuffs. I began to pull my hand in a painful effort to squeeze out of it but quickly realized this was a fruitless attempt. I glanced around looking for a small sharp object to pick the lock. A screw or a nail of some kind could be my answer.

Another ATV was approaching; it's familiar rumble growing louder as it neared the camp. My head snapped towards the basement door as the sound of footsteps slow and deliberate echoed on the floor above. A door opened, and muffled voices reached down to where I was trapped.

"Ah, I gather you got my message this morning. You're just in time. Come in!"

"Where is he? Where's my son?"

"You didn't bring law enforcing friends with you, I hope?"

"No, you fool. You threatened me not to, or Isaac would pay you sick bastard."

"Now, now, sticks and stones love. It was a ploy to get you here. Of course I'd never hurt our son. I love him too you know."

"Where is he, Cayden? Where's Isaac?"

Panic and worry strained Sheba's voice as footsteps resumed quite loudly above.

"Relax. He's not here. I lied."

"What!?"

"He's safe. I had to lie to get you here in order to help me with...a problem."

"What the hell are you talking about Cayden? I want my son!"

"You'll have him. But first you have to help me with something."

"Do you have any idea how much trouble you're in? The cops are looking for you because of that girl you assaulted. You need help, Cayden. I've said it a thousand times. I will not have our son picking up on your bad habits."

"You know damned well I did not assault anyone. I'm sorry if my flirtatious nature disturbs you but you knew that the day we met and found it charming as I recall."

"Yeah, that was a mistake I don't need reminding of. I'm not going to cover for you anymore. I'm done helping you. This has got to end. I'm going to Marcus to turn you in."

"You'll do no such thing if you know what's best for you." Cayden said coldly.

"Is that a threat?"

"What do you think?"

"Stop playing games, Cayden. I can't take any more crap at this point. Someone robbed Dolly's restaurant. Emma's been shot. Jade's missing. Shall I go on?"

Silence ensued briefly.

"What is that look for? Oh, please don't tell me you had anything to do with this. You wouldn't dare."

"No, of course not love. That's insane. I've been out here all along."

"Cut the crap. Just tell me where Isaac is, or I swear to God…"

Sheba's voice had begun to crack and waver as she spoke of Emma getting shot. My revolt for her fakeness broiled inside me. They had been such close friends for many years. How could she steal from her own best friend? Those two upstairs were one of a kind as far as I was concerned. It made me sick. I held back from calling out.

"Easy now. I told you he's not here, but you'll be with him soon."

Cayden's tone was flippant as he spoke.

"I don't believe you."

Footsteps resumed as they resounded from room to room. Their voices became indistinguishable at times as she searched far off rooms. The war inside me of whether or not to call out was becoming a losing battle as it appeared Sheba could be the answer to my salvation after all. It was becoming difficult to discern who to trust these days and who not to.

Whether calling out for help would put Emma's life in further danger crossed my mind. Yet I felt a reasonable belief that she would be safe if she continued to stay in the hospital with Marcus watching over her. The choice was becoming clear. There was no way I would stay here, quietly allowing him to do whatever he pleased with me. I had to take the chance for my own safety. I began to scream as loud as I could.

"Help me! Sheba, help! I'm down here! Please get me out of here! Sheba!!"

I screamed and hollered until the footsteps reached the door and it flung open. Sheba came running down the stairs in a shocked rush while Cayden's slow and deliberate descent followed her.

"Jade! Oh my God! Cayden, what the hell are you doing?"

She touched the handcuff holding my bruised wrist, then whirled on him.

"Give me the key you son-of-a bitch!"

He obliged willingly and without restraint. With shaking hands, Sheba unlocked me and I automatically rubbed my wrist. Sheba's eyes were consoling and sympathetic as she helped me to my feet in a protective manner.

"This…is what I need your help with, my dear, if you want to see Isaac again." His tone had become soft.

"You've gone way too far this time. I want a divorce and I want my son. You will let us out of here now!"

She began walking towards him still holding my hand. He grabbed her roughly by the shoulders breaking the grip she had on me as I stumbled backwards. She shoved her weight back towards him trying to push him out of the way when he raised his hand and caught her square across the face in a resounding 'smack'. The surprise on her face had her reeling backwards. She lifted her hand to cover the cheek he had hit. Then, before she had the chance to recover, he reached behind his baggy flannel shirt to withdraw a pistol that he now pointed towards Sheba's head.

"Get over there with Jade! Now!"

She took a few cautious steps towards me, and reached out her hand for mine. I stood there motionless with my back to the wall as her hand found my arm and held on tight. He smirked at the looks of fear on our faces then turned to walk back up the stairs.

"We leave at nightfall. I'll come down to get both of you then. In the meantime, if I hear a peep from either one of you, you're going to be eating lead."

The door slammed again as the lock turned once more trapping us in.

"Don't worry, Jade. I'm going to get us out of here."

She whispered quietly, never taking her eyes off the basement door.

"You might be interested to know your husband was the one who shot Emma and robbed Dolly's, too."

I whispered back.

She slowly turned her head to face me, letting go of my arm at the same time. Her eyes grew wide and her face began to pale as she digested my words.

"That's impossible. That can't be."

"It is. And he did. He told me himself. You said he had problems, I heard you talking upstairs. It turns out his problems are bigger than what anyone expected."

"It can't be."

She had a forlorn look on her face as she stared at the floor, repeating her shock at this new revelation. I still didn't feel pity for her given her valiant attempt to rescue me, or her apparent disdain in Cayden because she chose this path for herself. She betrayed my aunt and I couldn't quite forgive her just yet. The only pity I did feel was for their child, Isaac. What a sad life to grow up in, what hopelessly lost parents to have.

"You really didn't know?"

She looked at me again in bewilderment.

"No, how could you say that? I haven't even seen Cayden in weeks until now. He hasn't come home since I kicked him out. I knew he had problems, but I never thought he'd do something like this.

I came home from the hospital after visiting your aunt to find a note on the kitchen counter and my son nowhere in sight. The note was from Cayden. It read to meet him here at one o'clock if I wanted to see my son again, and to tell no one. Do the police know he robbed Dolly's and shot Emma?"

"Not that I know of. Your husband threatened me this summer at my aunt and uncle's party. I told Jackson about it. I'm sure it won't take him long to figure out who has me."

Not to mention my own personal translucent eyewitness, Sam.

"I'm truly sorry, Jade. My husband's completely lost his mind."

I said nothing more, but moved from the wall to sit back down on the cot hoping Sam and help would arrive soon.

"All I know is Cayden turns into something else when he drinks. He always has. That was one of the biggest red flags I noticed when we were dating. But like a dummy, I thought my love could change him for the better.

I stuck it out. He didn't drink all the time. But I did notice just now, upstairs, that there was an open bottle of Vodka on the counter top. Hard liquor makes him completely and inexplicably irrational. I still don't know why he'd attack Emma like that?"

Sheba walked slowly over to the cot and sat down next to me.

"This is all my fault. I'll take full blame for what has happened going all the way back to our wedding day, a day that should've never happened. And yet, Isaac came from that so I couldn't regret all of it in retrospect. He's the only good thing to have happened to me since meeting Cayden."

I sat there not wanting to listen anymore but I said nothing as she continued nostalgically.

"You see, Cayden and I tried for years to have a child but I could never conceive. Just when we had given up due to age and repeat failures, Isaac came along. But he came with a price, poor health and lots of medical bills. I don't mean to complain; I wouldn't trade Isaac for the healthiest, sweetest kid in the world.

But I'm the one who has always been in charge of the bookkeeping in our household. I told Cayden of our money troubles we've been having as of late. In the past three years we've had a few scares with Isaac's health, and the bills haven't stopped rolling in since. Even with the menial health coverage Cayden got with his job, it just wasn't enough to keep us afloat.

It's what drove me to do what I did. Stealing from your aunt. Something I deeply regret. I was desperate, that's all there is to it. I needed money and I didn't think anyone, including your aunt, would notice. I was wrong. Cayden started drinking more, then that incident with that teenager happened for which he has apparently been hiding out here to escape being captured. That's why I kicked him out. I couldn't handle the monster he was turning into."

Sheba's voice wavered and her eyes filled with tears.

"All I can guess as to why he did the unthinkable and hurt Emma was because I used to complain how well off her and Marcus are. How perfect their lives are and how they have more money than they know what to do with.

Emma once told me that Marcus comes from a very well-endowed family and that when he turned eighteen, he inherited more money than they needed. It's what kept the restaurant going in difficult times over the years. But overall, the restaurant has become a small fortune in and of itself. It's the most popular business in town along with the most beautiful rental cabins anyone has ever seen. I was jealous. I think that rubbed off on Cayden.

He took it upon himself to take away some of that perfection. To take what he thought was his. I don't expect your forgiveness for what I did to your aunt. I know I don't deserve it."

Tears were now streaming down her cheeks freely. After a moment of silence, I spoke slow and deliberate.

"My aunt doesn't have a selfish bone in her body, Sheba. I'm sure she would've given you as much money as you needed to take care of Isaac. All you had to do was ask."

"I know she doesn't. She has always been so good to Isaac and to us. I guess I couldn't swallow my pride enough to ask for any more than what she had already given over the years. I was ashamed to have to need someone. I've always been a bit too independent for my own good."

"Well your guilt over this is between you and my aunt. I have nothing to do with this."

She wiped her eyes then turned her head to look at me.

"How did you know I stole from her?"

"What?"

"At the hospital, you accused me out of the blue of stealing from her. How did you know?"

"A friend told me."

"Do you make a habit of listening to your friends when they could have been speculating?"

Sheba's tone was full of inflection.

"He wasn't speculating. He saw the files you altered and the inaccurate recording in the finance books of deposits you made on behalf of the business. The authorization she had given you to access the business account made it quite simple: plus the fact that Emma trusted you.

She wouldn't even consider you as a suspect when she started noticing discrepancies in the till. She figured it had to be a miscalculation. Her trust runs deep, a character trait that is a blessing and curse at the same time in this case."

"Who is this friend of yours?"

I looked up into Sam's face. He was back. Sheba appeared baffled as she continued to watch me.

"Gus is showing Jackson and Marcus the way. I have to go back and lead them here. It's rough terrain and the going is slow. Just know help is on the way."

"And Cayden?"

I could see from the corner of my eye Sheba turning her head from side to side trying to figure out who I was talking to.

"He's sleeping on the couch. Hold fast, Jade. I'll get you out of here."

"Who are you talking to?"

I turned to face Sheba's inquisitive stare.

"The friend who told me about what you've done. His name is Sam. His spirit was just with us."

The corner of Sheba's mouth twitched ever so slightly. Her fixture was solid like a statue, and for a minute I didn't think she would say anything at all. She just continued to sit stoically in some kind of trance.

"Are you kidding me? A ghost? You're saying you can see ghosts?"

"Yes. And I can speak with them, too."

"Sure. Okay, umm, well Jade. Tell your little friend to get us the hell out of here then."

Her voice was soft and slow like she was speaking to a child who didn't understand something.

"He's doing the best he can. He says Jackson and Marcus are on their way. They'll be here shortly. And don't think I don't notice your sarcastic tone. I could care less if you believe me or not."

She sighed loudly and rubbed the back of her neck.

"Jade, I'm sorry. I'm just stressed. Well, they'll never get here before nightfall, and I refuse to stay down here all evening. I know this area and to put it bluntly, it's a bitch to navigate. That's why ATV's are the best way in and out. Now, how to do this."

Sheba stood up and started pacing around the room. One hand rubbed her chin and the other rested on her hip as she moved around gauging windows and inspecting junk that was scattered about the basement floor.

"Ah-ha! I'll use this crow bar to bust open the door then beat Cayden senseless with it."

"Sheba. Come on. Sam said to wait. He also said Cayden's sleeping on the couch. Doing anything now might wake him."

"Perfect!"

She glanced back at me from across the room.

"Sam isn't here. Not in the physical sense anyway. Fine. I have a better idea."

She put down the crow bar quietly then tiptoed across the floor and up the stairs.

"What are you doing?"

I hissed at her, but she ignored me, continuing to climb the stairs. She retrieved a credit card from her pocket. Looking back towards me, she waved a hand then placed her ear next to the door listening for any sounds coming from the other side. After a few moments of silence, she wedged the credit card between the door and lock, gently working on the latch.

I had quietly followed her up the stairs not knowing what else to do. I couldn't very well stay down here if Sheba did escape. Cayden's wrath would be destructive and I didn't want to take the full force of it. A few times the card slipped and made a discernible scratching noise, which in the quiet and volatile environment sounded more like a bomb going off.

"Shhhh! Keep it down Sheba."

She shushed me back and continued working on the door. The door gave a slight jerk open in what seemed like an eternity but in reality was only minutes. Adrenaline began coursing full throttle through my veins at the danger we were about to face. Sheba gave a quick glance behind her to make sure I was ready then waved her hand to follow her. Ever so slowly, she pushed the door open so as to diminish the creaks and cracks the hinges were making.

Once open far enough, she stuck her head out to peek into the living area. She glanced back at me again with a smirk on her face that told me we were good to go. One step after another we made our way out of the basement and into the living area. The outside door to freedom was so close I fought myself not to run full blast towards it. Cayden's sleeping form on the couch caught my attention first and foremost. An empty vodka bottle rested lightly in his hand. Soft snores filled the room.

"I'm going to grab the key to the four wheeler. Meet me outside."

Sheba's words were so soft I barely understood what she wanted me to do. But her actions were clear. I made my way to the door and unlocked it, checking on Cayden frequently to make sure he didn't stir. Then I snuck out as quickly as I could. I ran towards the ATVs parked next to each other near a small shed and stood there waiting, hearing the minutes tick by in my head.

What was taking her so long?

Finally, Sheba scurried out and ran towards me.

"I want you to hold on tight because we're going to have to make a mad dash for it. I have a feeling I know where the search party is. We'll try and cross paths with them."

Sam had re-appeared and was standing next to me. He tried grabbing my arm. First looking back towards the house then at Sheba. His hands swiped right through my own and goose bumps danced up my arm at the attempted contact.

"Jade, don't!"

He started to say something else but the roar of the engine starting up drowned out his voice. The camp door flew open and a red faced Cayden came stumbling out.

"Hey! Get back here!"

The empty vodka bottle was still in his hand. I wrapped my arms around Sheba's waist and hung on for dear life as we jolted out of the yard and down a small dirt road. The sun was beginning to set and darkness seemed to be closing in fast. The wind was cold and it whipped at my face, stinging my eyes.

"No, no. Jade!"

Sam's voice was hollow and hard to place as I whipped my head around looking for him. There, up ahead, he stood; fainter than ever before like a soft cloud or morning fog. A look of sheer horror masked his features as his eyes pleaded with mine. Ice slithered down my skin at the danger they inflicted. We drove by him in a flash and I reached my hand out to touch him.

His arm reached back as he struggled to connect again. He appeared weak all of a sudden. Helpless. In fact, he seemed to be fading a little more each day since we met. So strong and pure in the beginning, touching me and feeling his warmth, and now a mere wisp of wind as he tried to hold on but could not keep up.

"Wait. Sam! What is it? What's wrong?"

But he was gone. I turned to look back and saw nothing but the fading sun on an empty trail. Sam was gone.

"Stop. Sheba, stop! Please!"

"Are you nuts? Cayden could be following us. I'm not stopping. Just hang on Jade. We're almost there."

I no longer recognized where we were. Fatigue and fear had drained me. In fact, it was all I could do to keep my head from dropping onto my shoulder. My arms loosened their grip around Sheba's waist and I suddenly felt dizzy.

I physically felt the loss of connection to Sam and somehow became weaker because of it. That was foolish thinking, I knew. It wasn't sensible. What was sensible was the last time I had eaten. It had been this morning. Cayden had given me nothing to eat or drink all day.

My throat was starting to become dry with thirst. Still…Sam was gone. And one day isn't all that long to go without food or drink. Where did he go? Why can't I feel his presence anymore? Could there be more than hunger causing me to feel as empty as I do? I nearly slid off the four-wheeler as Sheba took a sharp turn. Her arm reflexively reached back to hold me in place.

"Hang on, Jade! Almost there!"

We had reached another clearing high up on a ridge. Sheba cut the engine and climbed off. Sirens wailed somewhere in the distance. I could see off to the left the town below. The sun was still making its way westward, its' comforting light fading from the cruel day.

"Where are we?"

Sheba had walked a few yards away into the dense trees and started clearing branches off a vehicle. I slowly climbed down from the machine to watch her in surprise.

"Sheba, what are you doing?"

She didn't answer me nor did she look my way as she continued clearing off the hidden vehicle. She returned to where I was standing and held my arm.

"I'm really, sorry Jade. He's crazy. He'll hurt Isaac if I don't do what he says."

"So that's what took you so long to get the keys? You were conspiring with him?"

"No. He caught me as I was walking out the door. He was pretending to be asleep much to my surprise. Waiting for the opporture moment to blackmail me into playing along. He told me his plans and that I had to take you here, where he hid the getaway vehicle. He's crazy Jade. I have to do what he says. He'll hurt Isaac if I don't. I just know it. Please try to understand."

"I don't believe you! You knew his plan all along."

"No. I didn't. I swear, Jade! I don't want any part in this. He had made some snide joke a while back about taking you hostage but I laughed at him. I never thought he'd actually go through with it!

And I never imagined in my wildest dreams he'd bring our son into the middle of this but I was wrong. I feared something was terribly wrong the second I got home and found that note saying to meet him at the camp."

"Sheba, why the hell didn't you just go to the police right away?"

"Stupid reason, really. I was afraid. I started to believe that Cayden would hurt Isaac and I didn't trust the police to find them in time."

I had a thousand more questions to ask but just then the sound of another ATV approached from the distance growing louder and louder until it flew around the corner. It skidded to a stop and the rider removed his dark helmet. A ball of fear began to twist painfully in my gut.

Oh Sam, where are you? I need you.

A sick premonition haunted my thoughts, strong and oppressive. I was not going to get out of this alive. Jackson's face appeared before me and I closed my eyes as pain tore into my chest at the thought of never being able to say good-bye.

"There's my girls! Are we ready to fly? I'm being followed."

As Sheba had confided, any indication of Cayden's drunken sleep-filled stupor was gone as he hopped off the machine with a black backpack slung over his shoulder. He walked towards me with a steady gait and razor sharp eyes.

"Surprise! Thought you got off safe and clear, didn't you?"

There was acid mixed with sarcasm in his tone as he touched my cheek. I had already started pulling away from Sheba the moment I saw Cayden but she held fast and begged me to just do what he said. Her voice was hollow and forlorn.

"Oh no, you don't. You can try and run Jade but you won't get far."

I kicked at him and caught him square in the shin. He jumped back sharply then grabbed me from Sheba's grip.

"Feisty little thing, aren't you?" He sneered.

My attempts were futile compared to his brute strength. Within seconds my hands were once again bound in front of me, this time with rope. I started to scream again but Cayden's hand clamped down hard on my mouth.

"I really wouldn't do that if I were you."

He nodded to Sheba and her desolate face nodded back. She avoided eye contact with me as Cayden shoved me into the back seat of a newer hunter green pickup truck that Sheba had been uncovering in the woods. Cayden sat next to me keeping me in check. Sheba got behind the wheel and started to drive off down another dirt road that led onto the state highway.

"You're going to get caught Cayden and you're going to prison for this, both of you!"

Cayden laughed and turned to remove the .38 revolver he had in his jacket pocket.

"Oh, I think not. I've got lots of leverage. You see, my wife has no choice but to help me because if she doesn't do what she's told, she'll never see her son again. And once I get the ransom for your pretty little face, *you'll* never see me again."

"You're holding your own son hostage? What is the matter with you?" I snarled at him.

Sheba's eyes were welling up but she kept her attention on the road in front of her.

Cayden's smile vanished from his face as he raised his hand to hit me. I shut my eyes and prepared for the blow.

"Don't you criticize me, you spoiled little wench! You know nothing about hardship and sacrifice!"

I opened one eye to see he had lowered his hand.

My survivor's instinct told me to stay quiet but my shock and anger overpowered instinct.

"You're crazy!"

The corner of his mouth twitched ever so slightly.

"Just so you know sweet heart, once your aunt and uncle pay up, I'm going to shoot you. Maybe I'll shoot you in front of them, make it more interesting."

I glared back at him, hot tears of anger and fear brewing over.

"What makes you think my aunt and uncle have that much money? They're small town business owners for crying out loud. Even my uncle's previous inheritance wouldn't last you one year. You're a greedy, selfish person and money runs out fast with the likes of you."

"Little do you know! Sheba found all kinds of investments and stocks they have worth millions when she was stealing from the business account. She wasn't able to touch that of course. It's not just the business and surrounding resort that's worth money, it's your aunt and uncle.

And they have no children of their own to spoil. You are the closest thing to a daughter they've ever known. An only child yourself and Emma's brother living far away making his own money, living his own perfectly rich life, wanting nothing to do with the business fortune. You, in a way, are the sole heir to a very comfortable lifestyle. Not to mention what your own parents have in investments to offer up for your release."

I turned my face away from his in disgust.

"You make me sick."

He chuckled softly and brushed my dark hair from my shoulders. I cringed from his slimy touch.

"You certainly have a way of attracting trouble. First with your murderer boyfriend, Jackson and now with us."

Sheba shot him a strange look in the mirror but said nothing. He either didn't see it or ignored her.

"We all want something here. Sheba wants her son back, whom I have hidden in a safe location. Jackson wants a bit of redemption. You want your freedom."

"Why are you doing this?" The words were but a whisper now.

"Well, I'm not doing it for my health. I already told you! I'm here for payday. What other reason is there?"

He let out a maniacal chuckle and wiped his brow with the back of his gun wielding hand.

"We're not very nice people, Jade. Sheba and I have been plotting this for a while now. Embezzling from your aunt just wasn't cutting it after five years. The fact that we weren't getting caught gave us the incline to push further, deeper. Hit 'em where it hurts. They don't need all that money anyway. It's ridiculous!"

His tone was growing deeper, angrier as he continued.

"I had no part in what happened to Emma. How was I supposed to know you'd take the initiative to rob the safe after I told you about the stones? I'm guilty of embezzling and helping your sorry ass with Jade like you demanded. I just want my son back dammit!"

Sobs rocked her body as she tried to keep the vehicle on the road.

"I should just drive us all into a tree right now and end this!"

He had leaned forward in his seat so he could place his hands on her shoulders in comfort. I contemplated lunging at him but my hands were tied and my advantage was weak.

"Now, now dear. What purpose would that serve? Then you'd never see your son again because if the crash didn't kill you, I would."

And with that he sat back and buckled himself in while keeping his gun pointed in the general direction of Sheba and myself.

"We were in over our heads, anyway."

He continued on.

"Might as well keep trudging on down the path of unrighteousness. So I planned it all out to rob the restaurant. Using the four-wheeler was perfect. Hard to track those buggers considering they can go where other vehicles cannot."

Sheba's eyes remained on the road. She removed her hand from the wheel long enough to rub her face where he had hit her. She placed her hand back on the wheel and only glanced at Cayden briefly before returning her focus to the road. My mind reeled suddenly at the magnitude of my situation. And the immense amount of sadism that emanated throughout the truck from Cayden's delusions.

"Cayden, there's a cop car behind us. I thought you said you borrowed this truck."

"I did borrow it, from my cousin Lou. He doesn't know my secret. He thinks I'm using it for camp. Maybe the coppers don't know it's us."

We had left the dirt road and were traveling north on Highway 45. Robbins Pond Road was just ahead to the left, the place where Paulding Light could be seen. Another cop car just ahead of us coming in our direction suddenly turned on its flashers simultaneously with the one behind us. I prayed Jackson was in one of the vehicles.

"Sheba, turn here now!"

The truck turned violently down Robbins Pond Road as gravel spat up into the air behind us. I dared not breathe relief or hope too highly for freedom until I was out of this truck and far away from these people. Because the sun was still out and nightfall was still over an hour away, the guardrail where onlookers usually convened was abandoned much to my relief. My life and Isaac's were at stake here; there was no need to drag more innocents into it.

I felt a hand on my hair pulling me away from the window. Cayden had yanked my head to face him so that he could put duct tape on my mouth. The patrol cars were still a ways behind us on the long stretch of highway so the truck had a small window of time to roll to a stop. Cayden proceeded to drag me out roughly by my neck, the gun pointing at my head.

"Shit! This isn't how it was supposed to be! How did they find us so fast?"

He was hollering at Sheba who had exited the truck as well and joined me by my side.

"I don't know! It's not my fault, so quit yelling at me!" She yelled back.

Cayden flung the backpack over his right shoulder, as the sirens behind us grew louder. We had already made it down the hill and out of sight into the thick underbrush by the time the police reached the guardrail.

"Now what?"

He ignored his wife's question and kept shoving us along the dense brush just parallel of the clearing, out of sight from potential gun fire.

"Why didn't you just make the call from camp? No one knew you were out there. What were you thinking driving out in the open like this? I mean, where were you planning on taking us?"

"Shut up! I'm trying to think!"

We had been walking for what seemed like hours and my legs were starting to buckle from over exertion. Cayden's pace was fast and relentless and the constant jabbing of cold metal against my back gave me not a moment's rest. I had tripped and fallen a few times only to be hauled roughly to my feet again and shoved onward.

"There isn't enough signal at camp; my cell phone is useless there. Besides, it's not as inconspicuous a location as I prefer. It was only meant to be a pit stop so I could grab the money. I'm sure it made the top ten list of places to check."

We were deep in the forest now heading south of Robbins Pond Road. A quick glance behind me told me we were alone. Cayden stopped every so often to simply listen and think. Only the chirping of birds and startled chipmunks filled our ears. But we all knew this place would be surrounded in a matter of minutes.

He had nowhere to run. It would soon be over. A shiver ran down my spine as he nudged the gun barrel deep in my back again. I had had no water to drink since that morning and the day was rather hot. I was getting dizzier by the hour and felt an overwhelming urge to simply collapse.

In a matter of moments, I would. Just when my feet began to surrender its monotonous trudge and the exhaustion wrapped me in a tight embrace, Cayden stopped.

"Ah ha! There! Just ahead. We'll camp out there until I think of a way to get out of here."

I lifted my weary head to see what he was pointing to. Just up ahead, seemingly half buried by years of natural vegetative dominance and decay sat an old decrepit building of some kind. It appeared to be in a half crescent form with empty cavities where garage type doors hung. But now it conveyed an open and desolate blackness beyond. Brick had been its foundation and construction media and the roof, or what was left of it, was old tile.

Large gaps now took the place of most of the tile, and piles of rotted lumber rested nearby as if someone had attempted to repair or rebuild, then gave up on its existence. What was left of the abandoned building did not appear to be very large, half the size of a small home. My first inclination was that of an old bomb shelter but Sheba's voice cut into my thoughts clearing up the matter of identity.

"Well I'll be damned. This must be the remains of an old roundhouse."

She looked from one confused face to the other.

"Where all the trains would convene and where the tracks could be turned so as to send the train on to its next outgoing destination. It's like a train station. But I thought everything from those days had been removed just as the tracks had."

She walked up closer to the gaping holes where the garage type doors had been and looked down into the dense grass.

"No trace of any track left. Wonder why they left this here."

"Probably because it would cost too much time and money to tear it down. So they just left it. Either way, it makes a good hideout for now."

Sheba ran her hand over the rough moss covered brick. She seemed to be talking to herself as she walked along the building frame.

"Not one trace of graffiti or vandalism. No one's ever been here before I would bet. It looks untouched except by nature herself."

I had collapsed down the minute Cayden walked away to gather branches and twigs. I gazed up at Sheba's back. She stopped as if feeling my stare then turned to face me.

"Oh, you poor thing. You must be thirsty."

She had snapped out of her trance-like state to walk over to the backpack resting a few feet from me and grabbed a big water bottle from it. A lump of green paper caught my eye from within the backpack. The money that had been in Emma's safe for emergencies. Anger filled me again, broiling over my insides like a wave of fire.

She untied my wrists and removed the tape from my mouth after warning me not to scream. I glared at her, snatching the bottle from her outstretched hand, gulping down as much as I could before coughing and sputtering. I wiped my mouth with the back of my hand as Sheba took a swig of the water. Before she placed the bottle back inside the backpack, a glint of something else caught my eye. I leaned over to get a better look as the stone around my neck began to glow. The object inside glowed back in answer to its mate.

"You stole my aunt's necklace! What the hell is wrong with you? Money wasn't enough? That was a family heirloom? You've gone too far, Sheba."

Her eyes widened like someone who's just seen a mountain of shiny gold. She blinked a few times and broke her trance on the stone around my neck to hush me.

"Shh, shh, keep it down! Please! You have to believe me when I say he's taken us both at his mercy. I never wanted it to go this far. I was afraid and dumb. I didn't know there was another way without risking my son's life. I'm so sorry, Jade. I'm going to get you out of here, I swear."

Cayden was walking back toward us with an armload of twigs and branches for a fire.

"Cripes Cayden, it's too hot for a fire and they're gonna know we're here if you light that."

Sheba nodded towards his small brush pile. He straightened up after dropping the last of it and wiped his nose on his sleeve.

"It's a diversion. I'm lighting it tonight to draw them in as we slip out onto the highway, steal a vehicle and skip town."

He glanced at the roundhouse behind us before picking up the dropped load of twigs and bringing them into the building. He leaned down and situated rocks in a small circle before laying the branches within. Sheba rolled her eyes at his back, then stood up to help him.

"Cayden, I really don't think it's a good idea. They'll find us long before night falls."

His voice turned into a growl.

"Listen, we have leverage with Jade as ransom and they won't be able to touch us whether they find us or not. In the meantime, this is the plan! Now back off Sheba, this is my show and I'm calling the shots!"

He briefly waved his gun at her before turning back to the task at hand. I waited until their backs were turned again then made my move. With my hands now free and my mouth clear of tape, I ran like the wind out of our small clearing and into the trees yelling as loud as I could in the hopes anyone would hear.

"Help! Someone please help! I'm over here! Please!"

Loud crunching sounds echoed behind me before strong arms embraced me, pulling me to the ground. Cayden had caught up to me within seconds and clamped his hand down on my mouth. Sheba was right behind him panting heavily by his side. She bent over and placed her hands on her knees to catch her breath.

"Why the hell did you take the tape off her mouth?"

His words were directed at Sheba as she continued to catch her breath.

"You just noticed now? Huh!"

She let out a sarcastic laugh and he glared at her while pulling me to my feet.

"Don't make me shoot you, both of you!"

I struggled free from his hand over my mouth and spit out the frustration and fear that had been compiling for the past several hours.

"Go ahead! Do it, you coward…!"

I had barely spoke the words when his hand pressed down harder, not only blocking my mouth but my nose too, cutting off all oxygen. I lurched my body back trying to break free to no avail.

"Cayden, you're suffocating her! Let her go!"

Sheba was trying to pull his grip from me but he knocked her to the ground. I began kicking and punching at him, connecting numerous times with his skull until he pushed me back onto the ground and started to choke me. I gasped in a quick breath before his hands moved from my face to my neck. Sheba was back pounding at him and hitting him. He backhanded her in the face, knocking her out cold. I fought with all I had but Cayden was stronger.

"You little bitch! You just had to go and ruin it for everyone. Don't you know had you just cooperated I would've set you free? But now you've screwed yourself over."

Little pinpoints of dark matter filled my vision as the surrounding trees and sky molded into one colorful mass. Cayden's body had me pinned down and darkness began to shut everything out like a black curtain. I saw rapid-fire movie-like scenes of my childhood: me running through the backyard at home when I was about six or seven. I was being chased by the neighbor boy and my tiny laughter filled the air like distant echoes. I saw my life at different stages, from elementary school, to birthday parties, to family functions to high school.

Then there was Dylan's face when we first started dating. He was lifting me in the air and twirling me around. And yet my heart was empty even then, I just never knew it. I never wanted to believe someone who made sense to me was completely wrong in the most important ways. A best friend and companion he had been yet both of us were destined for different paths.

My vision changed and Jackson's face floated before me. Every living fiber within me awakened to his look, his touch, his very presence. A single tear rolled out of the corner of my unblinking eyes as they stared hollowed and unseeing at the sky above. I saw now he had been my purpose. All signs had pointed to him long before we met.

I knew this now with such conviction. I loved him like no other and knew his heart was good. Perhaps it was all a part of the gift, or perhaps it was death itself allowing the veil of life's uncertainties to finally lift. Suddenly his face changed and grew older as he looked at me.

Our hair was gray and our faces deeply lined as I realized this vision had not yet happened. A young man joined us on a park bench with a small girl in his arms. The young man looked just like Jackson and the little girl resembled myself in so many ways. I was looking at our children's children. That was the last thing I saw as death took my hand like an old friend and led me home.

Kathleen Wickman

CHAPTER EIGHTEEN — PHANTOM'S CROSSING

"Get your hands off her!"

A rock flew out from the trees and connected with Cayden's head.

"Ow! Son of a bitch!"

Cayden's hands released their death grip to deflect further hits as his eyes scanned the trees for the perpetrator. From the shadows, Sam stepped out with another rock in his hand. He flipped it once in the air and caught it in the same hand. I gulped in air and rolled over onto my side, coughing and sputtering while facing the two men. Through hazy vision I saw Cayden sizing up Sam's plain eccentric clothes and his lack of any kind of weapon other than the rock. Cayden stood to face him squarely, temporarily forgetting his victim lying on the ground.

"Who the hell are you?"

"Someone you can't kill. Step away from her and meet your fate."

The sun was setting fast as Cayden walked over to Sam an evil smirk on his face.

"Hasn't anyone told you farmer boy that you don't bring a knife to a gun fight?"

Sam stood in his place staring back at Cayden with unblinking eyes. He said not a word as Cayden pulled a gun out from the back of his pants and raised it squarely at Sam. I lay there as still as I could. Coughs still wracked my body as I struggled to catch my breath.

Sam caught my look for a brief moment then glanced back at Cayden. I prayed I'd become as invisible as Sam used to be. But right now Sam was not invisible. He was vivid and sharp and angry as he continued to level Cayden with an intense stare.

And much to my amazement, he was visible not only to me, but to Cayden as well. However this was possible, I did not know. One thing I sensed deeply was the fact that I felt connected to him again. I felt the pulse of his life just as much as my own.

"You're not too bright, farmer boy."

And with that he fired at Sam. The first shot made my body jolt. A flock of birds resting in a nearby tree took flight at the loud sound. Cayden's blood drained from his face as he watched in disbelief as Sam continued to stand there, unflinching.

"How the hell...?"

Cayden looked down at his pistol stupidly, then back at Sam.

"I told you I can't be killed. And I'm not a farmer boy. I'm a railway worker who has wielded sledgehammers bigger than your body. Now put down that puny weapon and fight like a real man."

I watched Cayden's mouth quiver ever so slightly at what he was hearing and seeing. He took a hesitant step back.

"I don't believe you!"

He fired again and this time Sam had stepped in front of a tree. The bullet went through him, slamming into the tree trunk behind him causing splinters to fly. Sam shook his head, grinned then looked down at his very solid, very real looking body.

"Nope. Still missed. But keep at it until your bullets run out, by all means."

Cayden turned and bolted for the roundhouse and the backpack full of money he had left behind. Sam was by my side in an instant, kneeling down next to me. The sun was setting quickly.

"Jade! Are you alright?"

My voice was raw and scratchy as I slowly rose to a sitting position.

"Yes, I think so."

I rubbed my neck where Cayden's hands had been. It felt tender and bruised.

"I just need a minute to catch my bearings."

"He's coming back, Jade. I have to get you out of here before he does. Can you stand?"

I reached out for Sam's extended arm and to my never ending surprise grasped flesh and bone. It still baffled me how a ghost could be so tangible.

"Follow me."

"What about Sheba?"

Sheba was still lying motionless in the grass a few feet away.

"We have to leave her. We don't have time, Jade. She'll be fine. She chose her fate and it is to be with Cayden, as evil as he is."

"What if she didn't? What if she wasn't lying and she had no choice? Sam, we can't just leave her. She has a son."

Sam looked frantically in the direction Cayden had run.

"Jade. I sense he'll be back for Sheba any minute. We don't have time to move her."

He reached for my arm as I knelt down by her side. His touch had become cold like a northern December wind. Even though it wasn't quite October, the temperature had begun to drop and darkness was setting in fast. Sheba let out a soft moan.

"Jade come on! He's coming!"

My head jerked up at the sound of branches cracking. I jumped to my feet and followed Sam through the clearing. No sooner did I run five yards when my foot caught the edge of a rock. In my fervor I had looked back over my shoulder to see where Cayden was and did not notice it jutting out of the ground.

My arms went flailing out as I tumbled forward. I let out a yelp of surprise before connecting with the earth once again. Sam stopped at the sound of my voice and started running back to me. But it was too late. Cayden had reached me and his tone was visceral when he spoke.

"Say goodnight princess."

I could just make out the shape of his face in the twilight. But I could see the gun he held plain as day. I could do nothing but stare wide-eyed back at it. As if on cue, a train whistle tore through the still night air alarming all three of us.

I turned my gaze to Sam and his surprise matched mine. The whistle shrilled again, sending shivers up my spine. The tracks that used to run through these parts were long gone. Where the hell was the train coming from?

The soft rumbling that accompanied the first shrill grew louder. The ground began to shake violently as if a monster was charging through the forest. Cayden stopped jerking his head in all directions in an attempt to locate the origin when he saw the shocked look on my face. He slowly turned around and screamed.

Sam pulled me up underneath my arms, dragging me out of the way as a blinding light seared through the trees. It looked just like Paulding Light the way it glowed so brilliant but instead of diminishing mysteriously, the light grew more and more vicious as it approached us. Smoke belched from its large stack as the outline of the train's body became conspicuous. And a massive body it was. I stared in awe as the dark phantom approached, metal grates bared like sharp teeth.

"It's Raven!"

Sam shouted then wrapped his arms tighter around me as we hunched in a nearby bed of wilting ragweed out of Raven's path.

"Hold on Jade!" He yelled above the roar.

She was close now. I could almost feel her hot breath of smoke as she rounded the corner on invisible rails. Cayden dropped the backpack and gun and started running like mad in the opposite direction. Raven was right on his heels.

She charged past Sam and myself as we huddled together. It was incredible to discern whether the wind had suddenly picked up or if it was truly Raven's speed that caused my hair to fly behind me in a twisted, wild mess of curls. I blinked rapidly not daring to miss a thing. Sam's voice was tiny in the roaring wind and thunder of the train.

"He's running towards the ravine. If he doesn't stop, he'll go right off!"

It was hard to see anything now in the pitch black of night. Raven's glow emitted the only semblance of light as she went past. I hesitantly walked out behind her in time to hear a terrified scream. I looked back to where we had been hiding but Sam was no longer there.

Raven had cornered another invisible rail and headed north through a dense cluster of trees. She never damaged a single branch as her roar faded and eventually vanished into the great beyond. Nothing seemed disturbed in her wake. Crickets chirped softly in the far off distance and the muffled rush of water filled my ears. Everything else was quiet and untouched.

"Sam!"

I hollered a few more times but heard nothing. A hand clamped down on my shoulder. I jerked my body around in surprise.

"Sheba! You scared me."

"Where's Cayden?"

Her tone was hesitant and leery but her eyes were pleading and frightened. My mouth dropped open and before I could answer her, she asked me again.

"What happened? What was that thing? What did you do to him?"

"Nothing. I did nothing." I stammered.

"He's dead." Sam answered her question but it fell on deaf ears as she continued to plead with me.

He appeared behind me now. I turned to face him as he went on.

"He ran off the cliff in terror of Raven. He landed in the river below. He's gone."

"Jade, answer me!" Sheba was trembling now, demanding an explanation.

I looked back at her with unabashed relief and exhaustion in my voice.

"He's dead."

She stared at me for a few seconds trying to register what I had meant. Then she took a few steps away and dropped down onto her knees. She rubbed her hands over her face then cupped them over her mouth in a gesture of shock over what she had just seen. The three of us eventually made a slow trek back to the old remains of the roundhouse.

I was sore, tired, thirsty, hungry and anxious to soak in a hot bathtub for the remainder of the night. When we reached the brick building, I leaned against the stone to catch my breath. My hand brushed the cold rough edge. Suddenly, my body went rigid. In a matter of seconds, the sun was up again, barely. It appeared to be late afternoon by the setting sun.

There were voices everywhere. The building I was just standing next to was completely restored and empty of any trains except for one. She was massive and pitch black; standing there patiently awaiting orders like a metal soldier. This had to be Raven.

I looked around for Sam but only saw hundreds of unfamiliar faces. Sheba was nowhere to be seen, either. They all had deep voices or so it sounded, as they all blended together in my ears. Their words were incomprehensible but the clipped edge of intent was clear.

Danger was looming. That much was obvious. With dirt and grime on their faces, they scrambled in every direction, some of them running right through me as I stood by the outer wall next to Raven.

"Get her out of here! Go!"

I jumped as a large muscled man in overalls yelled to the engineer. The engineer gave a quick wave of his cap in response. Another head peered out at a different window. This face I recognized just barely.

Sam was sweaty and dirt stained, his face weary from long hours of preparation and hard labor. This was the shipment I had heard about, the one that finally provoked the Archaleux to retaliate. The materials on Raven were going for construction on a new developing railroad town that was to expand on the current one of Watersmeet. A land long claimed by the natives. Not just any land, but holy land. Protected land, sacred and untouched.

Rage filled the local tribesmen. I could feel that rage now as it coursed through my being. I waved to Sam and hollered out but he looked right through me. A strange instinct told me to run through the open valley ahead of Raven.

I ran as fast as my feet would carry me temporarily forgetting about Sam. I heard loud voices coming from a makeshift camp settlement nearby. Only then did my feet slow and I walked inside the first tent to listen. A young boy had come running into the camp just ahead of me.

"They're almost here!"

He went on to say revenge was painted on their faces for taking what had once belonged to them, their weapons were held staunchly in their hands, swinging them as their pounding footsteps rattled the earth. The first gunshots rang out and I left the tent in time to witness a large mass of war-painted men tear through the trees towards Raven. I continued to run down the valley as Raven hauled her heavy load and slowly gained speed behind me, catching up with every chug. Arrows whizzed past my head.

Some of them ripped through me but I felt nothing. Only redemption pounded through my veins. The raw emotions swirling inside me felt not so much of my own, but of those around me. This time, I wasn't just watching the past unfold; I was living it.

Feeling what they felt, doing what they did. None of it made any sense to me as I kept running ahead of Raven. Fighting was taking place on both sides of the track now, and to my horror, I watched as men were butchered mere feet from me. I clamped my hand to my mouth and kept running.

Sam was firing shots back trying desperately to keep the warriors from climbing the train. One had evaded Sam's attention and snuck up the narrow ledge until he was close enough to wield his machete at Sam's head. Sam was engrossed with something ahead of him. I screamed and ran towards the train as the warrior swung the axe.

Every single fiber of my being surged into one immense super cell as I charged at the warrior, screaming at the top of my lungs. My body suddenly felt light, swift and impossibly fast like the wind as I launched myself an incredible distance to connect with his bare mahogany chest just as Sam pulled his head inside the train and slammed on the break switch. I grabbed a hold of something metal and obtrusive just as the train lurched. My body physically slammed into the warrior's as he fought to hang on.

"Don't you touch him!"

I screamed at the warrior, his intent fixated on Sam's re-protruding head. Sam was still unaware of the close call he had and was ignorant of the threat that still remained behind him. The warrior failed to see me but he indeed felt something. For as my body had hit his, I had watched as his eyes widened in surprise. I slammed my fist into his chest and once again made contact. The warrior let go of his grip and dropped to the ground as Sam finally noticed the danger he was in.

The warrior retreated into the woods just as Sam fired his shot missing him by yards. I could see he wasn't concerned as much about what had just happened behind him but by what was happening in front of him. I took my eyes off of him to look ahead. My mouth dropped open and I almost fell from the train at the sight before me.

Ahead was the most decorative native in the group. A large man with a massive headdress and sparkling necklace of stone stood up the hill from the train's path. He stood tall and proud, unmoving as a statue in the middle of the tracks not more than ninety yards in front of Raven. He was all muscle and shone in the setting sun like a gladiator from the Roman Empire.

I knew he had to be the one they called Keeja, chief of the Archaleux tribe. In his outstretched hand he held something that glowed majestically in the fading glory of daylight. The emerald green glow grew brighter as he waved it across the tracks and shouted to the heavens. The sun hurried its descent beyond the trees evading the tragedy that was about to befall this once peaceful town.

His voice booming, he yelled at the train as the ground began to shake. The train had picked up too much speed by the time Sam had switched on the breaks. Raven would not be able to stop in time as the tracks ahead cracked in two before our very eyes. Keeja walked off the tracks and stood watching nearby as Raven barreled down.

Sam jumped out and I followed suit. We hit the ground hard and both gained our feet but someone blocked our escape. She nearly blended into the trees but as we approached, she stepped forward with anger in her brilliant sky blue eyes. That anger was directed at Sam. She was tall and graceful, like a statue. Her hair was pulled back and hidden under a velvet hood. She wore a warrior's belt for which she now reached down and grabbed a knife from it.

"Sam."

Worry filled my voice but Sam never took his eyes off of the woman. I knew he could not hear or see me as we both continued standing there. Her eyes were locked onto Sam's and were filled with contempt. Her arm flung back with the knife still clutched tightly in her hand as she began to charge towards us.

I stood there frozen in fear then jolted as an explosion rang violently through my ears. The woman's face went completely white as the knife slowly fell to the ground. She grabbed her chest and dropped to her knees. I jerked my head over at Sam to see him standing there with a sullen look on his face as he slowly lowered the gun to his side.

Another terrifying scream tore through the surrounding trees. Sam and I turned to see Keeja running towards us. The sight of the woman's ailing body crumpled on the ground his primary focus. As he reached her side and cradled her head in his hands, an intense sadness filled my soul. The overwhelming ache I swore I had felt before. I dropped my head and bent over slightly to try and relieve the tightness I felt inside.

It was then I remembered when and where I had felt this way before. The evening Nikki and Heather first brought me to see Paulding Light. The first time I saw Sam. He had been a silhouette of a man holding a lantern in the blinding white ghost light of Raven.

This had to be where the curse was first born as I watched in horror as Keeja turned his ravaged face from the woman to Sam after his attempt to heal her went forsaken. Something around the woman's neck began to glow. And as if in response so did the stone in Keeja's hand. He raised it once more and shouted the words that have haunted Sam's family for generations to come. The ground swayed under my feet as dizziness over took me. All sound grew muffled and distant except the sound of Keeja's voice. I heard the strange language and somehow understood exactly what Keeja was saying.

"May you find the one for which to make you whole, give you new life, only for her to be taken from you as you have done to me!"

Everything around us seemed to halt. Noise, movement, everything as Keeja continued holding her. His mouth never opened again yet I heard his heart speak.

"My beloved Sirene. May twenty-five angels guide your spirit home for each year of life you were given. And may someday our souls be one again."

I knew now Sam had simply been in the wrong place at the wrong time the day the curse was born. I could see now Keeja had been stricken with a delirious grief that ran much, much deeper than the death of his loved one, Sirene. This is a great chief who is watching his holy land being taken from him. His home is being destroyed. And now, his soul mate has been killed even though she instigated the attack on Sam. It doesn't matter in his eyes that Sam was just defending himself. He's out for revenge because he's furious at what Sam symbolizes. Sam's people in Keeja's mind had brought death, despair and loss of freedom. The magic he holds in his hand has made him drunk with power. There is no turning back. Dark clouds had moved in and a rolling thunder rippled through the sky, breaking my trance on Keeja and turning my attention heavenward. Sam had torn his fixation off of Keeja too and looked up. Another loud crack followed by a horrific crashing sound had my hands flying up to block my ears. I whipped around to see Raven had crossed the broken tracks and began to derail.

Metal grinded against metal as she buckled under the collision. Men began fleeing everywhere to escape her impending fall from grace. Two sidecars near us lurched sideways and cracked free from the others heading directly towards where Sam and I stood. I screamed in terror and reached for Sam as he too began running in the direction where Keeja had stood.

But both chief and woman had disappeared. A large dark shadow loomed over us, completely blocking out any remaining light of day. I stole a glance back to see the railcar about to topple us. I tried reaching for Sam but my hand went through his body as his feet carried him ahead of me.

The ground shook violently and explosions jolted my body as the railcar crashed just feet behind us, tearing down trees in its path with the velocity with which it skidded towards us. Just then Sam tripped on some dense brush and went reeling down hard knocking the breath clear out of him. I stopped in a frantic attempt to pull him up but once again I couldn't make contact. He still did not know I was even there for I was trapped in the past, his present, helplessly watching his fate unfold before my eyes.

As the train careened at us all I could do was simply drop my body over his. I felt him take his last breath seconds before the train crushed us.

***

Phantom's Crossing

I've experienced a few dreams in my lifetime where they were so incredibly surreal it took me a moment upon waking up to distinguish what was real and what had been the dream. This was one of those moments as I found myself standing beside Sam's outstretched body on a makeshift gurney. Was I back in reality or was I still having a vision? For a split second I felt a suffocating panic well up in my throat at the prospect that maybe I had just died, too.

Could this really be the end? I glanced around feverishly at my surroundings and ascertained that I was standing in a white tent. No one was in it except Sam and myself who continued to lie motionless on the gurney. His head was bandaged and his right leg appeared to be broken.

His face was blood stained and purplish in color. His eyes were closed. The panic subsided as it suddenly occurred to me that I had not died and that my vision had not ended. Relief washed through me in also realizing that Sam had not died either as a soft moan escaped his cracked lips. I reached for his hand but felt nothing but air.

His fingers twitched at the soft breeze my touch created. I had no concept of time or space. I knew what events had just happened that led us here, why Sam was hurt but could not recall when or how we got here, or how much time had passed. All I knew was that it was dark outside. When I closed my eyes for one brief moment only to open them again, sunlight streamed in to the tent and people were bustling about.

I was still standing in the same spot, looking down at Sam's still form. Watching the sheet covering his chest slowly rise and fall giving the only indication of life. Sam's face looked much better. The blood had been wiped away at some point and he had been given fresh garments and clean sheets. But his injuries still looked to be serious.

I stood there for God knows how many hours, days, listening to others around us speak of Sam's accident, oblivious to my presence. Every now and then something would catch my attention.

"Not sure what else we can do for him. He's incredibly lucky to have made it this long." A deep voice said.

"Does Grace know?" This voice was soft, feminine.

"Yes. She's in an infirmary herself and cannot travel until their child is born." The deep voice answered her.

A few seconds, minutes, days, weeks, however long it truly was, passed by. I once again picked up on voices and words being whispered inside the tent. The doctor was checking on Sam's condition and marveling at his survival.

"Lucky man. How that train stopped just inches from crushing him completely."

"Yes, doctor. We found him just beyond a large oak tree that inevitably saved his life. The large trunk stopped the railcar in its path. We found debris all around him yet…" A young male voice replied.

"Go on. What was it you were about to say?"

The young man hesitated.

"Well doctor, it's rather peculiar really. The destruction in the car's path was devastating and yet there was literally nothing on or near Sam's body when we found him. No metal, debris, branches…it looked as if he were protected in some kind of bubble. The area around him was clear."

They were talking about Sam's condition as the room faded away again along with voices that grew ever softer.

"…leg broken by his fall down a small hill in his attempt to escape the train. Head injuries from the rocks he crashed into…"

I had tried protecting Sam. My mind wandered and my brow furrowed. Could I have been his saving grace? His guardian angel? It was absurd and impossible. But a nice thought indeed. My face softened as I looked back down at Sam's face.

I rested my eyes for a moment then blinked in surprise to see Sam staring wide-eyed back at me. I smiled at him, but he just stared in confusion.

"My wife. Where's my wife?"

In such clarity as I'd never heard him speak, Sam had awoken and was completely alert, if not somewhat alarmed. An orderly nearby noticed and called for help.

"Nurse, get over here! He's awake!"

A man and woman approached Sam's bedside and tried calming him down as he continued pleading for his wife. But there was no consoling him.

"She's fine. Now you must relax or you'll bust your bandages open."

"I need to see her. And the baby, where's my child?"

They kept telling him over and over that Grace was fine but never answered his question about the baby.

"Everything's okay, Sam. You must lie still." The nurse was trying to comfort him in vain.

"Where are they?"

The nurse wiped his brow with a wet washcloth and hushed him quietly in reply. She gave him something that apparently made him sleepy. Within moments, Sam calmed down and fell back into a deep sleep. When the noise of day and harshness of light faded to be replaced with a peaceful silence of night, the nurse returned to check on Sam.

He was awake again and staring stoically up at the ceiling. She said not a word as she fussed over him. Checking on bandages and attempting to feed him soup. Sam opened his mouth only to ask the same questions again. My heart ached at the desperation in his weak voice.

"Please. I know something's wrong. I know you're not telling me the truth. I must know. Please tell me where my wife and child are."

The young nurse hesitated and her face pinched tight at the intensity in his eyes. There was indeed something she didn't want to say. But Sam would not give up. He needed to know his family was safe. In a hushed tone I myself barely heard, she answered him, her face mere inches from his. I moved in closer to hear her.

"Grace delivered a healthy baby boy two days ago. She was in route to be here by this afternoon against her doctor's wishes so soon after having a baby. Her and baby Elijah made the journey with her cousin Edward as chaperon..."

She trailed off not wanting to finish. But Sam grabbed her arm and shook her with surprising strength.

"You must tell me." His eyes implored hers.

She swallowed hard and went on.

"They were ambushed by highway robbers. Something went terribly wrong and Grace was shot. They were all killed, Sam. I really didn't want to be the one to tell you. I'm so sorry."

Her voice cracked as she stood there helplessly, watching Sam as he digested her words. His head turned slowly in my direction as he looked right through me. I felt his pain all the way down to my toes as I stood there helplessly. The room grew darker again as my body suddenly became very cold. Strange how I could feel anything at all if this was only a vision. Before another day could dawn over the valley, Sam had lost his will to live and died that very night.

Kathleen Wickman

CHAPTER NINETEEN — THE ULTIMATE SACRIFICE

"Jade! Jade! Wake up!"

In a knee-jerk reaction mixed with irritation at the double time rhythm her hollering had incurred upon my heart I had snapped at her in response.

"WHAT?!"

My heart was pounding rather loudly in my chest as I jolted awake at Sheba's incessant jostling of my shoulder. *Where the hell was I now?* My brain was backfiring in its feeble attempt to register present day and time.

"You scared the shit out of me!"

I grabbed at my chest while sitting up and rested my back against the cold stone wall of the roundhouse.

"I scared you? Are you serious? You passed out and I couldn't wake you. Your eyes had rolled back in your head and I *scared* you?!"

I rubbed my head and dislodged a few dried leaves that had stuck to my hair.

"I don't know what happened." My breathing settled as did my heart as everything came into focus.

Sam was standing over me looking down with worry on his face. He knelt down before me and brushed some dirt from my check. His hand felt warm and full of love. I smiled weakly up into his face.

"Are you alright?"

Sheba's voice was strained as she implored my face.

"Yes, yes I'm fine. How long have I been out?"

"Well, it seemed like hours but was only a matter of minutes actually."

"Really?"

I looked up at her, trying to stand. I felt I had been gone for days. My gaze locked onto Sam's again as he stood with me.

"How is it I can feel you again?"

He smiled his beautiful breathtaking smile and answered humbly.

"Because you have saved me. And it's almost time for me to go."

"What are you talking about?"

Sheba had one eyebrow raised and stared at me as if I had hit my head. I ignored her not wanting to let go of Sam's touch as he continued to hold my hand.

"We're all a part of one another, connected in more ways than most of us realize. We all bleed, we all cry, we all love, and eventually we all die. I felt you that day Raven went off her tracks. I felt your spirit lying next to me. You had a purpose even then, before you were even born."

He laughed in amazement at his own words.

"Jade, this life is so much more complex than we even know. You only see one third of its mysteries but someday, when you take your final breaths, you'll see it all. And it will all make sense to you. I just want to thank you for everything."

"You *saw* my vision? You saw me there?"

"I felt everything you were going through while lying here unconscious. And in your vision you felt everything I did at that time. Like I said, we are all connected but you and I more so because of your gift. I did not see you that day on the tracks, but I did feel something guiding me. And now I know it was you.

My son had lived after all. Here all this time I had thought he was killed in the roadside ambush. They had got it wrong, Jade. He wasn't even with Grace. He had been left behind with a friend as she and Edward made their journey to see me. I knew it the moment I saw Jackson walk into your house that day wearing his badge displaying *my* last name. The pieces just fell into place."

He took a step closer so that our bodies were mere inches apart. I looked up into his deep clear gray eyes wondering what else he was about to say. But instead, he leaned down and softly kissed my lips, startling me and sending my heart into arrhythmia again. I stumbled back a step when he broke the kiss as he smiled down at me.

"Thank you." Was all he said.

He faded again into nothing as sound broke through the silence of the night.

"Jackson!" I called out at the sight of him clearing the trees.

The moon was full and bright in the night sky, casting light on the field we were standing in. He was in full uniform with flashlight swinging. I started to walk quickly towards him as he in turn took hasty steps towards me. Worry mixed with relief played across his face.

I stopped abruptly just in front of him, hands by my side, as he reached out with both of his to clasp my shoulders then enfolded me in a warm hug. My eyes drooped slightly as my mind wandered back to the last dreadful hours. Immense relief flooded through me at how lucky I truly had been to escape with my life.

"Jade! Are you hurt? Should I call for an ambulance?"

"No ambulance. I'm not hurt, really."

He pulled away to level me with that intense stare of his trying to decipher whether I was being honest or not. I smiled weakly in reassurance. I wasn't hurt but the last few hours had left me drained and empty. I wouldn't have fought him if he dragged me home by one arm, just so long as I didn't have to move anymore.

My legs were stiff and sore and I plopped down on a nearby stump to rub them. Jackson knelt down beside me.

"Thanks to Gus I knew exactly where you were. Or thanks to Sam rather. They tracked me down near your cabin as I set out searching for you. I got here as quick as I could."

Jackson chuckled softly at the weird course of events that led him here.

"I trusted him, Jade. As crazy as his story sounded that a ghost named Sam knew where you were, I trusted. We sent patrol cars out and cornered Cayden on the highway. One in front and I was following behind. All I cared about was getting to you. When I reached the creek at the bottom of the clearing, I heard that unearthly train whistle. There aren't any tracks left in this area. The sound of it made my blood run cold.

Gus directed myself and the other officers to where Cayden had fallen into the river. We found his body a few miles downriver from here. Your uncle and the other officers are down there now recovering the body. Once he was out of the equation, I knew it was time to move in and find you. We're still searching for Sheba as well. I feel she's in on this somehow.

I turned around to look where she had last been standing a few feet behind me but she was now gone. She must have run away when Jackson approached.

"She was just here Jackson a second ago. She must've bolted when she saw you coming. Running away isn't conducive for an innocent person, that's for sure. Sam tried to stop me when we escaped from Cayden's cabin. I think he was trying to tell me something, or warn me. We've got to find her."

"Jackson, she's been embezzling from my aunt for quite some time now. Cayden was the one who shot Emma and robbed the safe in her office. Sheba says she had nothing to do with it but I'm not so sure."

He nodded his head in agreement.

"I linked the robbery to Cayden after we couldn't find him either. He's been up to no good from the very start. If Sheba is capable to abandon reason for insanity in order to steal from her friend's business, she's capable of anything."

Just a few miles through dense trees and up the valley was the guardrail where many had once convened to witness Paulding Light and its mysteries. No one was there now I was sure given the threat to public safety Cayden had inflicted. I thought of Raven and Sam and couldn't help but wonder if I'd see either one again.

"We will find her, Jade. Come on. Let's get you out of here. Your uncle will be pleased to know you are safe."

He radioed Marcus and told him as much and gave his location.

"We're leaving now, Marcus and we will meet you on Robbins Pond road in twenty-five minutes."

Marcus insisted on speaking to me so that I could assure him that I was fine and in no need of medical attention. He didn't sound too pleased that Jackson had broken off from the main search group to go off on his own to find me and told him as much in a brief exchange. But Jackson seemed to expect such reaction.

After the radio contact ended, Jackson shook his head and gave me a side-ways look.

"I used to be a 'color inside the lines, by the book' cop until you came along. Shit, now I'm breaking all kinds of codes. Your uncle is going to have my head on a platter when we get back."

I smiled at his attempt at light humor.

"I'm sure it won't come to that. What more could happen? Cayden was the real threat and now he's gone. I'm glad I could remove some starch from your stiff blue-blood collar of yours."

He laughed at that but just as quickly, it died and his face returned to business again.

"Still, I know I shouldn't have abandoned everyone to look for you. But when Gus told me where to find you, I didn't want to waste another second. You've become too important to me. I had to see for myself that you were safe."

I looked up into his face and smiled reassuringly.

"And safe I am. Take me home please, Jackson."

I smiled softly and leaned my head into his chest as he put his arm around my shoulders. He hesitated for a second while glancing around the area one last time. He appeared to be listening to the night for any type of sound before guiding me from the tiny moonlit clearing into the shadows of the forest beyond.

Kathleen Wickman

CHAPTER TWENTY — DO OR DIE

The walk back to Robbins Pond road seemed to take forever. The sound of our crunching feet on twigs grew louder and more omnipresent the further we went into the forest. The moon's glorious brightness cut through openings in the blanket of leaves overhead and led the way as we made our journey out of the madness the day had been.

I began to drift into a sort of daze letting Jackson guide me with the arm that still remained secure around my shoulders. My mind played back all that had happened. It was only when Jackson's grip tightened sharply around me that I snapped to attention. His footsteps stopped abruptly as did mine. He let me go and to my alarm, I watched as he reached quietly for his holstered weapon. My eyes grew wide as they met his steely ones. Both his hands held firmly onto the gun as he slowly turned around to look into the shadows. I was now standing behind him in rigid fear of something only he could detect.

"Jackson, what is it?"

I had taken three steps back when he had reached for his gun. My back now bumped into a large boulder and I stood there with eyes wide open. He turned my way as his gaze locked onto the rock behind me. His next words were whispered sternly.

"Get behind me, Jade. Come here, now!"

I immediately took one hasty step towards him when something cold and hard pressed into my back.

"Don't move, Jade. I don't want to hurt you, but I will if I have to."

It was Sheba. She had been hiding behind the boulder and now stepped out from its protection to point what I know knew to be a gun into the small of my back.

"I need something from both of you. Jackson, you're going to help me escape by leading me to your car and driving us out of here. I know I'm surrounded and won't be able to get out without your help. And Jade, you're going to help me heal my son. There's magic in your blood. Your aunt told you that you are descended from the Ottawa nation but in truth, you are from the phantom tribe, Archaleux. Keeja's blood runs through your veins. I've read all about the Wounded Healer's stone. It only answers to one Shaman or leader by glowing emerald. You are that leader now. I saw it glow around your neck the day I was standing outside Emma's office. The day I learned that she kept the second stone hidden in her safe. All I needed were the stones because stealing money was no longer enough. I have one in the backpack I salvaged when Jackson came to your rescue. The other, well…the other you're wearing of course."

Her words were like a twisted poison in my ear as she spoke them from behind. Without turning around to face her, I shook my head incredulously.

"Have you gone mad? I can't help you or your son! What makes you think I know anything about magic stones or how to use them?"

She hadn't restrained me physically except by holding the gun to my back until I said these words. I felt her free hand reach around from behind and grab me around the throat, pulling me back into her chest. Like fireworks shooting across a clear sky, another vision hit me so hard—the air left my lungs and in one split second, all revealed itself.

I saw Annabelle walk to the front door and open it.

"What are you doing here?"

"Is that anyway to greet a friend and co-worker? I'm here to talk, Annie, about today."

Sheba's breath was heavy with the stench of whiskey.

"There's nothing you can say, Sheba. I've decided to tell Emma as soon as she and Marcus get back from their vacation. I don't believe you when you say you're done. That you won't steal from her anymore. I have to do the right thing."

"Look, I only did it for my son."

"Yes, you've already told me your justification to your crime. But it is still a crime, Sheba. Why don't you get that? Now please leave."

Instead of leaving, Sheba pushed passed Annabelle and sat down on the couch.

"Five minutes. Please Annie, just hear me out. I'm asking you as a friend."

Annabelle walked back into the room and stared incredulously at Sheba's placid demeanor.

"We're not friends. We stopped being friends the second you stole from someone who trusted you and supported you."

"I'm not leaving until you hear me out."

"Jackson will be back any second Sheba."

"No, he won't. I just watched his truck leave five minutes ago. I know you two are fighting. He won't be back any time soon."

"I'm calling the police then. And when they get here, not only will you be charged with assault but also with embezzling."

"Assault? I haven't touched you! You call the cops Annie, you'll regret it."

But Annabelle was already making her way to the phone. She heard Sheba jump off the couch and run at her to stop her. In a flash, Annabelle avoided being tackled and ran into the master bedroom to grab the gun Jackson kept in the nightstand. Sheba threw up her hands in surrender as Annabelle leveled the gun at her chest.

"Back off Sheba!"

"Okay, okay. I'm leaving."

They slowly made their way back down the hallway. Sheba walking backwards, hands up in the air as Annabelle drove her towards the front door. When they reached it Sheba stopped.

"Keep moving, Sheba. I mean it. I'll shoot."

"No. You won't. I know you, Annie. You're too soft and sweet. You don't have it in you. Look at you. Your hand is starting to shake and beads of sweat are appearing on your forehead. You can't kill me."

Annabelle let out a screech as Sheba lunged at her and for a brief moment both women had their hands locked on the gun as it now pointed at the ceiling. Sheba shoved against Annie's tiny frame, knocking her backwards. She caught herself before hitting the floor as Sheba gained control of the *weapon and turned it on her. Annabelle back-stepped to the mantle. Her head whipped around for something to use. Her eyes locked onto the figurine of the dancing man and woman resting on the mantle. With both hands Annabelle clutched it, her only feeble shield and weapon.*

"Don't do this! It's not worth it Sheba. You're drunk and unreasonable right now. Just drop the gun!"

"Annie, you know too much. I'm not going to jail and I know I can't trust you to keep your mouth shut. It's a pity, really, that you had to stumble in on me stealing from Emma. If only you hadn't called me on it, I might have forgiven you. But now you see, I have to keep you quiet forever. I refuse to go to jail."

"Fine. I won't say anything. You have my word."

"I don't believe you."

"Jackson will figure it out. He'll know you did it. You underestimate him."

"Jackson is the one who killed you. Or so it will seem to the world. Now, I know you know where the magnanimous hiding spot is for the legendary emerald stones. Tell me now. If they can't cure my son, I'll at least be able to sell them on the black market and be able to keep up with his health bills. Robbing the restaurant just isn't cutting it."

"I'll never tell you."

"Pity. I must say. Fine. I'll find out on my own. I have my ways. The fact that you and Jackson are fighting makes it so much better for my cover.

He was supposed to be my happily ever after until you came along. Now I'm taking it back from you."

"You're a married woman lusting after another woman's man. How low can you get, Sheba?"

Annabelle scoffed vindictively before continuing.

"Besides, he wouldn't touch you with a ten foot pole. He told me so. I know you don't have it in you Sheba to pull that trigger. Just put it down before you do something stupid."

"You little bitch."

Annabelle could see she was wrong in her approach and proceeded to throw the figurine at Sheba's head and run but the shot rang out before she could release it. Her beautiful lithe body crumpled to the floor like paper mache. Sheba pulled on the base of her black gloves after gently placing the pistol on the floor by Annabelle's feet. She thought of returning it back to Annie after fighting it from her grip but thought better of it.

Sheba knew deep down Jackson loved her. He had to love her. He just had to. It didn't matter that they had never been together or exchanged affectionate niceties. He never touched her in the way he used to touch Annie.

But Sheba knew the first day he smiled at her, that he loved her. She just knew. He had to love her. Now it was time to rip the place apart and find the stones.

I had come to from my trance and leveled Sheba with my newfound findings.

"It was you! You killed Annie! She knew about the embezzling when you had first started stealing from my aunt. She caught you red handed and so you killed her.

You've been jealous of her all along, as you have been with me."

I could see over my shoulder her face registering with surprise but only for a second before twisting into anger. She bent down momentarily to grab the black backpack she had left near the rock.

"Did your little ghost friend tell you that? It doesn't matter now. You will do as your told. You will help me, Jade. I promise to let you go afterwards. I have no reason to kill you. Once my son is healed, we are leaving to a place where no one will find us. All you have to do is wave the stones over his body."

This entire exchange from the second Sheba walked out from behind the rock until this moment seemed like hours, and yet only minutes had passed. I recalled Cayden luring Sheba to the camp by using their son as bait. He had told her Isaac was hidden in a safe place. It was obvious to me now that she was in on it from the start and their charade was to make me trust her so I would willingly go with her without a fuss.

That was what Sam was trying to warn me about when we sped off on the four-wheeler. He had known she was taking me back into Cayden's trap. And chances are, she knew where their son was.

Jackson had remained quiet during our little exchange but kept his gun focused on her. His face hadn't changed except when I went into my trance.

The last thing I saw before I phased out was his eyes grow wide in alarm as the blood drained from my face. I'm sure he must've thought I was about to pass out for that is how it feels when I have visions and yet I kept my balance and stayed standing.

Sheba kept a tight grip around my neck with the crook of her arm and changed the aim of her pistol from my back to Jackson's chest.

"Drop your gun, Jackson and lead us to your vehicle."

To my horror, she placed the gun against my temple and commanded him again.

"Last chance. Drop it or she's done."

"I thought you needed her Sheba to heal your son."

"As long as I have the stones, I'll take my chances. One thing I know for sure is I'm not going to jail and if I have to kill her or you in order to keep that true, so be it."

He waited no more for an opportunity to strike. Abiding her wishes, he dropped his gun and kept his empty hands shoulder high in surrender. She told me to walk as we made our way towards him. When we got two steps away she stopped.

"Turn around and keep your hands up."

He did as he was told.

My heart was pounding loudly in my chest at this point.

Sam, I need you! Help us, please. I screamed the words in my head.

Just then, a hauntingly familiar voice drifted ever so lightly upon the night breeze. Beautiful and smooth like honey. It was Stephanie's voice speaking familiar words of so long ago. Words I had yet to figure out or comprehend at the time but now understood. No one else seem to hear it but me for none reacted as I did.

"Take heed of your gift, Jade. For with its powers, there is a price to be paid."

"What price, Steph?" I had asked all those months ago.

"His life." She was speaking of Jackson. In her one moment of clairvoyance, before saying good-bye, she had been referring to Jackson. My heart told me so as her voice died on the wind. A single tear escaped from my eye and rolled down my cheek.

Sheba had taken the spare weapon out of Jackson's back holster and searched him for others he may have harbored. When she was satisfied that he was un-armed, she threw his weapons as hard as she could into the darkness behind us and forced him to lead the way. She made sure he walked a few yards ahead of us so as not to turn around and try to take her by surprise.

Another voice cut through my mind. It was Sam. Shrill and sharp he called to me.

"Don't let her take you, Jade! It's all over if you get into that car with her."

I turned my head sideways to see him walking with us. We were nearing Robbins Pond road where Jackson's squad car was parked. Jackson spoke up at that point, unaware of Sam's presence as was Sheba.

"Sheba, you can't win this. My unit is waiting for us. They won't let you pass."

"If you haven't noticed my dear, I'm in control here. So long as I keep your precious angel under my hand of fate, they will let us pass."

I spared a glance at Sam again and his face mirrored mine. Both of us had suffered long enough losing the ones we loved to hands of fate. It was time to cut that hand off. It ends with me. Strong conviction mirrored our faces.

I'm with you. You can do this. Are you ready?

I heard his words in my head and nodded '*Yes*'. With a look of pure concentration and determination, he swung with all his might and connected with Sheba.

"Oh!"

She let out a startled yelp, releasing me and stumbling backwards. This bought me enough time to wrestle for the gun in her upraised hand as she fought to gain balance. Her build was bigger than mine and she had more muscle mass than me, which made things rather difficult in securing the weapon from her. But the mere fact that my life was on the line gave me a surge of adrenaline. With a burst of strength, I managed to lower her arm down. My knee shot up and connected with her stomach then my elbow with her face.

I was entirely filled with red-hot anger at all that she had done, all that she planned to do. I resolved not to go down without a solid fight. Her fist reared up and smashed me in the face making me see spots as I reeled back. Without a second lost she aimed the gun at my chest as Jackson ran with all he had stepping in between us, holding me out of harm's way just as the sound of gunfire echoed through the night.

Kathleen Wickman

CHAPTER TWENTY-ONE — BROKEN

I lunged at her again just as Jackson hit the ground hard. She was temporarily stunned to see she had missed her target and hit her dearly beloved instead. I shoved down the panic pushing inside my chest and tackled her to the ground. Our bodies were twisting and rolling on the rocky dirt floor as I desperately tore at the gun in her hand. Our arms were tangled together as something warm dripped down my face and threatened to blind me as it neared my eyes.

But I blinked it away while slamming her hand down on the ground in an effort to dislodge the weapon. In one last ditch effort I tried twisting her arm to get her to drop it. Another loud crack ripped through the night sky jarring my body with it. We stared at one another, eyes both wide and riveted in surprise. Then slowly a glaze crossed over Sheba's stare and dark shadows replaced the light in her eyes as life's candle began to burn out.

I let go of her and dropped backwards propping the upper half of my body up by my elbows. I watched as Sheba closed her eyes for the last time. Her spirit appeared and stood next to an empty body. She looked down at what she had once been. Then looked up at me.

"Jade!" Her voice was hollow and confused.

Pity washed through me and I looked back sorrowfully but said nothing.

"What's happening Jade?"

"You don't belong here anymore."

Her brows knitted together at my words then she began wailing.

"I can't see Jade. Where are you? I can't see! It's so dark all of a sudden. Jade!"

I turned my head away as her voice and spirit began to fade into the night. She was searching for something she could not find. I prayed she would not be lost and blind forever. That forgiveness would find her on the other side.

When I turned back she was gone. I wiped what had been blood dripping down my face and crawled over to Jackson's still form. I saw instantly that he had been hit in his side.

"Jackson!"

I shook him gingerly and received a moan in response. I rolled him over from his side onto his back and to my relief saw him looking up at me. He managed a weak smile before whispering.

"I'm glad you're safe."

His voice was so far away. I blinked back tears while holding his head in my lap.

"You're going to be fine Jackson. Just hold on. I hear voices in the distance. Marcus will be here soon. He'll call an ambulance for you."

"We're still three miles from Robbins road. They'll never get here in time."

He winced in pain as beads of sweat broke out on his forehead and the color in his face grew one shade whiter.

"I have a confession, Jade. I wanted to take the stones, to destroy them. I thought they'd break the curse. I was foolish and desperate."

"It doesn't matter anymore. Just hold on. Please."

"Promise me you'll be happy. I need you to be happy."

"Jackson, don't talk like that. You're going to be fine."

I was crying openly now.

"I'm so sorry I didn't believe you about Annabelle. Can you ever forgive me?"

He smiled weakly again.

"I already have. Nothing you can do will make me stop loving you."

He tried reaching for my face but his hand stopped inches from my cheek then dropped lifelessly to the ground.

"No!"

Tears were falling like a river now. I wiped my eyes with the sleeve of my shirt and looked up into Jackson's wispy face. He was standing over his body and looking down at me. He had a soft glow around him and his voice was solid and strong. He looked to be at peace and no longer in pain.

"Please don't go, Jackson. I love you."

"I know. You're a strong person, Jade. You always have been. You will get through this. I promise you."

He seemed sad now, not for himself but for me. Sam appeared again and for the first time, generations separated by bridges of time looked upon one another a mere arm's length away.

"You're Sam?" Jackson implored him curiously.

"That would be me."

"Thank you for watching over her."

"I did my best, son. But like you said, she's a strong girl. She didn't need me, or anyone. My work here is done."

Sam nodded to something in the trees then smiled at us both. I turned to see what he was looking at and my jaw dropped open. There, just inside the clearing was the spirit deer; white as pure snow and glistening in the moon's rays. He was massive just as I had remembered him to be the first time I saw him.

He snorted once, his enormous rack spread wide and glorious. He nodded at Sam then took a few steps forward. By the time he reached us he had transformed into a man. Not just any man but the leader of Archaleux himself, Keeja.

He stood over me now. I had not moved one muscle and still remained by Jackson's body. I tried speaking but no words came out. And then the great phantom chief spoke in a voice that was surprisingly tender and soft.

"Granddaughter. You have come from me. In great anger I cursed the heavens which resonated back to earth and punished those who took Sirene from me. Our son knew not his mother as he lie coddled safe at our haven while the fighting erupted a hillside away. My wrath I could not foresee ricocheting onto you, my child. And for that, I am sorry."

He looked up at Sam and Jackson's spirit standing side by side and spoke to both of them.

"I ask forgiveness for the years my anger burned through your lives. My heart ached for

Sirene's spirit to come back but her journey was complete. My powers could not save a soul that wished only to join her ancestors in the sky. But you Jackson; you still have purpose here.

Your sacrifice has broken the curse and with that, by the powers greater than me, I can grant you life anew. Your love has brought peace to both our families."

He said the last part as he looked back and forth from Jackson and I. Neither Sam, Jackson or myself said a word as we watched, transfixed on Keeja's large form bending down next to me. He wore a white fur shawl that hung loosely on his wide muscled shoulders. White leather buckskins covered his lower half. His chest was bare and around his neck hung a different array of necklaces each containing multi-colored stones.

The only one missing was the emerald green stone I had seen him wave in my vision just before the tracks cracked in two and Raven took her fateful plunge. He smiled at me, his deeply lined face spoke of stories and journeys I could only dream of understanding. How I longed to know what those dark eyes have seen. Where he and our people really came from?

Before I could even hope to ask he reached for the stone around my neck. I instinctively reached up and unclasped the latch, freeing it from my neck and dropped it into his upturned hand. The one stone began to glow again at his touch, brighter than I had ever seen before. The area around us was washed in crystal clear light as the emerald faded into the background. Keeja touched my face with his free hand and I closed my eyes to better feel the warmth and love he carried in his heart.

I blinked in wonder as he waved the stone over Jackson's inert body. He began muttering something quietly and foreign then looked up at the heavens as if pleading for help. A soft prayer, a blinding light and for a moment, Jackson's body was swallowed up in it. When the light faded, I dropped my hand from my eyes to see only Sam standing there, his face pinched and eyes wide, fixed on Keeja.

I waited for what seemed like centuries before a gasp of air whooshed into Jackson's lungs. He coughed and sputtered a few times and the most beautiful sight looking back at me were those brown eyes I feared I'd never see again.

"You're back!"

He sat up slowly and I threw my arms around his neck, nearly choking the breath clear out of him again. He instinctively wrapped his arms around me in return then tried to get some distance so as to catch his bearings. Sam had walked over to Keeja who had now risen to his feet. He beseeched the chief's gaze.

"I, in turn ask your forgiveness for not only taking Sirene from you but for our disregard to your land, inadvertently destroying your freedoms and your sanctity. No words can express how deeply sorry I am."

Keeja raised his head slightly at Sam's words then slowly lifted his hand to shake Sam's. Both men smiled at one another as Jackson grabbed my attention again.

"What happened?"

He seemed disoriented and lost as he looked around at his surroundings. Pinpoints of flashlights were now dancing through the trees, as the sound of voices grew louder. The rest of Jackson's unit arrived and for the first and last time all day, I knew everything was going to be all right. I looked away from Jackson and back to where Keeja had been but he had already transformed back into his sacred albino form.

Just outside of the dense forest he stood tall and proud. His gaze fixed on us as help arrived. The other officers stopped short the moment they caught glimpse of Keeja, their mouths dropping open in surprise at the unearthly sight before them. I smiled in gratitude and thanked the good Lord above. With a wise look of complete understanding and love, he bowed his massive head once then turned in one graceful movement and leapt into the shadows beyond, disappearing completely.

The stone he had used lay resting by my side once again. I gathered it up gently and stuffed it into my jacket pocket as Marcus broke through the crowd of officers. Dropping to his knees, he grabbed me aggressively into one of his bear hugs. I tried reassuring him that everything was fine.

Jackson felt his side where he had been shot but instead of torn skin and clothing, not a scratch could be seen. It was as if he had never been shot in the first place.

"We heard the gun shot but couldn't find you at first." Marcus was talking a mile a minute.

"I knew it had to be Sheba. We had been searching for her this whole time."

Jackson still seemed a bit confused and rubbed his disheveled hair.

"Jackson, are you hurt?" Marcus turned his attention towards him now.

"I don't think so."

"Best not to take chances. Jade, you're bleeding. I'm going to call for an ambulance. You guys hang tight for a second. I'll be right back."

With that Marcus was on his feet again and jogging away.

"What happened?" Jackson asked again.

"You might have hit your head when you dove in between Sheba and myself. She tried to shoot me."

"Yes, yes, I remember that. I remember being shot then it felt as if I were in a dream or something. I remember someone being there with me, someone familiar, a friend maybe. I've never seen his face before. I died, didn't I?"

The last comment he said as if more of a statement than question. I tried not to answer.

"Shhh, it's okay Jackson. I'm here now and I won't leave your side until you tell me to."

"Jade. I must know. Did I die?"

"Yes, you did. I watched as your spirit left your body to stand next to Sam's."

"I was with my great-great-great-grandfather and I didn't even know it." He shook his head.

"Now I know what it's like to see what you see, minus the dying part."

"Try not to dwell on that aspect of it. You're back now. And everything is going to be fine."

Relief chased away the clouds in his eyes as he looked at me.

"I'm glad you're okay."

Sam had not left. I looked at him when Jackson spoke of his 'dream'. I whispered the words 'Thank You' to him. He tilted his hat, smiled and vanished into the night.

"You're okay, right? You're still bleeding, Jade."

"My head hurts but that's only because Sheba punched me."

Jackson shook his head in disbelief.

"She lost her life because of greed. What a shame. How did you ever get the gun from her?"

"I just didn't give up, I guess. I knew the second I stopped fighting, it would be over and I would be the one lying on the ground right now, instead of her."

"You must've had guardian angels watching over you because Sheba's the toughest broad I know."

"I most certainly did."

The brightest star in the sky winked down at us at my last words as we leaned in to hold onto one another in a silent promise to never let go.

Kathleen Wickman

CHAPTER TWENTY-TWO — THE BEGINNING

Jackson and I were sitting downstairs in the den at Marcus and Emma's house. I had come over early to help with the Thanksgiving fixings only to be shooed out of the kitchen. He was making fun of me not being allowed to help.

"Seriously, did you set a house on fire with your cooking abilities at one time? Is that why Emma won't let you help?"

I answered him in the same flabbergasted tone.

"Could it be that she *seriously* doesn't need my help? I mean are all women mandated into cooking for major feasts? Are you going to club me over the head next and drag me into your den?"

Excitement filled his beautiful brown eyes.

"Hmm, that sounds most intriguing. We are in a den already and I don't think I need a club to have my way with you."

I laughed out loud as he leaned over and assaulted my neck with kisses.

"Stop it! That tickles. What has gotten into you?"

He smiled in return and stretched his legs out in front of him, crossing them on the coffee table.

"My aunt is going to break your legs if she catches you with them on her coffee table."

"Yes, ma'am."

He cleared his throat in mock seriousness and sat up straight, placing his feet firmly on the floor and turning his body towards mine.

"Here, let me help with that."

I hadn't worn my necklace since the day of the attempt on my life two months ago. But considering this was a special occasion and the jewel was truly magnificent in its own right I didn't have the heart to lock it away forever. A negative stigma had begun to form around its purity even though Keeja had used it to restore life in the end. The stones had provoked so much fear, greed and evil prior to that point, it was hard to look at it for a while so I had kept it locked up in a safe I had in my bedroom closet.

I allowed Jackson to fasten the necklace as Emma's voice reached my ears. I heard her greeting guests arriving for the Thanksgiving meal. My mind wandered back to Emma's injury and that dreadful day. One good thing that came from the nightmare was Isaac was indeed found safe and unharmed at cousin Lou's house in the next county. The same cousin Lou that Cayden had borrowed the truck from.

My heart warmed a bit at the confounding reality that for the first time since my own gift inducing accident, someone believed that I could talk to spirits.

Jackson never doubted Gus and because of that, I am still here today. They headed off Cayden's escape forcing him to turn onto Robbin's Pond Road, where Raven's light draws visitors year round from the east coast to the west. It was her ghostly light that, in the end, stopped Cayden in his tracks. Emma had found out in her hospital bed much to Marcus' chagrin about my kidnapping but once learned of my safety, was able to recover more quickly and has now made a full recovery physically if not mentally as she scuttled above us upstairs.

Her hasty footsteps making their way all over the kitchen along with others as more guests began arriving. Mentally, she is forever scarred by Sheba's betrayal and death. It was a tough pill to swallow indeed to learn a truth that had been unraveling for the past year when Emma had suspected Sheba of stealing. And yet, she gave Sheba the benefit of the doubt in the hopes of transformation as any good friend would do.

But Sheba continued down the dark trail of deception, falsely believing she would never get caught. After all, Emma only monitored the situation, never confronting her until she knew one hundred percent that Sheba was guilty. And when she did, she did so in a manner in which to help Sheba but Sheba had denied any accusation or help. She was lost beyond recovery at that point. Prior to then, all Emma had was speculation, doubt and missing money and inevitably a broken heart. At one time, they had been good friends. It was still visibly hard to see Em cope with that kind of tragedy. Much to my surprise, after Emma was released from the hospital, she confided her own guilt when she confessed that she had hired Sheba knowing she had come from a troubled past riddled with petty crimes.

"Not all people who do bad, stay bad, Jade. Sheba had been a good person who had hit a patch of bumpy spots in life. I had believed she was capable of being a better person than what her

actions depicted. There had been a lot of good qualities inside her that I recognized.

I wanted to help and in the process, a friendship formed. She had done much good for the business and helped me out in many situations professionally and personally over the years before snapping and resorting to this. I especially saw what wonderful things were happening when Isaac was born. How much it had changed her and the love that seemed to grow in her. Not just for her child, but for those around her.

She was growing up, becoming responsible and accountable. Or so I had thought. I feel responsible for all of this."

I had wrapped my aunt in a fierce hug as we both cried. I told her none of this was anyone's fault. How is it reasonable to ever believe we have power over other's actions or intentions? Emma had a tremendously loving and giving heart.

There is no fault in that I had told her. Sheba had lost appreciation for that heart and for morality that is ingrained in each and every one of us from birth. Tragically, that was Sheba's own fault. I can still see aunt Emma and I sitting on her couch all those weeks ago crying in each other's arms, shortly after the tragedy.

A soft brush of air caressed our faces and dried our tears and our hair danced slightly in its wake. I opened my eyes and lifted my head. Emma looked around too at the *empty room*.

"Strange. I don't recall opening any windows…"

"You didn't."

I whispered the words over her shoulder at a man standing near the fireplace staring intently at us.

"Tell her not to change. To stay exactly the way she is. Tell her Scruffy says so."

Scruffy had walked a few steps closer to us on the couch and knelt down by Emma's side. His bright blue eyes twinkled behind dark lashes. His hair was dark and curly at the ends. He looked to be twenty years old. For such a young face, he had a noticeable five o'clock shadow, darkening his face further and perhaps being the reason for the nickname. He was rather handsome from head to toe and only had eyes for Emma.

"Jade? You look like you've seen a ghost. Are you alright?"

I shifted my eyes away from Scruffy to simply say 'yes'. She tilted her head so strangely at me that I continued.

"Remember that day in your office when I told you I can see ghosts? Well..."

I proceeded to share what Scruffy had just said.

"Who's Scruffy, Aunt Em?"

Her eyes grew wide and her hands lifted to cover her mouth as her face paled.

"How do you know about him? No one knew about Scruffy, not even your mother."

"Because I can see him now, Auntie. His spirit's with us. He asked me to tell you he's still wearing the red and black bracelet you made for him."

At that she surprised me with laughter. Her face lit up and she shook her head in disbelief.

"There's no way you could have known about any of this, Jade. Marcus doesn't even know about Scruffy. I don't talk about my past very much. No one approved of him because he came off as the 'bad boy' type and he was a few years older than me.

I was a senior in high school when we met. He was twenty-one. He gave the impression of rough and tough but to me he had been sensitive, kind and funny and so we hid our relationship from others. As far as anyone else was concerned, we were just casual friends.

But Scruffy was my very first love, long before I met Marcus. We even talked about getting married. My mother, your grandmother, was pretty strict. She'd have torn my hide if she knew I was tangled up with him.

After I graduated, he continued to stay behind to work for his father in construction and attend a local community college while I went downstate to MSU. One weekend he came to visit me but never made it. He died in a car accident. Jade, that was over twenty years ago, why is his spirit still here?"

"Tell her not to worry, I'm only here to remind her she's not alone. She still has wonderful family and she will get through this. She has you."

I smiled at him and shared with Emma his encouragement. She hugged me again and thanked Scruffy one last time, for everything. He touched her face and her eyes closed as if she could feel it. He winked at me and was gone.

"Now do you believe me, Auntie? I told you I wasn't lying when I said I could talk to ghosts."

"Yes. Yes, I do. And I'm sorry for doubting you. It's not every day you get visited by your ex-boyfriend."

"Who's ex-boyfriend?"

Marcus, with impeccable timing came walking into the room with half a sandwich stuffed in his mouth. He asked with casual interest appearing not to have witnessed the entire conversation as he plopped down in full uniform onto the recliner and switched on the television. Emma ignored his question.

"When did you get home?"

He continued flipping through channels more interested in what was on T.V.

"Just a second ago. I came in through the back door. They moved Survivor to next week! Ah, can you believe that?"

Crumbs fell out of his mouth onto his shirt as he complained in obvious irritation. Emma and I still sat facing each other on the couch, eyes wide open like saucers, neither saying a word. Then as if on cue, we both started laughing and the unspoken message was understood. This little secret we'll just keep to ourselves. Marcus wouldn't like it much had he just saw what his competition had looked like.

The memory faded and reminded me also that now Emma believed me as well and the feeling of support felt good. I no longer felt insane, vulnerable and alone. I regained my composure and knew we had better get upstairs quickly before they ate all the Thanksgiving food without us. The voices above us were growing louder and my stomach was starting to rumble.

Jackson had clasped my necklace and sat staring at me with a peculiar look on his face. I turned back to face him squarely.

"Jade, you okay? Have you seen another ghost? You seem so far away."

He looked around the room warily and I laughed softly in response.

"No. No ghost. Just memories."

"Thank you." I smiled at him lovingly.

He returned that beautiful smile so much like Sam's.

"For what?"

"For saving me."

He brushed my hair back from my face.

"The way I see it, we saved each other."

I closed my eyes as he leaned in and pressed his lips to mine. He pulled me closer to him on the couch and I wrapped my arms around his neck not wanting this feeling to ever end.

"Hey you two, get your butts up here! Pre-dinner cocktails are ready!"

He broke off the kiss and laughed.

"They don't even trust you to make the cocktails. What a shame."

He was chiding me as we walked up the stairs together, hand in hand.

"Hey! Give me a break." I chided back.

"I've cooked a few meals for my uncle and he's still standing. Besides, now that we're together,

I have officially elected you to be my guinea pig for my soon to be cooking experiments."

I heard him swallow hard before answering.

"Maybe you should try on Chunk first."

"He's fat enough. It's amazing he's still alive after all these years."

Jackson wrapped his arm around me as we greeted our family in the sunroom facing the lake. Soft music was playing as everyone mingled together. My heart swelled at all the familiar faces staring back at me. My mother and father were here along with my childhood friend Taylor.

She had just arrived yesterday and I realized how much I missed her face. She came over to me as the sun began yet another decent over the not yet frozen lake. It's orange rays penetrating the sunroom casting us all in an angelic light. I hugged my friend as Jackson walked over to talk to Marcus, Hawk, Duvall and their wives.

"I'm so happy you found someone, Jade. Jackson is a great guy. Hey, did you hear that Dylan is engaged?"

My eyebrows rose slightly at such an immediate declaration that at first I didn't know what to say. Taylor's expression was full of expectation at my possible responses.

"Wow. That was fast. I'm glad he's happy."

And even though I knew my friend meant well, I hoped she could see how at peace I was with my life. Not because of who was in it, but because of who I had become through all the trials my gift had given me. A curse in itself that had indeed turned into a blessing for it had brought me to Sam. And that in turn had brought me to Jackson. Sam's intervention brought two stubborn hearts together. I was stronger because of him and more confident at what I could do.

I found purpose in helping people and by first helping myself accept who I am even if others did not understand. Taylor had yet to learn about my gift and I hoped someday I'd have the opportunity to tell her but for now I smiled at her for what I had said, I meant. I planned on taking the long road of the rest of my life getting to know Jackson in every way humanly possible, first starting with a turkey dinner.

"Come on girlfriend, let's eat!"

Nikki, Johnny, Heather, Eric, Jordyn and her boyfriend joined us at the dinner table and just before sitting down a brown and white blur burst into the room with two bigger dogs chasing him. Scooter was back from his brush with fate as he attempted to save my life that day. The bullet had missed him and the ingenious little beast knew how to play dead until we had disappeared into the woods. He had hobbled all the way home with Bella and Bruno following behind where Marcus found him later that day and knew immediately something had happened to me.

I now reached for him but he brazenly ignored my attempt and flew past me carrying one of Bruno's favorite stuffed animals in his mouth. Bruno was dead set on getting it back even if it meant knocking over the dinner table. I laughed out loud at my furry friends and thanked God again for everything this day had bestowed on us. A second chance, a true love, good friends and a loving family all under one roof, it just doesn't get any better than that.

Luckily the dogs missed the table by a hair as they raced into the next room, Marcus on their tails, literally.

"Alright you three, into the kennels! Now!"

Emma laughed too and gave me a quick squeeze before sitting down. I gazed outside as something caught my eye at the edge of the yard near the lake. The sun was just above the tree line now and the air was getting cold.

"Where are you going now?"

I glanced at Jackson as he was about to take the seat next to me. I apologized quickly and grabbed my coat from the coat rack in the corner.

"I'll be right back. Start eating without me."

Before he could say more I was out the door and down the steps. Running to the lake while pulling my coat tighter around my chest. I stopped short of the water's edge and tilted my head slightly to the right.

"Hey."

Was all I managed to say at first as Sam just stood there in front of me, his back to the water.

"I thought you had crossed over."

He shook his head slightly.

"Not yet. I wanted to say good-bye first. And to make sure my grandson is being nice to you. He's a bit temperamental."

"Yeah, I've gathered that."

I chuckled softly thinking back to our first days when I arrived in Paulding.

"But he's mellowed out a lot."

"Good."

"I also wanted to thank you Jade for your selflessness and courage. You loved Jackson even before you realized it and you never gave up. Your gift allowed you to believe in the curse in order to break it and I'm grateful for that. Now I can finally go home to be with my family."

"It's going to be weird not having you here anymore Sam. I'm going to miss you a lot."

"I'll miss you too, Jade. But I promise I won't be far. Whenever you want to talk, I'll listen even if you can't see or hear me anymore. Where I'm going is only a breath away after all."

"Paulding Light won't be the same without you either. Will we even see Raven's light anymore?"

"Oh she'll be there, people are still counting on her to show. Unfortunately she will forever be stuck in a time loop-hole unable to leave, unable to stop."

"That sounds really sad."

"Remember she's just a train, Jade. She can't feel anything, she doesn't even know."

"She?"

"Well, you know what I mean."

"Yeah, I do."

"You'll still see my lantern though if you ever go back to Paulding Light."

"How can that be, if you're leaving?"

He winked boyishly, his radiant smile making me smile in return.

"I stuck it with Raven. When the wind blows a certain way at night, you'll see it's red glow dancing on the horizon. Can't let the onlookers down now can we?"

I wiped my face with the sleeve of my coat to no avail. Hot tears kept running down my cold cheeks.

"I love you, Sam."

"I love you too, Jade. I would've liked to think if I had had a daughter, she would've been a lot like you; kind, loving and thoughtful. Take care of my grandson."

"I will."

A sob caught in my throat as in one split second he crossed the lake then turned back to face me. I could still make out his stunning smile so much like Jackson's as he waved, turned around and walked into the dying light of the sun.

Kathleen Wickman

About the Author

Kathleen Wickman was born in Norway, Michigan. Her love of the written word began at an early age when she entered a poetry contest through her local school and won publication. From there, her love grew to short stories and descriptive papers.

Kathleen first visited Paulding Light as a teenager. An eighty mile journey it was from her hometown to Watersmeet, Michigan where the infamous "ghost" light can be seen at night, year round. Upon arriving at the guardrail where many onlookers gather, the most brilliant white light flooded the vehicle, leaving Kathleen and her friends stunned. Within seconds, it vanished. The most confounding thing about the Light was that those standing near the guardrail had not witnessed anything at all. In a way, the Light was an illusion. Young and old gather year round because there is indeed *something* peculiar and mesmerizing about this phenomenon that is said to grace these parts for over one hundred years.

In her many trips to see the Light over the years, she has spoken with onlookers who have traveled from all over the country to witness Paulding Light and its mysteries. Paulding Light was featured in an episode of Unsolved Mysteries as well as Ripley's Believe It or Not.

Kathleen resides in Iron Mountain, Michigan with her beloved dog Buckley.